SO-ARO-326

Blood of My Brother III: The Begotten Son

By

Zoe & Yusuf Woods

RJ Publications, LLC

Newark, New Jersey

The characters and events in this book are fictitious. Any resemblance to actual persons, living or dead is purely coincidental.

RJ Publications
ywoods94@yahoo.com
www.rjpublications.com
Copyright © 2009 by Yusuf & Zoe Woods
All Rights Reserved
ISBN 0-9817773-5-X
978-0981777351

Printed in the Canada

September 2009

1 2 3 4 5 6 7 8 9 10

DEDICATIONS
By Zoë

I believe that at least once in a lifetime we are bestowed something so incredible, something almost indescribable because of its magnitude; that it changes our lives and makes us the best that we could possibly be. I recognize what I have been so greatly blessed with and I give eternal thanks for that. Husband, I love the way that you love me. You are the best…always know that. *Vorrei morire per voi.* In dedication to my love for all time, Yusuf I love you!

By Yusuf

To my beloved wife; I am nearly overcome with emotion as I try to define my gratitude and love for you. You are everything that constitutes a true wife to me. At the thought of my struggles, you have been by my side every step of the way as we climbed any mountain set before us. You have loved and supported our family in any way possible and I thank you! We, thank you. So with my deepest affection, I dedicate this book to you.

We would also like to extend this dedication to all of the victims of the devastating fires that occurred in Coatesville Pennsylvania. Our thoughts and prayers are with you.

ACKNOWLEDGEMENTS

Through Allah's blessing we would like to thank everyone for the love and support that you have shown to the saga of Blood of My Brother. Please enjoy the story!

Yusuf T. Woods

I would like to acknowledge **Shamone Woods** (hold your head up; we'll get you home soon). **Kevin Black**: 'Real men do real things and we love you for that.' **Earl Black**: 'I told you I have you, now if commissary sold cars, you'd have one.' **Jay "Jasir" Hines**: 'What's up?' **Butter** from Riverside. **Tarik Hargrover**, NJ, Hanif up Schuylkill on 2 A, I see you, **The real Goldie. B**. NJ, and last but not least I said if I had a chance to speak I would always keep it real…free **Big Meech**, Det., free **Akbar Pray.** NJ, free **Guy Fisher.** NY, free **Jason Poole,** D.C. and even with the hate free…**Fly Ty**, Philly. I would especially like to thank Richard Jeanty for this lovely opportunity, my staff at Man Up Publications and to my cleaning company Ford Enterprise for taking care of the thousand pieces of scrap paper around the office so that I could see my desk. To my soldiers in the pen, here we go again! I got your letters and you are not forgotten. To prove it, some of your words are now a part of mine…

Remon "Mone" Gibson, "Strong Island, NY
I'm sending an unconditional love to Latara Little, my kids (crew), and my family. Without y'all there would be no me. Thanks for loving me and being there when I needed y'all the most, at the bottom. At the bottom you find whose there for you and your family will always be there for you no

matter what you're going through. C.B.S. (Can't be
stopped). Thanks for the love Yusuf Woods.

Abdullah Warrick
To all my brothers and sisters in the struggle who are not
merely persisting but are excelling under all circumstances
who have not and will not compromise their integrity, and
to all those who are holding down their loved one's, I
applaud you!!
Yusuf and Zoe Woods, continue to show the youth that the
"Grind" continues and that the legal hustle is what's
happening.

Mark "Spark" Nelson, D.C.
I send my love to all my loved ones and friends. My heart
goes out to all the real men whose name kept its value once
they were tested by these walls and gun tower. There's
always light at the end for the bonafide.

INTRODUCTION

From the window of an abandoned home, Roc looked out into the streets of Philadelphia with blood-filled eyes. Never in a time of war would he think that he would not have a solution for his enemy. That suddenly changed the moment he realized the true identity of his brother's killer was his mentor, the only person that he ever loved like a father and the most dangerous man he knew - Mr. Holmes. With the need for revenge overtaking him, Roc began to prepare for a fight he wasn't sure he could win, even with the help of the Get Money Clique. But for a promise he made to his father, he would die trying.

The strategic game of chess that began with the pushing of a pawn in the *Blood of My Brother* series symbolizes one of love, loyalty, blood, mayhem and death. Who will be the one to announce checkmate between the two Kings left standing - the teacher or the student? In the end, the streets of Philly will never be the same.

1

After the viewing of Lil Mac's body, a line of sixty-two cars accompanied by twenty-one limousines rode through the streets of North Philly, showing him the same love and respect he showed them. The sun found its way out from behind the clouds as the leading driver now out of Philly, drove down an old country road moving at an easy pace, watching the trees fly by. He passed through two open steel gates with two men standing on each side. The cars continued to move slowly through the private cemetery and stopped alongside a clear road.

While the preacher spoke kind and loving words above the casket, Roc had his team positioned throughout the crowd, looking for anyone or anything that they felt shouldn't be there. "Roc, there's a car here at the front gate saying that they know you, but they won't lower their window or give a name. They said something about the feds and me being one." Roc replied through his ear piece, "Let them through."

Moments later, a black tinted Maybach pulled to a stop and a tall muscular man dressed in black, carrying an umbrella, jumped out of the passenger seat. He opened the back door for Mr. Holmes who stepped out to be met by Roc as he stood at the edge of the grass. They embraced.

"I'm sorry, Roc, I know how much you loved him; I came as soon as I heard."

"That I do," Roc said clearly.

"Have you heard anything about who would dare do something like this?" Mr. Holmes questioned.

"Nothing yet. It was done as smoothly as if I'd done it myself, the way they didn't leave a trace or trail. But we do know they were imported."

"You think?"

Roc held Mr. Holmes's stare. "Yes. It would be like if I sent them after you; once they served their assignment they would have to be eliminated because of what they'd know. That would mean an all out war." Roc's eyes tightened while still locked on Mr. Holmes, his mentor for over twenty years.

"You know, if there's anything I can do, I will."

"I know, Mr. Holmes, but whatever connections you have, I now have them too and will use every single one of them until I get even."

"I'm sure you will," replied Mr. Holmes.

"Roc, get Mr. Holmes out of here; the feds got word of that he's here and you now have three heading your way," Boggy said into the earpiece.

"Come on, they know," Roc held the umbrella to shield Mr. Holmes as the big man reappeared and opened the door. Safely back in the car, Mr. Holmes cracked the window an inch. "Roc, there is no doubt that you will find who did this but please make sure you stop wearing your emotions on your sleeve so they don't see you coming."

"Thanks, old head, but who says I'm trying to hide it?" Roc walked by and stared at Mr. Holmes's driver who was another large muscular man. Mr. Holmes raised the window, never taking his eyes off of Roc who stepped over to where Boggy was. "Get me out of here quick and tell the team from Pakistan that he knows," Mr. Holmes said to his driver.

"How can you be sure?"

"To be honest, he just told me," replied Mr. Holmes.

Roc watched the Maybach disappear out of sight before turning to Boggy. "Get everyone together at the old spot on block three."

"What happened?"

"I know who spilled my brother's blood," Roc answered.

"How, who told you? Mr. Holmes?" asked Boggy.

"In a way, yes. Always know that for a good switch-up to work, the change has to look the same as the prototype and if it's off in any way, a real player sees right through that bullshit."

"Roc, what are you talking about?" Boggy questioned, not fully comprehending what was happening and all that Roc knew.

"Look, he had two new bodyguards and they're men," Roc said.

"And?"

"He hates men; he says he can't be around anybody he can't fuck. He should have used military women. It would have worked better."

Later that night in a section of North Philly, Roc and another individual sat in the back room watching the screen as it showed the faces of his men taking their seats at the large round table in the center of the room. Clockwise from the right was Boggy, Manny, Raja, Buff, Haffee, Mohammed, Shamone, M. Easy, Fox, Top Dollar, Ayzo, Daz, A.P, and NayNay.

After studying the eyes of their soldiers as they always did, in search of any weakness and deception, they only saw loyalty. It was evident that they all wanted the same thing - revenge. Roc slowly rose to his feet and stepped out to the head of the table to start to speak. "I brought you all here for one reason and that is to take out the most dangerous man I know and get vengeance for the blood of my brother." As soon as the words left Roc's mouth, the whispering throughout the room stopped instantly and everyone's eyes became focused on him.

"I see I now have your full attention and-"

"Cut the bullshit, Roc, and give me a name so I can go finish the rest," screamed NayNay while jumping to her feet, cocking back her forty-five automatic as tears of sorrow and anger for the only person she truly loved slowly came down the side of her face.

"Yeah, Roc, fuck that anticipation shit, this isn't a game and I don't see nobody here laughing. Now who did it?" added Fox.

Roc lightly nodded his head up and down, understanding the many emotions in the room and placed his hand on Mohammed's shoulder. "Be easy, Killer." Mohammed had started to rise from his chair, ready to address the disrespect shown to his Boss. Top Dollar eased his hand under the table onto his gun while cutting his eye at Boggy, wanting to hear his name come from Roc's lips.

"You must be Fox, am I correct?"

"Yeah, that be me."

"Well, I have heard a lot about you in the last two weeks that I had with my brother."

For a moment Fox began to smile, but that quickly disappeared.

"But you must not know me to be talking to me in such a disrespectful way." Roc moved until he was standing face to face with only an inch separating him from Fox, and then continued," Or you must know that the answer to your question is Mr. Holmes and we're about to face something we have never seen before. So you have to be ready to die like everybody else in this room. I can see you're prepared to do that. The difference is you just don't care who kills you. Fox, you're not my enemy; that I know. It's your rage that gets in the way therefore making you a weak link in a time that only the strongest chain will win. If it wasn't for the love you have for my brother, you would never be in the same room as me."

Roc's voice drifted from NayNay's ears, and after hearing the name of their enemy, she slowly eased back down into her seat in a daze. Her heartbeat began to quicken as she remembered the feeling of power coming from the old man. He was handcuffed with blood running from his mouth and down his face as he pleaded - not for his own life but to her surprise to save hers.

It happened in the lower section of Mr. Holmes's yacht in the back master bedroom. At the time, the Get Money Clique was going to war with Roc and unable to get him so they kidnapped the closest person to him - Mr. Holmes. NayNay was in the hallway when she heard Lil Mac scream, "What? My Mom!" followed by a loud bumping sound. Wanting to make sure Lil Mac was all right, NayNay headed toward the room when suddenly Fox appeared from the stairway pounding on the door. Seconds later, Lil Mac opened the wooden framed structure and the beauty of the room caught her attention. The hatred mixed with confidence that she saw in Mr. Holmes's eyes as he watched Lil Mac leave behind Fox was what kept her gaze.

Now alone, she eased the door back open to see the blood pouring from his head and lip. She grabbed a towel, rushing to his aid when he stopped her. "No! Don't. This pain is nothing compared to what you're about to face." Noticing her doubt, Mr. Holmes continued.

"Lovely lady, I'm like no other person you have met or will meet."

"And you're telling me this, why?" NayNay questioned.

"Because of the love you possess in your eyes for that kid that is so anxious to prove he's a man. But he doesn't realize that he's not going to make it to be one. I say this also for the reason that any coward can kill but it takes

a real man to save a life and I want to save Roc's life, not his. But if he dies, so must Roc and that would be as if I killed my own son. Rule five states that a beloved soldier must not die alone for someone will always avenge his death. So I will if I have to."

Spotting the seriousness within Mr. Holmes's eyes, a confused NayNay started to walk away deep in thought when Mr. Holmes said, "Pick the phone up."

"What?"

"The cell phone on your hip"

"Yes…"

"Now dial 411 star 82187"

"This isn't even a number"

"Just dial it," Mr. Holmes demanded.

NayNay did what she was told then a voice said, "The upper room, how may I help you?"

"Don't be scared, now just ask for Apollon," Mr. Holmes instructed.

NayNay hesitated, recognizing the name as one of many for the devil from the nights she was forced to attend bible school as a kid. Letting out a deep breath, "C-c-can I speak with Apollon?" NayNay repeated while thinking this was a trick. It has to be a joke. Suddenly a voice said, "Hello, this is Apollon the soul taker, how and who do you want to die?"

NayNay released the phone, letting it fall freely to the lavish carpet. "Don't look that way; he's really not the devil. He just brings destruction and brothers just like him. But this doesn't have to happen. Just un-cuff me and turn your back, then this will all be over with, I promise."

NayNay slowly removed the cuffs. Twenty minutes later, she raced to the upper deck screaming, "Solo, he's gone!" Wiping away tears, she whispered to herself as if Lil Mac could hear her, "I'm sorry I lied, baby, but I wish you would let him get away."

The voice of a heated Fox brought her back to reality as he yelled, "How the f - my bad, I mean how can you say that? I ride as hard, if not harder, than anyone in this room," he said, meaning every word of his statement.

"Well, let's see." Roc circled the room and stopped behind Top Dollar, placing a hand on his shoulder saying, "Here sits the most dangerous man in Get Money, and really in the whole room." Roc paused to let his eyes roam from the left to the right, taking in the reaction to his words then he continued. "Please don't look shocked in any way; in war one must aim for the head and let the body follow. That's how I got a lead on the once-mysterious Get Money Clique; my first move was when you just got back from M.I.A., remember?" Top Dollar looked at Roc with fire in his eyes as he answered, "Yeah, I do and so do the men you sent." With a smile, Roc then began to explain the event as Top Dollar and everyone in the room listened attentively. Nearing the end of the story Roc stated, "As a kid, Top Dollar listened to Malcolm and spoke Martin while growing up in a time when the heart of a man was judged by the integrity of his actions, not what he said. But the trick to this story is that Top Dollar was taught by the same man that schooled his best friend, my father, and Mr. Holmes."

When the name of their new enemy was repeated, all twenty-six sets of eyes moved from Roc and locked upon Top Dollar. "And this person is the legendary Terrance Brown, a.k.a. "Billy D." At hearing the name that hadn't been spoken in public in over twenty years, Top Dollar jumped up with a force that knocked his chair across the room as he freed his gun in the same motion. He swiftly raised the hard, steel weapon in his hand, screaming, "Roc, you better keep him out of this, you dig? He has nothing to do with it. Holmes is our business and--"

Suddenly Top Dollar stopped in the middle of his sentence trying to decide who to shoot as he watched Roc disappear. Mohammed quickly moved in the path of fire, now staring down the barrel of the gun. He smiled. Boggy, moving with the same ambition, stepped next to Mohammed on his right while Shamone posted on his left with all their guns locked, ready to fire on Roc's word as they shielded him. Roc grinned as he whispered to Mohammed, "I'm glad to see you still got it but next time I'm not going to give you a warning that this will happen." Speaking out loud Roc said, "Stand down." Within seconds he was again back in front of Top Dollar, who still had his weapon.

Unconcerned, Roc began pacing the room again while explaining with his hands behind his back. "See, that's where you're wrong, Top Dollar. He has everything to do with it. My mentor is now dead to me therefore *his* mentor must die also."

The whole room watched as Top Dollar's veins started to pulsate in his arms and wrist as his gun hand began to shake. Roc stopped pacing and turned to face Top Dollar. He then placed two fingers from each hand in the air, making two L shapes to form a picture frame and said, "That's it, keep that look right there, like that." "Roc, I respect you but please don't play with me," Top Dollar said through tightened teeth as he eased his finger back on the trigger. "Play with you? Respect? Ha-ha-ha," Roc laughed.

"You know the reason I like that look so much? It's because I've seen it before, only it was ten times yours and I was in jail looking in a mirror when you took my mentor." Top Dollar lowered his gun to his side, now truly understanding Roc's pain. "I dig your point and I'm sorry for what happened, but there must be a way we can keep Mr. Billy D out of harm's way."

"You know, I love to see loyalty and I believe there may be some truth to your words, that's why the small army I have surrounding Billy D's summer home up in Maine is standing down until I say when. Earlier today I received word that Mr. Holmes will be on the 12:00 a.m. flight to Dubai out of an undisclosed private airport just outside of New York."

"Enough said. Get Money, let's move," yelled Fox as he headed for the door while checking his watch which read 8:25 pm and then he stated, "We should be there by ten with two hours to set up." Reaching it, he started turning the doorknob when he noticed he was standing alone. He turned around when Roc motioned for him saying, "Fox, let me speak to you for a minute, will you?"

Roc wrapped his arm around his shoulder and whispered into his ear while walking him back to his chair. "Listen, if you keep it up you'll be wearing that red cap." "Red cap?" Fox repeated, confused. "Just know you don't want that. Now have a seat and shut up." Roc then began to fill the Get Money Clique in on his plan.

"On this plane, there will be three very important, rich, and powerful people. One of them being Mr. Holmes and he will be dressed in black because it represents power. There will be two bodyguards for each person. I was able to purchase the last two seats at a deal from a married couple that suddenly with a little help, decided that they didn't need a honeymoon for a hundred thousand each, so they'll be looking for a couple. That means, NayNay, you're in play." " I wouldn't be able to live if I wasn't," she replied.

Roc continued, "I know you've been around Mr. Holmes before but I know you can fool him, Ms. Jones, the same way you did me," Roc smiled. "I'm sorry, Roc, but I had to, the same way I'm going to do him. The only difference is he will die."

"Haffee, by Mr. Holmes knowing you the least over the years you're the only one from our team that he may not recognize. So you must run point beside NayNay as her husband. A.P. and Fox, you will be their bodyguards, Fatel you will be the bag man so here, you'll need this. Mohammed?" On cue Mohammed quickly entered the back room returning with a midsized box. Roc opened the box to reveal several plastic Mack 11's and vests with numbers hidden from one to ten on them. One by one he handed them out until he came to Fox and asked, "Now are you better?" Fox replied, "Yes and I apologize, Roc, for any disrespect I may have shown to you. It's just that if Mac was here and I wasn't, he would ride extra hard for me and I'm going to do the same, I promise." Fox accepted the vest and gun. "Now I'm about to make him proud."

"I believe you will." Roc watched how Fox firmly gripped his new weapon then began to clarify, "I wasn't speaking of a physical chain, Fox. Remember, it is only the chain of thought that will help us remain." "I knew that," Fox whispered while watching Roc move across the room when he was pulled to the side by NayNay. He thought to himself, *"Get Money will be the King of this city when it's all said and done. Right after I handle the old man for the disrespect shown to the family, then I'll handle you, Roc, for the disrespect you have shown me."*

"Nigga, is you alright?" Boggy questioned, wrapping his arm roughly around Fox's shoulder as he followed his stare and said, "I know that look better not be because you're thinking some crazy shit. If you are, the moment you make your move I'm going to be waiting!" Boggy backed away from Fox with his two fingers in a shape as if they were guns pulling the trigger as he laughed. "I'm the only one you need to see!"

"Yeah, laugh now, die later," Fox said under his breath.

After NayNay brought Roc up to speed about what happened between she and Mr. Holmes, and the odd feeling she was having as if she was being watched at all times, he repeated the story for the sixth time making sure he heard right.

"Now you're positive he said the name Apollon?"

"Yes, Roc, why, was I right? They're the ones who killed my baby?"

"God, I hope not."

"Do you know them?" NayNay questioned, trying to get any understanding to the name that once spoken turned Roc's eyes to something so dark they almost looked lifeless. "No, their boss," Roc said as he walked away without speaking another word. NayNay was left standing there, puzzled.

As his mind became disarrayed he started thinking, *"What does Diego El Sovida of the Corporation Assassins have to do with this?"* He then returned to the back room and sat next to the same individual whose eyes were still glued to the screen and asked, "Do you think they can handle it?"

"They better, because this may be the only advantage we have," Roc responded while he started to dial one of the four numbers only given to members of the Corporation - * 411.

2

Mohammed finished making sure that the Get Money Clique had the airport blueprint memorized to a tee. Knowing there was no room for mistakes, they each exited the small row home in North Philly to the surprise of Detective Brian who whispered, "I'll be damned, that's Roc's house," while lowering the high tech binoculars from his face.

"Now you see what I mean. Something big is about to happen."

"Maybe it's not Michael. It could be they're all just here to mourn the death of Mac Miller." "With guns?" Detective Michael said as he pointed to the exposed weapon on Daz's hip whose shirt rose while jumping in the back of the van. "And I'd bet my badge if I still had it." Detective Michael shot Detective Brian a furious look. "I said I was sorry, Michael, I know you're still not holding the bad tip against me?"

Paying the apology no mind, Detective Michael continued, "If we stop that vehicle, they all will be carrying unlawful weapons and drugs."

"That could be true but if I was to get on board with this operation it would have to be done by the book because I'm not also going to lose my badge, do you understand me?" Detective Brian declared while pulling the tinted Ford out into the street three cars behind the black B.M.W. x5. Top Dollar was behind the wheel and was following the van. "So this means you'll help me put these bastards behind bars?" Detective Michael questioned hopefully. "We'll see, but why don't you start by giving me a debriefing?" "Okay, after I left you at the crime scene I pulled up to Temple Hospital to get a peek at the young thug, Lil Mac, so that I could mark him off my list. But it was like a military war base as two armed men stood on each side of the emergency room entrance, while three men held the reporters at bay as they tried to rush the approaching black Escalade. You should have seen it, Brian. These guys are like animals, they even pushed B. Gumble to the ground. The Escalade then came to a stop with Odell Miller, a.k.a. Roc, stepping out like he was the fucking King of England."

Detective Michael let out a deep breath, hating the fact that Roc, his crew, and the Get Money Clique were still free. For over five years he and his partner, Detective Rayfield, had been building a case against Roc when the Get Money Clique came out demanding respect which forced an all out war, giving Detective Rayfield the link between the two crews that could have landed both teams in jail. But before he could reveal the evidence to Detective Michael, he then went missing to be found a year later on the day the war began between the two teams.

Detective Michael knew the date and the way the body was found was a message for him to back off but it actually only made him push harder, leading him to break the rules. He did it without hesitation, losing his shield along the way. Detective Michael vowed to make every last person who had something to do with the death of Detective Rayfield pay with their life, no matter if it was in the ground or in a cell.

He continued: With my eyes locked on Roc, I slowly moved on the outer rim of the circle until I made it to the edge of the building making sure nobody was paying him any attention. Detective Michael raced around to the front of the building. He stepped through the front doors letting his investigating skills lead him. As his eyes searched the hallway, he quickly checked the door knobs of each room he passed. In the middle of the hall, off to his right, a door popped open. Detective Michael dipped in and moments later he was searching the several boxes and shelves that lined the wall. He found a box of gowns. Holding one of them up in the air, he noticed the whole back was missing. *"What the hell, it's for Rayfield."*

He hastily stripped, leaving nothing but his underwear and socks on. With his gun in hand and no where to put it, he ripped off the neck of another hospital gown and used the rope to tie his weapon around his thigh. He then did the same with his wallet. Detective Michael removed a wheel chair from the corner and rolled it from the room. He eased his way to the entrance of the emergency room waiting area.

Looking through the window, he saw Manny standing up against the wall on the right side with his hands tightly gripping two Mack 11s as they rested inside his Carhart front hoody pocket. Raja had positioned himself in a chair that sat in the middle across from Manny and Buff. Within the newspaper on his lap, was a tech nine automatic. Buff quickly placed a clear clamp over the door handle, securing it.

Detective Michael wondered why it seemed as if Roc's men were about to go to war instead of saying a prayer for their injured loved ones when he eased the door open and began to enter. He then noticed there were several members of Get Money present, many with the look of fury and Detectiveermination to seek revenge upon their faces. His eyes stayed on Roc, who was moving through them like they weren't even there. Then suddenly the door slammed hard against the wheel chair. *"Aaaaa, watch it...what are you doing?"* *"What I'm doing is securing this room now get the fuck out of here!"* demanded Fox, placing his foot on the front of the chair before kicking it and forcing Detective

Michael to go flying in reverse out of control and down the hall.

Detective Michael, ready to blow his cover positioned himself to jump free from the shaking chair when a man in a white coat approaching the waiting area gripped the two black handles. "Excuse me, sir, are you okay?" "Yes, yes," Detective Michael answered, falling back down in his wheel chair. "Thank you; I was just trying to stand up to test the strength in my legs."

"Excuse me, Dr. Woods, we moved Mr. Miller to the back room on the second floor as you requested, and everything is ready." "Thank you, Nurse Thurman. I'm going to get them right now. Sir, if you will excuse me," said Dr. Woods. Detective Michael watched Dr. Woods walk off into the waiting room while whispering with a grin, "Thank you, Ms. Thurman, indeed."

On the second floor Detective Michael hid in the cut by the elevator when suddenly he heard the echo of three different sets of shoes followed by the voice of Dr. Woods as he explained, "Gentlemen, usually I wouldn't allow this but his wish is to see you both."

The sight of sadness that covered Roc and Top Dollar's face as they entered the room immediately made Detective Michael happy as he thought, "I wish the young bastard would live so I can kill him like I'm going to kill the rest of you punks, the same way you did Rayfield." He quickly blended back into the crease of the wall. Twenty minutes later, Top Dollar was the first to appear, slowly walking down the hall using his silk handkerchief to dry his eyes. "Yeah that's right, feel the pain like I did," Detective Michael said to himself. Moments passed when Roc followed, pulling Dr. Woods out behind him while he was looking around and making sure that they were alone.

"Dr. Woods, what are his chances?"

"I'll be honest with you, it doesn't look good but if he makes it through the night he will have a 50/50 chance."

"And the girl?"

"She'll be fine; your brother took most of the impact."

"Okay doctor. I need you to do this, get her off this floor for 24 hours. Can you handle that?"

With a look of perplexity, Dr. Woods answered, "Whatever you need." Roc began to walk towards the waiting room when Boggy appeared right beside him asking, "How's he doing, is he alright?" "Oh he'll be fine," replied Roc and then went into this wallet and pulled a photo out that Top Dollar couldn't see. Get this to Mohammed and tell him to follow it to the tee."

Hearing Roc's demand, Detective Michael eased into the elevator. Outside he watched the entrance closely from the front seat of his Buick when just as he predicted, Mohammed stepped out into the darkness. The distant look in his eyes puzzled Detective Michael but his next action caught him completely by surprise. He watched Mohammed slowly look in both directions, then without warning instead of taking the steps he jumped over the edge of a twenty foot high handicap ramp, disappearing out of his sight.

"Oh my Lord, where the hell did he go?" Detective Michael rushed from the car removing his gun as he raced to the edge of the ramp just in time to see Mohammed roll in between two cars, seconds after that the light to a Ford Mustang followed by the sound of the engine came to life. "Come on you sick son of a bitch!" Detective Michael raced back to his vehicle stepping on the gas in hot pursuit of Mohammed. He pulled out the parking lot as Mohammed made a right onto Broad Street. Detective Michael followed his suspect for several hours through the roughest section of North Philly. Mohammed slowed down, making a left onto First St. where dope fiends and prostitutes covered the

street and porches. Detective Michael drove three cars back through the nearly pitch black alley due to the shot out street lights. He now realized why his fellow officers called this section the Lost World, because in his many years of being on the force, he may have been here once.

He eased into an open space and parked while watching Mohammed exit his car. "What the hell?! This man really needs mental therapy," said Michael as Mohammed, whose face was now covered with all black Kiwi war paint, looked from the picture in his hand to the faces of the junkies laying on the warm summer ground. Displeased, he jumped back in his car and drove down one block after another repeating his actions. For several days, Detective Michael followed Mohammed on his nightly ritual.

Feeling that it was leading no where, he was about to call it quits but his natural instincts refused to let him. Then it happened one night that started the same as all the rest. But this day, as the dirty Ford crept through the darkness of Norus Street, Mohammed suddenly ran up the steps with his gun drawn at his side. He knocked before placing his ear to the door. "Oh shit!" Detective Michael screamed, spilling his coffee out in disbelief as he fumbled to retrieve his gun. He exited just as Mohammed began to descend the steps with the now unconscious man hung over his shoulder and yelled, "Police! Freeze or I'll shoot!"

Mohammed had a devilish grin on his face as he stepped in front of a car, using it as a shield while firing the powerful forty-five automatic several times, 'BOOM-BOOM,' forcing Detective Michael to dive over onto the opposite side of an abandoned vehicle for cover. He landed on the ground next to an elderly man that was trying to light a match and whose clothes had seen better days and asked, "These guys around here don't respect the law at all do they?" The man finally got the match to light and placed a *glass crack pipe to his mouth taking a heavy blast of the white rock. He paused, holding the smoke in a few seconds before blowing it in the Detectives face, "No, son, they don't." Detective Michael peaked over the hood of the car and watched until Mohammed's tail lights disappeared from his vision.*

"So what happened to the kid?" questioned Detective Brian, interrupting Michaela's story while keeping his eyes on Top Dollar as they moved in and out of traffic on the PA Turnpike. "Like I told you, after making it to my car while returning fire I chased him for twenty minutes until I ran out of gas," Detective Michael lied. "But what I think is that it has something to do with Lil Mac Miller."

"What? Come on, Michael, the kid's in the ground."

"I don't know. There's something fishy about this…"

"Listen, don't start with this bullshit, I'm warning you!"

"I know, but…"

"There are no buts; I watched them place that young kid in the ground at the sad age of 19 without it making one newspaper in this whole damn city. Like these kids aren't dying out here due to guys like him." Detective Brian pointed at Top Dollar as his blood boiled. "So he's our target and every person like him that preys on the weak minds of young men to do their dirty work. You understand me?"

Detective Michael didn't hear a word that Detective Brian said, as he was lost in his own thoughts, thinking, *"They're all my targets and I'm going to do what it takes to bring justice for the death of my partner even if I have to die myself."*

"I said do you understand me?" Detective Brian repeated his question louder, while shaking Michael.

"Yes. I understand, but why are you turning off here, they're not?"

"Yes, but we are."

"Wait, Brian, they'll get away and you know something is about to happen. I can see it in your eyes."

"You're right. I do feel something terribly wrong is about to take place but past that yellow pole is the New Jersey State line and we have no jurisdiction there." Detective Michael studied Fox closely when the two locked eyes with each other as Top Dollar got the ticket at the N.J. toll booth before pulling off.

3

At approximately 8:30 pm in an eight bedroom, four bathroom, three story mini-mansion located in upstate New York, several men patrolled the perimeter while Mr. Holmes relaxed in his master den seated in his tailor-made Burberry leather chair with his feet crossed, resting upon the antique 1860 cherry oak desk as he spoke with his two imported hit men.

A 300 lb man armed with a 9 mm tucked in his waistband and an M-16 in his palms stood off in the corner making sure they weren't disturbed. Just a few feet away another man posted on the outside of the door did the same.

"First off, gentlemen, let me compliment you on a successful mission," Mr. Holmes smiled, passing each man a Cuban cigar. He then stood up placing one to his lip with the obese body guard putting heat to it in a second. "Thank you, Paul. Now as I was saying, Apollon and Balial, I like to take care of the people who take care of me, because in the end we're all we've got." "I agree," said Apollon with his short trademark answer and deep raspy voice. Balial didn't say anything as he kept his vision locked on the men in the corner from the side of his eye while thinking, "*I can smell the fear in your blood and I hate the scent of weakness so if you try to make a move, you only have a third of a second before I put a bullet through your heart.*"

Mr. Holmes continued, "And for such a good job, I have this for you." He gave a light nod and the Paul placed a suit case onto the desk. He opened it to reveal two hundred thousand dollars. "That's yours." "Thanks, but no," stated Apollon. "Mr. Holmes, what my brother is trying to say is we thank you dearly but we can't take your money because our service isn't for sale. We only work for one person, that's Diego El Sovida," Balial explained.

"Is that so?" Mr. Holmes asked as he paused, taking a moment to look both men in the eyes while pulling on his cigar to let his power be felt through the room before he continued. "Then how did I get you to handle this?" Mr. Holmes released the smoke through his nose with a confident smirk upon his face. "That is easy, for now you owe a favor to a man that has everything like yourself, so I can only imagine what will make you even. But if I'm not mistaken, a soul taken is a soul owed, am I correct?"

Mr. Holmes's smirk slowly eased away as he shook his head up and down wondering how the men knew rule number 3 when only Corporation members had access to that information and there was only one book in the world with it and the man who possessed it would die before he revealed even a letter. "Don't look so shocked, Mr. Holmes," Balial said, as he and his brother removed their hands from their suit jacket pockets that were rested on the handle of their forty five automatic to reveal their rings from the Corporation that matched Mr. Holmes. "We just like the killing side better."

Mr. Holmes, still not satisfied, used his phone, texting several secret letters. Seconds afterward, their rings began to light up. "You believe me now?" "Yes but you have only finished half of my request."

"And the rest?" questioned Apollon.

"Kill Roc"

"But don't we need the okay from all the members to do that?"

"Not if you make it look like it was of natural causes," Mr. Holmes smiled, taking in another deep pull, watching Apollon shake his head up and down, loving the thought of the challenge and the power of taking down his next victim. "It's done."

Mr. Holmes gave another light nod and Paul retrieved several bottles of champagne, popping them one by one. Mr. Holmes's intercom light started to flash, "Excuse me." Mr. Holmes picked up the phone from its base with a smile still on his face but mentally he was furious that someone would disobey his orders.

"Hello, who's this?"

"It…it's me boss," Jack answered nervously.

"I'm sorry, Jack, but what did I tell you?"

"Not to disturb you for anything, but Diego El Sovida called and is waiting on line three. I tried to get him to call back but he stated it was very important that you two speak now"

"Well you should have tried harder." Mr. Holmes disconnected the phone, hitting three.

"Diego El Sovida, why didn't you call me on our secure line?"

"This line is safe I presume?"

"Yes, but you would have saved Jack's life."

"Well some people have to be sacrificed for the rest of us to continue to live well in life."

"Yes, there has to be consequences for every man's actions, even if it's not their own," Mr. Holmes stated, thinking of his beloved student.

"I'm glad you agree. Now are my people still there?"

"Yes, I'm looking at them right now."

"Good, because I just received a call from Roc asking for permission to speak with them."

"Did he say what he wanted?"

"No, because I already told him he could but you know that could never happen right?"

"It depends."

"On what?" Diego El Sovida asked, knowing Mr. Holmes was up to something.

"How well can they play."

"Don't even play, Mr. Holmes. Eliminate them immediately, because Roc can't know I was involved."

"I'll handle it."

"Okay and remember you owe me and it must be done in the next six months."

"Don't worry, I give you my word, and it's worth more than anything I possess."

Mr. Holmes hung up, now realizing why Diego El Sovida didn't use the Corporation line it was because killing a member was something beyond death and just the thought of it sent chills up his spine. Mr. Holmes eased back in his seat still with the smile on his face and asked, "Apollon, do you play chess?" "Yes," he replied. "Paul, grab the board for me will you? No, not that one, the red piece, I like to feel as if it's do or die when I play."

Once the pieces were set in position, Mr. Holmes attacked out the gate striking first, taking two pawns in a row. His action brought a smile to Apollon's face. While waiting on the open space to move his bishop, he retrieved a pawn while threatening Mr. Holmes's knight and giving it no option of escape. Mr. Holmes searched the board for his best move while already in his head, subtracting the knight from his plots. He eliminated another pawn to gain control of the center of the board. Apollon's next move eased his queen out of the backfield to the front line just before the pawn. Spotting this, Mr. Holmes thought as he moved, "*Roc would never had made that mistake, for he knows better than to bring your most powerful weapon out in the open before your opponent is seriously damaged. It could only cost you your own life because if it's lost, so is your life.*"

After making several sacrifices, using his only knight left, Mr. Holmes called "Check," placing Apollon's queen in harms way. Balial, who became caught up in the high level battle of the minds, shook his head from side to side as the words exited his lips, "Fatal mistake, Bro." "If only you knew how much; check mate in two moves."

It wasn't what Mr. Holmes said that sent a funny feeling over Balial's body it was how he said it. He then quickly shot his eyes in the direction of Paul's corner, finding it empty. He briskly turned his head to make sure he wasn't being set up, when the side of his face slammed into the barrel of Paul's 9 mm, who pulled the trigger, 'BOOM', killing Balial. Apollon's light skin complexion turned red instantly as he jumped to his feet with Paul's gun following his every move. Looking Mr. Holmes dead in the eyes he said, "You have pulled a stratagem on me, now you must pay." "As I stated earlier, I'm a man of my word and if you find some way to win this game, you'll be free to go."

Understanding his option, Apollon calmed himself and began to restudy the broad. He lowered his hand to move his queen then suddenly flipped the board over in Mr. Holmes's direction sending pieces everywhere. Paul squeezed the trigger twice but the distraction made his response seconds off, giving Apollon all the time he needed as he side stepped Paul while sending his right foot hard into the side of his knee cap and separating it on contact. "Aaaaaahhhhhh," the big man fell towards the ground with a roundhouse kick connecting to the back of his head knocking him out cold as he collapsed to the soft rug. Apollon moved with the quickness of a true pro while dropping to one knee, he stuck Paul with a sharp pen-like weapon in the pressure point of his neck. The object seemed to have come from nowhere and then it was gone.

Standing, he was again face to face with Mr. Holmes, "I'm going to love killing you for my brother... 'BOOM-BOOM,' Mr. Holmes pulled the trigger on the Ruger. He vowed after being kidnapped by Lil Mac to never leave home without it again. Apollon looked down at the smoke coming from the gun in shock, then to his silk shirt that now had several bullet holes before stumbling to the floor.

"That's another mistake Roc wouldn't have made. He would never have taken my paying you to kill as a weakness, as if I couldn't kill for myself." Mr. Holmes removed the 9 mm from the center of Apollon's back, tucking it in his waist band. Hitting the intercom button, he said, "Jack get in here with some help to clean up this mess and bring four body bags." Within moments Jack rushed in with Al.

"Al, make sure this room is spotless."

"Yes sir, Mr. Holmes."

"And Jack, the next time I give you an order, please follow it."

"I will, Mr. Holmes, I promise."

'BOOM-BOOM-BOOM,' Jacks lifeless body fell into Al's arms. "I know you will," Mr. Holmes tossed the hot 9 mm onto Al and then strolled from the room.

An hour later, Mr. Holmes entered his master bedroom, fresh out of the shower to see an extensive layout of high class designer suits with matching ties laid out across the bed. He began to let his fingers roam over the many different materials. His butler, Travis, then appeared from a side door with a large box that contained shoes to accompany his attire. Sensing his presence, Mr. Holmes said without facing him, "Travis, you know you can always tell a good suit by the feel of its texture?" "Indeed, sir, for it's the suit that communicates a man's position without him saying a word. Your shoes, sir." "Place them over there," Mr. Holmes nodded towards the black marble dresser as he held up two double breasted suits, one brown and the other white.

"Now which one do you like, Travis?"

"If you're asking my opinion, sir, I would go with black because it always represents power."

"Black it is."

Mr. Holmes tightened the rose gold Rolex on his wrist, placing the finishing touches to his flawless appearance and then headed outside to the waiting limousine where a large muscular man held the door. Another man stood on post three inches away at the doors opening, scanning the area for any thing that looked out of place. Mr. Holmes stepped one foot into the back seat then paused, reaching into his black suit case to get a small wrapped box with a red bow. "Oh, Travis, before I forget, send this package to the address on the top when I call you." "Consider it done sir." Taking it Travis noticed the lack of a signature, "Sir wait, who should I sign it from?"

Mr. Holmes shut the door, lowering the dark tinted window asking the big man still posted, "What's the name of that fella 2 Pac was beefing with?" "Biggie Smalls" "And what's the name of that song you listen to all the damn time like Roc?" "Warning, but Roc liked 2 Pac," the man corrected. "That's it, and you're right."

Mr. Holmes smiled devilishly and slowly disappeared behind the tint. The limousine maneuvered through the rough traffic of New York City with the vision of the large skyscraper reflecting off the fresh waxed paint job as Mr. Holmes relaxed with his hands behind his head while he thought, *"By the time I get back in town, Roc should have calmed down and be ready to listen to reason or his fate will be the same."*

Mr. Holmes pushed the touch screen television to catch the ten o'clock news, seeing that it was about to start. *"Ladies and Gentlemen I'm Molly Weiss from C.V.T.V. and welcome to another episode of In These Mean Streets. Today things have been in an up roar. I'm going to start with Victor Antigeo, better known as Don Antigeo, alleged to have murdered the number one boss of Bosses of all five mob crime families in New York to gain power. Antigeo has been indicted and the charges still have not been disclosed. Then back home in the city of brotherly love, a young man had a shoot out with two police men that ended deadly with one officer injured and the other dead. The suspect was also killed."*

"Damn, young soldier, it couldn't have been that bad to go out like that. But I'm damn sure not mad at you for fighting," whispered Mr. Holmes before answering his corporate phone. "Hello"

"Mr. Holmes."

"Roc?"

"Yeah, it's me, old head." The sound of Roc's voice instantly made Mr. Holmes smile. He didn't sense a drop of tension as Roc continued.

"The reason I called is to give you a warning."

"A warning, huh?" Mr. Holmes's smiled quickly transformed to a face that showed no emotion while his grip on the cell phone tightened extremely as he lowered his eyes, giving Roc his full attention.

"Yes, somehow the Get Money Clique thinks you had something to do with Lil Mac's death."

"Roc, that's insane. I could never do anything to hurt that boy without hurting you and you're like a son to me. This reaction, I don't understand."

"Me neither, that's why as soon as I heard their plan I called you right away. They got word that you may be leaving the city and they hired a hit man that will be hiding behind the disguise of a red capped man. He has been paid for an up close kill so there shouldn't be any trouble for you to identify him. He will be the one wanting to carry your baggage."

"How many will there be in all, Roc?"

"One, they believe he's the best, old head."

Mr. Holmes looked at the phone that was now dead. Puzzled, he was wondering if he took Roc's words out of their context at the funeral. The glowing red light that flashed in the night brought Mr. Holmes from his thoughts. *"I know my boy wouldn't let me down,"* he said to himself as the man with the darkened face waved the limousine through the security gate at the edge of the landing strip. The man then pocketed the neon sticks as his eye suddenly became distant at the sight of the passenger while his mind placed him back behind enemy lines when he was in the war in Iraq. Without losing the vision of the tail light Mohammed said into his earpiece, "Top Dollar, he's on his way."

4

The lights were dim in the basement of Roc's mother's luxurious summer home as several women sat around the bar sipping on strawberry daiquiris to the soft sound of K.C. and Jo-Jo's remake of '*If You Think Your Lonely Now*,' played in the background. The ladies who were now feeling a little tipsy enjoyed a passionate conversation on how to love a man. Sakara, who was the wife of Haffee, sat at the head of the bar with her hair laid down and her Dior shoes removed from her feet, relaxing while nursing her second drink. Next to her on the right sat Flirtatious, Luscious Chocolate, and China who were the company of Boggy and just happened to all be exotic dancers.

Roc's mother, Mrs. Miller, sat at the end stool, appreciating the delightful gathering that Roc put together for her in such a trying moment for their family. Roc's beautiful wife, Gizelle, stood behind the cherry oak woods structure refilling everyone's drinks when Sakara explained her point deeper, trying to give a better understanding. "Don't get me wrong, if a man isn't doing you right and you have tried everything there is to be done then you have the right to leave him. I just believe that if a man is willing to try to better himself than we should stand by him that's all."

"Shit, if my man is acting up and he don't get it right the first time I tell him, the only place I'm going to stand by his ass is in the line at the bank. Shit, you don't know?" said Luscious Chocolate. "That's right, girl, cuz ain't nobody got no damn time to be babysitting a grown ass man with all the major players wanting all this!" Flirtatious agreed, running her hands over her body before giving Luscious Chocolate a high five.

"Please, let me get this correct, you're telling me if times were to get hard for you and your man that you wouldn't stick it out to find out if it would work?" questioned Gizelle. "No, no don't get me wrong," Flirtatious said in the best voice she could to sound like Sakara. "I would stick it out and probably bend over and grab my ankles for another player with a bigger bank roll, yeeeaahhh." The two women broke out in laughter.

"What about you, China? Have you ever been in love, because by the way these two young ladies are talking, they haven't," questioned Roc's mother. "Love?" China repeated and then paused, looking as if she was searching her brain for the answer. "Come to think of it, Mrs. Miller, I never gave it any thought. I'm a stripper who lets men and women touch me anywhere for money and a lot of them are married, so if that's love, I'd rather take the money and keep my heart."

"Yeah, I keep getting scratches on my clit from all the wedding rings that be going through me," Luscious Chocolate. Mrs. Miller smiled as she shook her head in disbelief. "No, child, when you find love you won't be able to keep your heart because it'll already be gone. You just pray to God that it doesn't come back. That's why a woman that knows love is so willing to do what she needs to in order to make it work. See, when I first laid eyes on Larry Odell Miller Sr., Roc's father, I was walking with my mother on our way to the hair stylist which we did together every week."

Mrs. Miller shot a look at Sakara that made her pretty white teeth show as she smiled in agreement. "Well, Mrs. Miller, I got three married men daily, sexing me crazy and I don't have to listen to their problems, cook, or clean and they all spend a thousand or more on me a week," said

Flirtatious. When the comment reached Sakara's ears, she spit the red drink across the floor as she began to choke. China jumped from her seat, patting Sakara on the back. "Ms. Sakara, are you okay?" "Yes, it's just…that's what I pay my cleaning lady without her weekly tip, aaahh," Sakara laughed while she yelled, "Betty," into the wall intercom for Mrs. Miller's cleaning lady.

"Yes, madam?"

"Can you come down here? I'm sorry I have made a mess."

"No problem, I'll be right there."

Flirtatious looked around the room at everyone, laughing with eyes of hatred for Sakara as she yelled, "Yeah I know it's funny and I bet you those women that are sitting up in their pretty homes all high and mighty like you were laughing too until they tasted my clit and ass on their husbands' lips." The ladies laughter grew even louder but Sakara stopped instantly as she noticed Flirtatious's stare saying, "Oh, honey, they are nothing like me; I can smell a skank on my husband from a mile away. That's why I give him everything he needs from a woman and more at home!" "You think so?" Flirtatious replied. "Baby, I don't think, that's a word of uncertainty, I know this!" Sakara held her hand out so everyone could see, "Tiffany's 4 ct platinum setting ring." The diamond sparkled throughout the room. "See, baby, you're going to have to work almost a year straight with no breaks to get this." Then next…come the house, cars, and food. Then maybe you can worry about the problems of cooking and cleaning." The ladies continued to laugh until their stomachs began to ache, which only made Flirtatious more furious until she screamed, "Bitch!"

"Whoa, whoa, ladies," interrupted Mrs. Miller.

"I know this chic did not just come up in here and disrespect me!" stated a shocked Sakara while removing her diamond earrings. Then Gizelle grabbed her by the hand,

"Calm down Sakara." "Calm down? No, you better get ready in case these bitches try to jump me because I'm going to get old school and smack fire from the one with the hot ass mouth."

Gizelle tried to hold back her laughter as Sakara broke loose from her grip and jumped to her feet. "Now come on over here and I'm going to smack some sense into you because you done let my Dior shoes fool you." "Ladies stop it," Mrs. Miller said firmly. "Now come and have a seat all of you, we were having a good time so please lets not spoil it." Mrs. Miller's demands were followed immediately because when she spoke, which was rarely, every word possessed so much wisdom.

"See, this is the problem with our older people, Sakara I'm speaking to you, by not being patient enough to teach the youth what you know they need to learn. And our young people, I'm talking to you Flirtatious, you have to be patient enough to listen so someone will want to tell you something because believe it or not there are people where you're trying to go. Now come over here and have a seat while I tell China about love." Mrs. Miller patted the leather seat next to her. She waited until everyone got comfortable and began speaking.

"Flirtatious, you owe Sakara an apology."

"Sorry."

"That's bette.r"

"Now, China darling, love is a funny thing because you'll never know when it will hit you. It was 1971 on a Friday, I'll never forget that day as long as I live. My mother and I were on our way to get our hair done. When this fine man dressed in light blue cashmere sweater with a white butterfly collar and white wing tip shoes began to stare at me so hard it made my face smile as we walked passed him. But I knew he wasn't for me."

"What made you think that, Mrs. Miller?" Gizelle asked.

"Because you have to remember at the time, I was 19 with a full scholarship to UCLA and a GPA of 4.0. Everything I knew was upper class and then there was this man, who, while he looked at me, connected with my soul. He was writing down the neighborhood gambling numbers on a piece of paper; that right there told me he could only be one thing."

"And what was that?" The ladies asked in unison.

"A gangster. And my kind and his kind mixing, was unheard of so I never stopped my stride. We entered the salon and my mother said, "Carmen did you see how that hoodlum was looking at you?" "No mother I didn't notice." "Good, cuz that boy is nothing but trouble." After having my hair washed, I was placed under the dryer for fifteen minutes. So I closed my eyes and began thinking about all the lovely things I would do once I left Philly in a few months. Then I felt a tap on my shoulder and when I opened them, chiiiiillld I saw the most beautiful set of hazel eyes on this man that was drop dead gorgeous. The sight of him made my heart start to beat at a pace that was unrecognizable to me for this man whose hands carried a dozen red roses while saying sweet words."

Gizelle was looking at Mrs. Millers lips move but instead she was hearing Roc's voice as he said the same words to her that his father spoke to Mrs. Miller so many years earlier, "*Excuse me, Beautiful, it's said that love is the basic need of the human nature, for without it, life is disrupted emotionally, mentally, spiritually, and physically. You know I never did believe that to be true...until five seconds ago when I saw you.*"

Gizelle sat her drink down and headed for the stairs, still feeling a buzz while the ladies' voices echoed in the background. "Mrs. Miller, that's so sweet." "Baby you don't know the half of it; this man was everything a woman could ask for and more."

Upstairs, Gizelle walked down the hall toward the back bedroom where three men stood on post at the door. "Excuse me, fellas, but I need to get in there." Nobody moved as they looked passed her trying not to look at her ample breasts that seamed to test the strength of her silk blouse. Manny was the first to break the silence, "I'm sorry, Gizelle, but now is not a good time. If you can, go back down stairs with the rest of the ladies, we'll be gone in no time."

"Manny, I know you just didn't tell me to come back. Have you lost your damn mind?!"

"Gizelle, there's no disrespect intended."

"Oh I know there's not because your wife's at home and that's the only woman you can try to give an order to, now move!" Gizelle pushed Manny hard in the chest but didn't move him. "Damn," she said while thinking to herself, "*Lacey, you go girl.*" Boggy wrapped his arms around Gizelle's neck, pulling her off to the side seeing that Manny wasn't getting anywhere and asked, "Girl, what is you doing? You know it must be important business or I would have let you in the room so why are you tripping?"

"No, you're tripping, that line would have worked a month ago, but things changed, Boggy, the moment your street life touched my home and took my brother in-law from me. Now there are no secrets! All business is my business." Boggy stared at the serious look on Gizelle's face as a tear began to form in the corner of her right eye. Bending down, Boggy kissed her on the forehead. "I can't argue with that, Lil sis."

Gizelle eased quietly into the room to see the love of her life sitting on the edge of the bed with his back facing her as he spoke into the phone. "Yes, some how the Get

Money Clique thinks you had something to do with Lil Mac's murder."

Gizelle slowly crept up onto the bed and wrapped her arms around Roc's waist while resting her head on his shoulder. She waited patiently in silence until he placed the phone back on its hook then gently kissed him on his lips as if it could be her last time.

"So it's true…you're going after Mr. Holmes?"

"No, I wouldn't d-"

"Ssshhh, there's no need to lie, I'm here for you no matter what you have to do, baby."

Gizelle removed herself from the bed and walked around until she was face to face with Roc. "Love, I told you that you'll always have my support and I mean that." She then began to kiss him passionately, forcing his back down onto the bed. Her fingers slowly started to release the straps of his bullet proof vest that covered his muscular chest when he stopped her. "Baby, I can't. I'm sorry, my men are waiting on me." "Roc, ever since the death of Lil Mac, every time you walk out that door I feel like it may be the last time I ever see you, speak to you, or feel your body against mine. I understand that the people who did this to him will only respect blood shed so I must let you become your former self, for you to make it back home safely. But while you're here I will not be denied.

Gizelle's lips reconnected with Roc's, dancing to a song that only they could hear as she threw the vest to the floor, her nails ran along his rib cage until she pulled the wife beater over his head. Her hot soft lips began to kiss from his neck down to his six-pack while her freshly manicured fingers fumbled with his belt buckle to unleash his rock hard manhood. Roc, knowing his woman like every man should, knew Gizelle needed him more than anything right now. He pulled her head up from his chest to find her soft lips again before smoothly rolling her over onto her back. "You just lay right there."

He raced to the door, cracking it a little when Boggy said, "Come on, Roc, the cars are ready to move; we're waiting on you."

"I know but there has been a change of plans."

"What, a change of plans?"

"Yes, have a helicopter waiting to take us in an hour. That should make up for the delay."

"But what if I can't find one on such short notice?"

"Then buy one!"

"Okay player, you have one hour then I need you back on war time."

Boggy and Roc were more like brothers than partners. As they did their special handshake, Roc said, "My mind is always on war time, that's why we can eat in peace."

Re-closing the door, he paused to take in the vision of his wife wanting nothing else in the world at this moment but him. *"And she can have all of me,"* Roc thought as he removed each item of her clothing, leaving a kiss behind until she was completely nude. Loving the sight of his wife's natural beauty, Roc massaged her breast, taking her hardened nipple into his mouth. He started to suck, lick, and gently bite each one while vibrating his two fingers back and forth on her clit, sending a strong wave of pleasure through her entire body. A soft moan escaped Gizelle's lips as Roc started to kiss his way down her chest, making sure he touched all the right spots until his tongue reached the center of her clit. "O-o-o-h my God, Roocc." He moved his lips and tongue to match the rhythm of his finger moving in and out of her love box. After several licks, Gizelle gripped the back of Roc's head tightly as she pulled him closer, grinding her hips with every motion. Roc picked up his pace, tasting her juices that coated his lips while her legs began to tremble, "No, you're not getting away that easy," Roc slid Gizelle on to her side while easing his nine inch man hood deep inside her tight fitting paradise, "Uuuhhhh."

Not wanting to bring her a drop of pain or discomfort he slowly worked his manhood into her, inch by inch until her love walls gave in to accept his passion. Roc felt Gizelle's love box heating up as her wetness increased, placing his fingers between her ass cheeks, gripping them firmly while spreading them apart. He then began to thrust his hips forward long stroking her deep and hard, making sure he hit her G-spot with each motion. A clapping sound echoed off the contact of their bodies. Gizelle bit down hard on her bottom lip trying not to scream as thoughts ran wild through her head, *"Oh God, that's my spot Oooohh yes, he knows it too."*

Roc raised one leg in the air, kissing each toe before wrapping it around his waist without interrupting his rhythm. Then without warning he lifted her off the bed, locking his hands on her shoulders. He pulled her down closer to him with every stroke as his thick manhood repeatedly forced Gizelle's walls in with pleasure. Unable to control her moans, they grew louder as she began to climax. Her juices rushed down Roc's balls and legs as she lost complete power over her body. She quickly grabbed hold of Roc's neck, hoping not to pass out while she bit down on his earlobe, racing her tongue in and out of it while moans of joy echoed through out the room. Her body began to quiver as hot cum shot from her body. Roc slowly stroked his wife until her waves subsided as she whispered into his ear, "Thank you."

Roc gently laid her on the bed and headed for the shower. Minutes later he returned to find Gizelle sound asleep. He smiled, whispering back, "You can repay me later," before easing the door shut behind him.

5

11:35 pm at a private airport in upstate N.Y. several limousines approached the entrance while Fatel dressed in a red cap uniform, stood a few feet away from the other workers who were waiting anxiously to earn a dollar. His eyes rescanned the area as he spoke into his earpiece that was hidden by the large red hat. "Yo, Top, there's only three armed men that I can verify at the moment." "Okay, what's their location?" Top Dollar questioned from the front passenger seat of the limousine while looking through the front of the all glass structured building.

"The first one is twenty feet away from the entrance just pass the tip of the casino wearing a dark cream suit."

"With a white thin tie and his hair slicked back like he could be with the mob?" asked Top Dollar with his eyes glued to a pair of high tech binoculars locked on the man with the bulge in the front of his suit.

"Yeah that's him, his eyes haven't stopped moving since I got here like he's waiting on something to happen."

"Well he'll get it if he gets in our way," Top Dollar replied, meaning every word.

"The next one is on the opposite side, off to your right, sitting at the fifth table in the lobby of the Poland Mountain Bar."

"You're referring to the three hundred pound man eating that cheeseburger?"

"That's him."

"What's he gonna do?" screamed Fox who was listening in on the conversation.

"Don't sleep on him. It seems he may have some military training," explained Fatel.

"Who's the last one?" Top Dollar questioned while giving Fox a look that said, don't you start.

"He's right by the…"

"Wait, fill me in while I'm on the move, they're waiting for us," interrupted Top Dollar as a man dressed in a black tuxedo quickly walked by lightly tapping on the hood of each limousine giving them the queue that it was time. Top Dollar then exited saying, "Show time." He held the door open for NayNay whose long black hair was now dyed blond and neatly wrapped in a bun. She wore a short Elie Saab black dress with full Detectiveail in the lace that ran from her ankle up the side of her leg and back. It was designed with spaces in its pattern to give her easy access to the 380 strapped to each of her hips. There was also a small 22 tucked in the back of her sports bra. Her neck and wrist were covered with just the right touch of class as the white pearls she wore added a look of maturity to complete her role.

Haffee knew if his action was off in any way that Mr. Holmes was sure to spot it and that mistake may end up costing him his life. This forced him to be extra hype and ready to go all out. If Allah willed, this would be his last and final mission. As the souls of his Prada shoes touched the concrete, Haffee rose to his feet with the air of confidence and swagger of a billionaire. He gently ran his hands over his spotless blue and white three-piece suit to remove any unseen lint while checking his reflection in the tinted window. He straightened his tie as he said to Fox, "Perfect, now my hat." "What?" Fox replied. "I said my hat."

Top Dollar, quick on his feet said, "Here you go, sir," handing Haffee a dark blue cashmere London Fog brim hat. He adjusted it on his head, then wrapped his arms around the slim waist of NayNay saying, "Shall we go my love, revenge is awaiting us." NayNay and Haffee headed through the revolving doors with Fox and A.P. bringing up the rear, looking in every direction as if they were their bodyguards. Top Dollar hurried passed the Louis Vuitton luggage to the red capped worker from out of the trunk of the vehicle.

As he closely watched Fatel slowly approach a man in a black suit stepping out from the back seat of a Maybach questioning, "Sir, may I help you with your bags?" Slamming the steel door shut, Top Dollar handed the man a twenty dollar bill before dashing around the car and hopping into the driver's seat. He yelled, "Fatel that's not him, I repeat, stand down that's not Mr. Holmes. Damn he can't hear me."

Top Dollar dropped the limousine into drive pushing hard on the gas, sending rocks flying free from under the rubber tire as he raced for the back side entrance. Fatel had his feet planted in position ready to strike as he eased his right hand onto the 9 mm automatic that was in his uniform front side pocket. Small sweat drops began to form on the side of his face and palms while he watched and Italian man dressed in a double-breasted black suit under his three quarter length coat. The Rolex that was on his wrist gleamed in the night as he ran his hand through his silky salt and pepper hair: he was Don Antigeo. A known boss, Antigeo towered over Fatel with his 6' 2 frame saying, "No son, what ever I need I'll purchase while I'm there," as he stuffed a hundred dollar bill in the left palm of Fatel's hand.

Fatel looked from the money back to the man while his right hand crept to the edge of his pocket. Suddenly the voice of Top Dollar finally reached his ear. "Don't, Fatel, he's not the one." At that moment two of Don Antigeo's bodyguards stepped in front of Fatel's path. "He said he's alright, kid, now keep it moving," stated one of the body guards. "Thank you, sir," Fatel said stepping off just in time to see a man tap on the hood of that last limousine. "Damn," slipped from his lips at the sight of another red cap helping Mr. Holmes's body guard retrieved his bag.

Fatel quickly strolled over to them with a fake smile on his face, asking, "Excuse me sir, is everything under control, or is there more I can do for you?" Once again he slid his hand into his pocket.

"No we got it all handled," answered the large body guard.

"Please, Robert, don't be so rude; the young man can help me. Here son, you can take my suitcase, just don't let it get out of my sight and by the way, the name's Holmes."

"Okay, Mr. Holmes, thank you."

"No son, please hold it with your right hand."

Fatel looked at Mr. Holmes puzzled, as he slowly removed his hand from the handle of his gun, picking up the suitcase.

"Religious reasons, son."

"Will do, sir," Fatel said with hate in his eyes as his blood boiled from being so close to the man that took the life of his friend and leader.

Inside the airport, a smooth relaxing atmosphere moved through the not-so-crowded lobby as high class men and women became lost in the many options of fun while awaiting their flights. NayNay wore her dark sunglasses over her eyes to conceal the direction of her stare as she looked through out the room. Fox said, "Damn this place knows how to make a nigga feel right at home - free drinks, lobster, crackers, and shit. They even give you a phone so they can call you when your plane arrives. I guess it's so they don't interrupt this easy jazz playing on the intercom."

"I'm glad you're amused but get on point, here they come," said Haffee.

"I'm always on point," Fox replied as his eyes focused on Mr. Holmes's every move, thinking to himself, "Tonight the soul of Solo will ride again."

Don Antigeo's body guards showed their tickets at the front desk and were given a variety bag as the attendant said, "Sir, in there, you'll find several of the newest and hottest electronic devices like the new touch screen 3G phone that will ring twenty minutes before your plane departure."

"Thanks, what a ding bat, come on boss."

"You know, Jimmy, I'm feeling kind of lucky today. I think I'll try my hand at the casino."

"But, Don, you said we had to keep a low profile."

"I am, by leaving the country my family built, only to come back to fight another day!"

Don Antigeo walked passed Mr. Holmes giving him a light head nod in his direction as he entered the black jack room. Mr. Holmes, watching his men, began checking in, decided to excuse himself. "Fellas I'm going to use the restroom." "You want me to come with you boss?" "No, I'll be fine, I just got some advice from an old friend, but I believe he was wrong." Mr. Holmes's hard soled shoes echoed across the marble floor as Fatel trailed a few steps behind him waiting on the right moment. Seeing it, Fatel abruptly eased the suitcase back into his left hand to get his weapon, thinking, *"Pussy, when I'm done you'll wish you never heard of the Get Money Clique."*

Now only several feet away from the men's room, Fatel heard Top Dollar giving Mohammed his order, "Have the get away cars ready, Fatel is making his move, you dig." "Insha'Allah." Fatel watched Mr. Holmes enter the restroom with the door slowly closing, *"Time to meet your maker."*

Fatel stopped the door before it could shut. His hand was full with the feeling of cold steel; his 9 mm that had taken many people's lives and now would be no different. He walked in with death on his mind as he eased back the chamber, cocking the weapon when a motion caught his attention from the corner of his eye. Fatel quickly spun around with his eyes wide as Mr. Holmes jumped out from behind the door with a large knife, pushing it through his neck while rushing his body into the first toilet stall. The two men crashed hard up against the back wall. The blood raced from Fatel's neck as his body shook viciously as he tried to speak, "Aaaa...aahh." Mr. Holmes smiled, ripping the earpiece from his body and stepping on it.

"You won't ever get me that easily. Who do you think taught you youngins this shit? Oh you can't talk? Well I bet you know now!"

"Aaah," Fatel gasped for air, still trying to speak

"The reason I told you my name was not to be polite," Mr. Homes said, moving closer until he was an inch away from Fatel's ear. "I did it so you'll know the name of the man that took your life." Mr. Holmes pushed the knife in deeper, twisting it. Fatel's lifeless body went stiff.

Mr. Holmes placed his body on the toilet as if he was using it, then spit on the open-eyed face of Fatel. "Tell Solo I said hi." He then popped open his suitcase looking at the change of clothes that were inside and smiled, whispering, "A man that's not prepared for anything can only be prepared for failure."

Out in the lobby area, Fox sat impatiently with his hand tucked in his suit jacket with nothing but revenge on his mind. He said to Haffee who had begun to dial his phone just as Fatel entered the bathroom. "Listen, Haffee, this is the first time we're putting in work together so I'm letting you know now; I'm not with that waiting around shit. If he's not out of there in five minutes I'm on the move with or without you."

"Yeah I hear you," Haffee answered, really not paying Fox any mind. He placed the phone to his ear and said, "Hello, Roc, he just went in."

"Okay what channel are they receiving on?"

"Roc, is that a helicopter I hear?"

"Yeah, doing a little sight seeing."

"Up north I bet," Haffee questioned but already knowing the answer. Roc never left any loose ends, no matter who had to die to protect his family and team.

"Without question, I wish you were here to see me through this like always but I'll catch up with you next time, right?" The communication line suddenly went dead with Haffee not knowing how to answer his friend.

"Haffee, you there?"

"Yes, we're on channel eight."

"Okay," Roc switched channels then continued.

"I'm on it, now Get Money Clique, I need you all to listen closely: this incident took place a few weeks before my brother's death and I knew he would want you all to know the reason." Roc pushed play on the black handheld recorder to hear the sound of Shamone in his best cop voice say, *"Listen kid, I know it's hard out there for you to live and at times you got to do what you have to just to make it. That's why you're here instead of the station, to give you a chance to help yourself."*

"Help myself? Please, you don't have nothing on me. That's why I'm here and not the station." The Get Money Clique's eyes grew as they recognized the second voice to be Fatel as Shamone continued, *"Are you sure you want to play tough, you know it's hard being a gangster?"*

"You damn right and I'm all of it," Fatel replied.

"That's fine with me, I just pray that my partner who doesn't like you as much, doesn't find anything in that pretty truck of yours."

"He won't," answered Fatel.

A few minutes of just breathing could be heard on the tape then the crackle of a walkie talkie. "Partner, cuff the bastard. We got him," Mohammed yelled. "With what?" "A half a key of crack rock and a loaded 380 automatic," he responded. *"Copy, that's alright, gangster, stand up."* A *popping noise could be heard from Shamone releasing the button on his holster. "Okay, okay, how can I help myself?" asked Fatel.*

Hearing enough, Fox jumped up, "Where's he at, I'm going to kill him!" He then heard Roc's voice in his ear, "Sit down, Fox, remember what I told you!" Fox lowered himself back onto the cushion of the soft leather chair while searching his brain trying to remember what he was told. Roc restarted the tape.

"First you must tell me who you work for, starting at the top of the Get Money Clique. If you lie to me, I'll make sure you do every day of the 25 years you're facing." Again, breathing could be heard, with nothing else said for a moment and then Fatel spoke, "Mac Miller."

"Excuse me, what did you say?" Shamone asked.

"The head is Solo a.k.a. Mac Miller."

Roc pushed stop on the recorder and said, "For the consequences of disrespecting a Miller let alone the game, Fatel is no longer with us, but he must not die alone." "Don't worry, I got it, Roc. The target is in sight," NayNay responded. She pushed away from the gray marble table just as Mr. Holmes exited in a fresh tailored black suit. "He's on the go so we're going to split up."

"Hold up, I'm in charge here!" Haffee interrupted. "No, you're an overseer, so when I'm done, you can stand over him and see that he's dead," NayNay stated seriously before continuing to give her orders. "A.P., after you check on Fatel, I need you to take the back entrance and handle the big sloppy man on the right."

"I'm out," announced A.P. "Daz, you take the side door on the right, while the overseer here and I will go straight down the center. Fox, you'll be on a minute delay to do the clean up if all else fails. Let's go, we'll move into position in five." NayNay started to cross the floor, removing her glasses from her eyes so that she could see the pain in Mr. Holmes's face as she let every shot loose in his body.

Haffee was five steps behind, giving Fox a hard tap in the ribs with his elbow saying, "Come on!" The contact brought Fox back to the moment from the shock of Roc's words that he'd replayed in his head, *"Listen, if you keep it up you will be wearing that red cap."* Then AP's voice replaced Roc's through the earpiece, "NayNay, Fatel is gone." "Good, the bitch needed to die," she replied. *"Damn, Roc's gangster,"* Fox thought, as he caught up with the rest of this team.

Mr. Holmes entered the casino spotting an empty seat next to an Italian man with a dark tan as a quarter million dollars worth of chips sat in front of him. He headed for the seat when a slick haired man stepped in his path and said, "These seats are taken." Then the three hundred pound Robert stepped in his path, "Boss, sit down anywhere you want, and I mean anywhere." "Boys," the two bosses said simultaneously. The demand made the man slowly back away from the chair while each man refused to take their eyes off of one another. Mr. Holmes approached the empty seat asking, "May I?" Don Antigeo placed a bet of fifty thousand and nonchalantly said, "It's open." "Thank you." Sliding into the open spot, Mr. Holmes placed his triple black company card that read Holmes International Construction, into the center of the table. "Yes, sir, what would you like to start with?" "Double what he got," Mr. Holmes replied.

The dealer then dealt the cards to the several players through out the table while giving out the rules. "The game is black jack with twenty one being the best hand and ace and any face card pays double, all pushes lose." As the dealer continued to explain, Mr. Holmes with his hand resting on his mustache looking as if he was studying the cards said while barely moving his lips, "Please tell me you saw this coming, old friend."

Don Antigeo smoothly raised his cards to his face, stopping just above his mouth to prevent any unwanted law enforcement agent from reading his lips before responding, "To be truthful ,Holmes, I didn't even know I was under investigation. Don't get me wrong, by being who we are and what we represent I know we're always being watched by these scum bags. But it's nothing serious; you know, just paperwork for the tax payer's money. You would think that for a man with four federal district attorneys on his payroll, I would have gotten a heads up that they wanted me up in Washington. But now they have the right one this time. I swear, whoever is behind this is going to have his face dipped in a barrel of fucking acid."

"You're telling me nobody knew anything before they ran up into your summer home?"

"Nobody! I'm telling you, and if you didn't call giving me that warning, they would have gotten me. I just talked to the commissioner on my way here and he said that the issue is so secret that he doesn't even know my damn charges as of now." Don Antigeo closed his fist, slamming it down onto the wooden edge of the table.

"Just be calm, Antigeo."

"No, I promise you, friend, when this is all clear, and it will be cleared, whoever leaked one word to this cock sucker Special Agent Branson, their k-"

"Who?" Mr. Holmes interrupted.

"Special Agent Branson, you know of him?"

"In a wa-" Mr. Holmes's words were cut short as the sound of rapid gunfire rang out in to the air, followed by the sight of his bodyguard's head exploding in a mist of blood. "It's a hit!" Mr. Holmes screamed as he ducked, using the table as a shield when a shot hit him in the neck, dropping him to the ground. "Aaaaaaaahhhh," he yelled out. Thinking fast, Mr. Holmes raised his tie up to the gun shot wound and pulled it tightly to stop the bleeding. Chaos filled the room instantly with people racing in every direction to escape the wild gunfire.

NayNay, refusing to be held back, pushed a man roughly in the back out of her way and continued to fire with her vision still locked on a hurt Mr. Holmes. Robert, being trained for times of war, quickly removed his forty-five from his hip. He raised it as A.P. sprayed several shots into his upper chest. The impact from the rounds forced his large frame to the ground just as NayNay's trigger finger eased back firing several more shots into his already lifeless body just missing Mr. Holmes's head.

Daz with his gun locked, yelled, "Don't do it, this is not for you," as he spotted Don Antigeo reaching for his gun. Whipping it out, he aimed for NayNay who was closing in on them fast. Then suddenly a bullet slammed into his shooting arm and chest. The pain that rushed through the Don's body made him drop his gun before tumbling to the ground, as the remaining bodyguards instantly returned fire while also shielding their bosses with their bodies.

Sam, the other three hundred pound man, had his palms filled with two nickel-plated 9 mm's without hesitating to find a target, letting bullets fly, he rotated his aim from NayNay to Haffee, 'BOOM-BOOM.' Don Antigeo's men stood their ground as the sound of their sub machine guns rag out, 'Tac-Tac-Tac." Daz was the first to feel the powerful impact from the automatic weapons as three shots crashed into the center of his vested chest plate, knocking him up onto the Roulette table.

Haffee saw the young man go airborne from the corner of his eye and rolled in motion, facing the opposite direction as he began to feel that this may get out of hand. Suddenly he shifted his state of mind as though he was back on a mission with Bo, Roc, Mohammed, and Chris. He started to sprint while zigzagging as he returned fire just to put space in between shots. NayNay, with constant pressure on her trigger aimed to kill as she was posted beside a wall watching Haffee take off running away. *"Look at this coward ass pussy not on Get Money,"* she thought and redirected her aim at Haffee, letting her gun trail him, waiting on him to cross her path.

Haffee retreated, making the body guards switch their target from him to NayNay. At that moment he rolled back around a table and swiftly flipped it over onto its side using it for a gun stand as he dropped down to one knee, resting his wrist on the edge and fired, 'BOOM-BOOM.' He blasted an Italian man in the head, sending him back over dead onto Don Antigeo who said, "Holmes we got to make a break for it while our men still got them penned in." 'BOOM-BOOM' several shots echoed in the distance as Mr. Holmes removed his Ruger from his waist. "Don, I don't know about you but I'm going to fight my way out." "Will you just listen to reason?" the Don pleaded. "Yeah I am and the reason is war!" replied Mr. Holmes.

Haffee, now in his zone, screamed, "Triangle offense and Fox, get in here!"

"I thought you'd never ask."

"NayNay, either shoot me or be ready to move in on three."

"Sorry."

"One, two...three!" Haffee rolled to his feet firing with only one thing on his mind...to finish what he came to do. NayNay followed, rolling out from behind the wall on his right, blasting from each hand just as Fox raced in from the left side. Fox went pass A.P. who was slowly creeping forward when a series of bullets breezed by his head. On instinct he raised his gun yelling, "Solo, I got you baby!" 'BOOM-BOOM-BOOM.'

His first shot hit the 300 lb man in the right shoulder, shredding the muscle, then in his left. Fox continued to make contact, 'BOOM-BOOM-BOOM,' as four shots went down the center of Sam's chest, making a cross like symbol on the man. "God bless pussy!" With only one guard left standing, he quickly dropped his weapon, surrendering. "All right, all right you got me, I give up!" "I know," NayNay said pulling the trigger on the 380 until it kicked back empty. The team, with their weapons locked, cautiously approached Mr. Holmes and Don Antigeo who were both shielded by their bodyguard's dead bodies as Haffee demanded, "I'll give you to the count of three to come out."

At the same time, the voice of Top Dollar entered their ears, "The call for back up just came over the scanner. You have two minutes, then we all meet at the right side exit no matter what, you dig." "Two...three," Haffee said, pulling the trigger, followed by the others. The smell of gun powder increased through out the room. "NayNay, ID the body and we're on the move!" NayNay moved the two bodyguard's corpses to the side as she said, "You don't have to worry, their de...gone?!"

Quickly raising her head, NayNay looked around, spotting a side door slowly closing, she dashed off, her legs moved with quickness as she ran out into the hallway catching the two injured bosses off guard as they waited on the elevator. She took off at full speed firing, 'BOOM-BOOM.' A shot caught Mr. Holmes in center of his back and sent him into the arms of Don Antigeo. The elevator door opened just in time with Don Antigeo hurriedly pulling Mr. Holmes through the metal structure and placed him up against the back wall. "No, Don, stop. Leave me to fight. I'm finished and I will not die alone," stated Mr. Holmes as he fought to catch his breath. "I won't hear of it, old friend, and if you didn't help me, I wouldn't be here."

"But you don't understand. Leave me, Don, only one of us can survive."

"Nonsense, I'm going to get us both out of here."

"Never, I swear to you."

Mr. Holmes used his sweaty finger to push the Don, letting out a deep breath. Then he suddenly spotted the barrel of NayNay's gun sticking through the small open space before exploding, 'BOOM-BOOM.' She got three shots off before the door slammed closed while hearing the Don scream, "Holmes, Noooo!" as he dove to shield Mr. Holmes from the hail of bullets.

"NayNay is he dead?" yelled Haffee into her earpiece. NayNay concealed her weapon as she rushed to try and pry the elevator doors open to confirm her kill. "38 seconds remaining, let's go," Top Dollar declared intensely. "NayNay, I repeat is the target dead?" Haffee again asked. NayNay struggled to reopen the door to hear the voice of Don Antigeo utter, "Just hang in there Holmes, you'll make it."

"20 seconds." NayNay felt the elevator begin to move so she started to give it one last pull to be sure when Haffee tapped her on the shoulder asking, "Is he dead?" NayNay slowly released her grip on the doors and turned facing Haffee's direction. "Mission completed," she responded.

Roc removed his earpiece while turning around in the passenger seat of the helicopter looking into the black painted faces of his men. "They say you never bite the hand that feeds you and I agree, but someone should have told them to never bite the hand of any body I'm feeding. Rule number two; a feared man that is loved can never die alone, for someone will always come to avenge him. Now let's finish this chapter." Roc gave the pilot the signal, "Okay hold on." The helicopter raced through the air in hope of closure.

6

Detective Brian pulled into his reserved parking space in front of the 39th precinct. Throwing the car in park, he sighed deeply out of frustration before looking to Detective Michael saying, "Now listen, Michael, there are a lot of people that want to see you get your job back, but if Captain Citric happens to find out that you're here we're all screwed. After all, the heat he took on your behalf from the Mayor, due to that lawyer Sam Clinton, you'll never be an officer of the law again."

"I know, Brian, keep a low profile, get what we need and get out."

"That's good but what I was going to say was to clean your self up. You can't go around your colleagues looking like that." Detective Brian lowered the rearview mirror, "Look at your self." Hesitant to face the reality of what he had become, Detective Michael slowly brought himself to see a reflection he didn't recognize. As his once sky blue eyes that seemed to appeal to women now looked like they had been tinted with bags resting under them from the many nights he went without sleep. The clean shaven face he used to have had been replaced with a full grown wild beard. He raised his hand to his face, running it from his cheek to his chin and back, feeling the texture, while noticing several gray hairs speckled through out it.

"This can't be the face of a man in his thirties."

"You're telling me. Now get yourself together. The shaving kit and everything you need is in the stake out bag as usual."

"No, Brian, I think I'm going to keep it. It fits me being undercover."

"As what, a bum?"

A sly grin crept onto Detective Michaels' face as he answered, "The hunter," before slamming the car door behind him. Detective Brian could only shake his head. Inside the 39th station, it was packed as officers moved through out the large room in a rush to close or make their next big case. Others sat behind their wooden desks talking on the phone, reading over important reports. In the back, prisoners were being placed into two separate 6 x 9 cages that were pass their holding capacity.

Detective Brian stepped into the hectic station letting his eyes roam over the room before giving the sign. On cue, Detective Michael entered the headquarters for the first time in five months. He took in a deep breath letting it out slowly, "I'm back," he whispered, placing his hands behind his back as he strode beside Detective Brian, as they passed several fellow officers who spoke only to Detective Brian.

Pam, the officers' secretary, stopped and said, "Detective you had a few messages while you were gone. I left them on your desk.

"Okay, thanks, Pam."

"No problem."

"Hello, Pam," said Detective Michael, while Pam gave him a questionable look before racing off.

"Hey, Brian," asked David as he shook Brian's hand. "Are we still on for the Sixers game on Friday?"

"Yes and have my money when your team loses too David. I'm not playing this time."

"You just do the same!"

"David, how've you been?" Detective Michael questioned.

"Don't speak to me ,you freaking scum bag and keep walking!"

"Brian, what was that all about?"

"I don't know. I guess he's having a bad day that's all."

Detective Brian approached his desk to find under cover Officer Dell wearing a Sean John sweat suit, laying back in his chair with his feet up on the desk. Clearing his throat, Detective Brian got his attention, "There you are, Brian. I would ask what took you so long but now I see. Where did you pick him up, on a DUI or armed robbery? Well, it doesn't matter, go book him and when you come back I got something to show you."

"Ha-ha, real funny, Dell."

At the sound of his voice, Officer Dell questioned, "Michael?"

"Yeah, who else would it be?"

"Damn, you look like shit, but I'm glad you're here. I want you to check this out."

Dell quickly punched in several keys on his computer then a very distant vision of Temple University covered three fourths of the screen. "What's this, bro?" Detective Michael inquired. "I'm going to tell you but that's enough of that trying to be black shit!" "Oh, my bad, bro." Shaking his head, Dell started to explain, "From this position it means nothing, that's why we overlooked it but if you do this." Dell continued to push keys making the picture zoom in for a close up. "Oh shit, I'll be damned," stated a shocked Detective Brian as a small black dot in front of the building became a man in a Temple sweat shirt with a 9 mm concealed behind his back.

"This is the Mac Miller shooting, how did you get this? I personally checked every inch of film in a five mile radius and there was nothing. It was like they knew just the right spot to hide from the camera."

"They did. But that was because they controlled them," Dell responded.

"That's impossible; these surveillance cameras are by the special crime unit (SCU) in Center City. It was put together by officers from all over and they're rotated every three months so they couldn't be infiltrated because if it was, the person would control 80 percent of our radio air waves and 90 percent of our camera vision."

"Brian, everything you said is correct and they still did it and this is how I know." Dell made the screen split into eight different views of the campus. "See, this is what the whole campus looked like to the SCU moments before the shooting at 4:35pm. Dell hit one key. "I can't believe it, the cameras have been moved," stated Detective Michael. "Yes, by two inches, just enough so that if you blinked you would never notice it."

"Then how did you happen to come across it?" asked Detective Brian, now giving under cover Officer Dell his full attention. "Actually it found me. Like you, I also checked all the videos especially after I heard Roc had a 2.4 million dollar reward out on the underground for whoever found his brother's killer."

"You know, I did hear something about his brother being shot six times by a forty-four caliber hand gun. So he goes and multiplies six times four, which equals twenty four and there were two people, now you have the number - 2.4 million. This man is passed crazy," said Detective Brian.

"Either that or he's a genius."

"And how's that, Michael?"

"When I was in college, I once read this Egyptian myth about this King of Warriors named Ryan the Brave. He would conquer Kingdoms with a team of hunters by tracking his prey on foot with just a spear and a shield. Once he captured them he would fight their three best warriors, one after another and if one would win they were all free to go. This went on for years with Ryan's land and power growing tremendously which sent fear through the hearts of many. The other Kings knew in time their land could only be next. So a massive team of six warriors was put together and set to kill Ryan. The team waited in the forest along side the only trail that led to Ryan's castle.

Coming home from a long day of battle, Ryan appeared in the distance, slowly approaching as they waited to ambush him. They attacked in the blink of an eye with Ryan fighting them off in true warrior fashion, killing four. With only two to go, a spear ripped through the flesh of Ryan's back as he dug his blade into the man in front of him. Falling to the ground, Ryan tried to fight to his feet but the last warrior showed him no mercy as he repeatedly stabbed Ryan's body five more times until he lay motionless. Feeling his job was complete, he raced off leaving Ryan dead.

Some time passed when a carriage moving along in its travels spotted the bloody bodies. Quickly several men jumped out to rob them of anything of value when one noticed Ryan's famous spear. He bent down to retrieve it when a weak hand grasped onto his wrist. "Help me." Back at his Kingdom, Ryan was forced to rest for several months but his soul lusted for blood. He then offered twenty four full bags of gold to any warrior that brought back the head of-"

"I'll be damned, how could I forget the tale of the four Kings?" Detective Brian again interrupted, now somewhat confused and thinking, *"Four Kings, six men…no it can't be."* Michael then said, "I know there was something up Lil Ma-"

"Michael, don't start! Dell, please finish."

"So as I'm watching this Buick with three males driving down a side street, a block before the campus at 4:35, it suddenly just disappeared. I'm looking and looking and it's no where in sight. Now I'm going through every camera position until I found their mistake. See, they moved every camera facing them except this one because it wasn't. It really was facing almost the opposite direction, but the eye of the camera takes in everything just as your eyes do."

"You mean like the side of the eye?" Detective Michael questioned, now understanding where this was going. "Yes and it caught this." Dell hit a series of keys bringing the file in motion as the Buick with the three males pulled into a parking space and waited. Moments afterward, with their eyes glued to the campus entrance, Lil Mac walked into their vision. He stopped short of the edge of the sidewalk with his eyes starting to roam as if to be looking for someone. Then they suddenly paused on the Buick. Sensing something may be wrong, Lil Mac reached for his gun, forgetting that he no longer carried it just as the man in the Temple sweat shirt exited the vehicle before it pulled off."

"See, the kid knew something wasn't right, he just didn't know what," stated undercover Officer Dell while continuing to watch the screen as he viewed Lil Mac reacting to the sound of a horn and racing to his Benz with NayNay behind the wheel.

Michael then said, "They always do, it's their animal instinct. He just thought he was safe because he was out of the jungle."

"Cracker, is you on drugs? No don't answer that. Here comes the part."

The officers became silent as they watched Lil Mac speaking to NayNay while missing the Buick return as it pulled in front of them, cutting off the route of escape. Lil Mac looked up to find the man in the Temple sweat shirt approaching five steps behind NayNay while raising a chrome 9 millimeter.

Lil Mac could be seen using his body as a shield for NayNay as the driver's side window exploded with a hail of bullets. "That's enough, cut it off," demanded Detective

Brian. "No don't, I want to see it. My partner is dead or did you forget about that?" yelled Michael. "No we haven't forgotten Rayfield, Michael. But maybe you have because he was a good officer of the law and not a thug. So, I will not disrespect his name by acting like his enemy to get them. That would mean he would have died for nothing and that can't happen, especially after Dell here just got you your badge back with a promotion."

"I did?"

"Yes, I must give it to you, you're good, but you're still not ready to hang with the pros. Now let me handle my business if you will."

"Be my guest."

Detective Brian's hands ran over the keys on the computer as he froze the face of the shooter along with another person. "Now this is only the second time a picture has been taken of these men." "Men? That's two pictures of one person," said Dell. "That's what I thought until now. But if I knew it then, I could have stopped this," stated Detective Brian, looking off into space, remember the sad moment. Michael's touch then brought him out of his daze as he asked, "What the hell are you talking about?" "I'm saying this is two different people, watch."

Brian reversed the file until he got a good shot of the driver then enlarged his face. Next he did the same to the shooter in the Temple shirt. "Damn, they're twins." "That's not the half of it." Detective Brian ran over to his desk and returned with an unmarked file. He looked around making sure they weren't being watched before opening it. "From this moment on, nothing can be spoken about what you're going to see and Dell, who else have you shown this tape to?" he asked.

"No one."

"Good, if you want to remain alive, keep it that way."

"Come on, Brian, it can't be that serious," said Dell.

"Why don't you be the judge of that?" *In 1993 a secret task force team was put together with some of the best police men on the east coast. I just happened to be a part of it also. They trained us extra hard doing things a regular cop would never do like bomb defusing, being taught how to read and speak Arabic, how to defend yourself with a sword, everything down to praying as a Muslim. After five months they told us they had received word that someone was going to try to commit a terrorist act on the World Trade Center and that the person had just touched down on American soil. Our mission was to secure one person, Shake MuJahid-Sabar, alive. He was believed to be the third most powerful man in the world of terrorism and we needed to know what he knew. I will never forget that day. We were riding four Hummers deep, heading in the opposite direction on the east side highway to a hotel where intelligence had a location on MuJahid, when out of no where the ground shook from the explosion, followed by black clouds of smoke and cries of pain, all this without the driver hitting the brakes to even think about stopping, we pulled up positioning the Hummers on the front side and back of the Plaza Hotel, leaving no chance for escape, so we thought. Now watch."*

Detective Brian entered several access codes and the Plaza Hotel appeared on the screen with the four Hummer doors flying open. Five men speedily exited each vehicle dress in all black with masks covering their faces, leaving only their eyes exposed. The audio was clear as the voice of the commander came through the speakers, "Men, our enemy is on the seventy seventh floor in room 237. They say he believes it's God's lucky number." "Favorite," *a soldier* corrected. "What, soldier?" "Favorite number, Muslims don't believe in luck." "Whatever the fuck it is, let's prove him wrong. Teams 1 and 2 there's a man waiting by the *elevator to escort you up. Teams 3 and 4 you'll be taking the back stairs. Now let's go and keep America safe."*

The commander raced off in a rhythm, moving in twos as a man in a black and gold Plaza blazer held open the elevator door. The ten men moved across the lobby floor with speed and swiftness, while at the same time their actions remained soundless to the point that if you blinked they were gone. Making you wonder if they were ever really there. One by one they packed in with the commander bringing up the rear just as the door eased shut, "Floor 77." "Yes sir."

Officer Dell and Detective Michael couldn't believe their eyes as they looked intensely at the screen as the nervous bellhop raised his head to push the floor button. "Oh shit! That's the same guy that killed Lil Mac!" Dell yelled knowing that whatever he just found out was way bigger than he could ever imagine. "And Shake MuJahid," Detective Brian added. "What?" asked Dell. Detective Brian pointed to the screen as the commander said, *"Weapons." The men on cue cocked back their specially issued Mack 11s sending a bullet into the chamber. "Commander, teams three and four are posted at the back door awaiting orders." Looking up at the moving flashing button of lights that were on floor 71 the commander said, "We move on 3, 2, 1." The door opened with the commander stepping aside. "Go!" In seconds the team moved securely through the whole floor with four men, two on each side of the hallway, when the sound of the enemy's door closing caught their attention. "Team two see what that was, the rest of you, on my signal."*

Five men quickly stepped out of rank and moved down the hall as the commander raised his open hand. The officer with the door ram stepped into position. Then by making a fist, the commander sent the point man in motion, placing his ear to the door to listen for any movement.

Hearing nothing, he checked the knob, slowly turning it to the right until it opened.

Surprised, they looked to the commander who dropped his hand giving the sign to proceed. The men quickly entered the room in striking position. The first four soldiers through the door spread out wide, two moving on each side of the room with guns drawn and locked on their shoulder. The eye scopes pressed against their face showed they were ready for action as the barrel of their guns rotated from side to side in search of movement. The anchorman, satisfied that the first room was clear, flashed two fingers twice and four more men rushed through the center to the edge of the second room. They then broke wide repeating the actions of the first crew. This continued through out the entire suite until the men yelled, "Clear."

The commander entered the room to see three dead bodies all with shots to the back of the head. He walked to the sofa where a man laid face down with his head buried into the cushion and picked him up by his hair to get a better look at his identity. "Shake MuJahid Jabar, they got to you first, you bastard!" The commander slammed the body to the ground hard. He started for the next body when he heard in his earpiece, the voice of a soldier from Team 2, "Stop or I'll sh-, oh it's you." The sound of guns being un-cocked echoed as the officer continued, "I thought we told you...BOOM-BOOM-BOOM." Several shots rung out before the line went dead.

All three officers stared at the computer screen as an incensed look could be seen on their faces while Detective Michael and Dell prayed for the best for their fellow officers. Detective Brian, knowing the feeling, broke the silence saying, "At the time we really didn't know what happened, but here's what we got from the hotel camera." *Detective Brian pushed another code as the vision of a man with his head down, quickly sliding through the stairway door appeared on the screen. He ran down three steps when the door opened with four armed men hot on his trail. On sight, their weapons became locked on his head. "Stop or…"*

The suspect with his head still positioned so that he wouldn't be seen by the camera, slowly turned around to face the men as he followed their command, while swiftly placing the weapon he possessed into the center of his back before raising his hands in the air. "Oh it's you." They discharged their weapons while lowering them as they stepped onto the level platform, surrounding the man and asked him, "I thought we told you…" Then, with the speed that could only come from years of practice, a round house kick crashed into his voice box instantly killing the soldier in mid sentence. Before the suspect's foot could fully touch the ground, he pushed hard off his other leg, sending it to the other mans temple, while in motion removing the forty-five automatic from his back. The momentum of the kick spun his body into the air as he leveled his gun off squeezing the trigger relentlessly just as his foot landed.

Officer Dell watched the screen as the last two bodies dropped before all being shot execution style. He jumped up with such force that he knocked his chair over, yelling, "Who the hell is this guy and how did he get away?" Detective Brian still feeling the pain of losing a partner on his watch as if it happened yesterday knew that being mad wouldn't help anything. He calmly placed Officer Dell's chair back on its right side. "Have a seat and relax, I'm going to tell you how and why he won't get away again. Look."

They watched as the suspect raced down the steps with his head turned at a ninety-degree angle only giving the camera a side view of his face. "At what, this no-good bastard getting away?" Dell continued to protest. Detective Brian, refusing to indulge in Officer Dell's emotional outburst, remained silent and pointed at the screen. The door re-opened to the stairway with several soldiers making sure it was clear, as four men quickly tossed dead bodies over their shoulders and disappeared down the stairs. Two men with spray bottles and masks removed the blood from the carpet. "Right here," Detective Brian's finger stopped on the upper right corner of the screen pointing at the man who just entered the picture with the commander.

"Wait, that's the elevator man, but how could he kill Shake MuJahid if he's there and the killer ran down the steps?"

"I thought you'd never ask." Brian rewound the tape to where the suspect started his retreat and enhanced the side of his face, "Fellas, thanks to Mr. Gates in 09, we now have the technology to get view a whole face with only twenty percent of it being visible." With another click, they were looking at the elevator man twice.

"So it was the twins?"

"No, the triplets," Detective Brian corrected.

"What?"

"You young Detectives got to start keeping up," said Detective Brian while rewinding the picture back to the lobby scene where the soldier first entered and moved the camera view to a man that looked just like the other, sitting in a leather chair with a cup of coffee in his hand and an earpiece coming from his ear. "Damn, it's another one."

"Yes and if you look closely you can see what he said as he spots us."

"Look at him watching the door like he knew ya'll were coming. But that's impossible right? You didn't know until the moment of departure." Detective Brian nodded his head in agreement while playing it in slow motion as the man's lips started moving: *They're on their way now."*

Shocked, Dell questioned, "So he is the one directing them?"

"I don't know but I bet my badge if you go back to your tape that he's the third man in the Buick," said Detective Brian.

"But who are these guys with this kind of power?" asked Michael.

"I don't know but that's what we're going to find out because they are now wanted for two murders. But the question is what does Roc have to do with all of this," stated Detective Brian, now in it for the long haul, when someone called out, "Officer Dell and Brian, after you put that prisoner away turn to that bitch, Molly. I think you need to see this." All three officers looked up at the T.V. to see, "Welcome to another episode of *In These Mean Streets*."

7

Midtown Manhattan, upon one of the highest floors in a New York skyscraper, a late meeting was called because of the sudden drop in the stock market. Eleven nervous people sat around a large oak wood conference table awaiting their boss, Barbara Hudson, to arrive. With the exception of Todd James, they were all worried that they may not have a job in the morning. Todd, with his cool and relaxed demeanor would have quit a long time ago if it wasn't for the promise that he made to his father. Even though a Porsche, Bugatti, fast women, and luxury condo didn't hurt, Todd, who was handsome with a 6'1" 235 lb muscular build, didn't have his heart in the corporate life. He tried everything from long hours to short days but nothing seemed to work for him. Todd knew deep down that there was something he was put here to do, but watching over another man's millions wasn't it.

Todd also knew that many of his peers disliked him and it wasn't because he rarely spoke to anyone in the room. In fact, they could care less. What they couldn't understand was how he was able to keep his job for this long, even though he was one of the best financial advisors that the Brooks Co. had ever seen. There were also a lot of other people that could get the job done, who didn't come to work late all the time or who at least dressed the part of a business man. Like today, Todd looked around at all the business suits and dresses that filled the room and felt sorry for them as he thought, *"Look at all these losers wasting their lives away doing fourteen hours shifts in a cell they call an office."* Laughing, he adjusted the close-knit Brunello Cucinelli cashmere zip-up sweater that lay just right over his Polo T-shirt. A pair of baggy cargo shorts and opened-toed gator sandals finished off his Miami Beach appearance, which was where he would be heading by way of the company private jet to party just for the night as soon as the meeting was over, if not sooner.

Todd tapped his fingers repeatedly on the edge of the table, becoming bored with the whole waiting ordeal. He started rise saying, "To hell with this, I'm out of here." Just then the conference room door swung open with Barbara Hudson and her personal assistant, Christian, walking through. "Mr. James, sit back down. Thank you," said Barbara without even looking his way. "Dumb bitch," Todd whispered under his breath while falling back down into his hard leather chair. "I heard that," replied Barbara.

The moment Barbara Hudson entered the room her presence demanded respect and everyone's full attention, she wouldn't have it any other way. She understood that in a business world ran mostly by men, to become her own boss she had to make sure she was on top of everything a minute before it happened. That's the reason she was here tonight. "Ladies and gentlemen, as you all know the Dow Jones Industrial average is down again for the week, this is the third week in a row. And even though our numbers are still slightly increasing, our competition is down 11.8 percent. So before our investors look at them and think of us, I need you to come up with something that will separate us from them completely so that they will never be our competition again."

Barbara's face suddenly turned dead serious. "I expect your full proposal on my desk in an hour and I promise you the best will receive a reward while the worse will be fired." Without another word, Barbara removed her black leather brief case and disappeared through the glass door, heading to her office as Christian handed out pens and extra paper.

Todd waited until the door closed shut before placing his tinted Gucci sunglasses over his eyes while resting his feet on the fresh paper laid on the table. He moved around in his chair until he made himself comfortable. Shutting his eyes, he hoped to catch a quick nap. A mischievous smile eased across Todd's face, as it felt hot from the disgusted looks he knew he was receiving. *"Look at him."*

Twenty minutes later, now at his desk a few yards from the master officer's entrance, Christian was searching the net looking for a great investment for Barbara when the phone began to ring. "Hello, Brooks Co., Christian speaking how may I help you?"

"Let me speak to your boss quickly, this is very important."

At the sound of Munro Thurman's voice, who was the CEO of Brooks Co. and one of the most powerful men in the business world, Christian became instantly enthusiastic. Being too scared to put Munro on hold, he dashed through the hall until he reached Barbara's office. Without knowing he raced across her Persian rug, finding Barbara at her desk reading over files. Christian placed his hand over the receiver and whispered, "It's Mr. Munro. Girl, you finally made it!"

Barbara slowly brought the phone to her ear. "Hello"

"Yes, who is this?"

"I'm Barbara Hud-"

"Never mind your last name, I asked to speak with the boss, not his assistant. This is serious."

"Okay, sir, I'm sorry."

Barbara pushed hold, frustrated that she couldn't speak her mind and hit the intercom button, "Mr. Todd James, could you come into my office please?" Back out in the conference room, Todd was in a deep sleep dreaming about two exotic models taking their clothes off while oiling up each other's bodies when someone tapped his shoulder waking him up. "I know you didn't just touch me just as Sue and Maria were about to…Ha ha, never mind." He looked down at his hardened dick.

"Yes I did, they're calling you, and you're probably going to get fired," said Pat, laughing. Todd rushed down to the office, finding the door open and Barbara with her back to him with her arms folded tightly, resting on her breasts as she stared off in a daze. He eased up behind her with his still hard manhood pressed into the crease of the ass print visible through her dress. Moving her long hair to the side he placed a gentle kiss on her neck when he noticed she had tears in her eyes. Turning her around to face him, she handed him the phone, "Here, it's Munro. He says it's important."

Todd took the phone, bringing it near his face then kissed Barbara on the lips saying, "No, you're important," and then slammed the phone down on its cradle. Todd knew Barbara wasn't getting the respect she deserved and one day she would but now wasn't the time. Barbara wrapped her arms around Todd, kissing him deeply as he gripped her ass cheeks in the palm of his hand, lifting her in the air when Christian came out from behind the door yelling, "That's right Todd, don't go for that."

"Christian, if you don't get your gay ass out of here!"

"Okay I'm gone but you don't have to be so damn mean."

At the sound of the door clicking shut, Todd continued to kiss Barbara passionately as he ran his hand up the side of her legs until her dress was above her hips. "I miss you," Barbara said, hating herself for not being able to stop her body from becoming hot as Todd's hand now moved back and forth over the thin material of her panties, rubbing her clit. A light moan escaped her lips as she began to move her hips up and down forcing him to match her rhythm. Todd, feeling her wetness as it leaked through her panties, started to remove them as the phone rang.

The sound brought Barbara back to her senses as she pushed Todd hard in the chest, screaming, "Get off me. As hard as I work around here for you and then those bastards upstairs don't even have enough respect to hear my damn name!"

The phone rang again just as her right hand slapped Todd across the face, forcing it to the side. "Okay you're serious," Todd stated, returning his stare forward while placing his hand to his face. Bringing it back he spotted the blood that covered his fingers from his busted lip and said through tightened teeth, "I know what you want." "What?" Barbara replied. "This," Instantly Todd ripped Barbara's blouse and bra open, leaving her stiff nipples exposed. He roughly took one deep into his mouth and forced her down on top of the desk. "I run shit upstairs," Todd yelled, raising her legs over his head and holding them tightly together by one hand while using the other to rip her thong free and tossing it across the floor.

Todd then pulled her body to the edge of the desk until just her ass hung in the air. He ran a finger through her wetness checking her readiness, studying her every move as her body responded to his slightest touch. Satisfied, Todd ran his manhood roughly into her love box without remorse, hitting an unmovable wall that refused him to go deep.

"Ooohhh shiiittt," Barbara screamed while she grabbed hold of her ass cheeks and spread them out wide in hopes of reducing the pain by giving him as much access as possible. She bit down hard on her bottom lip as she let out a grunting sound from the pit of her throat. The pain of her pussy walls being forced in became too overwhelming as she tried to escape from the desk. Todd continued to long stroke Barbara at such an uncontrollable and intense pace that her body began to welcome it. His large manhood inched deeper and deeper until it reached the bottom. The punishment of pain subsided and turned into pleasure, taking over her body just as Todd knew it would. "Oh yes, fuck me, you spoiled fucking bastard, fuck me!"

At the sound of her cry, Todd grinned devilishly in victory as he suddenly removed his still hard manhood. He looked down at the flow of juices running from her sex box down her asshole to a small puddle that formed on the rug. "Baby pleeeeaase don't stop," she begged. Todd, ignoring her, answered the phone, "What is it, Munro, that's got you constantly calling this damn phone and having my people disrespecting me?" he questioned firmly.

"It's your father."

Todd's heart dropped instantly as his strong voice lowered to just above a whisper asking, "What about him, is he alright?"

"Well, yes and no. As you know already your father was leaving the country on such short notice for a business deal."

"Yeah"

"Well that wasn't a hundred percent true. He is now on the run"

"Munro, you've got to tell me where he is now so I can go assist him."

"You know I just spoke with him and he said you were going to request that."

"Then he also knows I'm coming."

"Calm down, Todd. You know nothing else would hurt your father more than you getting caught up on the other side of the family business."

"You're right but--"

"No buts. He just wanted me to call you to let you know he was fine before you see it on the 12 o'clock news. Oh and before I forget, he said buy up all the remaining shares in Holmes International Inc. in the morning because after tonight it will drop extremely low. But he assures you it will rise again."

Todd had to smile because even in a time of crisis his father still had his mind on money. Hanging the phone up he looked down at Barbara who was using her hand and tongue in a synchronized motion on his shaft while working it deeply in and out of her mouth. Todd knew she was only doing it to please him but now wasn't the time. He grasped the back of her head, palming her long blond hair and began to sex her face wildly with long pumps that made her gag with each stroke. He kept up this pace until his hot cum shot deep into her throat. Todd then walked away leaving her open, wanting more of him. He sat in the large leather chair bare assed, checking the clock that read 12:05. He pushed the remote on the satellite T.V. until he found what he was looking for.

Barbara, upset that she let herself take her emotions out on her man when he only did things to help, wrapped her arms around his neck from behind the chair, kissing him softly on the ear and whispering, "I'm sorry for hitting you, baby." "I know and it won't happen again!" Todd corrected, while raising the T.V. volume as the voice of Molly Weiss came through the surround sound system.

"Usually, ladies and gentlemen, I would be bringing you this episode of "In These Mean Streets" from the heart of the city streets, but today is different because things have changed.. Instead of the streets, they have brought the madness here to Connell Private Airport, where only the rich and famous can afford to fly as their seats go from twenty five thousand and up. So who would have thought that several masked men armed with high tech weapons that are believed to have soldier like training, would storm this establishment with guns drawn and open fire?"

Molly began to walk as she spoke to the camera. "If you look here over my shoulder to the right, just beyond the yellow tape, you can still see on the floor of this casino, four white sheets covering the bodies the police believe are the bodyguards of the mob boss Don Antigeo whose story I reported to you earlier today and Philadelphia's Vernon Holmes, who police said they've been after for over 30 years and still have yet to build a case against him. A few moments ago I had the chance to speak with Drug Enforcement Agent Giles and this is what he had to say about his terrible event:"

"Well, Molly, it seems from what information we have now, that a murder hit was planned for mob boss Don Antigeo from a wiretap we received a few hours ago."

"So you knew his life was in danger?"

"Yes, to a certain extent. But any alleged mob boss or person with that lifestyle is always in danger. So did we hear someone wanted him dead? Yes, all the time."

"Agent Giles, could it be true that the hit could have been to stop Don Antigeo from possibly snitching, being that he was just indicted?"

"It could have been, Molly, because no one wants to go to prison let alone because of someone's mouth. But these shooters here may have missed their target which is nothing new. Luckily it wasn't an innocent bystander this time. It could be in fact one of the most violent and intimidating man known to the drug trade."

"Did you say drug trade?"

"Yes, for years many law enforcement agents have tried to put the infamous Mr. Holmes away and failed but today his luck may have finally run out as the suspect lodged several shots to his face leaving fingerprints as the only way to identify him. For that reason, Special Agent Branson from Washington came and retrieved the body."

"Then how can you be so sure it's him?"

"Because along with the body we found his wallet, pictures and private company credit card that was only issued to him"

"And Don Antigeo, have you heard anything on his whereabouts?"

"No, not at this moment but we'll get him. We always do."

"Okay now what's that in your hand?"

Agent Giles lifted Fatel's iced out G.M.C. (Get Money Clique) chain in the air, "Oh this here is just a little something for the hunter back in Philly."

"Todd, I'm so sorry, what can I do to help?" Barbara asked. "Have my Ferrari downstairs in ten minutes and buy every stock they have in Holmes International Inc, he won't need it." Todd replied. She continued to talk but Todd couldn't hear a word as he got dressed and then walked out the door with his mind on his father and both sides of the family business.

8

Meanwhile in Maine, a few hundred miles away in the middle of the night with only the glow of the moon peering through the leaves into the darkness, Roc lowered the night vision binoculars onto his eyes. He adjusted them until the sight of the three-story, black-walnut wood cabin that was surrounded by a quarter mile of trees, looked as if it was standing right in front of him. His eyes roamed while he studied the large structure and found himself a bit puzzled thinking, *"I've been here before, but how?"*

Shaking his head, Roc called, "Boggy."

"Yo, what's up, are you ready? I got the New York soldiers spread out in three different positions in sets of four and two with us," Boggy said excited and ready for blood. To him it was do or die and he didn't plan on being the one dying. "Here, look."

Taking the binoculars, Boggy scanned the area. "Now tell me what you see."

"Nothing"

"My point exactly; a man with his power would have some type of security. Are you sure this is the right address?" Roc questioned, getting a strange feeling in his gut.

"Yeah, this is the address our cop friend at the 39th precinct gave us. Then Alexis googled it and they matched Terrance Brown a.k.a. Billy D."

Suddenly the words of Billy D entered Roc's mind automatically as it was told to him by Mr. Holmes, *"Know in this life that for a good switch to work, the change up has to be the same as its prototype. If it's off in any way, to a real player you're next move will be telegraphic and that may cost you your life. Now remember every piece of game I give you is universal."* The statement made Roc think as he continued to inspect the darkness.

Moments before, while sitting in the plush dining room of his cabin, Billy D was getting his feet and shoulders massaged by two beautiful women as three other hung on his every word. Billy D, dressed in his silk pajamas with the matching robe, spoke over the crackling sound of the fire place. "You know I love you ladies, right?" "Yes," they all responded together. Terrance Brown was better known by all the women as Billy D because of his strong resemblance to the actor Billy D. Williams. From his silky smooth hair to the brown sugar complexion, they even wore their mustaches similarly. The only distinction was that instead of brown, Terrance possessed a beautiful set of green eyes that looked as if they glistened when he smiled.

Over the years, time had been good to Billy D and even though he was 70, there wasn't a single gray hair on him. All in all he didn't look a day over fifty due to his daily workout routine. Billy D removed his feet from the soft hands of Jada and Kelly and placed them in his Gucci slippers, asking, "My pipe please," in his calm relaxing voice that he seldom raised. Both girls raced off to the den, each needing to be the one to fulfill Billy D's wants, for there was something about him that many women couldn't explain. But if they were ever in his presence even for just a moment, they could feel their soul being touched by his charm, ambition, and gentle personality.

Billy D sat straight up in his favorite chair as Kelly placed his pipe in his mouth while Jada lit it. The girls waited until Billy D was comfortable and had taken several puffs, releasing the smoke in the air before they asked, "Billy D please tell us what happened when you met Ms. Peaches and Aunt Foxy?"

"You lovely ladies don't want to hear that story because a sucker is the main character."

"Well if they don't, I do."

"Me too, I always love to hear a story about a hero and a sucker!"

Billy D turned in the direction of the voice to see Peaches and Foxy standing in the doorway looking as rich and beautiful as ever. "You know a man couldn't be a gangster or a gentleman in this world if you women didn't bring him into it." "You got that right," the ladies said, giving each other high fives through out the room as Peaches and Foxy squeezed into the large chair with Billy D, kissing him on the cheek as he began to talk. *"Okay, okay if it will make you happy. It was Harlem 1976 at a time when us blacks didn't have a lot of respect but it wasn't hard to find. It's just a lot of jokers were looking in the wrong place,"* Billy D explained, as the passion and love for the struggle still could be seen on his face. "Like this sucker, that's why I shot him, but that's another story," Bill D smiled, remembering the lovely sight of a sucker in pain, and then he continued, *"In a second floor apartment on the east side of Harlem at 9:30 am, Peaches quickly threw on her best Sunday outfit as the smell of fresh cooked pancakes and eggs filled the air. After placing a light coat of lipstick on, Peaches crept down the hallway until she reached the tip of the living room where she saw Candy, hand feeding their gorilla pimp, Continental B.T. as he lay on the couch with his leg in a sling. Peaches made eye contact with Candy, giving her a wink. Understanding, Candy said, "Come on, Daddy, eat your food so you can get your strength back."*

As soon as Continental B.T. turned his head from the T.V. to the fork, Peaches power walked her way to the front door. She slowly eased the knob back and slid out into the hallway, saying, "God, that was close!" and let out a deep breath. Continental B.T., with a mouth full of food yelled through the door, "Bitch, where the hell do you think you're going?" The bass in his voice sent chills up Peaches spine as she stopped in her tracks and turned around with a half smile on her face and said, "To church, Daddy, it's Sunday remember? I always go with Sister Brown to morning prayer."

"Yeah well, not today. Foxy didn't come back in after ya'll left for your shift last night and this isn't like her to be late with my paper. You wouldn't know where she's at would you?"

"Nooo, no, we were together when we left but I had a john to meet and when I came back to the track she was gone."

"Is that what happened? Candy, hand me my cane," Continental B.T. requested as he started to get up.

"No Daddy. She said she didn't know."

"Ho! Have you gone deaf?"

"No."

"Then what did I tell you?"

"Okay here."

Continental B.T. got up off the couch and approached a shaken Peaches. He stopped just an inch away from her face and said, "Now, Peaches, look at me."

"But..."

"Bitch, if you ever interrupt me again while I'm talking or thinking about talking I'll crack your god damn face open to the white meat, you dig?"

"Yes, it will never happen again, Daddy, I'm sorry," Peaches said very apologetically.

"Now study my face, do I look like I could be lied to right now?"

"No."

"Shut up, Ho! I know you're hiding something so I'm going to ask you one more time before I put your ass on a stretcher." Continental B.T. cocked back his cane and demanded to know, "Where the hell is Foxy?"

"I told you Daddy, I don't know."

"SMACK-SMACK," Continental B.T. let his cane go with two swift swings, hitting Peaches in her leg first which forced her down onto all fours, "Aaahhhh." Then the second blow crashed into her spine. Candy rushed to Peaches's aid. "Wait, Daddy, if she knows she will tell you. But please don't hit her again." Candy whispered in Peaches ear, "Girl is you crazy? If you know something you better say it because he will kill you!" Candy pleaded. "Yeah but he said..." Before Peaches could finish her sentence, Continental B.T. gripped her up by the arm pulling her to her feet.

"Who is he?" Continental B.T. yelled as tears started to pour over Peaches face. She didn't know how much more pain she could take for a person she only met once. "SMACK." When the answer didn't come, Continental B.T. back handed her across the lips. Peaches legs collapsed but Continental B.T. refused to let her fall as he held her up by the back of the collar.

"Ho, I know you don't want me to bring this hand in reverse so who is he?"

"Okay, she's with the man that shot you."

"What?"

"Daddy, please don't hit me. I swear I tried to stop her."

"I kno,w baby, Daddy's sorry. Now have a seat and tell me everything that happened," Continental B.T. asked while caressing Peaches' back. "Candy, hurry up and get this girl some ice for her mouth. Can't you see she's in pain? Damn! Now go ahead and start from the top." Peaches wiped away the tears from under her eyes. "Well we was working the track to make your money, Daddy, when this man who was dressed too fly to be a john and too smooth to be a pimp stopped us saying," "Excuse me, ladies, if I could buy a few minutes of your time, what would

it cost me?" "I don't know about minutes but you can have me for an hour for twenty honey, and I'll give you a time you'll never forget," said Foxy, running her fingers down Billy D's suit jacket and stopping just short of his zipper. "I will say the same if not more when I'm done. Take this fifty for the both of you and I will only need half the time." Foxy quickly grabbed the money from Billy D's hand.

"Okay handsome, where do you want to go?"

"Right here"

"What, on the track?" asked Peaches.

"Oh he's nasty, I love him already," Foxy stated as she started to unbutton her top when Billy D pointed to the steps.

"Okay my feet hurt anyway," said Peaches, taking a seat.

Foxy didn't move as she questioned, "Man, are you serious?"

"Yes, beautiful."

"So you're telling me you don't want nothing from me but conversation?"

"Yes, and your mind," Billy D. answered sincerely.

"Okay but I'm not giving you your money back when you don't get off."

Billy D remained silent for five minutes until Foxy asked, "Why?"

"Ssshhh lets just watch this crazy world you call life."

While observing the block, they noticed women were jumping out of one car and into another like ghost with no direction. There were junkies lying on the ground with needles hanging from their arms as others stood in the alleyways taking lines of white powder into their noses to relax their minds. Homeless kids raced through the streets with hot water and soapy rags on sale for a dollar.

"Boy, let me have two of them, ooohh that man was super strong," said Rosie before rushing into the alley to wipe her self. Billy D raised his hand and pointed to bring the girls attention to the top of the stairs where a pimp had his powerful hand wrapped tightly around one of his girl's necks as the other prepared to strike.

"Emotional enslavement," rolled from Billy D's lips as he watched the pimp's right hand make contact with the woman's face. "SMACK" The sound could be heard down the block. Foxy shook her head and said, "Damn, she must have messed up Rocco's money real bad."

"Do you believe that justifies his actions?" Billy D questioned Foxy as he looked directly into her eyes while she refused to show fear and held his stare. "Hell yeah, if your man tells you to do something, obey without questioning it. If she would have followed the rules I bet her ass wouldn't be getting tossed to the ground right now." "What about an apology when a mistake is made from the woman; who if there (was no her, there was would be no me)? As she eats, I am fed, when I become disturbed and kick, she feels my pain over the months I grew preparing to face this world with only her protection to save us. I promise you by six months you have become one with her."

Billy D, without losing eye contact, slowly kissed Foxy's hand before placing it onto her heart. On contact Foxy's mind suddenly went to the last time she saw her own mother, she was standing in the doorway as her mother explained, "I know, baby, I don't like going out late at night and leaving you here alone either but I still have this house to pay for."

"Then take my allowance, mom, please don't go out. Something just doesn't feel right," Foxy still heard herself begging.

"Don't be childish. Mommy is going to be just fine," Gloria told her daughter while softly kissing her on the lips.

"I love you, Tia." Then she placed her hand on Foxy's heart, "All in here," before walking down the street in her super tight dress, fishnet stockings, and fur coat. The reappearance of Gloria's face brought back emotions that Foxy tried to hide deep down inside as her tears filled her eyes and she quickly turned away from Billy D, not wanting him to see her as being weak.

Billy D grabbed Foxy by the tip of the chin and did not let her break eye contact, "Look at me, the easiest trick in life is to camouflage your fears rather than admitting that they exist but you need not be afraid." Billy D then took his silk handkerchief from his top pocket and wiped off Foxy's make up and thick lipstick before gently kissing her on the lips as he continued, "To be the beautiful strong woman you really are, now look at yourself, and smile for me." He pointed to a glass window where she could see her reflection. When she looked, Foxy saw the same innocent little girl who wanted to be a lawyer to make whoever killed her mother pay.

"It's okay, let it go and if you want a chance at a new life, I will help you help yourself and Peaches. The same goes for you too if you would like to come but there's one thing I need for you to do," Billy D stated.

Peaches became silent, not wanting to finish the story when a knock came at the door and she jumped to her feet to answer it. As her hand reached the knob, Continental B.T. screamed, "Don't you dare open that door before telling me what words that sucker spoke."

"He sa-"

"That's enough," Aretha stated, stopping Billy D in mid sentence as she stepped into the dining room. "Billy D, they're here."

"I know. They've been for a few days, looking in the wrong spot."

"I know but Roc has arrived."

"Come on, Ms. Aretha, can it wait until he finishes the story?" The girls asked.

"No and don't give me them long faces; ya'll just going to have to buy the book, don't worry it's coming." Billy D still unmoved, ready to give his girls what they wanted, said, "And Roc will do the same until he makes the wrong move and will perish like all the rest." "Maybe not this time, Billy, I think he's got it," Aretha corrected.

"What?" Billy D walked to the plasma T.V. hanging on the wall and touched it three times to activate his surveillance system. Suddenly the screen slipped into four visions of the men hiding in the darkness as they surrounded a wooden cabin. Billy D studied Roc as he exited off a four runner joining his team. He hit the screen once more just leavening Roc with his full attention. The whole room watched the screen nonchalantly, having seen this scene so many times before while preparing themselves for the loud explosion.

Billy D raised the sound to hear what was in the mind of his next victim but still not proving to be an enemy. Roc put the binoculars up to his face one more time to give his surroundings a last look, whispering, *"Every piece of game I give you is universal."* Seeing nothing, he said, "I know there is something missing," just as Mr. Holmes's words entered his mind. Roc quickly moved his direction of sight to a white house just behind the target about a quarter mile to the right, then to the left at the same distance where a sky–blue, two-story house sat quietly. He slowly turned in a 360 degree motion, taking in everything when he stopped, with his back now to the target and smiled, *"For a good switch up to work, the change up has to be the same as its prototype."*

As his eyes locked on a three-story, black-walnut wooden cabin that was surrounded by a quarter-mile of trees, the only difference Roc noticed was the hidden camera inside the birdhouse and trees. He wouldn't have been able to spot them if Mr. Holmes hadn't given him the same one.

Billy D watched Roc's eyes on the screen as they seemed to be looking straight at him when he said, as if Roc could hear him, "I knew you was the one!" before facing the room, "Well, ladies, we have been made." "It's about fucking time," said Foxy as she and the rest of the girls in the room cocked back their chrome 380's and rushed off to their positions. Aretha, still in the doorway asked, "Should I call the men also?" "It depends on how smart he is," Billy D replied with a furtive grin.

9

Four months later at an underground Federal ADX prison in a secret location in Florence, Colorado, built to hold only the richest and most high profile criminals in the world, the sound of several sets of shoes echoed across the freshly-waxed floor. Special Agent Branson, accompanied by two guards, escorted his prisoner down the long hallway to intake. Still a little out of breath from the chase, Agent Branson with his right hand wrapped tightly around the man's cuffed wrist while his left finger pointed in his face, said, "I know you didn't think you could go anywhere on this planet and think you'd be able to hide from me did you?"

Agent Branson roughly raised the cuff up to the center of the prisoner's back. "Aaaahhhh," the man screamed out of pain.

"That's for making me sweat."

"That's it, I've had enough, I want to see someone from the Warden's office now! Wanted or not, I'll still have your badge by morning."

"Yeah and when you see them, tell'em Branson was here again, Hahaaaaa…now get your ass in there!"

Inside the intake center, Tom and James worked the front desk. When they spotted Agent Branson coming through the glass doors, they knew whoever he had with him was extremely powerful to have him here in this state when he hated the cold. Now the only question was just how powerful. Tom didn't hesitate to find out, asking, "Branson what brings you down here in this lovely weather?"

"Real fucking funny, Tom. This weather is only good for making a snow man," Branson complained while removing the handcuffs.

"But if it wasn't for us down here, you wouldn't have a job," said James. "You may be right and there wouldn't be another place safer to keep this man in a cage," Branson smiled as he pushed his prisoner in the back, "Now get against the wall, and spread them." Branson began to pat down his prisoner. "So who do we have here?" James questioned, wanting to know about the well dressed gentleman. "You don't know? Damn! You guys really need to get back to the eastside and out of this underground shit hole of a state."

"Aaayy, watch what me say about me home," stated one of the two Spanish American guards that accompanied Branson in his best English. "What! I'll say what I damn well please about this freezing ice patch of land. Matter of fact, why am I explaining *me*," Branson said making fun of the man's English before telling him to "Get out!"

"Me don't understand."

Agent Branson aggressively pulled open the door, "When you don't know who's the most powerful man in the room is, you shouldn't be in it with him. Now get out."

With little hesitation, the man stepped out the door only to have it slammed in his face. As soon as the door shut, laughter filled the air while Agent Branson turned to the other guy, "And what about you?"

"No English, me speak no English."

"I thought not, because you'll be picking up snow flakes in the morning with him."

"Branson you haven't changed a bit since I left you in Washington over ten years ago," confessed Tom.

"Don't remind me," Branson replied, continuing to do his search on the prisoner. Branson dug deep into the man's pockets, pulling out two large bank rolls of hundred dollar bills and tossed them to Tom and James. "So I guess this means his security level is orange?" asked James while running his thumb over the new crisp bills which was the code word for high. "No, blue gray." *Super-max protective custody*

"What?" The two said in sync while looking around, making sure no one was paying any attention before ushering them off into the side room and locking it. Agent Branson smiled at the shocking look on his friends' faces as the value of the man now registered who was standing before them. "Why didn't you say something? You know this man can't be around nobody but other blue-gray inmates. Now give me his name and his code number"

"This here is Don Antigeo." After logging Don Antigeo's code number into the system, they proceeded to fingerprint him when Tom became frustrated, "Shit, why isn't this ink sticking?" "What's the problem?" James asked. "I don't know, this is the tenth time I've tried to get his prints on paper and they're not taking. It's just coming out in one big blob." "Leave it," stated Agent Branson, stepping beside Tom. "Branson, you know I can't do that," Tom said as he quickly shot a look toward James before continuing, "Because we must be sure he is who he says he is."

"I know all that but it is probably just the sweat on his hand from the chase earlier but that can take all day to dry and I have to report back to Washington ASAP. The city of Philly is about to be uncontrollable, so if you can finish him up and do it later and let me get out of here I'll owe you one."

"Okay"

"But, Tom!"

"James, what can it hurt to bring him down in the morning and do it?"

James was ready to protest when Agent Branson tossed them both another roll of money. "I guess it will be alright for just this one time." They stripped Don Antigeo of everything but his gold cross chain and Rolex. Once showered they replaced his brown suit with three pairs of gray dress pants, four blue button up shirts with gray stripes, shoes and socks. Seeing that he was finished, the Spanish guard asked, "What floor?" while removing his handcuffs from his hip. "Relax Carlo, I am going to take this one, you're not clear to go on that floor," said Tom, taking the Don by his arm into the elevator and just as the door shut, Agent Branson waved bye with a look of cockiness, *"You just sit right here and I'll be back to make sure you see the justice you deserve."*

On the way down to section C which was four feet below sea level, Don Antigeo lowered his head until he faced the floor to avoid having his face captured by the camera in the upper right, when Tom inquired, "Now who have you pissed off to get here?"

Silence...."Okay you don't got to talk but it's only three kinds of people where you're going. One is a person whose presence and mind state are so powerful that he can't be around many inmates, because within days he will have his own army what would be willing to die for him at the drop of a dime. The second is a person whose knowledge and power are so strong that if it was ever to be let out into the hands of the wrong people, it would change the world as we know it today; from who really attacks the world trade center and the people who back it, to the reason they killed J.F.K. The funny thing is they say they're all connected. The last person is one that has the information on the whereabouts on a person like one and two. So the United States intends on keeping them alive to bring the other to justice."

The elevator doors came open with Don Antigeo stepping out to face his new home. He let his eyes take in the structure of the two level tiers with cells on each side and thought, *"I haven't been in the belly of the beast since my teenage years, but some things don't change. Remember, never hit the ground, keep your guard up and always strike first and get a knife as soon as possible."*

The sound of a mop hitting the floor made Don Antigeo jump as he quickly threw up his fist, throwing two punches in the direction of the noise when Tom said, "You can relax, it's just Amid, the head orderly around here and he'll show you where you're living quarters are and anything else you may need to know."

Tom re-entered the elevator and just before it closed said, "Oh and Don, within 72hrs I'll know which one of them you are, ha-haaa." Tom laughed as the door shut, closing in on his big smile. Then Don Antigeo reached out and grabbed the cold steel door, forcing it back open as he looked Tom directly in the eyes, "Never judge a man off of another man's actions because a gangster will make you look like an ass every time, Mr. Rubin." Don Antigeo removed his hand and let the door close, leavening Tom standing there in a daze and wondering how Don knew his real name when his shirt read 'Johnson' for the safety of the officers.

"Don't worry about Tom, he's more bark than bite."

"I've been bitten before."

Amid seeing the man's seriousness said under his breath, "I'm sure you have bitten also," before speaking aloud, "So if you will follow me, your cell is right this way."

"Amid, if you don't mind me asking you a question…"

"No, you can ask me anything. That's how I get paid."

"Where is everyone?"

"Oh it's mail time every day at five o'clock. Your mail will run across your T.V. screen for one hour only. So make sure you don't miss it because in this show there are no reruns. But for the right price anything is possible."

"I see."

"If you want to, my gambling room is open from 6am-11pm. If you need anything from Nurse Jackie down to Gucci socks, I'm your man."

"I'll be sure to keep that in mind."

The two walked in silence until they came to cell C-74. "Here you go, make yourself at home. Yo, Rob, pop 74 and Don remember if you need some thing, I'm just a call away." Amid gave Don Antigeo a half hug while in the same motion dropped something into his pocket as he whispered, "Don't worry it's on me."

As Don Antigeo waited for the cell to open, he could see a man who looked to be in his mid-thirties with a fine build, lying on the top bunk reading a book called *'The Victory of the Mind.'* The door popped open with the sound making the man jump up off of reflex while dropping the book. He slid his hand under the pillow before turning sideways as he jumped down using his body as a shield to hide the knife that he'd retrieved and placed it into his pocket.

"Yo, Amid, what the fuck is this? I know he's not coming in here! I'm not supposed to have a celly."

"Calm down, Nasir, I must have made a mistake let me check. No, it says right here 74 in the lower--"

"I don't give a fuck what that paper says, I'm not taking no celly and I mean that."

"But I don't think there's anywhere we can put him."

"You better find one," Nasir demanded, not letting Amid finish what he was saying. Amid searched the paper as Don Antigeo looked around at all the mirrors starting to hang out the cell bars trying to see what the commotion was all about and knew the chances of him going to another cell was no longer an option. Nasir had already struck first blood with the manner in which he spoke and the lions in their cages smelled it, so for him to leave would only be seen as a sign of weakness and force him to fight several battles before the war.

The Don eased the metal gate back and stepped in until he stood face to face with Nasir and said, "For a man to be victorious he must first see his victory, then believe that it is possible. Seeing is believing; for many bloody wars have been won just off of faith alone…and faith is to believe in your mind."

Nasir and Don said the last part of that sentence together and then Nasir asked, "So you read *The Victory of the Mind*?"

"Yes, Yusuf's a good author," The Don answered while giving a light head nod in the direction of the hallway. "He also speaks about always giving your opponent a way out to retreat," the Don continued. Nasir looked out at all the mirrors, "And you left me none, I just hope you're not good with whatever you got in your pocket." Nasir looked at the well-groomed man up and down, thinking, *"He looks harmless, but if he gets out of line I'm going to handle him. Plus he looks intelligent, maybe I can learn a few things from him before I get out of here in two months…fuck it."*

Nasir stepped out of the way letting Don Antigeo into the cell. The Don could still feel tension in the air but knew it was nothing he couldn't handle. He reached into his pocket while Nasir who was back on the top bunk with his book back in hand, only this time he wasn't reading but instead, he watched the Don closely as his hand came out with a cell phone in it. Don Antigeo moved the phone in his hand, taking it in from all sides seeing nothing funny; he pushed the button to turn the power on. Nasir thought, *"I may have misjudged him, this man is dumber than he looks, playing with that phone like it's a new toy. Damn it's only a phone, use it already."*

The Don's next move really made Nasir question his own judgment as he walked over to the toilet and flushed the small phone, laughing as he said, "You know that's the first bugged phone I didn't have to pay for."

"Bugged? How could you tell by just turning it on," Nasir questioned suspiciously. "That's all I needed to do, but I wish you would have asked before I got rid of it." Nasir pulled his hand out from underneath the pillow again, this time with the same kind of phone.

Turning it on, Don Antigeo said, "Yes, they got you too."

"You sure?"

"Positive; see the transceiver is in the battery and that's why the bright glow is almost as if the lights going to blow. Let me guess, he brings you a new battery every day?"

"Yyyeah," Nasir answered hesitantly, feeling embarrassed to admit he'd been had. "That's how they get what your plans are, see." Don Antigeo pushed in five numbers then entered four more when a female voice came through the phone, followed by Nasir, *"Are you sure you're coming home, baby?" "Yes, I promise in two months as soon as I go to court and tes-"* Nasir grabbed the phone from Don Antigeo's hand and slammed it to the floor. "That's it! I'm going to kill Amid!" he screamed.

The Don in his cool laid back voice said, "I think you should finish your book first and it will show you how to have some fun with Amid while becoming stronger within yourself at the same time." "How do you know all this, uuhh, what was your name?" "Just call me Don, you know it seems like ever since I was a kid I was prepared to become nothing more than an outlaw, mobster, heathen, gangster, thug and whatever else you want to call it...he prepared me to be it." "Who?" Nasir asked, needing to know the answer. The Don smiled and began to make his bed, "Good night."

For the next few days, little was said between the two but Don Antigeo made sure that after Nasir read a chapter from his book then he would quiz him on what he should have learned before schooling him by giving him a story out of his life of experiences, hoping that Nasir would learn from his own mistakes before it became too late.

10

Three weeks had passed and Don Antigeo and Nasir were beginning to talk a bit more but the Don knew that Nasir didn't trust him or anyone, keeping the knife he had strapped on each side of him at all times. But outside of the cell things were much different, for Don Antigeo was slowly becoming a noticeable man of power throughout the institution that held two hundred of the world's most dangerous men.

In a place where money was like air because everyone had it, a man's heart, word, and actions became the only way to be defined him and the Don welcomed it with open arms. He began his day with a short prayer before receiving his morning newspaper and meal from Moe. Once finished he would stop by each of the only two single cells at the end of the tier saying numbers and letters through the door for hours. "A3 to D1," then smiled saying, "There's always tomorrow. See you then." He then walked off, visiting the underground yard with artificial lights that were so high tech that it was hard to tell that it really wasn't the sun. There, Don Antigeo would read a book a day for lunch, calling it food for thought.

Amid's statement was true that every thing was for sale at a nice price, as the Don received five new double-breasted suits from Moe weekly with shoes to match and a chef-cooked meal that was prepared for two and dropped off each day at five. After enjoying another tasteful meal with Nasir not touching a drop of his, Don Antigeo stepped out onto the block for his evening walk when Amid appeared in his path, giving him a half hug and quickly placing a bankroll of money into his suit jacket. Amid whispered, "Here's your winnings from last night and a seat will be awaiting you as always but that's not the reason I interrupted your walk." "Then what is?" the Don asked, upset. Everyone knew that he used this time to give his brain a moment to relax, free from any thoughts but revenge.

"I'm sorry, Don, but it's the Russian. He sent me down here for you. I tried to tell him no but I couldn't and I know he can't ever get out of that cell but it's just something about him, like he's got this control over me."

Okay now you go back and tell him that I'm a man of my word always and I will see him the first thing tomorrow morning like always."

"You see what I mean? It's as if he knew you was going to say that because he also told me to say that the Islamic Day began after the Maghrib prayer that came in at 5:01pm, which means if 4…"

"Which means I'm late," Don interrupted with a smile. He liked the mind game of the Russian, who they say is too strong mentally for any one person to be around for too long or he will control them. As they headed for the man's cell, Amid said, "You do know you're the only person here that speaks to their kind of people."

"And?"

"You haven't heard the story? There were two other men who used to stop at these single cells for two days straight then on the third day they were found dead in their cells, both having committed suicide."

"And?"

"Don, you're not scared?"

"Now that's a good question but I'm not the one you should be asking that. The only crime Cyrus has done was possess intellect and he chooses to use it how he feels. So anybody that fears wisdom should fear him. But I welcome it."

Ten feet away from the cell, Amid stopped, not wanting to see the eyes again that haunt him in his sleep as he thought while walking off, *"How did he know the Russian's real name? There's something up with him, but what?"*

Don Antigeo walked up to the cell window to see Cyrus seated in a chair, dressed in a three piece snow white suit, eggshell-colored shoes and a black tie while holding a glass of red wine. Spotting Don Antigeo, a large smiled instantly, "I'm glad to see you got my message. The kid fights so hard to deny me."

"Well I'm here."

"So let's begin. Knowing that this is your brains down time, it will need ten minutes to 'switch' into motion, but I should be done before then, ha-ha," Cyrus laughed. "Well C2 to E4."

Two hours later, Nasir exited the cell with his eyes scanning the block as he watched the hands of the people around him and not their faces. He entered the gambling room to find Don Antigeo's chair empty. "I know there was something up with this guy." He then exited the card room, placing his only free hand on to the knife in his right pocket as he bumped people out of his way while looking into cells for Don Antigeo with fury in his eyes. The feeling of betrayal sent chills up his spine.

Walking fast, he noticed Don Antigeo twenty feet away, standing alone. When they locked eyes, the Don had a warm smile on his face and placed one finger in the air, giving him the sign to wait as he said, "D3 to F1, check...D5 to F3 checkmate."

"Wait friend, let's play one more," Cyrus asked.

"There's always tomorrow. I'll see you then," the Don replied before approaching Nasir, watching him closely as he moved his stare down to his hand saying, "I see you're finally ready to make your move."

"What?" Nasir asked harshly while grasping hold of his weapon tightly, ready to strike. "The book, you are done right?" Nasir looked down, seeing the book in his hand, forgetting the reason he had come to look for Don Antigeo in the first place. "Yeah, yeah." "Good, now tell me what you have learned and how you're going to handle the situation with Amid." Don Antigeo waved Nasir on, now having company for his evening walk.

"I will do nothing," Nasir responded.

"Correct, and why?"

"Because he is the best kind of enemy, he can only hurt me by the things I allow him to do."

"And you possessing this knowledge does what?"

"It gives me the advantage of using Amid any way I please."

"Indeed, but the correct move would be?" Don Antigeo questioned as they finished their first lap.

"To befriend him, that way I can learn what he truly knows without him knowing I'm onto him."

"True and what would you become?"

"...the worst kind of enemy."

"Today you have passed."

"Now that that's out of the way," Nasir rubbed his hands together anxiously and asked, "Tell me what happened with your friend, Roc?"

"Yes, good old Roc. Where was I?"

"You were at the part where after you found out that Mr. Holmes was at the airport to kill you because he knew that once the war started between him and Roc, your power would tip the scale for Roc."

"Yes and Roc being a student of Mr. Holmes's, he could only think the same. *Outside the cabin, Roc lowered the binoculars from his face and looked to Boggy saying, "Have the men stand down, they're leavening." "What? Nah, fuck that, Roc, you know I would never second guess your decision but if this nigga, Billy D, is going to be feeling some kind of way when he wakes up and sees R.I.P. Mr. Holmes with his birth date and 09 next to it on the news, then we got to do away with him now."*

"Then don't." Boggy was about to protest then decided against it when seeing that look in Roc's eyes. The same look he had before he shot Ron G and many others. The look that said he had an ace in the hole somewhere and when given the chance it always proved to be deadly.

Boggy spoke through the walkie talkie, "Okay men pack it up we're going home, drinks on me."

"I didn't say everybody. We're not going anywhere just the New Yorkers"

"I got you," Boggy said with a smile knowing Roc all too well.

"Team 2, you move out first and team 3, you cover them." Roc watched the hidden camera as they followed the six four wheelers making their exit down the long dirt road while looking for blind spots. Not finding any, he yelled, "It's time, we're moving on my lead, now!" Sensing this was his best moment, Roc pulled onto the dirty red clay road at a nice pace of 30 mph while keeping the camera in his peripheral vision as he approached the cabin. He began to pick up speed by the seconds 35, 40, 60, 70...just as the first camera was turning in his direction he demanded, "Triangle offense." "That's right, player, let's do what the fuck we came here to do," said Boggy who was the second man behind Roc in a line of six men. He quickly pumped the brakes twice, falling back three spaces with Buff on his hip doing the same. Riding his bumper closely, Manny and Raja maneuvered around the two as they pushed the bike to the max, shooting passed Shamone who pulled into the driveway next to Roc.

"Manny, watch the eyes in the trees on your right," Roc warned. "I'm seeing it." Roc waited until they circled the cabin making it to the rear and said, "Boggy, I'm giving you the ball so you're playing Kobe on this one."

"Thanks, you know I love to shoot too, ha-haaa."

"Okay well I'm about to give you a pick."

Simultaneously, inside the cabin the women dashed off in different directions as Foxy yelled out, "Heather, you and Jada cover the front two windows and don't let anybody get passed you. Peaches, you get the others to cover the rear." Foxy continued to command while Billy D calmly watched the monitor, saying to himself quietly, "Come on, soldier, where are you? I know you're out there."

"Billy D!" At the sound of his name he slowly turned to see Aretha with a Mack 11 gripped tightly, saying, "The motion sensor just went off so he's close, we must get you to the safe room now baby, let's go." Billy D stepped beside Aretha, kissing her on the cheek while easing the automatic from her hand. "No you go, the kid has proven that he's a worthy opponent that came to fight, and I must respect that."

"Are you sure?"

"When haven't I been?"

'BOOOOOM,' Aloud explosion echoed just as the words left Billy D's mouth, making the whole house shake, followed by several gun shots. He raced off with Aretha protected under his arm, shielding her with his body while his gun moved back and forth in front of him, searching for the first victim.

Making it to the safe room, he made sure Aretha was secure as she pleaded, "Baby, please, if you must go, promise me you'll be back!"

"That, I can't promise but if I do die it was supposed to happen. Just know that they can never take away what I did for my loved ones so in reality, I'll always be here."

Billy once again kissed his mother, stating, "Because we're all we've got," before placing the piece of dry wall back over the hidden door. Several more shots could be heard coming from the front room, followed by a loud crashing sound. Billy D ran towards the action, loving the feeling of the way his blood charged through his veins while he freed the forty five automatic from his hip. "I hope he fights as hard as I think he will," Billy D said as he reached the front room from the kitchen entrance and had to strain his eyes to see through the debris, dust, wood, and drywall fragments that were in the air. He dropped low to the ground feeling something wasn't right and then swiftly placed his arms in the cross position, moving them from side to side repeatedly. Suddenly he noticed Heather's head pinned under the frame of a four wheeler. Three women let off shots covering Jada who tried to free her as another four wheeler rammed through the cabin structure just missing Crystal by a few inches when she jumped to the side as it came to a rapid stop.

Crystal being one of the best trained,, quickly jumped onto the hood of the bike and with two large steps she was standing on the back of the bike's carrying rack, firing through the large opening, 'BOOM-BOOM-BOOM'. Crystal's first shot caught Shamone off guard, hitting him in the upper chest. The second was just below it, going straight through his vest. As he hit the ground, Crystal knew he was a goner on contact. "Teflon, bitch," she whispered while swinging her aim to Roc as he ducked low, zig-zagging toward Shamone's falling body and using the darkness as his cover.

Breathing hard, with the feeling of shots just missing his head, Roc wasn't disturbed but the moment he saw Shamone's eyes rolling back in his head, rage filled his body as he grabbed hold of his friend and soldier, pulling him out of the line of fire. The voice of Boggy asking, "What's happening over there Roc, Shamone you need me?" came clear in Roc's earpiece just as he made it to a large tree and placed Shamone behind it. "Hang in there, help is on the way," Roc said to Shamone, dialing his cell phone. He then lifted Shamone's vest and put his hand over the wound to stop the bleeding.

"Laila"

"Don't try to speak, Shamone, just relax."

"No I –I- can't, Laaaaila illa Allah," Shamone said in Arabic, praying to god before taking in a deep breath and again called, "Laila illa Allaahhhh," just as his body went motionless. "May Allah have mercy on us all, Shamone," Roc slowly raised the phone to his ear, "I called you too soon, but don't go no where. They will need you in a minute, I promise."

Roc slammed the phone down, breaking it so that they wouldn't get a trace on his location. Then he ran his hand down Shamone's face, closing his eyes before raising as his veins once again started to pulsate from his hands and neck. "No, I don't need you but they're going to need help...go!" Roc yelled, giving the word while stepping out from the tree with a glock in each hand and firing. With the first shot, Crystal was hit in the foot, "Aaaaahhh! She screamed, fighting back in excruciating pain. She re-aimed her weapon as another shot crashed through the metal license plate.

She focused in on Roc's neck and began to squeeze the trigger just as he fired again. When she realized what he was aiming for she screamed, "Retreeeaat!" and jumped free from the bike at the moment it exploded. 'BOOM,' the loud blast started a chain reaction as the second bike exploded also and killed Heather instantly. The impact knocked Jade back across the room.

Crystal landed on the hard wood floor as the side door slammed open with Boggy behind it, pulling the trigger of the tech nine sub machine gun that was raised high and killed three girls in his path as he moved forward. Buff came *from the back with two 9 mm's. He gripped tight, aimed low and pointed at Crystal cutting loose. She used the momentum from her fall and rolled as the shots cracked the floor behind her.*

Buff quickly adjusted his hands to lead his next shot to match Crystal's speed. As Crystal felt the shots getting closer she knew she had to do something to stay alive. She kicked her good leg out onto the sofa frame and with all of her strength she pushed off, sending her body in the opposite direction with her gun free. Catching Buff off guard she fired, 'BOOM-BOOM.'

The shot grazed Buff's ear from her unsteady arm. The next hit him in the shoulder, knocking one of his guns loose as he fell halfway to the ground on one knee. Billy D smiled at the smell of victory, easing his finger back on the trigger when Roc appeared in the corner of his eye and fired shots that blew Crystal's body back across the floor as he landed shot after shot into her chest plate until his gun cocked back empty. Dropping it to the floor while continuing to fire from his left hand, Roc removed another gun from his waistline. He cocked it back using his jeans while with one smooth motion bringing it up next to the other gun and making both chambers dance as they jumped back and forth with action.

Billy D watched the men at work and respected their efforts but now he would see what they really were made of. He stepped out from behind his shield of the wall with his left arm in a 90 degree angle, pointed to the right as his right hand rested on top of it, aiming straight while firing at both Roc and Buff. He hit Buff dead in the center of his neck, sending him crashing to the floor. At the same time he was backing Roc out of the house frame. Billy D quickly changed the aim of his right hand's weapon onto Boggy whose back was to him as he pinned Jada to the wall with bullets and fired.

A bullet ripped through the lower side of Boggy's shirt and the outer coat of his bullet proof vest that was intended for his kidney. On instinct Boggy knew by the time he turned around he would be dead so he faked left and on the sound of the next shot he was already moving right. He sprung around, spotting Billy D and fired. The two began to exchange shots back and forth with Boggy moving in closer with each shot. Roc saw his chance and raised his gun as he eased passed the front of the bike, back into the house. He crept up on Billy D and fired.

At the rear of the cabin, Peaches and Foxy noticed their mentor caught in a heated battle as they fought to keep Raja and Manny from gaining entry. Peaches continued to fire while looking from Manny to Billy D. Seeing Roc now only several feet away from Billy D, she let off several more shots in Manny's direction before turning to run and help Billy D when Foxy gripped hold of her arm, still returning fire and screamed, "Bitch I know you're not going anywhere!"

"But Billy D..."

"Don't worry; he'll take care of himself; he always does but we have to hold our position because where there's no order, there's nothing."

"Rule six, you're right," Peaches answered, taking one more look at Billy D, who sensed that soon things would get a lot more intense based on the look in Roc's eyes that only pure death would satisfy.

Billy D abruptly moved his hand in a criss-cross motion from over to under hand using the speed in which he moved his arms as he fired to distract when he suddenly hit the safety button, sending the clip flying through the air. As Roc and Boggy's eyes moved with the object for a second, it gave Billy D the time he needed to release a flash bomb, 'BOOOOOOM.' The bright light appeared, blinding everyone in the room with thick smoke that made them gag.

Moving into action, Billy D smiled thinking, "It works every time."

On reflex Roc dropped low, pulling his shirt over his nose to minimize the smoke inhalation while straining his eyes and looking for Billy D, which he was unable to find. Continuing the search as the smoke began to slowly thin out; he spotted Boggy with his head held high.

"Boggy, where did he go, did you see him?"

"Yeah I saw the pussy!"

"Where?"

"Oh the pussy is right here," answered Billy D, stepping out from behind Boggy with his gun cocked and pressed firmly under Boggy's chin. "You see me now. Pretty motherfucker, ain't I? Now tell your men to drop their guns or I'm going to blow your friend's head off his shoulders."

"Okay, okay don't hurt him; this is my beef," Roc stated to give the command as Boggy yelled, "Roc!" with the rage of a caged beast. The two locked eyes while Boggy continued, "It's ride or die always and now is no different. He shoots me and you shoot him and every motherfucker in the room. So go ahead and pull the trigger, pussy, I was born to die in battle!"

"And I believe you mean every word, that's why I grabbed you and not Roc. So what's it going to be - loyalty or revenge? You have three seconds to decide our fate. One..." Boggy's face tightened as he braced himself to meet his maker. "Two"

"Okay everyone stand down."

A tear of anger eased down Boggy's cheek, watching his friend that once promised just as he did, that if one was ever captured to never surrender to the other team, for they both knew the price of the game. As Roc dropped his gun, Raja and Manny were escorted into the living room at gun point by Foxy who asked, "Billy, do you want me to kill them now?"

"No, Roc here is right. It's my actions in the past that have him here today, fearing my actions in the future. So today he must defend himself against me in the present. One on one, meaning one gun, one clip, one heart, one man and the winner will decide the fate of the other if you agree?"

Before Roc could answer, Peaches spoke up, "But Billy D, you're way older than him."

"Yes dear but..."

"What I have in youth can be an advantage or a weakness," Roc interrupted.

"So we will meet out back in the heart of the woods in a half hour. Will that be enough time for you?"

"More than enough," Roc stated firmly.

"Foxy, give these men back their weapons so they can feel comfortable."

Billy D took Boggy's gun, breaking it down into pieces and dropping it to the floor as he said, "Everybody but him," and walked away.

"But what if they try something?"

"They won't. Ttell her why, Roc. Because you..." Roc finished the sentence, *"Must always be the man you say you are."*

"For?"

"Your words mean more than money."

"You better say it because the American dollar isn't worth nothing today but a man's value is going up by the minute and I'm worth about a trillion, ha-ha-ha. You boys got yourselves in some deep shit."

"It's nothing I can't handle," Roc answered.

"I hear that." Billy D started to leave then stopped in the doorway and turned saying, "Oh and Boggy..."

"What pussy?"

"When I'm done it will be one face, one tear...yours!
Ha-ha-ha." Boggy and Roc stared at each other confused,
wondering how and what Billy D really knew.

Out back in the center of an open field, Billy D now
dressed in all black with his London Fog hat cocked deuce
ace on the side of his head, stood back to back with Roc.
"After fifteen feet begin to fire," he said. Roc nodded his
head in acknowledgement while scanning the faces of the
twenty men that secured the side line that seemed to have
come from no where. He thought, "They had to be here, why
didn't he use them?"

"Lock down, lock down. All inmates report back to
your cell, lock down!" The C.O.'s voice spoke from the
loud speaker stopping Don Antigeo in the midst of his story.
"That's enough for today; tomorrow you will tell me what
you have learned."

11

The next day Don Antigeo awakened to the sound of a light tapping on his cell door. His eyes cracked slightly while still looking as if they were closed to see a man with his attire for the day, freshly pressed on a hanger draped down his back. There were also two brown bags which contained their breakfast and a Philadelphia Times newspaper resting under his arm.

Don Antigeo rolled from his bunk and got himself together by brushing his teeth, washing his face, and trimming his hair before making eye contact with Moe. He gave him a light nod as Moe yelled, "Pop C-74, Copper. Here you go, Don, nice and hot as always. There are two bagels with cheese and eggs over easy, orange juice and coffee black with two sugars. "That's fine; you can sit it next to the T.V." Don Antigeo passed Moe a hundred dollar bill and asked, "You did get yours also?"

"Yes, thank you, Don. I'll see you at lunch," Moe eased the bars closed. The Don dropped Nasir's bag on the floor next to him where he was doing his thousand push up for the day, saying, "That's food for the muscle." As he finished up his last two hundred, he questioned, "Why are you buying him breakfast?"

"Because no matter how far we make it in life, the people you take care of and that take care of you, is all that you will ever have, you got that?"

"Yeah, I got it but you're already paying double as it is, just by buying from him when you can get it for half price from Amid."

"What?"

"I said why pa…"

"I heard what you said; I just can't believe you would speak it. Let alone repeat it," The Don interjected while helping Nasir to his feet until they stood eye to eye. "Nasir, I like you and I see it's hard for you to trust anyone but we'll get beyond that. For you to live as long as I have, you must understand one thing; that there are only two sides in this world. For example, we have this cell here and the block that is just inches away but if I have to do just once you hear me, I said once, what Amid is doing to walk down that hall, I will remain in this cell for life."

Nasir watched the calm mild demeanor of the Don who continued to speak with emotion when he thought he spotted a spark of fired deep in the shell of his eye. "We don't condone or support his kind in anything but suicide, you got that?"

"Yes"

"Okay, now get dressed."

Don Antigeo finished his breakfast while reading the money section and smiled. An hour later up on the second floor in the back room on the tier, Don Antigeo opened the door to the law library. Stepping in, he removed the cob webs from his path as the still air invaded his lungs. He looked around at the many shelves filled with law books from every different country in the world that seemed to have not been touched or cleaned in years.

The Don ran his fingers along the rim of the wooden frame, retrieving it back black from all of the dust. "Come on," he yelled. Nasir hesitated to enter before giving into the Don's call, "Have a seat," demanded Don Antigeo while his hands moved over the A and B section, stopping at the C's. He removed a book on Columbian law, dropping it down hard on the table in front of Nasir. "What's that?" "Food for your brain," Don Antigeo replied.

Nasir opened it and glanced at its contents. "In there, Nasir, you will find two important things; one is the mistake of the men before you that were here or another hell like it. And the second is the mistake of your government, either way you need to know them both." The Don looked over Nasir's shoulder at the index and advised him to read page 287. "On A-1 of the Columbian Cartel?" Nasir asked confused.

"Yes and I'm going to tell you why. Remember the two cops I was telling you about?"

"Who, Detectives Brian and Michael?"

"Yes, well this time they were accompanied by a cop named Officer Dell."

Detective Brian and Michael's eyes were glued to the T.V. when cheers of joy and high fives erupted through out the 39th precinct as newsperson Molly Weiss informed viewers that the identity of the dead body was that of Mr. Holmes. Seconds later at the sight of the G.M.C. chain, a hyper Detective Michael tapped Detective Brian's arm, informing him, "It was them."

"Who?"

"I told you we should have never turned off. Damn! I knew it, a hunter's instinct is never wrong."

Officer Dell closed the space between them and whispered to Detective Brian, "What is he talking about?"

"I don't know. Michael, explain yourself will you?"

"Look," Detective Michael quickly pointed to the chain. Still puzzled, Brian said, "And?"

"You still don't get it do you? G.M.C., Get Money Clique."

"I'll be damned, that's where they were going."

"Will somebody please fill me in?" Officer Dell demanded.

"Well me and Mr. Angel here were tailing these thugs earlier today just before this happened." As Michael brought Dell up to speed, Detective Brian's mind was moving double time as he watched the screen's background

closely for anything he may have missed while Molly signed off, "Well, ladies and gentlemen, you heard it here first live from In These Mean Streets."

At the sound of Molly's statement, Detective Brian's vision shot to the clock on the wall, 12:12 am. He hastily gripped his coat from the chair and ran off, waving Detective Michael and Dell to follow. They rode the elevator down to the police main garage where many cars and trucks were recently searched and waiting to be taken to be impounded. There were two B.M.W. 525's, a 300 C, two jeep Cherokees, one corvette, three vans with secret compartments, a Bentley GT and a black Porsche sitting on twenty-inch rims.

Edward, who was in his mid-forties and fifty pounds over weight, working the desk behind the large steel cage, was watching Law and Order on an old black and white 13 inch T.V. A loud dinging sound from the elevator gave him a warning that someone was coming and he looked up to see Detective Brian and undercover officer Dell with a prisoner. Edward stuffed another Krispy Kreme donut in his mouth while turning his attention back to his show.

"I know that fat piece of shit saw us coming."

"Michael, take it easy, what's wrong with you? When this is all said and done, we're going to get you some help," Detective Brian stated.

"I don't need no help, I need justice for Rayfield."

"And we will get it, now relax and let me handle this."

Approaching the small opening in the cage, Detective Brian put on his best fake smile, "Edward, old pal, long time no see. How's life been treating you?"

"No, Brian!" Edward answered without looking up from the T.V.

"No what? You don't even know what I'm about to ask you, Ed."

"Whatever it is the answer is no."

"Come on, don't be like that, Ed. I just need a small favor that may help me crack this big case I just got the jump on and it may get us all promotions. If you do this I promise to put your name right under mine on the arrest report."

"Promotion?" inquired Edward as his left eyebrow rose up slightly.

"Most certainly, I'm onto something big, Ed."

"Okay, you got my attention. How big?"

"So big that I can't give you all the Detectiveails at the moment but I can be sure that you won't have to work the graveyard shift in this piss infested basement they have you calling an office. Ed, I've known you a long time, you deserve better than this."

"You're right and you know what? I'm sick of this dump and look at me: I'm out of shape since they stuck me down here in this shit hole. But I'm still not trying to get fired."

"Eddie, look at me, does it look like I would get you fired? Let alone myself. Ed, I'm all in with this one too."

"If you put it that way, you can take the heat for us both if your plan don't work"

"Agreed!"

"Okay what do you need?"

"Some cars."

"You got it...anything else?"

"Yeah, there's one more thing. Have you heard of an Egyptian myth?"

"No."

"Well, Ed, it deals with numbers, how you saying one thing, and mean something else."

Twenty minutes went by and a tinted red Corvette driven by Officer Dell, rolled onto the street out from behind the gate, followed by a B.M.W. They pulled side by side at the corner stop sign and Detective Brian asked, "Now where's Michael at?"

"I don't know, he was right behind me."

"Well its 12:35, he must hurry up if we're--"

Just then, the sound of screeching tires filled the street as the black Porsche fish tailed onto the scene. "Here he comes now." Detective Michael pulled in between the two cars. "Michael, this is not time for your foolishness." "I know, I know, Brian, straight by the book, now let's go handle this." Detective Michael pushed hard on the gas, taking the car from zero to sixty in three point four seconds as Brian's voice came through his walkie talkie, "Slow down."

Paying the warning no mind, Detective Michael's eyes searched the car that to him could only belong to a drug dealer, from its plush interior to the specialized sport gear shift and surrounding sixteen speaker custom sound system. He pushed play on the ten-disc CD changer with the music of Lil Wayne 'A Milli' basing through the car as Michael slowly began to bob his head and stated, "To catch an animal, I must think like one." He then eased passed the turnpike exit, taking a back road.

Around the same time, over 30 miles away in a New Jersey project located in East Orange, the glow from the flames lit up the night as the several vehicles used in the Mr. Holmes hit burned to a crisp. The members of the Get Money Clique surrounded the fire, each with a half empty bottle of Belvedere in hand. The thick scent of hydro weed smoke filled the air as they stood in silence in the memory of Lil Mac.

Top Dollar took a long swallow of the hot liquid before pouring out an equal amount on the ground. "Drink up, soldier, because tonight vengeance has been served. Now, may your soul rest in peace," Top Dollar raised his bottle and vision up to the stars as if he could see Lil Mac while holding back his tears. He made sure he didn't cry, to respect Lil Mac's wishes and yelled, "We got the bastard for you, son, but it doesn't make the pain of your absence hurt any less. Nothing could, because you were like no other. You truly were the last of a dying breed."

Top Dollar removed the tear from his eye so they wouldn't fall before he continued, "But I swear, until I see you again, young blood, whether it be hell or them pearly gates, the Get Money Clique will continue to live through me, you dig? And Mrs. Miller has now become the mother of all of us so don't worry, we got this. You just keep my partner close until I get there." Top Dollar turned to face the Get Money members with his eyes still glossy, nodding his head slightly as they all raised their guns, firing twenty shots into the air which made a loud thundering sound that echoed off in the distance.

A few feet off to the side, several local hustlers raced back and forth to cars, serving junkies hand to hand while the wealthier ones posted up beside cars selling weight when the sudden blast made them all jump and grab for their weapons. "Yo! How the fuck they think they can come down here and just disrespect us making it all hot and shit?" stated a young kid named Rich while giving his customer two twenties of hard, white rock before easing his hand on the butt of his gun that was within his waistline.

"Yeah, who are they?" questioned Fred, doing the same. "Fuck it, let's find out if they came with De'ran." "Yo D, Let me holla at you for a minute," the voices called out. Hearing it, De'ran already knew it wasn't going to be anything good. "Excuse me I'll be right back, Top Dollar." De'ran stepped away from the Get Money Clique and made his way over to his homies, thinking, *"Here comes the bullshit."* He saw Rich, who hated him for how much money he was making through out the P.J., just as he stepped up from out of the car saying, "Yo what's the deal with you and these out of town niggas? It's one thing that you're out here grinding and getting money cuz you live here, so you get that pass. But now you're pushing your hand."

De'ran smiled knowing the card Rich was playing, divide and conquer, as he looked at all the mean stares that surrounded him. Nodding his head, he thought, "*Lame, you don't have the heart to ask me for nothing by yourself but for a deal on some coke, now you're questioning me. Okay you're right; fuck it.*" He then spoke out loud, "Why? Is there some problem, because I don't see them running to no cars trying to stop your money? Oh my bad, I don't hang out with cats that do that."

"What?"

"Don't get me wrong, ain't nothing wrong with it because we used to do it together but then I kept my mouth shut and focused on business."

"Nigga, you got life fucked up if you think I'm not going to speak up on the way I put on for my city."

Rich removed his gun, cutting his eyes at Top Dollar as several people followed his actions. "Okay, okay you want them gone?" De'ran raised both hands in the air giving up. "You damn right, they're not blood so they're food. Get them the fuck up out of here!" demanded Rich while voices echoing in agreement entered the air. "Well all you got to do is tell him; his company isn't welcome."

"Who? Nigga, get him here! What the fuck is this sucker talking about?" Without answering, De'ran waved to the tinted Audi A8 when the door cracked open with the dome light coming on and showing the identity of the man now crossing the road. The crowd became quiet as Haffee stepped onto the side walk, "De'ran, what's up, the cars get here yet?"

"Yeah they just pulled up out back but my man here wanted to say something to you before you roll."

Rich stood in shock seeing the legendary Haffee standing before him. Haffee was born in these very projects and many people believed that he was one of the best hustlers to ever come out of Jersey until he moved to Philly, only to send a truck load of bricks back to the city. "Okay, what it is, main man?"

"Oh-oh-oh…"Rich stuttered.

Puzzled, Haffee looked at De'ran asking, "Is this a friend of yours?"

"Yeah, something like that but don't worry, he must have forgotten what it was he was going to say, let's go."

As they walked off, De'ran looked over his shoulder at all the shocked faces, knowing that tonight he had just separated himself from the rest of the hustlers, placing himself in a league of his own. Out back, five plated luxury cars sat in a line as Zack handed the keys to Haffee, "They're all sports cars and I tinted them all like you asked." "Thanks, Zack, the money is up top waiting for you."

"Okay, but watch the Viper acceleration, it's so strong that if you push down too hard you'll be sitting on four flat tires."

"You don't have to worry about that, I can handle her," stated Fox, taking the keys from Haffee. "A.P. lets go, you're riding with me," Fox yelled. "Okay, you can have it, Fox, but everybody make sure you remember the aliases we gave you on your licenses because they work. If something happens, just pull over and play it cool; everything will be just fine."

The sound of engines roaring, followed by tires racing across the gravel invaded the air as NayNay and Daz shot out from the tip of the projects, leading the way in a black Mazda RX-8. Next was Top Dollar handling an all wheel drive Acura RL, followed by Fox and A.P., then Haffee in the R8. The four cars disappeared out of sight.

As De'ran and Zack started to head up the steps, a shadow of an image caught their attention. De'ran quickly grabbed his weapon, feeling it was Rich trying to bring him a move for his actions earlier. He pointed his finger directing Zack to move and take the front of the car that Rich had disappeared behind. While De'ran went for the back, Zack did what he was told.

Stepping out into the street, De'ran rounded the car when suddenly the high beams of another car caught him off guard and blinded him. Instantly he covered his eyes by reflex as the car jumped forward. He braced himself for the impact as the car raced towards him with a voice saying, "Look at me!" De'ran, still adjusting his vision, strained to face his killer, and on sight said, "Mohammed?" "As-Salaam Alaikum," Mohammed replied, tossing the keys to the last parked car into this hand, "You keep it, I can get my own, Allah Akbar."

De'ran watched as Mohammed's car shot from the block, then all four cars swiftly rolled down the ramp onto the two lanes. Top Dollar and Haffee stayed in the center as NayNay and Fox went right, moving at top speeds of 70 mph. Fox welcomed the vibrations from the powerful R.P.M. going through the palm of his hands while riding NayNay's bumper closely. They moved in and out of traffic to the sounds of Nas' *New York State of Mind* on Hot 97.

When the song ended Fox said, "A.P. check the CDs, they got to have something in this joint."

"Oh, we have Yung Berg."

"What!"

"My bad," A.P. tossed it into the back seat, "Soulja Boy?"

Fox turned his face from the road to A.P. and gave him a look that said, *"Nigga, is you crazy?"*

"I know, toss it. I was just testing you. But I got something right here," A.P. said before sliding the cd in and pushing play. As soon as the words, *"You can have whatever you like,"* blasted through the speakers, Fox hit eject then lowered his window and threw the CD into the oncoming traffic. "What the hell you doing, Fox? That's T.I., he's the man!"

"Yeah I heard, that's why I did it. Now beat box for disrespecting an outlaw." Fox pushed down on the gas pedal, flying passed a day dreaming Haffee, hitting his horn.

The sound got Haffee's attention. For a second he gave a light head nod and fake smile, and then he was right back thinking about what his life had become as the young hustler's face haunted him. *"Damn. They couldn't have been any older than fifteen to twenty, looking up to me in shock as if I'm Michael Jordan or Jay-Z."* The vision stuck in his head while the words of his Iman replayed, *"Fear Allah, Haffee, for your heart still has life in it but also possesses an illness, and one of the two will manage to dominate the other. On one side your heart has love for God, faith, sincerity and reliance upon him. These are what give it life and without this your heart will die. There is also a craving for lust and pleasure, so you strive to experience them. It's also full of self admiration, which can lead to its own destruction."*

"Is this the meaning of destruction?" Haffee questioned himself, looking at the forty five automatic that lay in the car's passenger seat. *Suddenly Top Dollar's voice came through the earpiece as if he heard the question and screamed, "Watch out, it's an ambush!" Haffee's eyes slowly adjusted back to his surroundings as the "Welcome to Pennsylvania" billboard drifted behind him. Just then, a red corvette flashing blue and white under cover lights pulled out several feet in front of him, blocking his path. Haffee's foot slammed down on the gas making the V-12 engine jump forward while whipping the steering wheel to*

the right, then quickly back to the left. He nipped the front of Officer Dell's vehicle and broke passed it.

Dell stepped on the pedal, crashing recklessly into him and raising the A8 into the air. It fishtailed sideways, killing the engine. "Dig, a soldier is down! Help is needed!" Top Dollar yelled, hitting the brakes before throwing his car in reverse. He pushed it, forcing the wheels to spin in place as smoke appeared from the burning tires. Top Dollar raced backwards heading straight for the red corvette saying, "Time to meet your maker, pig."

Officer Dell noticed the Acura coming and the look of Detectiveermination that was in Top Dollar's eyes. "Oh shit!" he exclaimed. Then he left off the brake and moved out of the way just in time to avoid a broad side collision. Top Dollar used the momentum of his speed and pulled up the emergency brake while working the wheel in a circle. This sent him spinning at a 180 degree angle and he stepped on the brake as the vehicle stopped with the driver side window next to Haffee's.

"Come on, get in. We got to go now!" Haffee tried the key again, getting nothing, "Come on, start," he yelled. Detective Michael raced from behind the PA billboard bobbing his head to "Hey Mr. Carter" feeling a newfound zone as his blood pumped and made him hyper. Detective Michael, with his eyes focused on Officer Dell moving out of Top Dollar's way, snatched up the walkie talkie and screamed, "Dell, there's no surrender, no retreat!"

"What the hell are you talking about? That man damn near killed me!"

"Well I'm about to show you. Brian, are you with me?"

"I'm right on your tail." Detective Brian's high beam lights flashed in Detective Michael's rear view as he lined the Porsche up with Top Dollar and slammed his foot to the floor, 50-60-70-75, the bright light that approached, rapidly made it hard for Top Dollar to keep his vision in tact as he pleaded one more time, "Please come on, Haffee, we have more company." Haffee tried the key once again, "Come on!" As Top Dollar slammed his door shut, Detective Michael stated, "Yes, try to run...I knew you were a coward, hahahahaaaa, but any one of you will do for now."

Only a few feet away from Top Dollar, hearing the call for help Fox u-turned to the right while NayNay u-turned to the left. She raced back down on the outside line of the traffic doing 80 mph as the powerful Viper stayed on the opposite side of her moving through the passing lane. Top Dollar saw the all black Porsche speeding directly for him and yelled, "Get out of there, Haffee." "Top, I got this!" replied Haffee, hitting the gas.

Top Dollar sped off greeting Fox and NayNay as they shot back passed him. Fox lowered his window, fighting back the strong wind to gain his position on the doors window frame. Detective Michael's eyes were so focused on Haffee that he didn't see the move that was in motion as Fox raised his hand and squeezed the trigger of the 9mm he held firmly.

"Michael, watch out! Oh shit, nooooo," Officer Dell screamed, seeing Michael's driver side window explode into pieces as his car sprung wildly out of control. Officer Dell turned off from chasing Top Dollar and rushed to aid his falling partner while asking, "Michael, are you alright? Please respond! Michael!"

More shots blasted loudly into what moments ago was a quiet night. Daz's body hung halfway out of the window firing on Detective Brian. The impact shook the frame of the vehicle as shots pierced its steel structure. Detective Brian lowered his head to just above the steering wheel, gunning the engine. He pulled in front of the R8 using Haffee's vehicle as a shield. He quickly looked his body over for injuries.

Haffee tried the key again refusing to leave; needing to test his destiny when he spotted Detective Brian searching himself. "This son of a bitch don't even know I'm in here," he thought and slowly removed his weapon from the seat and raised it to the windshield just as Detective Brian's instincts sensed movement and looked in his direction. He was face to face with the weapon that had taken many lives. "I guess it's going to be destruction," Haffee eased his finger back on the trigger as the picture of fear covered Detective Brian's face. "One way or another, something is going to happen!"

Haffee fired twice into the two side tires as the car came to life with him speeding off. Detective Brian jumped from the car, aiming his 9 mm and leading it with the momentum of the R8, "I got you know!" He fired, 'BOOM' and the driver side of the window exploded with the bullet just missing Haffee's head as it continued through , spider webbing the front windshield. Seeing that his shot was off, Detective Brian adjusted his aim a bit to the left, "Bye-bye!" he whispered while waiting as the R8 crept towards his line of fire.

Then unexpectedly he was under fire as Daz aimed for him, 'BOOM-BOOM'. Ducking down, Detective Brian jumped back in his car and pulled out yelling, "Dell, assistance needed, I'm under fire with one hot on my trail. I'm riding on flats and they're catching up!"

"Okay I'm on my way, just hold on, Brian."

"Michael, Michael, wake up!" Dell shook Michael hard on the shoulder through the window. "What," Detective Michael answered, seeing stars. "Come on, Brian needs our help." On just a touch, the Porsche roared to life. "I hear you were looking for me," said Detective Michael, repeating the words of Lil Wayne before fishtailing back into the flow of traffic, racing to aid Detective Brian with his gun jammed in between the window. He said into his walkie talkie, *"Dell, it's time!"*

'BOOM-BOOM.' *"Come on, Fox, we're out,"* said NayNay into her earpiece, pulling Daz out the window and down into the passenger seat. She moved through out the traffic until she pulled behind Top Dollar and Haffee, Fox followed. *"Team, they just placed the call for back up, I guess they thought they was going to make the bust their selves. Now roadblocks are being set up on exit 13 and 16, so here's the plan: Haffee you ride the next exit, get off on the back road and ride it to Harrisburg then double back,"* Top Dollar directed. *"One"* Haffee replied as his tail lights disappeared down the ramp. *"Fox, you're up, hit the next exit and take it to our spot in Williamsport."*

"Are you sure, Top? Because I'm here if it's war," Fox affirmed. *"I'm positive, we must separate, and we have to do it quickly before they box us in."* Fox saw the exit sign approaching and had a bad feeling about leaving his team in a time of danger as he listened to Top Dollar giving NayNay her instructions.

"You take number 11 and go to Reading, you know the spot?"

"Yeah but what about you, Top?" NayNay asked.

Top Dollar waited until she was midway down the ramp before he answered, *"Dig, baby girl, someone has to be the bait so the rest of ya'll can get home safe."*

Top Dollar raised his gun out the window letting off five shots into the night while hitting the gas and racing off into the open road. *"Nooooo, Top, don't!"* NayNay screamed, continuing down the off ramp as she watched Top Dollar doing about ninety around the bend when Daz's yelling got her attention, *"NayNay, look out!"*

She slammed into a cop car that blocked the road as several officers quickly appeared with guns drawn, coming *from everywhere surrounding the car. Two cars came down the ramp, cutting off any chance of escape, "Let me see your fucking hands or I'm going to blow your heads off!" The overweight officer yelled. NayNay turned to face Daz, "Get out, I'm going to take everything; without Lil Mac here, there is nothing left for me to live for. I'm only remaining here to get revenge for his death," she voiced. NayNay then turned her palms over to show Daz the deep cut marks on her wrists from her attempted suicide before raising them in the air as her left hand inched back for the gun hidden in her sports bra.*

Fox heard the demand to get out of the car followed by NayNay's statement and screamed into his mouth piece while slamming on the breaks u-turning, "Nooo, NayNay, please don't do this!" NayNay removed her earpiece, giving her the perfect opportunity. "Please don't," Daz pleaded. "Solo wouldn't respect this. If they didn't have the drop on us it would be different but not this way, he would never give them the pleasure to say that they killed one of us like this. Plus I feel like a bologna and cheese right now anyway."

"Well you can have mine," NayNay laughed, opening the door and being rushed to the ground. Daz followed with his face pinned to the concrete and said, "That's the smile I haven't seen in a while." "Shut up," Officer Edwards yelled before grasping onto the walkie talkie, "Brian we've got them. That Egyptian myth worked like a charm; how you gave them two numbers over the air then added them together, bingo! Here they come."

"Okay, Ed, just hold them. I'll be right there…"

"Come on don't stop, Don! You've got to tell me what happened to the girl," Nasir pleaded. "I will once you're finished and fill me in on what you've learned from that." The Don tapped the book then walked out the door.

12

At 3:34 am in the midst of the night, Don Antigeo tossed and turned with sweat covering his body, feeling as if his cell was closing in on him. Pulling the blanket tightly over his head, Don Antigeo bit down hard on his bottom lip as his mind endured the frightening nightmare for what seemed like the hundredth time.

An owl called out into the night as a man dressed in all black with his face painted black and forest green blended into a large bush that sat just inside the surveillance perimeter of the mini mansion. He waited patiently as several men patrolled in sets of two, a few inches away, none the wiser of his presence.

Hours had passed without him changing the slightest position with his mind only focused on the sight of his brothers. The front door opened and with his head still locked straight forward, sure to not alert anyone of his presence, Lucifer watched Mr. Holmes's every move as he handed over a small wrapped box before vanishing down the long driveway.

When his brothers didn't appear shortly after, he slowly placed two stainless steel rings with a short razor sharp thin wire connecting them together, on the middle finger of each hand. Rising from out of the bush into the open he stated, "I will attack them from the front, the back and from side to side." Whispering, the devil promised to God while looking at his watch, "30 seconds," speaking of the time remaining in the bodyguards two minute rotation. The two armed men turned the corner of the building heading towards Lucifer's way with their M-16's resting high on their shoulder while engaged in deep conversation.

"I'm just saying, what's up with all that gang banging up here in New York? This shit don't go down like this in Philly."

"I don't know but they're everywhere and they ride hard. You fuck with one of them if you want but I'm telling you this, you better not be faking it."

"Faking! Man fuck them niggas, if they come to my city its war because the only color we respect is green...you already know. It's not a secret; it's get down or lay down in Killadelphia. But I know whose fault this is, Nicky Barnes, he did this shit."

"What?"

"You heard me nigga, Nicky. That clown did this shit because that's what the fuck he really is. Rat ass nigga; he gave up everything he was, from the way he lived to the foundation of who he was...that's the only reason we're talking about him now. How he told on Guy and many others over a woman he didn't own, I mean this nigga started telling like he bought a bitch and he had a receipt. That move right there took the heart out of New York and these niggas left are just the veins, not gangsters!"

"I heard you, but..." The man stopped speaking as he heard a sound to his left and dropped his weapon into his hands. "You hear that?" James asked with alert eyes. "Yeah, it probably was a cat or some..." Before the words could leave his mouth, Lucifer appeared at his side swiftly wrapping his hands around James's neck with a wire that made a swish sound cutting through the air and his throat. The man was killed instantly.

"What were you saying?" The other man questioned while turning around. Lucifer quickly released his finger from one ring. The thin wire retracted back to the other like a rubber band cutting his neck open in reverse. He then sent a hard right kick to the man in mid turn, forcing his head high in the air and giving him the access he wanted. Within *seconds he had the rings wrapped around the man's neck as he slowly applied pressure. Several lines of blood started to appear while the man screamed out, "Aaaaaahhhh."*

"Please don't cry, it only turns me on when you beg for my mercy and not his. Now where are the two visitors?"

"They're over there," he replied looking in the direction behind Lucifer who followed his stare, looking over his shoulder. "Where?"

"In your ass, faggot! Aaaaaahhhh..." the man yelled before his neck was snapped from the force of Lucifer pulling and then releasing the body and letting it fall. He took off at full speed toward the mansion and arrived at a window where he placed his ear. After hearing nothing, he quickly began to cut out a large hole in its frame before lowering himself down behind a lavish sofa into what seemed to be a living room. He looked around the room several times carefully while his ears listened for the slightest motion. The whisper of voices danced from two rooms over that navigated his movement as he made his way across the two inch high rug soundlessly. He moved into the dining room, grabbing an apple from the fruit basket on the table, bit into it and placed it back in the basket right side up.

The door of the den was slightly ajar as he watched the three men in suits zipping up the last body bag; thinking that this was another deal that his brothers left with death instead of a handshake. He now understood their reason for a quick departure and backed away from the door while removing his cell phone and pushing the number six on speed dial. Placing it to his hear, he heard the sound of two rings that stopped him in his tracks. Lucifer lowered the phone while the other ring tone continued to ring in the air. He then slowly turned on his pivot, pulling the steel rings apart seeing the blood that covered the thin wire and tasted it before taking off at full speed down the hallway.

Busting through the door, his foot was immediately in the air sending a hard half round house kick into the first man on his right Adam's apple, crushing it on contact. The second man didn't have a chance as Lucifer, in his coming down motion wrapped the wire tightly on his neck, with the third man quickly retrieving his gun. The man backed up, puzzled from the deranged looking person that was holding his partner hostage.

"Let him go before I blow your ass to hell!"

"Sssshhhh, I'm trying to hear his heart beat slow and I just got back from there," Lucifer replied.

"I'm not playing with you damn it. I'll give you to the count of five." The man tightened his grip on his weapon, "1, 2, 3."

"Okay, okay don't shoot I hate guns," said Lucifer, releasing one ring sending it racing back around the man's neck. The third man now more confused with his eyes following the strange weapon moving back and forth. "This is yours," Lucifer yelled through tightened teeth while throwing a sharp knife through the air from his free hand that was taped to the tip of his wrist beneath his sleeve. It landed right between the man's eyes before he grabbed the ring out of the air and pulled it back hard in the opposite direction until the man's body went stiff.

Lucifer spit the apple out on the man's face, "Taste the forbidden fruit," he said before slowly walking over to the first body bag and ripping it open. When he saw the lifeless body of Apollon, rage filled his body making his skin hot instantly. He scooped up the body and put it over his shoulder. As he moved along he viewed a body of a man he didn't know, before taking Balial up into his arms and leaving the mansion through a side door. He ran through the woods handling the extreme weight with ease for a quarter mile back to their car where he placed the bodies comfortably on the back seat.

Lucifer then took two black Mack 11s with silencers and several other blades from the trunk and dashed off, re-tracking his steps as the trees camouflaged his movement. He pushed his legs harder and harder until he reached the back step, "Now you will know the teacher," Lucifer said, moving through out the house with blood on his mind and entered the living room and found two men kneeling over the three dead bodies. "Their souls were needed as well as yours." He pulled the trigger without waiting to see their bodies fall.

Going up the stairs he inhaled deeply with each step and whispered, "I smell the stink of your sin." Moving down the hallway he let the air out from his lungs and stopped at the fourth door on the right, "Now you must pay for them." As soon as he kicked the door in, he startled a blond-haired woman deep throating a man in the sixty-nine position whose face was buried in her hairy bush. Lucifer squeezed the trigger once as the muffled sound brought death again, dropping the woman's head to the mattress as the man's manhood disappeared in her mouth. "Hey, that's it baby," the man said just as the sound repeated and two shots were placed in her ass cheeks, hitting the man in the face.

"Burn in hell," Lucifer said closing the door behind him. Following a scent he continued to inhale deeply and moving his head as he followed his nose from side to side and came to the door of the master bedroom. "I smell the scent of your fear," he spoke, turning the knob to the right until it popped. Giving it a light push, the large wooden door opened just as four shots slammed into it.

"Yeeessss indeed, I smell your soul is frightened and why wouldn't it be?" At the edge of the door frame Lucifer readjusted his bullet proof vest pulling it up to his ear while ducking his head so as little as possible was shown before kicking his shoe off high into the room. Shots fired again, hitting the shoe as he located the direction that his enemies

were shooting from. Then, before the first shoe could hit the floor, he was in the air firing as he dove aiming at the spot. His attempt was off by inches as his shots hit the man in the shoulder. "Aaaaahhh," the man screamed. Lucifer landed and quickly rolled, locked, and fired to hit him several times in the face.

The sound of sniffing could be heard through out the room as he said, "I smell fear, but you have shown much heart." He moved around the huge room trying to understand the mixed scent when he spotted a wrapped box with a bow sitting on the dresser. Seeing it he remembered the face of the man who said, "Consider it handled, sir."

"He has to be around here," Lucifer spoke turning toward the large walk in closet that sat mid center in the back of the room. As he slowly approached it, inside Travis stood frightened and hiding behind a brown Dior suit with his 63 year old frame trembling. He watched the man who had just murdered Freddy with the swiftness of a marksman heading towards him sniffing the air as if the Sean Paul cologne his granddaughter got him for Christmas would be the death of him. Lucifer was only inches away as Travis prayed, "Oh God, please don't let this man eat me I sw-" He stopped just when the door of the closet swung open making Charlie jump as Lucifer ripped off shot after shot into the clothes before ripping the garments from the hangers. He didn't find anything as he looked to Travis's side while slowly raising his gun to level it off at Travis' chest.

Travis was quickly searching himself for anything that he could use as a weapon to defend himself. Locating nothing but the house keys, Travis braced himself by closing his eyes and squeezing his body tightly. When nothing happened he reopened his eyes to see Lucifer staring at the large painting of Mr. Holmes that sat in the middle of the room as if he spotted it for the first time. He moved in closer saying, *"You, and whoever had something to do with this will kneel before me and answer for your sins."* Then *Lucifer pulled the trigger placing several shots from each Mack 11, ripping the painting in half.*

"I will not stand for this, Roc, Roc, Roc," escaped Don Antigeo's mouth as Nasir shook him, "Don, wake up, you're bleeding! Don, Don, wake up!"

"What, Roc, what?"

"No, Don, it's me, Nasir. You was having that nightmare again."

"No, just a dream, I was just thinking of the life of a good old friend as if I was living in his shoes."

13

Still unable to sleep, Don Antigeo sat up in deep thought about Roc while finding it strange that even with the possibility of Lucifer connecting him to the Lil Mac killing that he would still call out to him of all people in his time of danger. Lying back on his soft pillow Don Antigeo closed his eyes and quietly spoke, "Make me proud, new breed," as he continued to think…

Roc stood with his back to Billy D's and his hand tightly gripping his 9 mm while at the same time his mind was relaxed, *"I have been here before."* The counting started, 15, 14, he observed the area closely, 13, 12, before studying the faces of the men and women that stood along the sideline and back. Then something caught his attention as the words of Mr. Holmes re-entered his mind. "I have truly underestimated your power, son, but as you know, Roc, a real man never falls for the same deception twice." 7, 6, Roc finally started to take a step forward as Boggy noticed the concerned look upon his friend's face. Roc then gave him a look that made Boggy nod in understanding. It was that look he had when he shot Ron G and others. Knowing that he had an ace in the hole and when given the change to play it, it had always proven to be deadly, Roc continued to creep as the counter yelled, 5, 4…and slowly he cocked back his weapon now truly understanding his enemy. "2, 1. Fire!"

Billy D quickly turned catching Roc a step too late as he raised his gun and locked it on the side of Roc's face just waiting on him to turn all the way around while easing his finger back on the trigger. Then he suddenly released it, shocked to see that Roc wasn't a step off, in fact his gun was aimed on the heart of the real Billy D. Roc moved in closer until he could feel the heat of his breath and said, "You thought I would fall for the same move twice?"

"Not at all but maybe once, I'm glad you didn't, Lil Rocky the Warrior. That means I would have failed, now put that gun down so we can get to know each other again because I see you've learned much over the years."

"What did you just say?" Roc questioned.

"Put the gun down?"

"No, before that," Roc moved the gun to Billy D's face as he answered. He remembered hearing the same voice but only it was when he was a kid at his father's side as a stranger said, "Lil Rocky the Warrior, so I finally get a chance to meet my future Corporate man." It was unbelievable to Roc. "So we've met before?"

"On several occasions, believe it or not. I was even there when you were born. How is your lovely mother?"

"So I guess you won't be mad that a person you witnessed being brought into this world is taking you out of it?"

"You wouldn't dare," Billy D stated with a confident smile.

"You shouldn't be so sure of yourself, Billy D."

"Uncle Terrance to you and I'm sure for two reasons."

"And those are?"

"One is because they say the real is a recognizable cause," Billy D answered and paused until seeing that he had everyone's attention then continued, "A person can always see traces of himself in someone else. That's why I let you live earlier, because I knew you would do the same."

"Just like you were waiting on me because you knew I would come?"

"Exactly. That's why two is so important because if you ever want to know how you fit into all of this you'll walk with me like old times and put that gun away. You're starting to make me nervous and you won't like me when I am." Billy D, not waiting on an answer started down the hill to the hike path. "You know in some strange way I believe you," Roc said while following Billy D's lead.

Aretha clapped her hands twice and said, "Come on, ladies, let's go inside and show our company some hospitality and make them something to eat." "Yeah I got something for ya'll to eat also," yelled Boggy while looking into Foxy's eyes and licking his lips.

On the trail Billy D asked, "Do you remember any of this?" Roc looked around taking in his surroundings then closed his eyes and was back as a kid again making his way down this very path with his father at his side while a man was behind, whose face he couldn't see but his voice still remained strong in his mind.

Roc heard the voice say, "Lil Rocky the Warrior, do you want to play a game?"

"Yes, sir. Dad, you going to play too?"

"No, son, this game you'll have to play by yourself but I'll be watching," Roc's father replied while he got on his knees in front of Roc to look him into the eyes. "Son, remember that in life it's never what you see or hear, it's always what you know. There will be times that you will feel that you're alone but you're not. Roc, remember your body is a sponge that takes in information from everything around it and even when you're not paying any attention it is, so you listen to it always."

"Silky Smooth, it's time," the man said.

"Okay, okay. Son, you hear me? Listen to your instincts."

"Silky."

"Alright," Roc's father, who was known by the name Silky Smooth Larry back in the day, stood to his feet giving Billy D a light head nod. Billy D quickly wrapped a blind fold around Roc's head to cover his eyes as Roc started to

resist and struggle against the strong man just before his father's powerful voice called, "Roc!" Immediately Roc stopped as Billy D began to give him his instructions in a low calm tone. "Lil Rocky the Warrior, don't be scared."

"I'm not."

"That's good, the reason I have this over your eyes is because it is said that the ability to see a situation as the other side sees it is one of the most important skills one man can possess. Who could lose a war when he's fighting against himself? Therefore you have to know every part of yourself first before that can happen. Now let me see your shoes."

Roc handed them over and could hear footsteps racing off with his father's voice now weakening in the distance saying, "Remember what I told you, listen to yourself. I'll see you back at the cabin." Roc started to follow just as he noticed another set of footsteps going in another direction. Two days later, dirty, sleepy, and hungry with leaves tied around his feet as shoes, Roc knocked on the first cabin door that the prototypes used to trick him and found his father and Billy D with a large smile on their faces.

Rushing to his son, Silky gave Roc a big tight hug, "Son, you have made your father so proud today!" He released him and turned to Billy D, "See, I told you never question my blood line. The best time was four days Billy D and my boy cut that in half. Now tell Money Man Holmes to top that." "Truly, Lil Rocky the Warrior has done great."

Roc reopened his eyes looking at a much older Billy D with a smile on his face for the memory of his father and asked, "So you moved?"

"You do remember?"

"Maybe."

"Good enough, let's continue."

They walked in silence as Roc paid attention to all the strange sounds around him. Then the blinking eyes of a snow white animal resting on a large tree branch caught his attention, making his muscles tense up. Billy D could feel the sudden change in disposition and tapped him on the shoulder. "You indeed remember. For you are now listening to your body but relax, it's only an owl.

They turned off the path and slowly approached a black painted barn that was hidden by the night "Do you recall this place?" "I don't know," Roc replied. "You must, this was your favorite. You would come down here by yourself even when you had some free time," explained Billy D, while holding the door for Roc to enter.

Stepping inside, Roc was surprised to see such a big difference from the dirty cobwebbed infestation outside to come just inches and be standing in a spotless firing range. "And this here was your best obstacle." Roc followed Billy D's pointing finger to see a big training field with skeet popping up from everywhere as cones, wooden stands and seven foot high nets were placed through out the room blocking the pathway. "You used to complete this in about two minutes flat, you care to give it a try?"

Gripping his gun tightly, Roc said, "Why not? A person could never have too much practice." Roc stepped to the center of the starting box and raised his 9mm. "Rocky, I think you should try the lockers on your right first." Roc's eyes roamed over the several gym lockers that lined the wall with names engraved in the center. 'E.T., Deek, Turtle, Aaron, Obama, Rocky.' There was another name after Roc's but white tape covered it. He slowly began to move it, seeing a T and O before Billy D grabbed his hand and stopped him. "That right there would give you to much of an advantage. Now that you see the locker, open it." Roc looked at the old master lock confused, asking, "How am I supposed to do that?" Billy D said, "Listen."

With his hands on the lock, Roc closed his eyes and seconds later he saw himself again at a young age, turning the lock to the right, then to the left twice, followed by another right and the lock popped open. He reached in the locker and grabbed the 22 automatic, the same model his father used to carry before stepping into the starter box checking the clip.

Billy D entered with his father at his side, "I knew we would find you down here, Rocky the Warrior."

"Why not? A person could never have too much practice. You taught me that, Uncle Terrance."

"You're correct, so don't let me stop you."

A young Roc waited for the light to flash green, and then began to let the bullets fly. He jumped over a mid high fence shoulder first, tucking it as he hit the ground and rolling with the impact. He came up firing at three skeet, hitting them dead center. As he got back on his feet, Roc raced through the fire laced floor before diving for the rope that hung from the ceiling, catching it with one hand. He crossed a pond while defending himself as another skeet shot across the top of the ceiling with flashing lights that faded from yellow to orange. The next color to come was red which indicated the enemy would have killed Roc. Another one popped up from the ground and Roc knew he had to think fast as the skeet above quickly closed in attacking the right side which was his free hand. The other rushed from behind and left Roc to react on instinct as he fired away hitting the one up top. 'BANG-BANG,' he released the rope just as he cleared the pond, dropping the gun from his right hand and quickly catching it with his left and pulling the trigger. Roc nailed the target with the orange light having just a drop of red in sight.

"I told you my son would be the next best, that's the advance test and he killed it."

"True"

'Clap-clap,' "Great, Rocky, you did it in under one minute; that's your new record."

Billy D's clapping brought Roc back to the present as he looked to the 22 in his hand. The strange scent of his father entered his nose, leaving Roc more confused then he had ever been in his entire life. At the same time he felt so prepared for the answer. "So I was trained to go in that room that day and get that gun to shoot that man?"

"Yes and no."

"What's that supposed to mean?"

"Come on, I'll show you."

They walked through the range until they came to a side door. "After you," said Billy D. Roc stood in the middle of the all white room in shock, the same way he did the first time he was there. He moved his head around, astonished by all the books that filled the room from the floor to the ceiling. There were six computers spread out on the white marble table.

Without thinking, Roc took a seat in the big comfortable chair that was in the middle of the room. "You see, your father was right; all you have to do is listen." Billy D stepped to the table, moving the computer to the side to reveal to Roc that his name was written the same as on the locker. "Don't just sit there, you know what to do."

Roc was listening to his body and let his hands roam over the keys. After several tries, his access was granted and he logged in to see that there were pictures of moments in his past that he didn't remember. But once seeing the photos, the memories began to replay in his head like it were just yesterday. Roc's eyes looked through the images when several seemed to stand out from the rest. One was of him and his father as they stood out in front of his new Buick with the words, '*His first understanding,*' written above it.

Roc looked from the life changing picture to Billy D and quickly stood to his feet. "What the fuck is going on and who the hell are you?" Roc questioned with anger. "What's wrong, Rocky? I don't understand; we were having such a good time. Why are you suddenly so hostile?" Billy D replied as he backed away from Roc's rage.

"Don't play with me. This picture was taken the day my father killed Big Jeff," Roc stated, grabbing hold of Billy D's arm. On contact Billy D pulled away with a force that stunned Roc as he stepped forward leaving less than an inch between the two. The fury in Billy D's eyes suppressed Roc's rage and Billy D answered in his signature cool, calm tone, "No, don't you play yourself. If you're asking me were you put in a position, yes, but for a reason. It was to uplift your people as a whole."

"How, by selling drugs and killing people?" Roc sarcastically questioned.

"By any means necessary and don't you dare stand in my sight judging my actions when I walked these streets at a time when a black man didn't have a drop of respect and for them to get it, they had to take it. So that's what we did and we did it so hard that they put their poison in our beautiful community for free. What you now call hoods and one by one our strong soldiers became addicted and controlled by the very substance that made your ass rich. You know why?" Billy D refused to wait for a response and continued, "It's because the most effective leader is the one who satisfies the psychological needs of his followers and that's what I did. Now I feed millions of families legally through organizations funded by my corporation. Come on, Lil Rocky the Warrior, don't look so surprised that you work for me," smiled Billy D.

"I know you didn't think all this was for nothing; your father and I prepared you for these moments but when he was killed, your mind locked and the things I taught my best student got suppressed from a form of mental distress. You forgot about all this."

Billy D moved his hand in a circle motion show casing the room, "And I thought you would let me down so I started to rebuild the plan with another student. Then we realized that you didn't forget anything we taught. It's just you used everything that your father taught you himself."

"And what was that?"

"To protect your family and I have to say, you did a hell of a job. But now your real challenge is yet to come."

Roc looked down at Billy D's outstretched hand and gave him a firm handshake. "Thank you for everything you've done but this is the ending of our beginning. I came here to bring closure to my life and for my family." Roc released Billy D's hand leaving his 9mm in his palm. "Now with the understanding we have made today, parting as non-enemies, I am officially retired," Roc stated.

Billy D began to clap his hands applauding Roc. "Rocky, that was a lovely speech, almost better than the one I gave. But still, you ran into my house killing two of my beloved people. Thirty-one years after those words left my mouth, not counting the many people before you that are in the ground. I said this to say we never truly retire. We're just getting a moment's rest, so please take yours and enjoy. But don't let your guard down because when you think it's over it's really just the beginning."

Don Antigeo finally drifted off into a deep sleep with a devilish grin.

14

Two weeks later, Don Antigeo, after showing Nasir for a month how to play chess, began to let him win and today was no different...or was it? Nasir called "Check mate," with joy. "I don't know why I keep letting you beat me. All I had to do was move my knight and I had you but instead I left it sitting there as if studying your motives."

"Don, at times I understand what you be saying because I was also an overseer of hundreds of people in my business but there's this look I receive from you, like you're sending me some kind of mes..." 'Knock-Knock' The sound of someone hitting on the cell bars stopped Nasir as he was speaking. "Nasir you have a lawyer visit," Amid said rolling the computer screen into the cell. "It will start in twenty minutes."

Don Antigeo watched Nasir's every move as he placed a suit on his back. He was thinking, *"Does he look nervous or is it just me?"* Don Antigeo already anticipated his departure but decided to test the water to see if he had progress. He grabbed his newspaper while pulling his chair in eye sight of the screen. He began to unfold it while pretending to get comfortable when Nasir said, "Excuse me, Don." "Oh I'm sorry, you need to be alone." Don replied and exited the cell with his trademark stroll on his way to the yard. He thought about his plan and the reality of what these six-by-nine cold, cement walls did to people.

Inside the 39th precinct, NayNay was placed in an interrogation room where she sat at a cold steel table with only two chairs as company for hours, while several officers watched her reaction to the isolation from behind the mirror.

Detective Brian questioned, "Michael, don't you think she has waited long enough?"

"No, just a little bit more. I still can see the fire in those animal eyes." Capt. Citric yelled, "I don't know about this damn fool."

"I hear you, Captain, but he's the one who made the official bust and with out him and his badge we wouldn't have a case. This is the best chance we have to get Rayfield's killer."

Capt. Citric now had his finger in Michael's face saying, "Okay, I'm going to let you do this but I swear, Michael, if you do another one of them damn foolish stunts to have the Mayor calling my phone for anything, you'll never be a cop again as long as I have a job in this city. Do you understand me?"

"The hunter doesn't get hunted, now give me that. I got a pussy cat in the cage that's scared that I must now tame." Detective Michael snatched his badge free from Capt. Citric's hand and placed it around his neck with a soft kiss before pushing the interrogation room door open with a hard shove. NayNay could feel her eyes becoming extremely heavy as she fought to stay awake when suddenly the loud slamming sound of the metal door being forced up against the back wall made her jump.

Detective Michael followed right behind it, closing it with the same force and then took a chair, adjusting it until he was positioned right across from his prey while thinking, *"Look at you, far away from the jungle and you're scared, tired, and you need a friend. Well I'm not going to give you any of the above."* The evil in his smirk was visible while NayNay was having thoughts of her own, *"Why is this man looking at me like that and not asking me if I want to speak to a lawyer like Top Dollar said he would? I need to go home and get some sleep."*

After ten minutes of giving NayNay his best poker faces and noticing the several drops of sweat forming on her forehead, Detective Michael slowly stood up, *"Now she's ready,"* he thought before saying, "You do understand that I'm about to send you to your cage for a long time don't you?"

"Don't listen to him, he's only trying to scare me like Solo said they would," NayNay took a deep breath as she ran her fingers through her hair and continued to stay strong. *"I got to pull myself together and do the things they taught me to do in this situation. Here goes nothing."* "No, I didn't officer. What did you say your name was?" *"That's right and once I get his name, I'm going to tell him to let me speak to my lawyer or I'll have his badge."*

"It's Detective and I didn't," Detective Michael said, beginning to circle the table while feeling the eyes of his prey following him with each step. "Well if you don't know, it's only right that I tell you in about twenty minutes you and your friend, Mr. Williams, Daz, are going to be charged with murder for killing a beloved police officer."

Back behind the glass window, Capt. Citric had steam coming from the top of his head screaming while heading for the door, "What the hell is Michael talking about? I'm getting him the hell out of there now! We have nothing to support a case of murder and we'll be lucky to make the assault on an officer charge stick. Detective Brian, come with me, I'm taking over."

Detective Brian quickly grabbed hold of Capt. Citric's arm that was reaching for the door knob. "Let's give him a chance. I think he may be on to something." Looking down at Detective Brian's hand, Capt Citric with his 6' 2", 280 lb frame that towered over most people he encountered, said, "If you don't get your fucking hands off me…"

"Oh I'm sorry, Captain."

"Don't be, because you, you…" Capt. Citric was so angry he began to stutter.

"Just brought yourself a ticket for two on the grave yard shift in the heart of North Philly handing out parking tickets if that lunatic does anything wrong to jeopardize this case. I'm telling you and Officer Dell over there."

"Me?" Officer Dell asked.

"No the other ass, stupid, yes you!"

"But, Captain, that's not fair!"

"Well welcome to Philadelphia because it's not fair here."

Captain Citric made his way back out the door slamming it. Officer Dell questioned, "He really didn't mean that did he, Brian? That's plain suicide; we couldn't last twenty minutes down there at night." Brian replied, "I don't think so," and turned his attention back to the mirror saying under his breath, "I hope you know what you're doing, partner."

He watched Michael ask, "Have you ever been to Muncy State Prison for women? No, I take that back; you're a big cat in this game you had to be in the feds."

"Sir, I haven't been anywhere and I want to speak to my lawyer."

"Well there's a first time for everything," Detective Michael continued to pace as more sweat appeared on NayNay's face. He then calmly said, "Can I ask you a question, Ms. Jones?" "What?" NayNay answered nonchalantly while pushing the hair from her pretty face. Then Detective Michael suddenly exploded, "Why the fuck did you do it?" He slammed both hands down on the metal table making it vibrate as NayNay flinched. "Was it because Rayfield was ready to bring you and that pussy group, Get Money thugs, down?"

"Rayfield, Rayfield…" NayNay let the name float around in her head as she tried to remember where she heard it from. Then it hit her, "Oh shit no," she said out loud as she began to block Detective Michael out thinking back to that night and praying that there wasn't any truth to Detective Michael's threat.

Her mind traveled back to the passenger seat of Roc's 600 Benz as they crossed the city line back into Philly. A Dodge Charger pulled out from the cut of an underpass jumping right on to their tail. Seeing the move in his rearview mirror Roc smiled while easing his foot off the pedal and dropping the speed to 50 mph, five miles under the speed limit. He made a right at the light then a left onto 51st street and just as he thought, the car appeared moments later on the same street. Roc now understood what was happening so he touched a button in his center console to activate his plane.

"Call Manny," he said into the voice activated dialing in his car.

"Dialing Manny," the car responded.

"Hello"

"Manny"

"Roc, you know you have two under covers tailing you!" Manny explained as he road five cars back to make sure his boss remained unharmed. "Yeah, that's why I called, to tell you to fall back," Roc answered. "But Roc…"

"I know, just fall back. I know who this clown is and he can be unpredictable but I can handle him."

"Okay but I'm here if it gets out of control."

"It will because it's way past that. Fuck the police, until they try to help people instead of just trying to put them in a cage."

Roc re-hit the button canceling the call before turning to NayNay, "Ms. Jones, I'm sorry for what you're about to see happen but this couldn't be prevented. As long as I'm black with money there will be cops harassing me because they believe that just because I make it out of the hood and became successful that I should give them information on my people. That will never happen. There's death before there could ever be dishonor."

The moment the words left Roc's mouth, red and white lights flashed in the background. "Here we go, you ready?" Roc questioned with a comforting smile that NayNay shook her head in agreement, "As ready as I'll ever be." Roc pulled to the side of the road with his eyes locked on his rearview as he reclined his seat back. The two Detectives approached the car with one on each side and their hands rested upon the hip holster.

The leading officer used the butt of his flash light to tap on the tinted window trying to get Roc's attention, while on the other side NayNay sat puzzled while the light entered the car in search of something through the tint as she watched Roc continue to listen to Pac's 'The Realest Shit I ever Wrote' until the song ended.

"License and proof of registration"

"Are you sure you want to do this while I have company, Detective Michael?"

"Positive, now get out of the car, Roc, I have a report that this car is stolen."

"From who, myself? I own the dealership."

"I don't give a shit if you own Ford, get out the car. You too, pretty lady, let's go."

Roc stepped out of the car, running his hand smoothly over his suit when Detective Michael pushed him hard against the door of the car. "Okay, Michael, I see that you're hands-on in this situation so I'm going to be the opposite with hands off."

"You do that, scumbag."

NayNay stood off to the side as Detective Michael frisked Roc. "Spread 'em wide," Detective Michael kicked Roc's feet apart. Once being searched and having handcuffs placed on him, Roc was forced to the ground as he *protested, "Come on, Michael, this is uncalled for, plus this is a twenty thousand dollar suit."*

"Then buy another one."

"I can but everybody can't and you only get one chance to make a first impression, ha-haaa," Roc laughed. After they searched his car for almost two hours and broke his lights, they found nothing. Detective Michael tossed the keys across the street into the night. "After you find them you can go," he said. Roc stood to his feet with the NayNay's help who came and sat beside him against Detective Michael's orders once seeing how bad he was being treated.

Back behind the wheel and moving through the streets of North Philly, Roc asked, "Are you alright, Ms. Jones?"

"I'm fine."

"Thanks for the support you showed me back there."

"Oh it was nothing."

"But it was, because no matter how far we make it in life, the people you take care of and that take care of you is all that you will ever have. So now you have me, if ever there is a time you need my support I'll be there." Roc flashed a friendly smile in NayNay's direction but as soon as he turned away the mood suddenly darkened as he activated the car phone saying, "It's time for Jihad," which was the Arabic word for war.

"Dialing Mohammed," the system confirmed.

"Assalamu Alaikum"

"Mohammed."

"What is it, Boss?"

"Is it that obvious?"

"Sometimes, but Manny just called."

"You remember the Rayfield move our friend is making?"

"Yeah I'm looking at the script right now."

"Well it just changed to a hand off situation."

NayNay slowly raised her head that suddenly began to feel like it was spinning, to look at Detective Michael while he paced the floor and stated, "You know you're going away for life." It was then that the picture immediately became clear to her as she remembered the morning she was watching the news while braiding Lil Mac's hair the next day after being stopped with Roc.

"Hello, I'm Molly Weiss and welcome to another episode of In 'These Mean Streets.' Yesterday a body was found outside of the 39th precinct, nude with his hands and feet missing. The body was burned so badly that it took over a week to identify it as being Detective Josh Rayfield."

"Rayfield, Rayfield…" NayNay whispered. Moments after that the slamming of the door with Detective Brian entering the room interrupted her thoughts just as Detective Michael jumped at her. "Bitch, you hear me? Don't just sit there you killed my partner and you're going to pay, I'm going to make sure of it!" He then gripped NayNay by the neck squeezing tightly as he pulled his free hand back into a fist, ready to strike and Detective Brian quickly grabbed a hold of him. "Stop now! That's enough," he said pushing Detective Michael out the door, "And don't come back until you cool off!"

In the hallway Detective Michael spoke in a tone low enough that NayNay couldn't hear him, "Did I do a good job?"

"Like you never left," Detective Brian replied shutting the door in his face.

"I'm sorry about my partner's actions Ms…?"

"Ms. Jones," NayNay stated.

"That's right, Ms. Jones. He's just upset, well, we all are, about the loss of Detective Rayfield." While explaining, Detective Brian studied NayNay's facial expressions trying to get a better understanding of their mystery woman. The fact that NayNay had never been arrested and a match for her finger prints couldn't be found, all the information they knew at the moment was from the I.D. that she had in her possession which said she was Michelle Jones. But Detective Brian believed it was a fake. Then there was her co-defendant who keeps repeating his platoon number.

Detective Brian was Detectiveermined to have her give him everything she knew and when she was done, be happy that she did it. He continued, "But I don't believe you're the one that killed him at all. As of now all the evidence is pointed at you unless you can help me find the real killer. Then you can walk right out that door and we'll throw out everything, I promise. And nobody will know you said anything."

NayNay noticed the officer's kind and sincere manner and tried hard to remember the words of Roc while still listening to Detective Brian say, "I know you don't want to go to jail and I don't want to see a lovely young lady like you go but my partner does. So right now he's trying to dig up any information he can to tie you to this case and you know what killing an officer means, right?"

"No, what?"

"That they'll kill you by way of lethal injection, so please help me help you."

Back behind the mirror, Detective Michael took the folder from under cover Officer Dell's hands. "That's my cue, fellas, now who wants to bet I'll have her crying to tell me everything in less than two minutes?" "You do that Michael and I'm going to handle Mr. Daz," said Officer Dell.

Detective Michael re-entered the room slamming the door and yelling, "I got your ass now." He tossed the folder onto the table. Detective Brian acted surprised to see the photo of the Get Money Clique that Michael stole from D's bedroom. He slowly began to drop the photo of each member on to the table in front of NayNay. There was Top Dollar, NayNay, D, and Lil Mac.

On sight, NayNay became lost in her emotions as her hand reached out trembling towards the pictures. A mad flow of tears started to flow down her face and Detective Michael smiled thinking; *"Now we'll finally know."* He then continued to push on, "We know your clique was within a five mile radius of Detective Rayfield's last call by your cell phone. Now my partner's telling me you're willing to cooperate."

NayNay shook her head up and down while more tears raced down her face. "To be truthful I don't want to let you off the hook so easily but Rayfield's killer is more important. Now tell me what you know before I change my mind."

"Okay, sir, I will just let me get myself together." She held the picture of Lil Mac tightly in her hand and looked at his handsome face, noticing that the love he had for her still could be spotted in his eyes. "I love you, Solo. I always have and I always will," she said quietly, replacing the tear covered photo back in place. She then dried her eyes with the back of her hand now remembering Roc's words.

Sitting up straight, NayNay looked down at the scars from her slit wrists and said, "First, let me say for the record that I didn't have anything to do with Rayfield's death."

"Ms. Jones we know so--"

"But I wish I did!" NayNay laughed, quickly cutting him off and yelling, "So kill me, just kill me because there's death before there could ever be dishonor where I come from! You can take that good cop bad cop shit and shove it because I'm a Remy Ma kinda bitch. Now I'd like to see my lawyer, Detective Michael, Mister I didn't say I remember you."

"You dirty heifer!" Detective Michael screamed jumping at NayNay for real this time as Brian fought to hold him. "Let me go or get her out of my face, Brian. And whatever we have on the bitch, charge her!" They led NayNay and Daz down the hall in handcuffs when Capt Citric approached saying, "Fellas, I don't know who these two are but we have to sneak them out the back because every news reporter in the city is out there along with four lawyers."

"So"

"So you can't let the media see this young innocent face even if she is the devil."

At RCFA women's holding facility, NayNay was rushed through intake with C.O. Ross giving her the cell number 210 on B block and a dirty blanket off the floor. NayNay walked down the long hallway as the women inmates hurried to the window to see who the fresh meat was. They began to bang on the window and scream out to get NayNay's attention.

"Hey, sexy"

"Bitch, look at me"

"Yeah, pretty, I'm going to kill you!"

"You better have your paper work because I hate snitches!"

NayNay tried to ignore all the comments as she stepped onto the sally port of B-block and waited patiently as the sound of steel bars crept back to allow her to enter her unit. The sound made a chill run through her body. She walked on the block where a 260 lb female guard waited. "Ms. Jones, I'm C.O. Harris and here is your I.D. You don't move anywhere without it, up there is the phone and this right there is my offi--"

NayNay walked straight for the phone without giving C.O. Harris time to finish what she was saying. Quickly she dialed zero then Top Dollar's number. 'Ring-Ring' "Come on, Top, pick up." 'Ring-Ring' "Please pick up! I promise not to make fun of you again."

"You sure?"

"Top Dollar?"

"That's who you called right?"

NayNay let out a deep breath and said with the biggest smile she could have, "Thank God, I was starting to miss your old ass already."

"Don't worry about nothing, baby, you're doing great. I'll see you tomorrow morning in court and I'll be there early to bail you out. So can you hang in there for a few more hours?"

"Okay, I will. And, Top?"

"Yes?"

"I didn't say anything to them."

"I know, baby girl, that's why I'll be there tomorrow, you dig?"

"I dig."

NayNay sat alone next to the phone fighting to keep her eyes open when C.O. Harris tapped her on the shoulder. "It's late, time for you to lock down," she said. NayNay made her way upstairs to her cell as inmates eyed her up and down. She reached cell 210 where two women, one thick and the other slim, playing cards on the bed. The cell opened and NayNay's tiny frame was behind it. The two women looked at each other before jumping to their feet, "Let us help you with that, girl," removing the blanket and pillow and introducing themselves. "Hi, my name is Jen," said the slim one and "I'm Sonya," the other one said. The ladies neatly made NayNay's bed that was spread out on the floor due to the overcrowding inside the prison. They began to ask her a hundred questions.

"What are you in for?"

"How did they get you?"

"Are you the girl they're talking about on the news that was shooting at the cops?"

"No, Jen, she's too pretty to do something like that."

"Ladies, please, I promise ya'll I'll tell you everything in the morning but right now I'm so tired, all I want to do is sleep."

"Oh go ahead to sleep cuz you do look beat. And hurry, Jen, get her a sandwich." Jen quickly popped open a new razor, using the open blade to slice the onion, cheese and turkey. NayNay after finishing her food was sleep within a few minutes with the vision of Lil Mac appearing in her dreams. *She was laying on their king sized bed as he slowly approached saying, "Baby, you've been through a lot today; now let me take away your pain." Lil Mac gently kissed her lips twice before invading her mouth with his tongue in a deep and passionate kiss. NayNay moved her head in her sleep to accept the warm feeling of his touch as if it was actually happening.*

Within seconds her body began to tingle as his hand circled around her hard nipples before the moisture of his hot lips invited them into his mouth. He then moved his hand down to her swollen clit and parted the outer lips wide as his middle finger quickly moved back and forth on just the tip of it. He could sense the silent fire building up inside of her as she moved her ass and hips from side to side while her wetness leaked from her love box to the crack of her ass.

NayNay's body called to be tasted and at the lovely scent of her sex, she didn't have to wait long as he went without stopping the motion of his fingers, sticking his tongue deep inside of her. "Ooooh, I miss you," escaped her lips, accompanied by a light moan as Lil Mac worked his tongue around her clit while his two fingers started to finger fuck her. Her legs started to quiver as she began to reach her orgasm and Lil Mac's fingers went in and out of her juices. He then quickly pulled it out from her soaked pussy and without warning slid them into her asshole.

Continuing to delight her clit with his fast tongue motion, NayNay moaned, "Ooohh shit, baby, I'm cuming."

The surprise of the instant pain mixed with pleasure sent NayNay into a moment of bliss like never before. She raised her legs high into the air and wide to give him full access to her body. Lil Mac gripped NayNay by her inner thigh, pulling her to him while at the same time sliding his dick inside of her. He wanted all of her; pulling and pushing with a strain until he was balls deep within her sex box. NayNay moved her tongue with a matching rhythm as their lips once again locked; just as a funny tasting liquid entered her mouth bringing her out of her heated sex dream.

She opened her eyes, stunned as Jen's naked body sat upon her face rubbing her clit in a circle motion while jerking her hips back and forth over NayNay's lips, whispering, "I'm cuming, daaaammn she's good!"

Sonya was at the other end of the bed with NayNay's legs high in the air as her tongue raced through her pussy lips while she stuffed a homemade dildo covered with a rubber glove deep inside her pussy. NayNay quickly blinked her eyes hoping that when they re-opened this would have all been just a nightmare but it wasn't.

When she re-opened them she no longer witnessed Jen, instead it was her step father once again molesting her like so many times before. Enraged, NayNay bit down hard until her teeth sunk into Jen's pussy lips. "Aaaaaaaahhh," Jen screamed, causing Sonya to pop her head up from the pit of NayNay's love box to see what was happening. At the same moment, NayNay's foot cracked into the center of her face and the impact of the blow sent her body flying back up against the steel bars. NayNay got the space she needed from Sonya, who outweighed her by over thirty pounds. She then pushed Jen to the floor and jumped to her feet before dashing to the desk and grabbing the razor from it.

NayNay was on top of Sonya in an instant, cutting her face and wrist as she held her hands up trying to defend herself. Jen sat back knowing she had to do something soon as she watched the blood pouring from her girlfriend. She was unsure of how much more Sonya could take and yelled out for help, "C.O. help, help please…C.O!" NayNay turned to face Jen with blood dripping from her hands, as the pretty girl that entered the cell with the innocent eyes was gone; they were overtaken with the look of revenge.

"You have tongued the wrong one this time, bitch!" NayNay screamed.

"No please, I'm sorry! Sonya made me do it, she said you'd like it."

"And you'll like this," assured NayNay and with just one quick motion swung the sharp piece of steel through the air cutting Jen across the face. "Aaahhhh," Jen fell to the ground and quickly crawled into a ball as NayNay stepped into to finish her just as the cell door popped open with four guards rushing in. They wrestled her to the floor while handcuffing her.

NayNay was placed in a single cell until the morning when a guard called, "Jones, get ready for court." She stepped out into the hallway and was placed in line with several other inmates. C.O. Ross watched her every move while she was being strip searched and just before the group was about to depart she pulled NayNay to the side.

"Ms. Jones, I'm coming to you about last night."

"Listen, whatever you want to charge me with just do it," NayNay stated walking away. C.O. Ross grabbed her arm and said, "You've got it all wrong, I'm not here as a C.O. I'm here speaking to you woman to woman. Can we do that for a second?" NayNay nodded her head in agreement.

"I know what those girls did to you; are you alright?"

"Yes, I'm fine."

"Young lady, I saw the look in your eyes after this happened. It's okay if you don't want to talk to me but talk to someone. You can't keep holding those emotions inside you like that; you have to let them go if you ever want to begin to heal. And don't worry about what happened to them because I threw away the paper work."

"I wasn't," NayNay responded without another word and headed for the door when C.O. Ross' next comment stopped her. "You know I too was touched improperly when I was a child. I didn't start to become a better person until I left behind any power he had over me." NayNay just turned around, following the line out the door.

At city hall in a large court room on the 32nd floor, Judge Brake sat at her bench reading over her morning cases. She came to one that said 'Important' in big bold red letters. She quickly read over the folder content. Once complete she slowly raised her head to scan over the many faces of unhappy family members, lawyers, and police officers but she was looking for one person and he wasn't there. Thinking that maybe there was some misunderstanding, she read his short note again.

"Dear Judge,

Even though the charges we have may not warrant this, we ask the

court to hold Ms. Jones in custody because she may be our only link in finding

Detective Rayfield's killer.

Sincerely,

Detective Brian"

The Judge banged her gavel calling, "Order, court is now in session." She reached for another case at the exact moment Detectives Brian and Michael made their way through the double swinging doors led by D.A. Rich. They greeted each other with a light head nod.

Judge Brake motioned her lips to say, "Are you ready?"

"Yes."

"Okay, I will now hear the case of the United States vs. Jones and Williams."

An officer escorted Daz out into the court room with his hands cuffed behind his back as he heard someone saying, "Inmate Jones you're up." The voice was a bailiff who turned the large key and NayNay stepped out of the crowded dark cell feeling something inside of her change as she looked at the women standing at the gate crying with anger and hate in their eyes. *"Damn you're so weak."* She was escorted out into the court room with her hand cuffs in front of her. She smiled at the sight of Top Dollar who waved as he whispered something to the elderly man in a blue Salvatore Ferragamo suit that was seated next to him. NayNay was shown to a hard wooden table, when a man in a cheap suit and glasses held his hand out, "Hello, Ms. Jones, nice to meet you. I'm Mr. Stewart, your public defender."

NayNay left his hand hanging in the air, flopped down into the hard chair and said, "Let's just get this over with. I'm guilty and whatever they want to give me, give it to me."

"Ms. Jones, you must not understand."

"Oh I do understand, they want someone to fry and I'm it. So what's he doing here?" NayNay pointed to Daz, who sat on the opposite side of the man. "Hey, cutie." Seeing his cue, the man in the expensive suit quickly stood up as the judge questioned, "Shall we begin?"

"Yes, your honor. Gordon Knox, counsel for the defendant. Hey, how're you fellas doing?" Gordon Knox said tapping Detective Brian and Michael on the shoulder as he passed them on his way to the table.

"Excuse me, aahh…"

"Mr. Stewart."

"Well, Mr. Stewart, I believe you're sitting in my seat. If not then someone paid a hundred thousand too much."

"Mr. Knox, there must be a mistake. The last time I checked, it was impossible for you to represent both."

"Your honor, if you would give me a chance to explain," Gordon Knox paused, waiting for several men and women dressed in suits to fill the last three rows of the court room. He bent down in between Daz and NayNay saying quietly, "Don't be worried, they're here to see me work. You can thank Top Dollar for bringing me by for this last dance."

"You hear that?"

"What?"

'BANG-BANG,' Gordon Knox stalled until the sound of the gavel entered the air as Judge Brake said, "Court is in session; you do know that?"

"My theme song, I know these people like the back of a book."

Rising to his feet he looked at Judge Brake directly in the eyes, "Your honor, I have just been informed by Mr. Williams here that he no longer wishes to be represented by counsel and would like to exercise his rights to represent him self, which means he'll sit back and say what I tell him, if he wants to walk out that door in twenty minutes."

Laughter filled the courtroom as Gordon Knox made his way back to the table.

"Is this true, Mr. Williams?" the Judge asked.

"Yes."

"Well, D.A. Rich will you please call your first witness."

"Your honor, due to the fact that the legendary Mr. Knox is here for some strange reason…the state would like to rely on the notes in our affidavit."

"Noted. Mr. Knox, do you have any objection to that?"

"Yes, I think I will," he answered back on his feet as he began to speak to this audience. "Your honor we all know that whole affidavit is futile. No where in it does it state that anyone of the many police officers that were on that road block could say that they watched my client do anything and it says right here on line six of page three; that officer Edward radioed to Detective Brian that he had made the arrest of my client and Mr. Williams. Do you see that, your honor?"

"Yes, I've read it and…"

"Do I need to say more? Don't answer that because I see that I must, if you will look to the original complaint, who was the arresting officer?" Judge Brake quickly flipped through the papers, "It says here Officer Edward."

"So I ask the state how is it possible?"

"Mr. Knox, I know you have been away from the court room for some time but the last time I checked, a fleeing suspect can be apprehended by an officer's back up."

In the last row the lawyer Sam Clinton whispered to his young intern, "It's amazing how he hasn't lost his step."

"What's amazing, Mr. Clinton? It seems to me he has boxed himself into a corner."

Sam Clinton smiled at his law professor and said, "Someone's in a corner but its sure not him."

Mr. Knox, while rubbing his hands together continued, "Your honor, you're right, I haven't been gone that long to not know the difference between a criminal and a suspect who is innocent until proven guilty. So officer Edward didn't see my client and Mr. Williams here who I must say is doing a great job as a lawyer, doing anything wrong. Therefore Officer Edward only had the right by law to detain them until Detective Brian came and identified them as the people he believed to be the criminals. But he did not have the right to search them a second sooner. In light of that, the gun must be suppressed and if my memory will do me any justice, I think I won a case like this in front of the Supreme Court in 19…"

"I know it was the Jackson vs. United States 1989. I am still the Judge, Mr. Knox." Judge Brake recessed the court for an hour. After the time ended and everyone re-entered the court room, she quickly got their attention. "I went over all of today's evidence and Mr. Knox is correct so by law I have to dismiss the weapon charge. But still, there are the issues of the assault and I believe there is enough to hold those charges over for trial. So until then, bail is set at $500,000.00 each. There will be no ten percent and Mr. Knox, please know the feds will be watching where the money comes from very closely."

"Very well, your honor, I can see the fix has taken over the place of law in this court." Mr. Knox looked to Top Dollar who mouthed, "I need more time," before adding, "Your honor, I believe you may have stepped outside of your boundaries of artery by making their bail so high on a C felony."

"Maybe but not mines," someone called out. The whole room looked towards the door to see Roc standing there in an all black suit. "I'll pay it," he said looking at NayNay and said, "I am here."

Detective Brian leaned over and said to Detective Michael, "I guess we're on our way to New York."

"But what about the jurisdiction?" asked Detective Michael.

"To hell with it!"

15

At 1:32 pm in the gymnasium of the prison, Don Antigeo landed punches to the speed bag at a rapid pace as the rhythm of the flickering sound relaxed his mind. A strong sweat raced down his body as he began to find his old groove. He spotted Nasir from the corner of his eye making his way across the floor through a small group of people and he was headed in his direction. The Don changed his vision to the clock above him and thought, *"He has been in there for almost three hours."*

Switching up hands without missing a beat, Don Antigeo at the age of fifty moved like he was still in his thirties as he bobbed and weaved his head around the bag while still throwing punches. "Easy, Don, you've been working so hard lately. I just knew I would find you here."

Don Antigeo threw several more punches before deciding to answer, "Yes I have, because I too will be leaving in two weeks and then we will be faced with the battle of our lives. So it's important to be prepared." He moved from the speed bag to the punching bag while asking, "How did the counsel meet go?"

"To be truthful it was confusing. In one aspect your life can be clear as a summer's day at noon, while another man's is darkening by the second like his destiny is in…"

"No, don't, Nasir. I think you should keep your thoughts to yourself until you have them all figured out and I'm sure in the end you'll make a decision you could live or die with."

Don Antigeo proceeded to work the bag from the top to the bottom when Nasir's next question stopped him in his tracks. "You mean like Mr. Holmes?" And with a smile Don Antigeo ripped the gloves from his sore hands, looking

Nasir straight in the eyes and asked, "Are you sure you want to know the rest of the story?"

"Yes, I read the case law you gave me and I've learned that a person must trust someone in life, because if Alberto would have trusted his sister he wouldn't have come to jail for life and I believe Roc trusted Mr. Holmes. So I must know to understand Mr. Holmes's mistake."

"Fair enough," Don Antigeo replied reaching for a pair of boxing gloves from the wall. He tossed them to Nasir, "Let's hit the ring."

Hesitant, Nasir said, "Are you sure?"

"Why not? It's only a little bit of pain." The two tapped gloves with the Don throwing a quick right jab as he jumped back into the story…

Roc was upstairs in the first brownstone he bought his mother, standing on the back balcony wearing a tailor made double breasted suit. With only the sweet mild sound of birds singing and a cool breeze blowing against his back, Roc witnessed the unique beauty of his city. He loved the fact that on the outside it seemed so calm and peaceful like any other day. But he could sense the difference in the air, for today would be a historical moment for the city of Philadelphia. And every known police officer and law enforcement agency in town would have their ears and eyes open on the big event. It was this understanding which made Roc wonder as he took a breath of fresh air into his lungs. Would his plan still work if put to the ultimate test? A sly grin came across his face as the wind blew his silk tie around.

One side of him was happy that he made it to this level of success and knowing that his father would have been proud of him every step of the way. On the other side he was sad that it had to come with the death of his mentor.

A hard tap connected to the thick glass of the balcony door made Roc slowly turn around to see Boggy standing in a dark blue Gucci suit, white shirt with a matching tie. "Roc, they're here," he said. "Okay, tell them I'll be there in a few minutes."

Boggy gradually began to shut the glass door when Roc called out, "Boggy, double check everything for tonight. They can't know what hit them until it's too late!" Roc made his way down the spiral stair case when a sound came from the back room stopped his stride. Knowing that no one was supposed to be there he crept toward it as he eased the P.89 automatic from the center of his back and cuffed the weapon behind his leg while pressing his ear to the door. Again hearing the muffled sound he eased the door open to see his mother, crying while resting in her favorite rocking chair with something in her hand.

As the chair moved back and forth, the steady rhythm of the look of affliction and depression were evident on her face alone. Roc's heart ached instantly at the sight of the damage he caused to her and prayed that soon he could take some of it away as he removed the group photo of his father, Mr. Holmes, Top Dollar, himself and Lil Mac from her hands. He pulled her to her feet wrapping his arms around her and said, "Don't cry mother, I'm here and everything is going to be alright."

"I know, baby, and if it wasn't for you I probably would have been gone from this earth already. But losing another loved one to a painful death, Roc, I raised them boys like they was my own children," Mrs. Miller yelled and cried out. "I can only think that you could be next." She squeezed Roc tightly while closing her eyes as more tears began to run steadily down her face.

"Mother, don't think like that, the…"

"Ssshhh," Mrs. Miller placed her finger to Roc's lips.

"Son, I never told you this and I didn't feel I would have to until now. When you were young, your father said you were different and I didn't understand his feeling because every parent that loves their child thinks their kid is special. Then that night you came home with your father after he sadly killed big Jeff and you saw it, I begged him to get you some help and you know what he did?"

"No, but please tell me," Roc answered anxious to know more about his father's actions.

"He held me in his arms like you're doing now and said to be patient, everything is going to be alright; our son will make us proud. But I couldn't forget that look you had in your eyes. The look of innocence in my baby was gone. Being a good wife I decided not to argue but if I saw the littlest thing go wrong with you…" Mrs. Miller placed her hands on Roc's cheek, kissing him gently and continued, "I sat back and watched the kids begin to follow you. I believe it was too much pressure for a kid your age to be responsible for the well being of others. I realized like many other occasions, your father was right. You were placed here to lead. For some people make mistakes and some make decisions and you my dear are a decision maker. So promise me, because my soul is telling me this is far from over."

"But, Mom, I told you everything was over and today will bring us closer. Then I can spend some much needed time with the two women I love the most."

"Baby, I know you mean every word but a mother's heart will never tell them wrong and I feel something terrible is going to happen so promise that you won't forget how to lead your own self. I need you and Jr. needs you, you're all I have left."

"Okay, Mom, I promise what ever it is you feel in the end I'll be the last man standing." Roc pulled his mother closer to him letting her relax in the crease of his shoulder. Rubbing her back, he slowly raised his eyes to the master dresser mirror noticing the reflection of his six foot frame still with the P.89 automatic held tightly as his eyes calmly darkened. A sudden movement to his left brought his attention to Gizelle as she stood in the crack of the door wiping away her own tears as their eyes met and she motioned her lips to say, "I need you too."

Outside, several limousines lined the side walk as Roc's team splitting in pairs. Mrs. Miller and Top Dollar disappeared behind the tinted window of the first vehicle. Boggy, with Flirtatious and China wrapped on each of his arms, got in with Chocolate coming in last. Haffee helped his wife get comfortable in the third car. Roc and Gizelle, who held Odell Jr. in her arms sat back, watching the four TV's in the last car. Roc said into his earpiece, "Top, it's time."

Seconds later, all together the vehicles pulled out into traffic. They rode through the streets of Philadelphia for twenty minutes making swift right turns every seven blocks which was actually according to Roc's plan. This led them in a five mile circle. Roc was content with the time given and questioned Mohammed through his earpiece who had been watching their every move in the distant shadow, "How many?"

"Roc, I don't know what Mr. Holmes had going on for them to act like this but you have their three detectives and two feds moving hot on your tail."

"So are we prepared to give them what they need to see?"

"Yes."

"What about you, are you ready to handle this?"

"Insha' Allah."

"That's good enough. Top Dollar, pick and roll, defend is in play on tenth street so have the driver bang a hard left from here."

Mohammed fell back a few cars with his eyes that were just above the steering wheel of a stolen Nissan, noticing the first limousine slowly approaching 10th and

Arch St, stopping at a red light. The quiet engine idled while the driver did drum lines with his fingers across the leather of the dash board to the radio. Then just as the crossing lights were turning from yellow to red, NayNay rushed through the intersection in a black Expedition pulling in front of the line with out missing a beat as the limousine continued to move at the same pace behind her.

"You're late."

"I know, Top Dollar, I'm sorry I don't know what's been happening to me lately."

"Is everything alright? I can have Fox take over if necessary."

"No, I'm fine. Plus I have to see the bastard put in the ground," NayNay answered, meaning exactly that. She stepped down hard on the gas sending the truck through the next light. "Ya'll guys stay down back there, we have company like expected," she said while adjusting her rearview mirror. Detective Michael made the left also in an undercover Impala when he noticed a sudden move that seemed strange to him and said, "Brian, can you see who's driving that truck?"

"No, not from here"

"Well I'm going in for a closer look"

"No, keep your position, Michael. As far as we know it's just a truck trying to make it to work."

"Okay."

"To hell with Brian, this is my case now and I'm going to do what I have to in order to solve it." As the car eased onto the expressway, Detective Michael decided now was his opportunity as he pulled over onto the passing line moving in and out of traffic, listening to 'Mr. Officer'.

"Michael what are you doing? Fall back in position before you blow our cover!"

Detective Michael refused to answer as he road pass Detective Brian without looking in his direction until he became side to side with the truck. Being unable to identify the driver because of the tinted windows, he screamed, "Damn! Brian chill out I was just trying to get a closer look because my instincts tell me there is something about this truck."

NayNay looked at Michael and smiled as she thought, *"I'm going to love doing this to you,"* before picking up speed. Twenty minutes later at a four way intersection just outside of Philly in King of Prussia, NayNay moved with the momentum of the traffic in a half circle when she lightly tapped the brake to let the two identical Expeditions waiting on the outskirts in front of her.

Fox waved from behind the wheel of the first one as he raced by followed by Daz. They eased beside NayNay at the steady speed of 65 mph and waited. Roc enjoyed the moments he had to play with Odell Jr. by throwing playful jabs at his chest and head yet still keeping his eye on the passing exit sign. "Jr., what did I tell you about keeping your hands up in front of your chin to protect yourself?"

"Okay, Dad"

"So when I throw a punch at you like this, you can hit me where?" Roc threw a wide punch in slow motion that his son ducked, saying, "Dad, me no hit you cause you my man"

"You got that right, because if you do you'll never forget it." Roc grabbed Jr. Up into a bear hug. Gizelle watched them share a laugh together while thinking, *"Maybe what he said to Mrs. Miller is true…everything could be over. He does look so much more relaxed; like he doesn't have a care in the world."* She smiled, *"Thank you, God, for giving me my family back."*

Gizelle leaned in giving Jr. a kiss on the cheek before closing her eyes and softly touching Roc's lips once then again while working her way into a deep passionate kiss. Roc sat his back against the plush leather to welcome the tender affection of his wife while still maintaining his stare out the window. He smoothly broke the kiss saying, "Baby, you know I love you right?"

"Yes, and I love you," Gizelle answered, starting in to finish off the kiss, not getting enough of her man when his words stopped her.

"NayNay, your exit is the one after this so let's make it. You've got five minutes."

NayNay slammed her foot down on the gas pedal making her vehicle jump forward as the speedometer shot past 85 mph leaving the other trucks in their position. The limousines followed her lead until the last one was side by side with the leading Expedition. Roc lowered his window as did Fox, catching his stare Roc said, "My brother said now you are ready to lead so now I'm about to see."

"And he ain't never lied."

"Then it's on you," Roc gave a light nod to the driver who in response took off in pursuit to keep up with the rest of the vehicles. Fox got in position beside Daz when it hit him, *"When did Solo tell him that?"* just before he looked at Daz, who was bracing him also.

Detective Michael was matching NayNay's speed still trying to get a peek at her identity as he suddenly had to jerk the wheel over to the left to avoid NayNay when she swerved into his lane and before he could react, two trucks pulled in front of him. Detective Brian's voice roared from the walkie talkie on the front seat, "Michael, what are you doing, trying to get yourself killed? Fall back into position so me and Dell can at least cover you."

"Okay but I'm telling you something's not right." Detective Michael hit his turn signal to get over to the non-passing lane just as the glow of red lights filled the inside of his car. Fox and Daz slammed down on their brakes and the loud screeching tires and dark smoke entered the air.

Detective Michael hit his brakes moments before crashing into the back of the truck, starting a two lane, eight-car collision. Roc smiled looking out the back of the limousine window with Jr. in his arms and under his breath said, "That should hold you."

An hour later at 1:00pm in Coatesville Pa, a small city just outside of Philly; hundreds of people covered the street and sidewalk in front of the Johnson Funeral Home, making it hard for the limousines to get through.

As they waited for the doors to open at 1:30pm, the head driver stated, "I'm sorry, sir, this is the farthest that I can get you."

"Don't worry, you dig? I'll handle this," Top Dollar assured, getting out of the car as Mrs. Miller grasped his hand firmly saying, "You be careful okay."

"If not for anybody else, I'll do it for you." He then closed the door behind him.

Dodging out into the middle of the street he yelled, "Excuse me, ladies and gentleman, if you don't mind, please make a path so that we can get through." Most people continued to move about their way with tears and pain in their eyes, paying Top's word no attention. Then someone yelled back, "Man, fuck you!"

"Who said it?" The second the words left Top Dollar's mouth, people stopped and turned, giving him their full attention now with tears and hate. A young man that was about 6'2", 260lbs answered, "I did, nigga."

The crowd parted as the man made his way to the front with several men and women falling in line behind him. Top Dollar saw the kid's size and the angry onlookers then decided to slide his hand onto the gun in his suit jacket pocket. He explained, "Listen, I didn't come here for a fight, I came to show my respects to a friend and fallen soldier and that's what I'm going to do. If I have to drop a few of you to do it, I will, you dig now?"

"We're all here for the same reason, what makes you any better than them, old head?"

"The fact that he's with me, Inch," said Aman, stepping out from the crowd in a fresh new suit, glossy eyed.

"Manny, what up?" the two gave each other a half hug as Inch whispered, "Man this shit is crazy, I can't believe he is really gone."

"Me neither, but we'll make it through this, that's my word."

After separating, Manny did the introduction, "Inch this is Top Dollar, Top, this is Inch, Buff's brother."

"I'm sorry, Inch; just know we all love Buff. Now let's go and show him how much."

Coatesville was the home of Buff, Raja, and Manny, where many people heard of the endless stories of them being some kind of dangerous killers. But to anyone that knew them and things they did for their community, it was hard to believe they would hurt anyone that didn't try to hurt them first. So when they spoke up, people listened.

As Manny and Top Dollar walked through the crowd, people stepped to the side while giving their condolences as the limousine rode in behind them. Inside the packed chapel, where standing room became scarce, the preacher spoke kind and loving words above Buff's body. Buff looked calm and at peace in his all white Valentino suit.

Once finished, Roc slowly walked down the long aisle with Boggy, Manny, Raja, Top Dollar, and Inch following. Roc was thinking of all the good times he enjoyed with Buff as he lifted the all black and gold casket into the air...

Roc was standing in the shadows of the basement as Manny and Raja sat around Buff's bed listening to him tell jokes. "So we're in the living room, it's me, my dad, and my date…some pretty white chick I brought home. I can't remember her name but anyway she said she needed to use the bathroom. And as soon as she was out the room my dad leaned over to me and said, "Son, do you know what the black man's kryptonite is?" I said no dad, what? This nigga going to say, "Dirty white women and fried chicken." Laughter filled the room…

The memory brought a slight smile to Roc's face as he just moved with the motion of lowering the casket into the back of the hearse. Mentally, he was in a much happier place with his friend…

They were at Club Soldi as it got more packed by the moment. Roc was dressed in his white suit with a sky blue Armani handkerchief and matching tie, scanning the crowd in search of Buff. He found him at the bar dressed clean in his all black shirt and slacks with a tailor made yellow suit jacket. Two beautiful women held on to his arm on each side. "Yo, Buff, I need your help. Can you take a ride with me? I got to see what's up with Boggy and them niggas. I know they should have been here by now," Roc said.

Buff knew just by the look on Roc's face that something was wrong and jumped to his feet before Roc could finish talking. "And he had class," Roc whispered while he recalled what Buff did next. *He tossed three G's onto the bar for the women and said, "Come on, we can take my car."* "And he was always there when I needed him," Roc was taught to never show his emotions and was having a battle with himself and lost as tears for the first time in years began to pour down his face. The odd feeling of wetness continued as the faces of Buff, Mr. Holmes and his father danced in his mind.

The street was now nearly clear except for the last of the family members descending the church stairs and Roc's team, who was standing around and watching the strongest man that they knew stare into the sky in a daze and crying.

Top Dollar started to head toward Roc when Mrs. Miller stopped him, "But…," he began to argue against. "No buts, let him get it all out. He deserves that."

Moments later Roc removed his silk Gucci handkerchief, wiped his face dry and turned, adjusting his suit to see Buff's mother standing on the last step. She was waiting for him with her arms held open wide while her lips said, "Come here." Roc entered her embrace, placing his head on her shoulder as he inhaled the lovely nature of her scent that he had come to love. "Roc, you know you and my son was in a lot of mess out in these streets. What it was; I don't know, don't care and didn't ask. My son brought you into my house and you ate out of my freezer and slept on my sofa," stated Mrs. Foster. Roc rubbed her back with her letting out a deep breath before continuing, "And he did all of this because he loves you like a brother. So please don't blame yourself because we don't. Thank you for paying for the funeral and everything but here, we don't need a house that big."

Mrs. Foster placed a set of keys in Roc's palm that he didn't take. "I'm sorry to hear that but I can't take it back."

"Why?"

"Because I didn't buy it, Buff did. And yes we were into a lot. So as men we have to be prepared for moments like this." Roc gave Manny a head nod and Manny looked around twice before popping the trunk of the limousine and taking out a large duffle bag. He handed it to Inch before Roc continued, "In that bag there is five hundred thousand and each month you will receive a check for eight, giving you a salary of ninety six thousand a year."

"My God, Buff's favorite number," whispered Mrs. Foster with tear filled eyes.

"Thank you, Roc. Whenever you need me, call," she squeezed him tightly.

"Don't say it like that, I'll still be there every Saturday because he may be gone but a part of him will always remain here," Roc pointed to his chest and started to walk away as he heard Inch say, "Roc I heard on TV that you were having a masquerade party for my brother and Mr. Holmes, can I come?"

Looking over his shoulder, Roc said, "Ask your mother."

"Yes, he can go anywhere with family because that's all we have…"

Don Antigeo back-peddled into the corner as the crowd that now surrounded the ring cheered him on as they watched him work his hands quickly up and down, defending off Nasir's attack. Nasir continued to throw jab after jab, making contact and cutting Don Antigeo just above his eye, but nothing too serious, which in turn made Nasir furious that the Don was still standing after eight rounds. Nasir threw an upper cut right off his jab that caught Don Antigeo in the chin making his head pop up before he smoothly covered it. Nasir thought that he'd hurt the Don but if he'd learned anything from Don Antigeo it was that looks can be deceiving.

He noticed the Don's leg suddenly begin to shake, "*I got your ass now,*" Nasir rushed up on him, leaning his weight forward and covering the Don's top as he attacked his body. Don Antigeo rode the rope wisely, lessening the blows as he shook his leg once more before faking to run to the left when Nasir pushed him hard with both hands back against the rope. Just as he turned, Don Antigeo slammed a hard right hand into Nasir's chin. The punch caught Nasir totally by surprise as he stumbled back and fell slowly to the mat. Fighting to regain his sight after the stunning blow, Nasir rapidly blinked his eyes to clear his vision. With his sight returning he saw men jumping up and down celebrating the Don's victory, and the Don was standing over Nasir with his hand out. Helping him to his feet, Don Antigeo stated, "I guess we can finish the story another time."

"You tricked me, you old bastard."

"And I hope it's not the last," they both laughed.

16

For the past two weeks, Don Antigeo had been giving Nasir as much space as possible, seeing that this was a very stressful moment in life for him. The fact that his court appearance was slowly approaching in the morning, had him pacing back and forth in his cell as he packed and unpacked his belongings for the tenth time. Don Antigeo noticed all this from a distance as he watched his every move while standing across from his cell talking to Moe, who followed his stare saying, "What's wrong with our friend is everything alright?"

"No, your friend," the Don corrected, watching Nasir wipe away the heavy sweat from his forehead. "At this minute, he's searching his soul for peace because he has a big meeting tomorrow and he will need to get his rest. So don't bring his breakfast until around eight."

"Okay, Don, but I'll be there for you at the same time as always."

"LOCK DOWN, LOCK DOWN! COUNT TIME," the P.A. system announced. Don Antigeo moved onto his bunk with his head sinking into the extra stuffed pillow while his hands held a Robb Report Magazine. He started to breeze through the pages in search of the next luxurious home he would buy when this was all said and done.

He spotted Nasir laying out a black suit, "Son, I would go with white. It represents a much more positive statement."

"You think so?"

"Believe me, it does," the Don smiled.

After an hour of Nasir changing suits several times, the Don stopped him, "Nasir that one is fine. Now why don't you come here and have a seat." Don Antigeo patted the chair beside his bed. He waited until Nasir was comfortable then said, "Know that every man must fight the war with in himself alone to truly say he is the controller of his own destiny and that fight. Even though it's with oneself, you must fight it like any other opponent. So what's the first thing your corner tells you that must be done?" Nasir replied, "Relax."

"So do that and I'm here for you as an ear to listen if you need to get anything off your chest. Just relax, get focused and prepare to win." Seeing the hesitant look in Nasir's face, the Don began to lie back down but before his head could hit the pillow again, "Don, wait, the reason why I have been so interested in Mr. Holmes and what happened to him is because we have a mutual friend of power that used to speak highly of him. His name is Diego El Sovida but I know him as El Smokes." Nasir took a hard swallow as if saying Diego El Sovida's name made his body dehydrated. "It's like you're a gift from God because you hold a valuable piece of information that will help me make the judgment needed for tomorrow. So will you please tell me what happened with Mr. Holmes?

"Anything to help," the Don answered with a demonic grin…

One night at Roc's club Soldi, it was packed for his masquerade party. This place was crowded passed its capacity as every hustler, businessman, and celebrity that had a connection to the city was present. The security guards received pressure from every angle as people yelled, "Man, open the fucking rope."

"Yo, we're going to get in regardless nigga, so you might as well get out the way."

"I know you heard what the fuck I said, back the hell up off the rope, nobody else is getting in," stated Melvin, one of the men that looked like an offensive linemen for the Jets, guarding the door.

"You're only saying that because you got the cops with you."

"What! This is Roc's club, fuck you and the police. Matter of fact, get him out of here for talking crazy."

Four men with shirts that read 'Security' grabbed the man up quickly by the legs and arms. "Okay, my bad get off me!" "Nah nigga, call the cops." They tossed him hard into the middle of the street. As the night moved on, the security continued to refuse to let any more people in unless ordered by Roc himself.

Shuttle Maybachs with arrangement routes from the airport rode through the club's three large parking lots, which was covered with luxury cars from one end to the other. Each vehicle possessed a very important person as they passed the many different people in costumes on their way to the main entrance.

As surveillance camera's monitored their every move closely, seeing them now only yards away from the front door, Haffee pushed away from the marble desk and said, "Excuse me, Gizelle, can you take over for me for a moment?"

With a sky blue dress on, that caressed every curve just right, Gizelle made her way to Haffee and placed a hand on his shoulder, "You know I will but, Haffee, if you really want to be done with the street life, you have to give the owner position a chance." "And I will, as soon as I get back," Haffee smiled at Gizelle in the distance, knowing she only meant well as she shook her head, seeing the elevator door close behind him.

Upstairs in Roc's office that overlooked the whole club, Roc sat by his desk studying the third dimensional surveillance screen while talking to Boggy and Manny who were seated on two soft black leather sofas.

"I'm telling you, Roc, these girls are animals," said Boggy, thinking of China and Flirtatious each having their lips wrapped tightly around his balls.

"But I thought we talked about you settling down and having some kids like mother asked you," Roc questioned without removing his eyes from the screen. "I know, Roc," Boggy lowered his head in disgust, looking at the deluxe carpet slowly shaking his head from side to side. He then lifted it and said, "No disrespect to mom cuz I love her dearly but them bitches can't get enough of me, ha-ha. It's on everywhere and anywhere, I'm telling you man. You know what I mean, Manny, if they came here right now I'm hitting ass everywhere, on the desk, on top of your shoes…everywhere."

The two smacked a high five as Manny laughed, loving Boggy for being the one way he knew him to be…him. Roc started to object when three quick knocks followed by another two pauses and another knock made contact with his office door. "Come in."

Haffee stuck his head halfway in the doorway, "Roc, they're here."

"I know."

"So what you want me to do?"

"Just notify Gizelle"

"Will do," Haffee replied and began to shut the door when Boggy yelled, "Haffee, come on, this shit ain't for us. You're on some real bull shit, killers don't retire."

"I know, Boggy, they die."

Haffee calmly closed the door, letting out a deep breath while resting his head back against the door. He hated the fact that he had to give his friends the cold shoulder but he knew that to give himself a chance at a new life, he had to leave the old one behind.

Back inside, Boggy asked, "Roc, what the hell is up with him, the first time we sent him out on a mission by himself we got to bail two people out and he came back with the Holy Ghost."

"Come on, Boggy, the man is Muslim."

"My bad, but you know what I mean."

"I do, but we don't know what he is going through. So as his friends we must support him in war and in his search for peace."

"You're right but it's still some bullshit."

Roc smiled at Boggy's statement as he rose to his feet, standing in front of the surveillance monitor that covered the back wall. His eyes roamed over the hundreds of people until he spotted Gizelle leading three men to the top V.I.P. suite. Roc touched the upper right corner of the screen and instantly eight cameras changed to a close up picture of Gizelle and the three men whose faces were covered by presidential masks of Clinton, Obama, and Reagan. She cut a banner that ready, 'Royalty Suite' on a taped off section which was the best V.I.P. room in the place.

The moment Gizelle removed the tape; ten barely dressed women came and stood at the entrance. Roc raised the volume to hear Gizelle say, "These women are her to keep you company and through those doors down there on the left, where the two bodyguards are standing, are rooms with a showers and top of the line clothing if you should need to change. If there is anything else that you may need, please don't hesitate to ask."

Roc watched the three men stare at Gizelle's backside as she exited before saying, "Now let's see what the rest of these players are up to." Roc touched the screen again as all thirty V.I.P. rooms appeared before him. He leaned back on his desk with his arms folded, enjoying the sight of the strength of his hands as he acquired players from as far as Africa to as near as the hand to hand hustlers around the corner, popping bottles with his boss.

Boggy and Manny now stood beside Roc as he touched screen twenty one where there were four men with gold and platinum teeth laced in diamonds, showing through their masks. "Now let's see what these New Orleans cats are talking about."

"Roc, how do you know they're from the N.O., they got masks on?" questioned Manny.

"Because they're where I put them, like the rest of these people. Remember everything is for a reason," Roc answered as their voices played through the surveillance audio. "I'm telling you, Whooie, these niggas down here is eating crazy, but they're killing everything moving. If we're bringing some of them choppers down here, this shit would be nothing to get some of this food around here," said EB, the hired gun of the crew while cutting his eyes across the V.I.P. section to where Biggs and Rob from North Philly stood. They were standing on a table with bottles of red Moet in each hand while their jewelry lit up the room, bobbing their head to the live act on stage.

"Chill, Whooie, we're here cuz a made man invited us and we're going to respect that, so maybe another time yah heard me," said Juluke.

"Yeah," EB responded raising a bottle of champagne to his lips while still hopefully watching his prey.

Boggy noticed the moment that Biggs caught the stare and quickly changed the screen to box eight and stated to Roc, "I want to see if this loud mouth nigga Biggs is real or faking it cuz I keep hearing his name in shit. Now he got some out-of-towner on his ass."

The screen gave a close up of Biggs's section as his eyes tightened on EB while he slowly stepped down from the table handing the bottle off to a pretty light skinned woman before smoothly tapping on Rob's designer jeans, he whispered, "Yo, I think these niggas are on some bullshit, plotting on making a move on us."

"Not here, this nigga would be dead before morning if they disrespected Roc's spot." Biggs nodded in agreement as he pulled out a big bank roll of bills, "Well fuck the plotting, I'm going to make their mind up cuz they can die tonight fucking with me!" Biggs walked over to a crowd of women dancing to the song, '*Turning me on*' and quickly started moving his hand back and forth over the money, shooting hundred dollar bills in the air making it rain.

Mean-mugging EB and his crew while a few feet away several bills landed in the crease of Butter's Brioni suit as he sat with his legs crossed beside his lady friend Belinda, locked in a deep conversation. "Butter, I'm talking to you."

"And I'm listening. You said some nigga named Fared is running his mouth about how much money I'm getting"

"Yeah, honey, and you need to handle that," Belinda took a small sip from her wine glass then continued, "And yesterday he saw me in a store and said something under his breath about how he's going to get you locked up, then get me back and I'm not having it…Butter, you hear me?" Butter watched a bill land on the rim of his crease then he spotted the others, he grabbed the five hundred dollars in his hand and looked in Biggs direction. He saw him and Rob both now making it rain.

Looking at Baby's people, Butter took the money and used it to gently wipe down and over his John Lobb shoes before tossing it to the floor. "Butter," his girl friend repeated. "Okay, love," Butter said not wanting to have to deal with something so small but knew he had to because it was big to Belinda. He let the air out of his lungs. Butter continued, "Love, when you let someone affect you, it affects me and that's only right because I care for you. But with this money comes hate, so I need you to have tough skin. You can't let someone that's a nobody affect me; look around." Butter paused making sure Belinda was with him before he asked, "You see every body that's somebody is here. Anybody that knows somebody is here and this Fared person isn't. The only way he could get here is by your mouth. So please don't leave him out he needs to drink too." Butter grabbed a bottle of chilled Don P. off ice and popped the top before turning the bottle over and pouring it into the bucket of ice.

"Now, make sure this is the last time you invite a clown in my presence." Butter released the bottle when the sudden movement to his left caught his attention. He turned his head in that direction and stood up at the same time, thinking, *"Not here, Biggs, Roc's not having this shit."* The New Orleans section was on their feet with masks off as Biggs and Rob headed straight at them. EB took a step forward when Juluke pulled him back behind him saying, "Woody you know already, I have never been a coward your heard and you're here with me so just play your position and nothing else cuz if Woody get out of line, Woody going to get his head busted."

Biggs and Rob were five feet away when Butter accompanied by Artie, Gizz, and KB from the Delaware section stepped in the middle. Butter and KB faced Biggs and Rob while Artie and Gizz calmed the New Orleans, "Come on, gentlemen, not like this. We came here to show our respect not to disrespect," said Butter.

"Yeah cuz only Mike Tyson gets paid for his fight shit, hell I ain't had to put my hands on a nigga in twenty years," yelled Artie. Biggs looked EB once over saying, "You're right," when he spotted the red flag hanging out his back pocket and screamed while trying to push past KB, "Nigga you blood! Well open your mouth and I'll eat your food pus…"

"STOP," KB said firmly. "If you disrespect that man, who I don't know but I do know Juluke like that, there's no turning back." The name danced in Biggs's head for a minute then he asked, "Is he from Chopper City?"

"Yeah"

"Damn, that's the bull Juluke; he's the one that got them things like snow man and 17.5. This clown looking at me like he wants my shit and he's with the mother fucking line," said Biggs out loud. Rob's mind quickly went into motion as he stopped the closest waitress, "Yo, take them N.O. cats ten bottles of whatever they're drinking and tell them it's on me."

Hearing that everything was calm, Roc removed his finger from the button that would have had several of his many thugs placed through out the floors, on the scene in seconds. "I guess the kid was going to put on for the city," Roc said smiling before heading for his private back room, "Have everything ready to go in twenty minutes."

Outside, a stolen Camero pulled to a stop in the center parking lot with Lucifer behind the wheel. His face was painted pearl white with black lips as red specks of dried up blood was mixed in. His eyes were observing the many people moving about when they stopped on the entrance. Seeing the three large security men that blocked his access, Lucifer slid his blade into place at the rim of his wrist, *"I will attack them from the front."*

Slamming the door, he moved through the lot blending in with the rest of the masked partygoers. He came to the edge of the street and slowly eased the two rings upon his fingers. A slight grin appeared at the center of his mouth as he decided to kill the smallest one first, in hopes that it would give the larger ones more of a chance to prolong their death.

Lucifer crossed the street taking the deep scent of what surrounded him when suddenly his eyes widened in anticipation, because instead of the usual aroma of fear, it was loaded with ambition and he could taste it. Lucifer was now so caught up in his next victim; he didn't notice the apple red Lamborghini Gallardo that came roaring fast down the one way street. Just missing him, it pulled across the oncoming traffic and parked in front of the club. The passenger door swung open with Barbara stepping out in a lovely red dress and lipstick that matched the car. Her hair was pulled back, revealing every inch of her pretty face and she walked around the car as the sound of her six inch heels strutted along the cement and she paid the calls from men no mind. She opened the door for Todd who was dressed in a pair of baggy Polo shorts, open toed sandals, an unbutton Dior shirt and a tank top that showed off his muscular frame.

"Hey, you can't park there, you have to get one of our valet in the parking lot to handle that," uttered one of the security guards. "Well I have you for now," Todd replied tossing his keys with a knot of money into the man's hand. He extended his arm while Barbara took it proudly and Todd finished saying, "That's five grand for five minutes, I believe that should do." "Yeah, yeah thanks," the man disappeared behind the steering wheel.

Todd approached the door without any thoughts of stopping when a man stepped in his path with his hand out, "Excuse me, this party is by invite only." The huge palm made contact with the center of Todd's chest and he looked from the hand back up to the man's eyes as he held the man's stare, visualizing swiftly knocking him out. Todd smiled easing the man's hand from his chest to his hand, giving him a firm gripped hand shake that matched the big man's strength. "Hi, I'm Todd." The other man checked the list moving in closer saying, "It's not on here."

"I never said it was," Todd answered refusing to look away. Lucifer saw the commotion and took one last inhale of Todd's scent before sliding by unnoticed. Barbara said, "No, I spoke with Roc, we do a lot of business together and he told me my name would there, it's Barbara Hudson."

Rechecking the list, the man shook his head up and down while opening the velvet rope. Still not wanting to be defeated so easily, the man asked, "This is a masquerade party so where is *your disguise*?"

"I'm wearing it," he answered.

"And what are you supposed to be?"

"The shit!" Todd said with confidence, bumping the man on purpose as he passed paying the words the man yelled no mind.

Inside, Gizelle led Todd to the third floor while NayNay who never used to drink, sat at the bar against Top Dollar's wishes, pouring herself a fourth shot of Cognac. "NayNay, what are you doing to yourself, stop it."

"No! For what, Top?" NayNay yelled, raising the dark liquid to her lips and drinking it straight down.

"Maybe because you're a beautiful young lady with her whole life ahead of her"

"My life died with Solo," said a slurred speaking NayNay, pouring another shot and taking it down also. She was trying hard to get rid of the feeling that she was continuously being watched, only to not find anyone there, like now. She looked around at all the faces in the room for the twentieth time.

"Stop drinking, NayNay, this is not you"

"Top, will you leave me the fuck alone? You're not my damn father as bad as you want to be, damn it. I'm grown; matter of fact why the fuck don't you got kids?"

"You're right, I'm not," Top Dollar stood to his feet but the pain from NayNay's words almost brought him to his knees. "Okay I'm going to go but please don't give our enemy back the power of killing you both when he took the bullets so he would die alone."

Top Dollar placed a few hundred dollars on the bar saying to the bar tender, "Make sure that's the last bottle you sell her because she's like my daughter and you don't want to meet an angry father, you dig?" NayNay watched Top Dollar walk away before swallowing another shot. She looked around again when she noticed two eyes staring at her. The woman knew that she had been busted and made her way over to NayNay, taking a seat next to her.

"Hello, I'm Pam."

"Ssshhh…don't speak," NayNay interrupted while roughly removing the woman's cast mask to see her jet black hair, soft mocha complexion, thick lips and dark green eyes. "Spy," NayNay said guzzling down another drink and loving the feeling of pain she received as the hot alcohol burned her insides on contact. "Aaahhh," she slammed the glass down hard on the bar. Still having the strange feeling, she looked around once more before quickly taking the bottle and the woman's wrist tightly. NayNay quickly pulled her through the crowded dance floor as she pushed and bumped people out of her way, "Move."

They approached the entrance to the private back room where a body guard stood posted. "I caught this bitch stalking me and she might be police." NayNay removed her stare from the man's eyes and looked to her waist line. Jesse spotted the shape of her forty five automatic, then with a short nod he stepped aside while thinking to himself, *"I must tell Roc about this."*

In the room NayNay sat the bottle on a bamboo dresser while removing the gun and holding it tightly in her right palm. On sight the woman began to plead, "I'm sorry please, I wasn't stalking you it was just…you're attractive and you like…"

"Ssshhh", NayNay placed her free hand on the woman's shoulder and gently lowered her to her knees. The woman unfastened NayNay's baggy jeans. She inhaled the enticing scent of NayNay's sex box through her red see through panties. She used the softest touch to free NayNay of her clothes one item at a time until she was completely nude. With her hand on NayNay's abs, she slowly laid her back onto the bed and NayNay opened her legs wide as the woman was about to stand and demanded, "No...crawl to me!"

Displaying a smile Pam's said, "Damn, bitch, I knew you was bad when I saw you." The woman raised her dress above her hips feeling the friction on her knees with each inch from the carpet and loving it. She ran her fingers through her own dripping wet pussy lips, then reached the bed and couldn't wait to explore NayNay's pink walls but playing the lady role tonight, she knew that rushing one moment wouldn't be accepted.

Slowly she began to massage NayNay's feet while at the same moment leaning in and starting to massage the tip of NayNay's clit by moving her tongue in a water wave motion making the middle rub the top as the end of her tongue flickered back and forth in the center.

The temperature of NayNay's body rose quicker than ever as she fought back the emotion to cum so soon. So in resistance, she palmed Pam's head whose touch ran chills of pleasure up her spine from the way her tongue and lips moved licking and sucking from her ass to her clit and everything in between. A loud screamed escaped from NayNay's mouth as she shot cum on the three fingers that Pam had inside her. The intensity of the climax mixed with the alcohol made NayNay feel as if she was spinning out of control and she couldn't care less. She grabbed the bottle from the dresser and drank down a few inches of the brown liquid once more, watching the woman take the fingers that were just inside her and kiss them before placing them into her mouth.

Pam removed the bottle from NayNay's lips and placed it to hers while seductively crawling onto the bed and up NayNay's body where she found her mouth, releasing her drink in it. Their tongues twisted together as the ambition to explore the rest of NayNay's body built with each second as their kisses became wilder when suddenly NayNay pushed the woman over onto her back then mounted the woman's awaiting face. The two were so caught up in each other that they didn't notice the masked man slide into the room.

Upon seeing them his blood boiled with rage and he then realized he could have been a part of the problem by not watching after her more closely, like his brother asked. He stopped at the back of the bed to find his erect manhood throbbing as the feeling of his anger coupled with lust took over just watching NayNay's ass swinging back and forth over the woman's lips as it was done to her.

The masked man moved in closer to get a better look at Pam's gapped open legs and exposed sex box. Hesitantly his hand stretch forward gripping the right one and raising it over his shoulder but when he went to grasp the other one, it was already there. The woman arched her back while aggressively working her tongue with anticipation of the man. Then without warning he rammed every inch of his manhood into her sex box, "Ooohh daaamn, shit o-o-h yes," the scream of pleasure echoed as the masked man's motion of penetration grew longer and harder. "Ooohh yes, fuck me harder!"

Hearing the words, NayNay turned and connected eyes with the masked man. Then as if in a daze she found his lips and they locked. Suddenly the door came flying open and in a second NayNay had her gun in hand and positioned on Roc as the masked man stood in the middle of the floor with a gun aimed at Roc also.

Roc yelled, "Mac, put that fucking gun down, didn't I tell you to stay in the shadows." NayNay quickly questioned, "Solo, is that you?" Knowing the eyes but thinking she was dreaming, NayNay ripped the mask from his face and on sight slapped him as hard as she could while raising her forty five automatic to his head in the same motion. She debated on killing him and herself as Lil Mac slowly lowered her gun with his hand before taking her into his arms and she began to cry. "Why would you do this to me, my heart couldn't take it, Solo."

"I know but…"

"There's no but, I'm this close," Roc interrupted as he put his thumb and index finger an inch apart while continuing, "From getting your lives back without taking one so that you can go back to college and finish what you started. So please do what I asked of you because right now I must convince three of the most powerful people in the world that I didn't cross the line and kill myself by killing one of our own, so here," Roc tossed a roll of money while looking in the direction of the woman. "Handle that and I'll see you in my office."

Seconds after Roc closed the door, Lil Mac stuffed the money in his pocket and turned his gun to the lovely woman now sitting on the bed and fired four shots into her frame. Confused, NayNay asked, "Why did you do that?" "Because of Roc I now understand a true chess player never falls for the same move twice and I did once when I let Boggy live and he shot me. Then with Mr. Holmes trying to have me killed. Now death is my only option for anyone and debts must be paid! Now get your shit and let's go." Back in the upper office, Boggy grinned while sitting in Roc's chair at the screen to the reaction of Lil Mac saying, "I knew the lil' soldier had too much heart to be dead at the hands of a coward that couldn't look him in the eyes as he pulled the trigger." Boggy with the same finger he used on Fox, placed them in the shape of a gun and pointed to the screen, pulling the trigger…."

Oh shit, you mean to tell me the kid never did die?" questioned Nasir. "I'm afraid the bastard didn't," the Don said standing up and checking his watch, 4:20. He looked out the cell door for the guard to pass. "Shouldn't you be getting your rest for your big day tomorrow?"

"I will, so did Roc pull it off?"

"What! Most likely if it's up to him, he did," the Don's voice dropped to a much deeper tone. "And did the corporation believe he didn't have anything to do with killing Mr. Holmes?"

"In a way…" Don Antigeo paused in the middle of his sentence as the night guard approached their cell doing his nightly stroll. But this night was different, he stopped in front of Don Antigeo saying, "Nasir, I heard about your decision and that's good but the lights are passed their time to be out so get them off!"

"But you never said nothing before, why is it such a big deal?"

"Because it's time for you to rest ha-haaa"

Nasir turned and killed the light, giving C.O. Tom just enough time to pass off to Don undetected, who with his back still to Nasir asked, "Why don't you tell me if Roc got away with it?"

"What do you mean me tell you, ha," Nasir laughed nervously.

"Come on, Nasir, every lesson I gave you was an answer and you still never thought to ask the question of why."

Nasir began to think about the many things that the Don taught him. "Nasir for you to live long in this life as long as I have, you must understand one thing, that there are only two sides in this world. What one are you on?" Nasir's eyes tighten as the Don's words from the gym came to memory, *"Easy, Don, you've been working so hard lately I just knew I would find you here."*

"Yes I have because I too will be leaving in two weeks and then we'll be faced with the battle of our lives. So it's only right to be prepared."

Shaking his head he thought, *"This can't be true, he's my friend."* Suddenly everything started to make sense with the words that Don Antigeo spoke only a month ago. "Tell me what you've learned and how you're going to handle the situation," Don Antigeo had questioned at that time.

"I will do nothing."

"Correct, and why?"

"Because he is the best kind of enemy, he can only hurt me by the things I allow him to do and know."

"And by you having possession of this knowledge, does what?" the Don continued to quiz.

"It gives me the advance of using Amid any way I please."

"Yes indeed, but the correct move would be..."

"To befriend him, that way I can learn what he truly knows without him knowing I am onto him."

"True and what would you have become?"

"The worst kind of enemy"

"Today you have passed..."

As Nasir came back to reality he slowly raised his head to find Don Antigeo standing next to him with nothing but the look of death in his once peaceful eyes. The Don said, "For a man to be victorious he must first see his victory then believe that it is possible to achieve." Nasir's respect for the man he shared a cell with just shot passed a hundred now understanding Don Antigeo's motive as he stood in the second most protected jail in the world. Nasir noticed a large blade in Don Antigeo's hand and asked, "I know the reason Diego El Sovida sent you and why but may I ask who you really are?"

"You heard of me coward; we used to have a mutual friend."

Puzzled, Nasir quickly tried to figure out the identity of his assassin. Then his eyes widened to the size of quarters as he yelled, "But it can't be, it's impossible." Nasir repeated his words, "The reason I've been so interested in Mr. Holmes and what happened to him is because we have a mutual friend of power."

"But I thought you were supposed to be dead."

"In a way but I couldn't go owning a man because my names is worth more than gold."

"But how?"

"See, when that pretty lady stuck her gun in the elevator and we locked eyes as I witnessed the fury in her soul, her weapon was on the center of my head with her finger easing back on the trigger. Just as she pulled it, she turned her arm placing five shots into the face of Don Antigeo, God bless his soul."

"So they wasn't there for you?"

"Yes, but only to show me on good faith that he could have killed me."

"The same way you did with Lil Mac?"

"Now you're catching on but it's too late."

Mr. Holmes caught Nasir by surprise gripping the top of his head and pulling it backwards while in a single motion bring the knife from one ear to the other. Nasir had a smile upon his face as he refused to put up a fight and instantly died.

After finishing the rest of the neck tie, by pulling Nasir's tongue through his neck and sending a message of a person being a rat, Mr. Holmes cleaned up the cell then dressed Nasir in his white suit, placing him in the bed as if he was sleep with a white towel wrapped tightly around the cut. Mr. Holmes tapped on the cell bars twice and moments later C.O. Tom popped open the cell door. Mr. Holmes started out of the cell then stopped, "I almost forgot." Removing his Rolex, he placed it on the wrist of Nasir while folding his arms neatly across his chest."

"Mr. Holmes, he's downstairs," said C.O. Tom. "Well we must not keep him waiting." Outside special agent Branson held the door to the awaiting Blackhawk helicopter for Mr. Holmes who embraced him with a half hug. "Nice to see you make it back boss, how did everything go?"

"It's done, now I'll finally get to have my justice in Philly. Your phone please."

"Hello, Travis"

"Sir Holmes, is that you?"

"Yes and you can deliver our friend his gift now."

As the helicopter moved through the sky, Moe lightly tapped on the cell door as usual with two breakfasts and a newspaper tucked under his arm. He got no response and eased back the cell door finding no sign of Don Antigeo and thought, "Something's not right here." Moe looked around and spotted the Rolex and began to follow the Don's instructions when he said nice watch. He remembered the Don saying, "You can have it but when you see it anywhere other than my wrist, burn everything around it."

17

The sun was still slightly noticeable as several luxury cars pulled to a stop on the runway of Pilatus Airlines travel station, where a high performance PC-12 aircraft with a four member crew waiting for their arrival.

Gizelle pulled Roc closer as they watched the sun disappear together for the first time in years from the back of a custom Escalade. Roc kissed her softly saying, "Just give me one second." Placing the phone back to his ear he asked, "SO you just dropped him off?"

"About three minutes ago"

"Thanks, Branson, if anything changes keep me posted"

"Alright but be careful Roc, the look in his eyes said he has something big planned for you."

"I'm way ahead of you."

Roc made eye contact with the driver who was cued to get their door as he put the phone back in place. The rest of the drivers followed pursuit releasing Roc's team along with the Get Money Clique into the clean evening air. A young man in a dark blue uniform with gold stripes and a huge hat hesitantly made his way over with his hand extended. "Hello, Mr. Miller, I'm Louis Katz, your pilot for your flight to Mexico. If there is any…"

"What did you say your name was?" Roc sharply interrupted.

"Uuhh…L-L-Louis Katz, sir. Why is there a problem?"

"Louis, haven't you flown for me before?"

"Yes to great Exuma, in the Bahamas."

"And I requested you right?"

"Yes."

"Then relax because you're family now or you wouldn't be here. I care for these people that are about to get on the plane and I'm putting their lives in your hands so I must be pleased with your service. Now get ready to fly and everything is going to be just fine, okay," Roc demanded shaking the man's hand firmly. "Okay thank you, Mr. Miller, and your flight will be ready for departure in five minutes."

Gizelle waited until Louis walked off and asked, "Roc, why did you do that to him?"

"Do what?"

"Shake him up like that, baby, or do you like to see people scared of you now?"

"Scared? Never! Because a scared person is unpredictable. They'll even kill themselves not to face reality. But on the other hand a drop of fear can never hurt, haa-hhaa," he laughed. "Now let's enjoy our vacation."

"Roc, you're so crazy."

Meanwhile off in the distance, approximately a hundred yards away, hidden by the arrival of the night, a clicking sound repeated from the inside of a hot wired Pilatus Airline service truck. Detective Michael took snap shot after snap shot from the passenger seat of Roc and his gang's every move. Detective Brian was next to him slumped down low with a pair of binoculars to his eyes as he paid close attention to the words coming from the headphone of the listening device aimed where Roc was standing.

They, along with the help of under cover officer Dell had been watching Roc for eighteen hours a day since the moment NayNay and Daz walked out of the court room saying, "Fuck you ,pigs," as they strolled passed. That was over three months ago.

Detective Brian hadn't noticed anything out of the ordinary other than Roc's lavish lifestyle and that at the time seemed unwanted by his suspect. But recently in the last ten days, Detective Brian thought he observed a slight change in Roc's actions and this moment just confirmed it.

Sitting up straight he passed the binoculars to Detective Michael. "What sticks out the most in this picture to you?" Detective Michael let his eyes examine the scene until he spotted NayNay. "I see this tramp getting away with murder" "No, look at everything."

Detective Michael continued to inspect the faces of Manny, NayNay, AP, Top Dollar, Daz, Haffee, Mrs. Miller, Gizelle, Fox, Boggy, and Roc. "Man, I don't see nothing but a bunch of low life monkey's that need to be put back in their cages."

"Michael, once again I'm going to act as if I didn't hear that but the next time you're going to have to fight this monkey sitting here."

"My bad, Brian"

"Okay, now focus."

Detective Michael watched the Get Money Clique make their way down the red carpet that lead to the jet stairs. "I see them leaving that's all." Detective Michael tossed the binoculars back onto Detective Brian's lap with frustration. "It's just the same thugs beating justice."

Detective Brian shook his head stating, "Maybe it's because we're so busy watching what's in the box and looking right passed what's on the rim of it." Detective Brian replaced the binoculars onto Michael's eyes and aimed the vision about forty yards back to the perimeter of the runway where fifteen armed men stood on point. "Damn, you would think they were at war!"

"My point exactly."

"But with who, they're together now right?"

"Now that's the million dollar question." Detective Brian took back the binoculars and zoomed in on Roc while trying to read his lips as he spoke with Boggy in a tone much too low for the device to pick up.

"Are you sure?" Roc questioned Boggy for the sixth time. Boggy looked at Haffee ad Sakara walking through the jet door hand and hand. "Yeah, Roc, I think I'm going to pass, I need to hit these streets."

"Come on, Boggy, you don't got to do that, you're a millionaire and I made sure of that so if you're going to turn my invitation of some time away from all this destruction down, then keep it real with me."

"The real is, Roc, the money, no matter how much it is, it can't ever give me the feeling that I get from breaking the plastic on a crate of a thousand bricks. The smell of all that raw knowing my nigga is about to eat heavy or the look of true loyalty when you change a young soldier's life that's trying to fee his family and maintain off of four and a half ounces. Then you front them their first brick, the look in the eyes of the haters when I say fuck it and pull the Lambo out and take it to the corner store in the hood with my jewelry out and all. Daring a nigga to disrespect me."

Roc's blood moved faster through his veins as he saw the passion in Boggy's words as his muscles flexed while he continued to talk with his hands. "Then there's the ride or die chicks that will give you head on the steps while you're making a sale, now that's my definition of success."

"I do feel you."

"Plus, I was never good at running."

Roc gave Boggy a half hug and as they embraced he whispered, "It's not running, it's a vacation."

"Now, Roc, whose turn is it to keep it real?"

Parting, Roc let out a deep breath because deep down inside he knew Boggy was right, saying, "Just remember to watch yourself, he still has one move left before his war can truly begin with me."

"Yeah I know he must try to get a level of understanding before he can kill you or you kill him," Boggy answered, speaking of the lesson they were taught as kids by Mr. Holmes. "*Anytime real money is involved, Roc and Boggy remember there will always be jealousy with it so you'll need loyalty like we have. When you're blessed to possess it, do your best to keep it and if ever separated, give them a way of warning. First show them some good faith for the love in your heart for them and if all else fails, try to get a level of understanding before you kill them.*"

Boggy then questioned, "But what the hell does that have to do with me?"

"Everything, because if he can't target me he must use the people I care about to send his message."

"Like you did with Billy D, but that made you a move ahead of him."

"Ssshhh, not too loud, it almost feels like I made a deal with the devil."

"Alright you better go before you're late for your quote unquote vacation."

"Boggy the only thing I'll be late for is my funeral."

Boggy smiled seeing that look once again in Roc's eyes while watching him ascends the stairs of the jet with the door closing behind him. Boggy turned for his car to find Fox standing behind him. "Nigga, you better hurry up before they leave your dumb ass."

"Nay, I'm cool with them leaving me cuz I'm trying to roll with your dumb ass."

"Oh, I get it. You're a hard rock and you want to see what my life is like. But do you really think you can stand it?"

"What you going to do, cut my feet off?"

"That's right little nigga, talk that talk. You know the last nigga that said that to me they had to put his toe tag in his mouth."

Boggy hit the button to unlock his G.T. "Get in." Sliding his CD in with the lyrics of Jadakiss's 'What if' vibrating from the speakers, Boggy made his way for the exit gate when a black Maybach Exelero raced through it doing about 100 mph. It just missed his car as the hoody wearing driver whose face he couldn't see, hit his horn, 'BEEP-BEEP' while throwing his fist in the air as he headed for the jet.

Fox almost snapped his neck as he followed the cars movement saying, "Wait, I know that car...but it can't be." Boggy pulled Fox back down into his seat. "Listen, your first lesson is to know when it comes to Roc, anything is possible. And two, here roll this box of blunts."

"And what's the lesson in that?"

"That you better learn how to do it on the go with out getting it on my interior or I'm going to bust your ass, hard rock."

A trail of dust flew from the tires of the Maybach as it raced for the jet that slowly began to circle the runway for take off. "Damn," the driver yelled seeing that he may be too late. "No, I got to do this now." He then lined the vehicle straight for the jet, pushing down hard on the gas and forcing the sport car forward.

On the jet, Roc reclined his seat back letting his head sink into the soft cushion of the plush pearl white interior. Closing his eyes on contact he began to question if he really had what it took to out think the person who taught him how to use his mind. Roc ran his hand repeatedly down the long beautiful jet black hair of Gizelle who was lying from her seat across his lap.

Unexpectedly the sound of Louis's foot steps forced his eyes back open. "Mr. Miller, sorry to disturb you but there's something you need to see." Roc pushed the divider to the side to see his mother sleeping with Odell Jr. knocked out as well, resting on her large breast. He made his way to the captain's cockpit, "Mr. Miller, look, what should I do?"

Roc saw the fortitude in the drivers face and said, "Stop and tell your people it's time." Closing the door as he left, Roc bent down kissing his mother on the forehead. "It'll all be over soon." He went back to his seat and smiled as the jet door opened with the blasting words of Nas's Ether flowing through the air. *"(I, will, not, lose) "God's son" across the belly, I prove you lost already."*

Stepping on the jet, Lil Mac readjusted his hoody on his face saying into his earpiece, "Mohammed, did they see me?"

"No but they're running your plates right now," Mohammed answered, hiding in a trash can twenty feet behind Detectives Michael and Brian, following their every move.

"So I got it from Roc, ha-ha." Lil Mac laughed walking down the aisle as his crew members looked and still couldn't believe their eyes. Even after the meeting at club Soldi. But there were still two very important people he needed to reunite himself with. He stopped next to Roc's section and the two brothers locked eyes, "I'm glad to see you could make it."

"I'm glad you stopped," Lil Mac said, smiling seeing Gizelle laying comfortably on Roc with a portion of her rear end hanging out in the aisle. 'SMACK!' Licking his lips, Lil Mac hit it firmly, watching Gizelle yell with her sweet tone gone as she pushed off of Roc who was grinning and she was on her feet in a second with her guard up.

She turned and froze as Lil Mac said, "You know I always wanted to do that and by the rate people have been shooting at me, I thought this might be my last chance." Gizelle with both hands now wrapped around her open mouth as she started to cry, couldn't believe her eyes as her shaking hands found the face of Lil Mac and kissing him on the lips. She wrapped her arms around him tightly, laying her head on his chest when she felt the two forty five automatics holstered on each shoulder. Gizelle slowly backed away, breaking their embrace and still looking at Lil Mac straight in the eyes. With tears still flowing, she saw that the innocence in Lil Mac was now gone and instead of joy, the sad reality of that is what she felt. She now looked in the face of a kid with the same frame but his eyes told a much different story of pain and hardship. Without leaving his stare, she said, "You know your restaurant is doing fine. I've been running it myself with the help of M-Easy until he did what he did to Roc and left the country, coward. I also kept all your school books if you ever get…" Gizelle became overwhelmed with emotion, refusing to hold them back she let them go. "If you ever get tired of making me cry or is that what you Miller men do best to the people you care about?"

She burst out into a loud cry while racing off to the restroom. Lil Mac grabbed a hold of her arm, "Gizelle, wait," she pulled free, shooting him a look that said *don't play with me.* Lil Mac looked to Roc, "That's one down, Mac, with one to go and you're losing."

"Which way?" Lil Mac asked. Roc pointed forward and Lil Mac pulled back the divider to find Top Dollar in a chair next to the door dressed in a cream Hugo Boss suit, brown gators and a brown hat lying over his face. Tapping his shoulder, Lil Mac whispered, "Now get your ass up slow or I'm going to blow your mother fucking head off, you dig?" Top Dollar's eyes shot open; stunned that he had been caught slipping. Seeing Lil Mac he quickly gripped him into a head lock pulling him into the arm of the chair. His other hand rubbed over his head rapidly until it burned.

A velvet box with a bow fell from Lil Mac's pocket. "Okay, okay, Top Dollar, you got it, you got it."

"I must not, the way you left the meeting and I don't see you until now."

"I know, Top Dollar, I'm sorry but its Roc, he says we're being watched 24-7 and I can't let nobody see me outside of the team or his reason for treason wouldn't be good no more, whatever that's supposed to mean."

"I don't know but do it cuz I haven't seen Roc make a wrong move yet."

"Real rap, Top, is he like that?"

"Real rap, but he's no Solo." Top Dollar released Lil Mac and rose to his feet. "I see you brought me a present."

"No, that's Roc's. I forgot to give it to him."

"Well, I'm going to step out so that you can handle your business," Top Dollar nodded his head in the direction of Mrs. Miller who remained sleeping. Lil Mac slowly approached the sofa taking a deep breath. He hated the memories of the many sleepless nights he witnessed his mother endure as she cried asking God why he removed him from her life. All the while, he stood helplessly in the shadow of what used to be his own home. Seeing his mother so peaceful forced him to wipe his face before anything could fall if possible. At her side, Lil Mac got on one knee, kissing her on the forehead then doing the same to Jr. whose eyes opened on contact, "It will all be over very soon."

"Uncle Macky! It's tomorrow already, time to play basketball cuz I'm tired." Mrs. Miller, without opening her heavy eyes smacked Jr. upside the head, "What did I tell you about that, boy? You're going to have people thinking you're crazy."

"I'm sorry, Grandma," Jr. said, putting his little finger to his lips saying to Lil Mac, as he tried to whisper, "Ssshhh, Uncle Macky, my dad said it's a secret. Remember she can't know." Mrs. Miller smacked him again. Taking the blow, Jr. eased his head back down on her chest, sticking his thumb in his mouth. He then winked at Lil Mac and said, "Tomorrow."

Lil Mac gave it a second thought, beginning to feel that maybe now wasn't the best time. He headed for the exit when, "Lil Macky, if you don't get back here boy," Mrs. Miller ordered and stopped him dead in his tracks. He turned to find her arms open wide as JR. jumped down with his little legs running as fast as they could pass Lil Mac and he screamed, "Daaaadd, I didn't tell her our secret, Daaaddd."

Mrs. Miller took Lil Mac in her arms and refused to let him go for five minutes without saying a word until she became satisfied that the mother and child bond was recharged. Then she stated, "Now come and sit, we need to talk." Lil Mac took a seat next to his mother; he was surprised to not see a look of happiness. Instead Mrs. Miller wore a study expression like when she would catch him skipping school. "So, baby, are you done?

"Done what, Mom?"

"Damn it, Macky! Don't play with me. I know all about you out there in them streets playing thug with that hot ass little girl of yours."

Lil Mac lowered his head, looking at the ground and said, "Nah, Mom, it's not even like that."

"Well explain it to me, because anything that could have my oldest son trying to convince me that a man laying in a casket came out of me when I can tell my son from anywhere in the world, it has to be worth listening to."

"I'm sorry."

"Don't be sorry, just tell me you're going to stop"

"But I can't," Lil Mac answered. It's gone too far now, blood has been spilled and lives have been lost."

"That's not true, I've been talking to an old friend and it all can end now with you by just giving your word and it's done."

"I've driven my poor mother crazy. Who would she know that's hip to the life of a hustler," Lil Mac thought as he listened to his mother.

"Mom, who are you talking to? I know not the police."

"Please, no but if you want out just say it."

Lil Mac didn't want to let another loved one down and answered softly, "Yes, Mom, if it will make you happy I'll give my word."

"Very," Mrs. Miller grabbed the jet phone from the wall and began to dial. "Hello," a male voice answered. "Yes, it's me and he's willing to say it."

"Okay just put him on and Carmen, this will be the end for him, I promise."

"Thanks. Macky here." Lil Mac took the phone nonchalantly and brought it to his ear, "Yeah."

"Lil Macky, it's nice to finally speak to you after I've heard so much about you."

"That's good, who's this?"

"Oh you don't remember my voice?"

"No, but why are you telling my mom you can stop this madness?"

"Because I can but for you only, your brother's situation is much different."

"And who are you?"

"Well, my friends call me Billy D."

Recognizing the name, Lil Mac took the phone from his ear and looked at it in shock then to his mother, thinking of Roc's words, *"Mac, this cat Billy D is playing on another level and his hand is in everything from Dad, Mr. Holmes and me. It's like he's playing a game of chess also but his moves are calculated generations apart."*

Lil Mac put the phone back to his ear and Billy D questioned, "Macky, you there, Macky?"

"Yes I'm here and I understand everything you told my mother. I respect you for that. But as long as Roc has an enemy I have an enemy as well. Like he taught me, its two faces, one tear…meaning when one cries so does the other. I think you need to have that old man give his word because the Millers are fresh out of warning shots. And if I see him first, that's his ass cuz I don't play chess, I play checkers the old fashioned way; you see your man, you jump him. So thanks, but no thanks." Lil Mac slammed the phone back on its hook.

"Baby, how dare you?"

'SMACK' Mrs. Miller smacked Lil Mac across the face hard. He held his check, checking to see if blood was coming from his lip before he was about to apologize. "I'm sor…" Then his mother cut him off, "Macky, how dare you disrespect me by using such a foul mouth in my presence. Now come here and give me a hug for making me so proud. Your father would have rolled over in his grave if he thought us Millers didn't always stick together no matter what."

Lil Mac walked to his mother's embrace. Smelling the scent of his cologne, she said quietly in his ear, "Oh and the next time you call yourself spying on me without me knowing change you cologne."

"So you knew?"

"You know it's my favorite."

Outside, Mohammed examined the two detectives as they watched helplessly as the jet left the ground racing through the sky. "I guess there's nothing else to see here," said Detective Michael. Detective Brian reconnected the three wires as the engine started. Pulling off he answered, "If anybody would know, it's going to be him."

Picking up the walkie talkie, Detective Brian asked, "Dell, how is our friend doing?"

"He's watching you take off through the gate, now he's getting out the trash can and he's on the move."

"Well make sure you don't lose him, he's our only lead."

"Copy, over."

"Brian, how did you know there would be someone watching us?" inquired Detective Michael.

"The same way they knew we would be watching them," Detective Brian's hand tapped on the gold and black book that sat on the front seat.

18

Back in upstate New York, just passed 9:00 pm where the eight-bedroom, four-bath mini mansion that now seemed abandoned stood, the side door easily opened by the force of Mr. Holmes's left hand. His right one held the Ruger tightly, as it was leveled off not knowing what to expect as he shut the door behind him.

Making his rounds, he moved through out each room finding his belongings, broken in pieces, sofas flipped over along with many things missing. "I know he didn't do this but who did?" Comprehending, there was only one way to get the answer to his own question, Mr. Holmes hurried for his back staircase and halfway up it, he suddenly stopped in front of a picture of George Jackson with red eyes. The words, 'Blood in my eyes' was written underneath. He pushed one eye in and a popping sound occurred, followed with part of the wall sliding open. Mr. Holmes went down the small hallway and made his way to his secret den where several 24 inch flat screen computers controlled his section of surveillance. It was connected to the twenty five cameras hidden through out the house.

Sitting in his large leather chair, Mr. Holmes entered several numbers into his iPhone, activating the system. He touched the part of the screen that read surveillance and said, "Play." Within a few moments Lucifer appeared emotionless and pulled the two rings tightly and killing James. This disk started at the same spot that Mr. Holmes left it.

After he studied Lucifer's attack, viewing it over and over again trying to find any weakness in the masked man, he quietly said looking at the screen, "I don't know how we missed that, there were three of you. But our day is sure to come." Mr. Holmes began to fast forward the disk to a more recent date and time, only pausing once to review the look of hatred in Lucifer's eyes as he placed several bullets into the face of his self portrait. He hit stop when he observed Detective Michael, Detective Brian, and Officer Dell on the screen walking though his back door in cleaning uniforms. "So routine," Mr. Holmes grinned as the voice of Detective Michael came from the speaker while knocking on the door one last time.

"Hello, cleaning service…hello. Is anyone home? I guess not." Detective Michael waved Brian and Dell on, the three quickly moved through the house dusting for finger prints. Detective Michael slammed a lamp to the ground before turning over everything he came in contact with. Mr. Holmes watched them enter his master den with Detective Michael trailing close behind Detective Brian and ripping the books from the shelves he passed.

He noticed that Detective Brian was actually ready the titles, *"Now what are you looking for?"* Halfway down the wall of rare first edition books, Detective Brian's pointed finger stopped and removed a hard back book titled The Great Men of War. He quickly opened it letting his hands roam over the pages. He stopped a third of the way through the book.

"Now let's see what we've got," Mr. Holmes said while zooming in on the page and began reading out loud with Detective Brian as he followed along with the movement of his finger. *"Ryan the Brave was forced to rest for several months but his soul wanted blood. He then offered 24 bags full of gold to any warrior to bring back the head of any man who supported the four kings. He specifically ordered that no one was to touch a hair on the king's head for vengeance would be his. Ryan's willpower helped him to recover quickly as his mind remained strong, many men returned with bloody palms as they received their gold with greed filled faces. Ryan internalizing the lesson of his forefathers knew money together with loyalty was hard to find. Therefore he assigned watchers to observe his men and men to observe his watchers. After only three months, he along with a team of twenty men set out on a hunt for blood.*

Their first attack was the kingdom of Sir Edwin IV who was backed by the powers of Rome. They fought tooth and nail for 36 hours straight until the very moment Ryan slid out from behind the huge drape of the center hall with blood covering his body. He slowly removed his dagger from the case on his hip, making his way toward the gold chair soundlessly then suddenly in one quick motion, before the guards could react he brought his sharp blade down through the air and locked it under the neck of King Edwin IV, whispering, "Only if your soul knew how long I have waited for this moment, it would have let you perish before now."

Speaking out loud for the guard's attention, he screamed, "This is your king y'all brawl so hard for while you fight to the death he sat here and refused to bare arms. So fight with me together or fight me to your death." Ryan stepped back in his defensive position as Sir Edwin's head feel freely to the floor. The word traveled quickly that Ryan was alive and now owned Edwin's army, which forced the remaining three kings underground only to be found and killed one by one. Years had passed so smoothly for Ryan until the day he faced Edwin the V."

Mr. Holmes laughed thinking about how Roc did the same with the Get Money Clique, knowing the rest of the story by heart, he began to fast forward passed Detective Brian closing and tucking the gold and black book into his jacket. He then noticed Detective Michael dusting the dining room table while looking around suspiciously from Dell to

Detective Brian who was off in a distance still searching made Mr. Holmes say, "Stop…now play." Detective Michael's hand quickly reached out grasping something and had it in his pocket so fast that Mr. Holmes almost missed it.

Confused, he questioned himself, "Why would he steal an apple…" then it him, "Fuck!" He quickly rewound the disk stopping just as Lucifer spit on a man's face stating, "Taste the forbidden fruit." "There," Mr. Holmes said quietly as he paused the frame as Lucifer bit the apple. He then placed the phone to his ear, "We have a problem that could blow the plan."

An hour later he stopped out of the shower into his master bedroom to find several new designer suits with matching ties lying out across the bed. He let his fingers run over the different materials and stopped on the exact suit he killed Fatel in, "Great choice sir," said Travis as he held a box that contained shoes to accompany the wardrobe.

"Travis, when did you get here?"

"The moment you called, sir."

"So is everything moving as planned?"

"Just as you said it would, I just wish you would reconsider and let me have some men escort you back to Philly."

"See, Travis, that's where I went wrong in the first place. Roc learned to be the best because he studied me at my best. These rent-a-soldiers I'm using could never win against him."

"Does this mean you want me to call the team off of Mr. Boggy?"

"No, that will bring me the time I needed to win after he's in the ground. The present, did you deliver it?"

"Yes, personally and the young one signed for it before speeding off screaming I was making him late for a flight or something."

"Great, did you get the whereabouts on everybody that I asked for?"

"Yes, I logged them in the navigation system but we'll only have until next week because Ms. Molly said that is your time."

"Then I guess we should be on our way."

A few hours later, Travis' foot eased on to the brake slowly bringing the speed to ten mph at the top of 12th St. at a wild block in South Philly asking, "Sir are you sure about this?" as he watched the heavy flow of drug traffic moving back and forth. Young men ran to cars in butter Timbs, wife beater shirts, and baggy jeans that barely held up the 9 mm's on their hip.

"It's the only way," Mr. Holmes replied. Travis stepped on the gas while his eyes watched the men on the roof whose gun's followed the flow of the cars. Several men rushed the luxury truck and tapped on the hood and windows that made Travis jump. The people were questioning, "Fried or Harry powder, what you want?" Unsure of how to answer he said, "Sir…"

"Be easy, Travis, and pull over in the middle of the block."

"Okay, sir, but watch it, these guys are thugs. They're not like us."

"I know, that's why I'm here," Mr. Holmes said, exiting and stopping in front of a row home where about twenty men and women sat on the porch playing Play Station 3 for money. The heavy cloud of weed smoke made Mr. Holmes cough as he walked up on the old wooden frame. Pardon me gentleman, can somebody tell me where I can find Stevie Richerson?" Mr. Holmes asked, feeling that guns were being aimed at him in the distance.

"Damn, old timer, who are you?" said Tim while pushing pause and sitting his joy stick down. Mr. Holmes could tell by the diamond Rolex on the man's wrist and jewelry on his neck, along with the silence of every one that he was the block leader. "I'm Holmes, and old friend of his."

"Oh we don't know nobody, I'm just wondering how you think you could just walk up here tossing a name around like it's sweet."

"Because I see his son, Stevie Jr, right there," Mr. Holmes pointed speaking of the young man with the other joy stick pretending not to notice Mr. Holmes by keeping his vision on the TV. Mr. Holmes then said, "There is also the fact that at a time of gang warring I used to own this block and everything between, all the way down 19th St and I stopped there because it was a church on 20th St. but all this was before I gave it to your uncle Tim. So, if you would tell him Mr. Holmes is here then you can show me through the maze where ever it's at now, it's had to change over years."

The crowd started laughing, cheering on Mr. Holmes. "Okay old head, that's what's up. You used to do your thing out here?" someone yelled. "Real heavy, youngster, real heavy," Mr. Holmes responded. "I see you still got some of that bread the way you pulled up here in that spaceship while niggas is out here starving," said Adam as he watched the visitor closely plotting for his come up.

"Starving, nigga," Mr. Holmes repeated, shaking his head in disgust. "Son, for one, you're not no nigga and two I never met a real man that ever starved especially when this is your community and you got the Chinese feeding their families and sending their kids to college off both ends of the street." They looked on, loving the spark of fire in the older man's eyes and got even hyper, "That's right, old head, fuck that!" In the midst of the commotion, Stevie Jr. stepped off to the side and dialed a number on his phone.

"Yo"

"Ay, Pop, you got company."

"What?"

Stevie Jr. could hear his father's glock coking back while yelling, "Clear everything up now!"

"Wait, Pop, it's not the cops. There's some guy named Mr. Holmes saying he knows you and gave you the block. Just give the word and its done cuz Adam and them already got him lined up."

"That's because he did now bring him to me and, son…"

"Yeah?"

"If you like your friends then pass on this one, ha-ha."

Stevie Jr. stepped back on the porch to see Adam now just a few feet from Mr. Holmes with his hand in his pocket, which Stevie knew had his stainless straight razor in it. Stevie Jr. rushed in between the two noticing Mr. Holmes's hand in his suit pocket also. "Follow me, old timer."

Stevie Jr. led Mr. Holmes across the street into an abandoned building. They made their way over the broken bottles, used needles, empty dope bags, and dirty wet clothes to the upstairs. In the back room, Stevie Jr. moved a huge dresser to the side to reveal a hole in the wall, stepping into the next row house over that was even filthier.

They proceeded down until they came to the basement door where Stevie Jr. grabbed two pairs of rubber boots from an old stove. "Here, put these on, you don't have to but if you want to save them gators, you should." Mr. Holmes tailed Stevie Jr. through the two feet high water as he watched rats dash from the steps into the water doing what seemed like swimming, 'Amazing' dipping under the structure of the stairs. Stevie Jr. did a special knock on the brick wall. Seconds later a section slide back.

Mr. Holmes smiled as he stepped into the plush basement that represented nothing but class from its Italian sofa, Asian style coffee table and a pair of custom made Barcelona chairs to find his old friend Stevie Blue at the bottom of the steps. "Money Man Holmes, what brings you here to South Philly to see little old me?"

"We need to talk."

"Well let's go upstairs."

The living room was even more beautiful as the sound of money machines working echoed from behind a closed door. "Blue, I see you're still using the old burned down house routine," commented Mr. Holmes, for outside looked as if the fire had destroyed the house. Behind the living room wall were three feet of burned wood with all the windows out, so if anyone looked in, they would see nothing but wood and ashes.

"Money Man. what's on your mind?" Stevie asked. Mr. Holmes brought Stevie Blue up to speed on everything that happened between him and Roc. "And he's even tested Billy D…and made it."

"So he's become that good?"

"Better, but there are still a few tricks I had yet to teach him so…"

"I'm in!" Stevie Blue said.

An hour afterward, Travis pulled into the large parking lot in West Philly placing the vehicle into park with Mr. Holmes still not believing this to be a true question. "Blue, are you sure this is right?"

"Man, no jiving. I was just as shocked as you when I heard."

"Sir, this is the address we have on him also," added Travis.

"Well I got to see it to believe it."

Stevie Blue and Mr. Holmes pulled back the double glass doors to see two toy cops sitting at each end of the wooden table. "Gentleman, please empty your pockets and place your belongings in the basket," said Jeffery, a middle aged man as he grabbed the metal detector from the table. "Sir, you won't be needing that, I'm only going to be a minute so can you tell me what room I can find Mr. Merrick in?"

"But every person must…"

"That's my belongings," Mr. Holmes interrupted, tossing a roll of money into the basket. "Now it's yours."

"Understood, now go down the hall and knock on the last door on your right, they'll get him."

Sliding the money into his pocket, Jeffrey opened the thick metal cage letting them through before locking it behind them. Finding the office, Mr. Holmes tapped once then walked in where several young kids that could pass as men, lined the wall mean mugging while they looked him up and down.

"Excu…" Mr. Holmes started to speak and stopped when a side door with the word 'Principle' on it, swung open with aggression as Money Bags Merrick walked out with a kid's shirt gripped firmly. He jacked him up in the air from the back screaming, "Kill Moe or whatever the hell they call you, the next time you pull a knife on one of my teachers I'm not going to call your dad so he can speak up in your defense, saying my boy didn't do it. I am going to beat your ass my damn self and then see if your father will fight in your defense. Now get out of here and take your ass to detention!" he shoved Kill Moe out the door.

"Next!" screamed Money Bags Merrick s his 6' 1" frame which was still in great shape at the age of 48 returned to his desk. "That would be us but I'm not good with following orders." Looking, Money Bags jumped to his feet in shock, "My eyes must be playing tricks on me because I know this can't be Stevie Blue and Money Man Holmes in the flesh. "Knock it off, Bags, and show up some love," they all embraced, enjoying several laughs together like old times when Mr. Holmes inquired, "Now that I see it, even though I don't believe it, what happened?"

"Well, me and Sammy 'Big Block' Gators was casing out the Pardent National Bank for several weeks when ... 'Everybody get the fuck down, boom-boom-boom,' screamed Sammy and he threw his mask while pulling the trigger on his Mack 11 pointed at the ceiling. He said, "Bags, hit the safe and do what you do, we got sixty seconds." I grabbed the nervous bank manager off the ground and rushed him to the back of the room to the large vault. I said, "Open it the fuck up now or I'll blow your fucking head off, you jive turkey." I heard Sammy yell "50 seconds," while he was forcing the tellers to empty their drawers. The thick steel door swung open and I was in my element. I ran to the first beam and picked up a money bag and tossed it back down. I could tell just by the feel of its weight that the bag contained fives. I reached the hundreds and quickly filled two large black duffle bags to the rim. Sammy called, "20 seconds".

I re-entered the center of the bank with a bag over my shoulder, tossing the other to Sammy. "10 seconds, let's move!" We followed our escape route through the back door and ran into the alley. Sammy said, "You go right, I'll go left and I'll meet you at the get away car." He took off down the alley and I made it a few feet from the tip of the block when the sound of screeching tires came from somewhere behind me. I turned while moving my feet to see a black and white police car with the drivers door open as an officer with his gun out yelling, "Stop or I'll shoot."

Sammy stopped slowly raising his hands above his head. I hoped that I wasn't spotted and rushed to the wall hiding behind a trash dumpster and watched the officer slowly approach Sammy as he removed his handcuffs. Officer Wilson demanded, "Turn around!" Sammy was hesitant but turned and as he moved a little to the right, I could see the cop's face clearly when I pulled the trigger, knocking Officer Wilson off his feet. Sammy "Big Block" Gator threw a fist in the air, shaking it firmly before taking off and getting away..."

"After that I had to lay low so I went down south, took some night classes and became a teacher after a few years. I came home and here I am with a normal life. That's why I have to say no to getting the old gang back together for one last run. It sounds great but these kids need me."

"That's understandable, Money Bags, and I respect it but everyone is going to miss your presence, especially Sammy "Big Block" Gator."

"How, he's still doing that bid for that armor truck heist and they just denied him parole."

"You in or you out?" questioned Mr. Holmes with his phone to his ear.

Inside the 50 foot high wall of Graterford Penitentiary's D block, like the five other blocks, was a world within itself and there wasn't any day the same in the place. The eight hundred inmate's housed on its tier were called animals and were policed by only two correctional officers to keep the order, if there were any.

Several men stood, surrounding one of the day rooms 32 inch TV's watching the B.E.T. series *American Gangster* when Sammy "Big Block" strolled passed hearing someone say, "Damn, that nigga Frank was doing the pussy out there like that."

"Hey, that nigga's gangster, he was making like a million dollars a day." Sammy "Big Block" being an O.G. to the heart, stopped in his tracks and turned toward the T.V. to give one of his own the respect they deserved when he spotted who they spoke about. His soul started to boil. "Excuse me, excuse me," Sammy said, making his way to the TV and pulling out the plug. "Hey, old timer, what you doing?"

"Yo, yo, I'm watching that shit!"

"O.G., you bugging, cut the TV back on!"

Inmates screamed and the crowd began to get wild. "I will as soon as I say this, but I damn well know you can give me five minutes of your time because I'm a real American Gangster and that you can ask your father's father. Not like that joker on TV."

"Plus old head from North Philly so he can say what the fuck he wants to say," stated Dro who was a professional boxer in for murder as he eased the eleven inch knife from his waistline and stepped up next to Sammy "Big Block." Sammy was one of the few men he respected in this zoological garden as he liked to call it. Dro's crew, Forty and Mark stood at each exit Sammy now had everyone's full attention, "You know it saddens me to see all you guys away from your friends and families in this struggle and know that the day has finally come where a man that didn't have the heart to face the actions of his own hands, instead uses them to point out his loved one to face here." Sammy's arms stretched wide at his surrounding then he said, "But still, he's praised openly and called an O.G. Well if this is an original gangster to you, don't ever call me one again. We are nothing alike. I am and will always be the protector of my brothers and sisters, never their oppressor.

'Boom…Boom.' "Come on and open up I need to speak with Sammy," Banged C.O. Dickson on the door trying to gain access to the second half of the block as Forty refused to move and yelled, "I said wait until he's finished talking."

Sammy resumed, "I'm not here to preach to you cuz ya'll young niggas are hard headed and your fathers should have done that before you got here. I'm just setting the record straight so you'll know the real from the fake and as sure as I'm standing here, that joker is faking it." Sammy then stepped off as the cheers and applause came. Forty held the door open for him and he was greeted by C.O. Dickson with his hand extended with a green sheet in his palm. "They changed their minds Sammy, you made parole." "Why wouldn't they? A gangster is need."

A short time had passed and Sammy 'Big Block' waited for the large metal gate to open. He was dressed in a gray suit, light pink shirt and matching tie. The wardrobe couldn't be complete without his trademark big block gators on his feet. He stepped out into the captivating evening air to see Money Man Holmes, Stevie Blue and Money Bags Merrick leaning up against a stretch white limousine. "What took you so long?"

The time reached a little passed 4:00 pm as the gang reached the office building of Ground Breaking Real Estate with Stevie Blue asking, "Money Man, do you think he's still upset about you letting Roc shoot him?"

"I didn't let Roc shoot him, I just didn't stop him. But he's bigger than that."

"I don't know; Popping Tags Shorty was always known to hold a grudge."

"If so then let him say no but until then he's still my partner."

Behind the front desk sat a ravishing blond who was painting her nails as Mr. Holmes requested, "I'd like to speak to your boss about the million dollar property he has for sale." The men were quickly shown to a side room and seated around a large marble table as another sexy assistant filled their glasses with champagne.

In a back room, Popping Tags rubbed his hands together from the good news of the money he was about to make on his mind. Popping Tags entered in a Gucci double breasted suit saying, "I'm sorry for keeping you men wai…" he paused on sight of his old squad with his fake smile easing away into a look of concern. He asked, "What's wrong?"

"I have a problem and I need your help."

"Say no more."

Popping Tags hit the intercom, "Sue, go ahead and close up. Tell everyone to take a few days off with pay. I think I'm coming down with murdering cold."

Mr. Holmes slowly stood up, "Now that we're all here I think it's about time to show the student that he could never beat the teacher, and this is why…"

19

On a beach in Mexico a week later, Roc and Lil Mac's feet moved with speed along the warm sand while finishing up the last of their three mile run. NayNay and Gizelle followed along on horseback. "Come on, Mac, suck it up. There's only twenty yards to go," Roc said. "I'm with you but this bag is hard to deal with, stuck to my body."

They finished and quickly threw on their body suits. "You okay?"

"Yeah, Roc, damn, I'm hurt but still a man."

"Well, the last one to the yacht in dancing with mommy tonight," Roc yelled, taking off for the peaceful sky blue ocean with Lil Mac hot on his tail. The Fraser yachts Benetti docked a hundred yards out form the shore, possessed the enjoyment of a luxury Villa, like a heliport, full gym, a state of the art entertainment center, formal dining room and multiple decks enhanced for the privacy of the guests.

Haffee, Sakara, Top Dollar and Mrs. Miller with Jr. on her lap, sat on the top deck enjoying the beautiful view. "Hey, I remember when I used to swim like that up and down when I was a young whipper snapper myself."

"You need to stop telling stories, Top Dollar, you an Odell hated the water and he knew I loved it," corrected Mrs. Miller.

"Who said anything about water, you dig?"

Mrs. Miller quickly covered Jr.'s ears saying, "Top Dollar!"

Roc had just beaten Lil Mac by a few feet and joined his people with water dripping from his body. He rushed to his mother, wrapping his arms around her body. "Roc, stop it!" she replied.

"Come on, Dad, that's not cool getting me wet like that," Jr. said. A waiter entered with a tray of fresh drinks, "Mr. Miller, now that you've returned, brunch will be served in twenty minutes. After that, you're mountain climbing trainer will be waiting patiently."

"Thanks, Clint, will you have the captain swing around to pick up my wife. If anyone needs me I'll be in my room," Roc made his way down to the cabin, passing Manny and AP as they shot dice on the pool table. "That's the number, young buck, what you waiting on, run that money."

Roc watched AP search his own pocket like he was the police as sweat covered his forehead and hands came up empty. He said, "Yo! I am dead, let me run to my room and get some more money and I'll be right back." "Nah fam, let me get that time piece until you get right." AP dropped his iced out Movado onto the table as Manny turned toward Roc flashing a set of loaded dice with a smile. Shaking his head, Roc continued down the stairs.

After cleaning himself up he flopped down on the bed looking at his reflection off the huge ceiling mirror. He let out a deep breath wondering if leaving was the right decision while questioning himself, *"What if they cross me?"* Roc let his mind drift back to the day…

After having a great time, Gizelle led the three masked corporate men to a private side elevator in club Soldi. They rode it to the roof in silence where Roc waited in the cool night air with his back to them, looking off into the star filled sky. "Gentlemen," he stated, hearing the door close behind them. Roc slowly turned, "I see you have chosen the faces of the men that let a hustler rule the streets in the past and soon to come."

Sunan Kudari, an Asian man with brown eyes, dyed black hair that was slicked to the back and standing at 5' 10" tall and 185 lbs, removed his Reagan mask. Adrian

Cortez was the head of one of the largest Columbian Cartels and was next to take off his Clinton mask as he stared at Roc with fire in his eyes that made Roc smile.

Diego El Sovida was the last to reveal himself, dropping the face of Obama to the ground with a grin, making up the men of the Corporation. Roc with no time for delay began, "Men there are several antennas through out this rooftop making our conversation impossible to bug. Now, may I ask what's so important that brought you al the way to the United States to see little old me?" Thinking to himself, "The first person to speak is the one that's neutral because if they all agreed, I would already be dead."

"Roc, the reason why we're here is because you are being accused of killing two members of the Corporation with out permission and as you know, the penalty will be worse than death."

"Okay, Sunan Kudari is the one," Roc thought as he said aloud, "Did you say two members?"

"Yes and I believe El Sovida has the tape of you asking for permission to speak with his assassin, am I correct?"

"Yes," answered El Sovida shaking his head. Roc closed his eyes knowing the game had just been changed in the ninth inning. He reopened them to notice that Diego El Sovida's smile had gotten bigger as he started to say, "I would nev..."

"Roc, please know before you say anything there are fifty men in your club, prepared to take you down along with your loved ones if need be," Adrian Cortez cut in.

"Okay, if you're asking me if I called Diego El Sovida, yes but did I kill them, no. If I was going to, why would I ask for permission on a phone that I know is recorded by the four of us?"

"Maybe you planned to use that as your alibi," Sunan Kudari insisted.

"I said I didn't do it and why are you pointing the finger at me in disrespect when you know you can't bring me or any Corporation member up on this accusation without a witness," Roc stated as his veins began to show. He fought hard to keep his cool when the action that followed pushed him over the top when Diego El Sovida yelled, "And I got one, you bastard! How dare you, after I did what you asked leaving their body on my door step with a note taped to their chest but today you will pay!"

Enraged from the set up, Roc roared, "I swear by the blood of my father that runs through my veins, if you bring a man that is respected by us and he swears he witnessed me harm anyone in our Corporation, I will walk to your men with my head hung low."

"How did I know you would say that," Diego El Sovida replied with his hand waving and said, "Send him up."

Roc couldn't believe his eyes when the elevator opened and M-Easy stepped out and stopped next to Diego El Sovida. "M-Easy, what the hell are you doing?"

"I'm here to tell the truth."

"The truth, what! So you're going to sell me out for money?"

"Roc, stop!" demanded Sunan Kudari before turning to M-Easy. "Please, young man, will you enlighten us on what happened?"

"See, Roc said he knew Apollon and Balial were the ones that killed Lil Mac so he put a plan together to get rid of them. Once everything was in placed, Roc had them come over."

At that moment, things for Roc began to go in slow motion as he quickly pleaded to his friend, "Don't do this to me," while thinking of the summer M-Easy went to stay with Diego El Sovida. "Why didn't I see this coming?"

M-Easy finished, *"Roc walked them into the back room and I never saw them again."*

"So it's like that?" Roc asked through tightened teeth while he removed the forty five from his waist. He knew that he was the only one there with a weapon, thanks to his security team. Roc now had control of their lives in his hands. *"See how easy things changed,"* Roc thought.

Adrian Cortez started to protest then stopped as Roc released the clip and handed the gun to Sunan Kudari, *"A man's word defines his being, so take it."* Roc stepped to face Diego El Sovida, *"If this is the end, let's get it over with."* Together they headed for the elevator where thirty men waited at the bottom. Sunan Kudari broke the silence, *"Wait! This man never said he actually witnessed Roc kill them. Sir, did you see them die?"*

"No but I know he did it, he kills everything," M-Easy answered.

"Don't we all, but you just saved his life." Diego El Sovida glimpsed at Roc who had a mischievous grin on his face. But it was the look he noticed in Roc's eyes that told him he had to put an end to this situation soon. Roc mumbled so that only El Sovida could listen. *"Remember what the note said."*

Paying his words no attention, Diego El Sovida stated, *"If they didn't come out, Kudari, where did they go? You know he killed them."*

"Maybe out another door, El Sovida. I'm not saying this is over with; we shall and will get to the bottom of this. If he or whoever did it, they will pay! But the issue at hand can't be completed now. Therefore please remember it's not good to show your emotions so strongly when the answer is uncertain. You could make an enemy that wasn't originally there."

The three men re-entered the elevator with Sunan giving Roc his gun back. *"If you didn't do it, you have nothing to worry about and you will still have the right to clear your name. But if you did do it, you'll have everything to fear…"*

Roc was still laying on the comfortable king sized bed, deep in thought as the constant bumping sound coming from Lil Mac's room next door forced him to get up. He knocked on the connecting door while easing it open to see Lil Mac pulling at the colostomy bag that was attached to the left side of his body until the sensation of pain became too much for him to endure. Lil Mac then banged his fist on the dresser top, only to try again. Blood covered his hand as it reached for the bag once more when Roc snatched his wrist away.

Shocked, Lil Mac looked in Roc's direction now aware of his presence with tears of anger in his eyes. "Let me go! I'm sick of this shit being a part of me."

"Hopefully you don't have to wear it much longer. Dr. Woods is flying out next week and then we'll know if it can come off. Now get cleaned up, the food is ready," Roc said, spotting the flashing light above the door which notified him that brunch was being served. "And hurry up because you smell like shit, ha-haaaa," responded Roc. "Real funny, Roc, real funny!"

After brunch, Manny, Haffee, Roc and Lil Mac were led down a long mountain trail by Doug, their rock climbing instructor. They stopped at the rim of a three level waterfall where a twenty five foot wall was placed for beginners. Doug said, "Gentleman, you have been up this wall several times, today we will do it for speed."

"What about that one?" replied Roc pointing to the fifty foot high waterfall.

"No sir, Roc, you're good but that still may be a little too dangerous for you and your team."

"Well we like danger, Mac you take point. Haffee, you play the right wing. Manny, you go left and I'll bring up the rear," Roc stated.

"Roc sir, please be careful. One slip-up after you clear the first wall and you will fall to your death," responded Doug.

"Then you better make sure you catch me."

Lil Mac leading the pack stepped to the wall looking for the best path to attack with room for his two wingmen. Spotting it, he tightened the safety rope around his waist as he blitzed the wall with a passion, honored that Roc would entrust their lives in his hands. Lil Mac used his 6'' 1" frame to his advantage making it halfway up the first part of the wall in no time. He secured the two ropes into the mountain structure before dropping them to Manny and Haffee. They moved with speed, advancing at the same pace across from each other. Roc brought up the rear, loving the feeling of nature's power as he moved through the strong current of water rushing over his face.

Doug watched their operative-ness as they proceeded to the third level when Roc yelled, "Triangle offense." Lil Mac gripped the rope tightly before kicking off the wall, feeding the slack of the rope into the support ring and sliding down until he was now in the middle while Manny pulled his body up into the front.

Roc followed suit but stopped next to Lil Mac. Haffee quickly moved over to the left side of Lil Mac as if they made a wall that protected each side from being invaded. "Damn, these guys must have done this before," Doug said in amazement.

Returning back to the yacht, the men were met by Gizelle and NayNay who said with her hand extended, "Lil Mac, your present keeps ringing." A soon as he saw it he remembered the velvet box with a red bow was delivered for Roc at mom's house. Roc quickly unwrapped the box to find an iPhone with a note that read, "Son, no one can become strong without things like adversary, resistance and problems. These are all struggles that make our inner self grow stronger. Therefore a threat foreseen is half avoided."

Distinguishing the hidden message, which was a quote by Thomas Fuller, Roc turned to Manny demanding, "Call Boggy, they're going to try to kill him now!" Just then, the phone began to ring. Roc placed it to his ear and the voice of Mr. Holmes asked, "Are you ready for this?"

20

A thick cloud of kush weed smoke flowed through a packed row home in North Philly. Boggy, Fox and Inch as well as some of Boggy's block runners sat in a circle surrounding two local junkies, Jeff and Blue as they stood in the center of the living room, waiting on their prize to be revealed while preparing to fight. Jeff was the taller of the two, standing at 6'1" and 175 pounds. Blue was only 5' 10" and 190 pounds.

"Let's get it popping," yelled Boggy letting the gray smoke escape his lungs before passing the blunt to Buff's little brother Inch saying, "Now remember what I said. You weren't with me nigga and if you go to jail, you got to sit until they give you ten percent. I don't know what Roc was thinking about."

Boggy placed an eight ball of crack onto the night stand and spoke, "The winner by way of knock out will receive the best fried cocaine in the city along with an all expense paid around the world trip on Nekea. "On cue, Nekea, who you could tell used to be beautiful before the drugs, walked down the stairs wearing an old thong that vanished into the crack of her large stretch marked ass with a matching bra. She walked in the center of the circle, opening her legs wide while sliding the thong to the side and revealing her big hairy love box lips as two glass pipes fell from her insides. Picking them up, she laid them next to the eight ball. "These are for us baby and I'll be up stairs waiting," she said. The crowd went into an uproar of cheers as they smacked her ass as she passed by.

"Man, I love this shit. Fuck the Onyx Night Club, this is the strip thuggin," yelled Fox snatching the blunt from Inch's lips. Jeff watched Nekea's ass jiggle back and forth up the steps thinking, "I'm going to hit that ass one time then she got to go, she's not smoking up all my shit!"

Immediately, a right hook slammed into his eye and several stars appeared in his vision. He fought to keep his balance. Blue smiled, seeing Jeff stumbling back and let a hard left go, following behind the right to his jaw. Jeff's feet flew out from under him as he crashed into the circle of onlookers that pushed him roughly to the floor. Someone punched him in the back of the head.

Blue was back on top of him in seconds as he rushed him, swinging haymakers and jabs. Jeff tried to duck while attempting to make it to his feet when a punch landed to the side of his rib cage, making him fall back to the ground. Jeff knew that if he stayed there he was as good as finished. He quickly rolled over onto his back hearing Blue's footsteps and began to kick wildly. The sole of his holey Nike slammed into Blue's forehead and sent him back across the room into a man, making him spill his beer on his self. The man yelled, "Oh, you stinking base head!" He mugged Blue in the face and pushed him to the floor.

Already on his feet, Jeff wrapped his arms around Blue's waist, lifting him high in the air and bringing him down as hard as he could on his neck and back. "HAAAAAHH," Blue screamed in agony as his shoulder blade cracked. He lay there limp and Blue screamed, "Alright, I give up; you got it."

Jeff squeezed him tightly from the back around the neck choking him while pulling him up to his feet. Spit covered Jeff's forearm and wrist as he squeezed tighter before running Blue's un-resistant body face first into the wall. Jeff turned to look at Boggy screaming, "Put another piece of rock on the table and I'll kill him!" Again the crowd was hype as they watched Blue hold on for dear life. Boggy started to give the okay when his phone started to ring.

"Hello. What? Calm down, Alexis, everything's going to be alright I'm on my way." Boggy jumped up checking the chamber of his 9 mm before tossing the keys to his Ranger Rover to Fox. "You drive, let's move!"

The three made their way for the door when asked, "Do you need any of us?"

"No, this is squad business….and Jeff, let that nigga go!" Boggy slammed the passenger door to find young Bucky, the neighborhood kid that did every kind of hustle for a dollar, standing at his door begging, "Come on, Boggy, let me go with you. I can watch your back like no body else."

"I'm telling you this street life is too much for you right now. So get back up the block and do what I pay you to do and that's to yell when you see the cops, that's all," Boggy instructed.

"Please, Boggy, you said it's ride or die and I got my own gun." Bucky removed a 38 revolver from his jacket pocket. "See, and my shit don't jam it pops at will," he said. Boggy shook his head at the sight of the 14 year old kid holding a weapon like he was ready to take a life. "Bucky, you really want to go with me?"

"No doubt," Bucky answered hyped up, pulling on the locked door.

"Then if you're really hard, kill a nigga on twitter then take it to trial and beat it. Then you can ride with me." Fox pulled out into traffic as Boggy dialed Mohammed's phone, reaching his voice mail and stated, "Yo, Mohammed, somebody tried to break into Roc's club, I'll meet you there."

Ten minutes later the Range Rover pulled to a stop in front of Soldi to find Alexis, one of Roc's club manager's in tears. Boggy was out the truck in a second with rage in his eyes for the thought that someone in his city would think of disrespecting their place. He asked, "What happened?

"I was at my desk going over some paperwork for the shipment to Miami when I heard a noise coming from the back office. I thought it was Roc or you so I went down to the hall and saw four men in masks with guns searching Roc's office, they were looking for something. I got out of there before they could see me and that's when I called you."

"Who else did you call," Fox questioned.

"Nobody, I work for Roc, I know the rules," Alexis replied.

"Alright you did good, now get in the truck," ordered Boggy while turning to Fox and saying, "Come on, you take the back, I'm going through the front." Then he spotted Inch exiting the truck, thinking not again, "No you stay here and look after Alexis, I can't have your blood on my hands. Roc would kill me then Buff once I get we're I'm going."

"Come on, Boggy, I went on route with Buff before," Inch pleaded.

"I know, now get in the Range."

Boggy cased the door open to the dimly lit club, slowly closing it behind him. He paused in a shadow of darkness and listened to see if he could here any movement. He moved low down the center row of an aisle using the booth for cover, stopping behind a large beam that gave him a view of the left side of the club. With his gun leveled and his eyes on the back door, he whispered, "Now."

Seconds after, Fox appeared in his sight proceeding through the back door with two glocks pointed and moving them back and forth in front of him. Boggy gave him a head nod in the direction of the elevator and repeatedly ran his finger up and down on the hand grip of his pistol, anxious for the action he was about to face. "Roc this is what we do, never run but I'm not mad at you."

The elevator doors came open with Boggy walking out first and Fox followed, covering his back. The two moved through the hallway with their weapons motioned and waiting on the slightest movement to put it to an end. They carefully secured every room they passed until they reached Roc's office. Boggy placed his ear to the door and heard movement, he stepped away slowly and whispered, "They're still here," pointing to the door and giving Fox the signal.

Fox raised his foot preparing to kick it in when Boggy with a puzzled look on his face, raised his hand and stopped him. "What?" Fox said. Boggy shook his head, "Youngster." Before leveling off his gun and pulling the trigger several times. Screaming came from behind the door, "Now!" Boggy ordered. Fox kicked the door open to find two men. One was hit in his mid section and the other had a gun shot to his right leg.

A shadow of a man dashing for cover caught the attention of Fox as he stepped in the room firing 'BOOM-BOOM.' The flash from his gun lit up the room's darkness as he shot the first wounded man in the face and the next in the chest. In his stride he took cover beside a flying cabinet as a shot that was aimed for his head missed him and slammed into the metal cabinet nearby.

Boggy reloaded and returned fire using the light from the hallway to catch a glimpse of the man for a second before his bullet entered the man's neck and he collapsed. Boggy swung his firearm towards the remaining man but before he could complete the motion, several shots forced him back out the door.

Fox smiled at the fact that it was now one on one. He moved his head gradually forward to the edge of the cabinet to get a peek at his opponent's position. A spark suddenly blinded him as a bullet ricocheted a half inch from his face. Back shielded by the cabinet, Fox took in a deep breath as he thought, "*This motherfucker damn near took my eye out. I'm going to kill 'em.*" Then the words, "It's ride ordie time," entered his ears as Boggy rushed back into the room with his gun aimed and leveled on the man whose weapon was pointed at Fox. He fired two shots into the desk top frame, hitting the man in both legs. "Aaaaahhhh," fighting back the pain the man swung his gun on Boggy just as three shots ripped through his chest. Fox, visibly angered, watched the body fall with Boggy jumping onto the desk and emptying out his clip in the man's figure.

Boggy quickly began to search the body of the three uninvited guests when the sound of rapid gunfire erupting, demanded his attention. Standing up he ran to the surveillance monitor with Fox at his side. He activated it to witness Inch standing in front of the Range squeezing the trigger of his Glock-40, engaged in a heated gun battle between him and Sammy 'Big Block' Gators as he raced for his get away car with Money Bags holding the door open.

"Come on!" Boggy and Fox took off for the stairs, making it to the second floor. While outside Sammy 'Big Block' Gators dove into the passenger seat as Money Bags Merrick's foot smashed down on the gas pedal asking, "Is it finished?" "You better say it," smiled Sammy 'Big Block' while removing the detonator from his jacket pocket. "Bye-bye," his hand made contact as Money Bags watched his review mirror seeing Soldi suddenly explode.

21

Moments earlier, inside a Dunkin Donuts, Detective Michael and Detective Brian sat in a booth by the window that gave them a great view of Market St. Detective Michael with a lot on his mind from the news he had just received an hour ago, stared out the window at a man in a freshly waxed Benz with his music blasting as he was stopped at a light. *"There's another drug deal that should be behind bars,"* he thought.

"Michael, Michael!" Detective Brian yelled.

"Huh?"

"I said, what did the lab come back with on that apple you took?"

"I don't know, it hasn't come in yet but he said as soon as he finds a match to the DNA he would fax it to me."

"Who's he? Because today on my way to work I stopped by the lab center and they said you haven't brought any evidence in there in quite some time," questioned Detective Brian while studying Detective Michael's face.

"Because I didn't take it to the center, I thought I'd try something different this time."

"But what if there's a connection with the blood sample we took from the rugs. The evidence won't stand up in court."

"At least we will know the evidence."

"And what's that supposed to mean?"

Detective Michael looked at Brian in the eyes and was about to answer as the voice of Officer Dell came through their walkie talkie. "Requesting Detective Brian or Detective Michael respond, copy" Clutching his radio from his hip, "This is Michael, Dell, what's the status?"

"He finally stopped."

"Where?"

"At a small row house on 7th and Diamond in North Philly"

"We're on our way." They quickly took their belongings while Detective. Brian tossed a ten dollar bill on the table and ran for the door. "Come on, Michael, if you drive we'll be there in five minutes."

Ten minutes later a Chevrolet Malibu crept down 7th St and Detective Michael was behind the wheel. His eyes roamed around in the gloomy night and he still almost didn't recognize Officer Dell in his disguise as he stood with a full beard, black Kufi, and Levis jeans that were cut off at the ankle. Detective Michael pulled over at the end of the block and killed the engine as they waited for instructions.

Officer Dell made sure he wasn't being watched before going down the small alleyway beside an old lifeless house. He quickly unlocked the back fence undetected, looking around once again and said, "Now come down the side alley and make it quick because if they spot Michael, he's as good as dead."

Finding Dell, they blended into the shadow of the houses until they reached a window. Peeping through, Detective Michael was the first to spot Mohammed as he came down the stairs making his way to the kitchen. Removing his weapon from his holster, he stated, "This man is an ex-war solider who was dishonorably discharged for over aggressive force. He's known to be armed and dangerous and is already on the run for two murders while wanted for questioning in several others. So shoot first and toe tag him later!" Detective Brian being the officer in charge said, "Okay this is how we're going to do this, Michael you take the back door. Dell you jimmy the window right there," Detective Brian pointed to the weak frame of the basement window and continued, "I'll take the front door and once every one is in position we move in on three."

Detective Brian watched as Dell gained access with ease before walking around to the front door. Detective Michael approached the old wooden frame, thinking, *"Now we will know the truth."* Then stated, "One in position" "Two in position" Brian taking in a deep breath and letting it out slowly, began to count, "One…"

Inside the kitchen, Mohammed ran the warm water over his hands three times then the same for his mouth and nose, in preparation for Isha Prayer. He entered the living room laying his rung on the floor and withdrawing his shoes. In a calm tone he said, "Allah Akbar," while raising his hand high to his ear before crossing them onto his chest. He lowered his head to the ground, locking his vision on the center of his rung and refusing to move them. Mohammed gave all his attention to his Lord. He began to recite the Qu'ran, "Bismillaahir Rahmaanir Raheem," when Detectives Michael and Brian entered the room at the same time with their weapons positioned on him.

"Put your damn hands above your head slowly!" yelled Detective Michael.

"Qul Huwallaah Ahad"

"It's over, Mohammed, now slowly lock your hands behind your head and this is the last time I'm asking."

Undisturbed by his visitor's presence, Mohammed continued to fulfill his obligation as a Muslim. He believed that to break his prayer in a time of anger, is an act of disbelief. "Subhana Rabbiyal."

Detective Michael gave a nod as they both quickly rushed Mohammed on queue. Detective Michael rammed his knee hard into Mohammed's chest from behind while roughly pulling his hands behind his back. "Aaaahhh, laa ilaaha illallahu," Mohammed yelled as they slammed him down aggressively in a hard wood chair. Detective Michael then slapped him hard across the face. "Now shut the hell up with that damn crazy talk!"

Mohammed tasted the blood from his lip and began to speak even louder while refusing to break his concentration. "I said stop it," Detective Michael screamed with his hand in the air ready to strike again when Detective. Brian snatched his arm and stopped him. "Wait, let him finish."

"Finish what? Talking gibberish?"

"No, begging for forgiveness."

"And how the fuck do you know?"

"Because he's saying, God I seek refuge in you from Satan the outcast."

Mohammed slowly raised his head to see the three officers and smiled before spitting his blood filled saliva in the face of Detective Michael, saying, "I knew I should have killed you and shelly as I planned."

Fear and anger instantly took control of Detective Michael's body as the name of his wife rolled from the mouth of a known killer. "Aaaaahhhh, you bastard!" He hollered while kicking Mohammed with all his might in the chin and sending him crashing back over the chair onto his back.

Rushing him, Detective Michael began to pistol whip Mohammed as speckles of blood flew with every blow when the butt of the gun slammed into Mohammed. Officer Dell reacted and fought to restrain an out of control Detective Michael. "Stop, Michael, you're going to kill him!"

"Yeah Michael, we can't let him get off that easily. He must face justice." They fought for another few minutes to get Michael back to his feet and calmed down. "I'm fine, I'm fine. You can let go of me now." Detective Michael readjusted his shirt.

"I pray that Allah permits me to die at the hands of my enemy then I would be granted paradise," Mohammed stated.

"Then if you don't cooperate, your prayers will be answered," replied Michael, placing Mohammed back up right on the chair in the center of the fairly lit living room where there was nothing but one small safe and a lamp sitting on a night stand. The motion of Mohammed's phone vibrating made Dell jump, thinking it was a bomb. "Don't worry, I'll get it," Detective Brian placed it to his ear just missing Boggy's call.

Detective Michael snatched the lamp and removed the top, placing the bulb an inch away from Mohammed's face. "First you're going to tell me how you know my wife. Then you're going to tell me who killed my partner, Detective Rayfield, now start talking!"

Mohammed began coughing to clear the thick liquid from his throat and again spat at Detective Michael, hitting him on the leg and asking, "Are you sure you want to know the truth about the people you cherish so deep in your heart? Haa-haa!" Mohammed laughed.

"This man is crazy, Michael. Come on get up and let's take him to the station."

"No, I want to hear this now!"

"But you can't possibly think you can believe any thing this maniac has to say."

"Well, let me be the judge of that."

"Yeah, Brian, he wants to know," said Mohammed, now meeting Detective. Michael's stare with the same rage and hatred while continuing, "I met your pretty little wife the same way you did, through Detective Rayfield."

"What?"

"Remember the day you were assigned as partners, you talked all about being a D.E.A, haaaa…"

"Captain Citric walked an anxious Detective Michael through the 39th station stopping at a desk that read 'Detective Josh Rayfield.' Rayfield was sitting in his chair with his feet up on his desk as he spoke on the phone with one of his informants, "I don't give a damn if his mom died, the wire tap runs out in two days so you have to make the buy before then."

"But…"

"There are no buts! I don't care if you got to make the purchase at the casket, just make it!" Detective Rayfield slammed the phone down on the cradle. "Sorry for keeping you waiting, Captain."

"No problem, Rayfield, I'd like you to meet our top rookie, Detective Michael, your new partner."

"What!" Detective Rayfield was on his feet quickly. "Will you excuse us, Michael? Captain, you've got to be kidding me. I can't take on a partner right now. Let alone a rookie, he's not going to do anything but slow me down."

"I know but you're the best detective I've got and you said it yourself, you don't have too many years left. You have to pass that knowledge to someone, why not the best in the nation if we've got him. Not only that but I'll owe you one."

"Owe me, I like the sound of that but it's going to be big!"

"Rayfield, I'm sorry about that, just dropping me off on you."

"Don't worry about it kid, you see that stack of folders on the left side of my desk, that's our case load."

"Yeah."

"Well, that's where you will start." Beginning, Detective Michael read over several cases when he spotted a file on the right with Roc's name written on it in bold red letters. Picking it up, he asked, "Detective Rayfield, what about this one?"

Seeing it, Rayfield snatched it from his hand. "There's nothing happening with it, I said on the left side."

"I know, I'm sorry but I heard so much about the famous Roc, I know if we bring him down it would be kind of the big break I need to become D.E.A."

"So does everyone else but I'll tell you what, you close all those cases and I'll think about letting you in on the case I'm building."

Two years later inside a courtroom, the jury came back with a guilty verdict on all counts for Ericson "ET" Turner. Detective Michael turned to Rayfield and said, "That's the last one."

"I still don't think you're..." "Come on, Rayfield, I cleared that case load three times and nothing personal, but if you don't want to let me in I'm going to the captain and have him give it to me on my own..."

"Haaaaa," Mohammed continued to laugh, "You asked him for this after he begged you to let it be. He knew it was so much bigger than that small mind of yours! But no, you had to get M-Easy locked up and that was your first major mistake..."

Inside a stolen tinted Maxima with Mohammed in the driver's seat, Shamone was in the back seat while Detective Rayfield occupied the passenger seat saying, "He lives in the third house from the end. I tried to tell him to back off M-Easy because I knew this would happen the way Roc cares about him, but tell boss if he gives me a little bit more time I think I can bring him over also."

"And who's that?" *Mohammed asked while pointing at the woman handing Detective Michael his bagged lunch.*

"Oh that's Shelly; she's a friend of ours. I introduced him to her."

"But what if she gets in the way?"

"I didn't say she was my friend."

Mohammed lifted the armrest to reveal a large yellow envelope filled with hundreds. Detective Rayfield immediately slid it into his pocket saying, "Now you're talking my language, while exiting...."

"I don't believe it you piece of shit!" Detective Michael yelled, stopping Mohammed's story while throwing several punches to Mohammed's face. "Why would you lie on him like that Rayfield was a good cop and friend?"

"That's enough, Dell, go and get the car while I clean this man up for booking."

"Mohammed shook his head to clear his vision and gather himself after being hit in the head. "It's funny how those same words got him killed and you also. Rayfield wasn't the first or the last we have in..."

"That's enough, on your feet buddy!"

"Wait," Detective Michael took hold of Detective Brian's hand that held Mohammed's handcuffs. "I deserve to at least hear it." Detective Brian was uncertain about this but stepped to the side as Michael handed him the lamp. He then quickly raised his gun to Mohammed's forehead and cocked it, "You know, Mohammed, your paradise is really close, I can smell it and I will grant your wish if you tell me who killed Rayfield."

"That's easy but why don't I tell you the reason first," Mohammed smiled.

"Remember...in the visiting room at CFCF county jail, Haffee sat at the table in a hard wood chair waiting on his lawyer Sam Clinton. Detective Rayfield and Detective Michael walked in asking, "How are you doing, Mr. Mayo?" Haffee stood up quickly and headed for the door with Detective Rayfield blocking his path. "Let me out of here pig! I'm not with that rat shit."

"Mr. Mayo, please have a seat, we just want to talk to you and you don't even have to say a word if you don't want to," he replied.

"Yeah you're right." Haffee knocked hard on the glass window, "Yo, C.O., get me out of here and take me back to my cell," Haffee's request was paid no mind. Detective Michael stated, "See, it's not that easy to get rid of us."

For hours they offered Haffee several deals to cooperate against Roc. Everything from letting him go, to paying him money. He refused every offer. "See, Rayfield, I told you this good for nothing piece of shit wouldn't know a good deal if it bit him in the ass."

"Haffee jumped up again and threw a punch at Detective Michael hitting him right in the face. HE tried to follow with a short left just as Detective Rayfield gripped him from behind as his partner got himself together. "You dirty bastard!" Detective Michael screamed before hitting Haffee with several punches to his rib cage and ending with an upper cut to the face. Twenty minutes after this the detectives were on their way back to the station. Detective Rayfield's phone rang.

"Hello."

"You know he must die now for the disrespect."

"But he didn't start it"

"I don't care, boss said finish him…"

Mohammed looked into Detective Michael's eyes and said, "But he couldn't finish you so I finished him but only after feeding him dog scraps for a year with piss calling it formula sixty! Ha-ha-ha," Mohammed laughed again, loving the look on Michael's face.

"You bastard, you fucking cock sucker!" Detective Michael's finger eased back on the trigger ready to fire and remembering the day that Mohammed spoke of, like it was yesterday. The lamp suddenly fell to the floor out of

Detective Brian's hand, breaking the light bulb and sending the room into complete darkness. Mohammed's feet dashed across the floor. Detective Michael swung his gun to where he sensed the movement as did Detective Brian.

They both pulled the trigger as a loud scream erupted at the time of the guns going off. Officer Dell couldn't believe his eyes as he watched from the kitchen door way. He ran into the room finding the light switch, he quickly got to the floor scooping up a bloody Detective Michael in his arms. "Breathe, Michael, just breathe and relax. Don't worry you'll be fine. Officer down! I repeat officer down on 7th St, officer in need of assistance."

Detective Brian re-entered the room after chasing Mohammed saying, "He got away!" Just then he observed Detective. Michael's helplessly laying there. "Oh shit!" Brian rushed to his aid asking, "What happen?"

"You know what happen, you shot him!"

"I did? It was a mistake, it was dark. I'm so sorry, Michael."

Michael was on a stretcher in the back of ambulance within a matter of minutes while undercover Officer Dell jumped in with him. Detective Brian stopped him, "No, I'm going; he's my partner," he said. Without moving, Dell looked to Detective Michael who shook his head in agreement. The EMT placed an I.V. into his arm and Officer Dell jumped down walking passed Detective Brian without saying a word. He headed over to help the fifty officer's searching the area for clues.

The red and yellow lights flashed in the night as the ambulance made it to Temple Hospital. Detective Michael fought to keep his consciousness while continued to lose blood. "Hold on Michael, hey can this thing go any faster?"

"Sir we'll be there soon."

"Michael you hear that!"

"Brian."

"I'm here Michael"

"How did you know?"

"Know what?"

"How did you know about the apple when I never told you?"

Detective Brian stared out in a daze as they removed Detective Michael from the ambulance and wheeled him into the emergency room.

22

Roc wasn't sure how he was to take Mr. Holmes question and asked, "What do you mean by am I ready…for what?"

"I don't know I guess while trying to get a level of understanding with you, I got a little out of hand but I think you should be the judge for yourself."

The phone disconnected, leaving Roc more confused while his mind shifted into overdrive because knowing Mr. Holmes, there was something up his sleeve and there was something different about his voice. Roc hoped that he could put his finger on it when his thoughts were interrupted as the phone rang once again.

"You've got mail." The first picture that came through on the phone caught Roc totally off guard as he witnessed the premiere brown stone he brought his mother burning to the ground. The next photo showed his club, Soldi up in a blaze of flames as well, followed by a snap shot of Detective Brian, Dell and Detective Michael surrounding Mohammed's home.

"Nooooo!" Roc screamed as his hands began to tremble and the fury built within him. He brought his arm back, ready to toss the phone deep into the ocean then the ringing sound that came from it stopped him, "What do you think? I went a little overboard. I know, Roc, you don't have to tell me but things happen. And there can be a lot more where that came from."

"And what do you think I'm going to be doing while you're trying to destroy everything I've built?" Roc questioned firmly.

"Just what I taught you to do, always play to win. That's why I hope that you will accept this level of understanding."

"What are the terms?"

"At six o'clock, I will be live on Molly's show. Make sure you're watching and you will know then."

Tossing the phone into the water, Roc looked at his watch. *"5:30 pm, there's not enough time,"* he thought reaching for his own phone. Roc tried Boggy's number once again and got no answer. He dialed Mohammed, who picked up on the third ring. "Boss"

"Mohammed, I may have a location on Mr. Holmes."

"Okay, boss, give it to me and I'm on it."

"Mohammed, why are you breathing so hard?"

"Oh, them Kafurs gave me four cracked ribs but they're not broke, I can handle it."

Roc could hear Mohammed taping himself up in the background and said, "Stand down."

"But, boss, I can handle it, just give me the address."

"I know you can but I need you to do something more important."

"Name it."

"Take care of yourself and when you're done, make sure Boggy is alright also."

Roc lowered the phone from his ear, staring out into the open sea as the powerful yacht sliced through the large wave. Gizelle walked up beside her man, placing her arms around his waist. "You know everything is going to be just fine, baby. All you have to do is ask God for help."

"That's it," Roc quickly picked Gizelle up high into the air kissing her enthusiastically. "You know sometimes I don't know what I would do without you," he said, kissing her again. "Have everyone meet in the movie theatre now."

"Okay, you know it's great to see you're finally putting things in God's hands."

"Baby, I will one day, I promise but right now I'm going with the devil."

Roc walked away as Gizelle stood there lost as he dialed * 411.

At 6:06 pm from a comfortable seat inside the movie room, Roc studied the background closely as Molly began to talk, *"Welcome to another episode of In the Mean Streets."* "It's his home in South Philly"

"I know the address," shutting his phone, Roc sat back and listened as Molly introduced Mr. Holmes. *"Ladies and gentleman, today I have a surprise for the world as I bring you an exclusive interview with the one and only, Mr. Vernon Holmes." The camera zoomed in on a relaxed Mr. Holmes dressed in a double breasted Armani black suit and peach handkerchief with his legs crossed, taking a deep pull of his Cuban cigar.*

Molly continued, "I know what you're thinking but agent Giles said...well, he was wrong."

"Indeed so," Mr. Holmes added, letting the smoke escaped his lungs.

"Mr. Holmes, now that you're here and well, thank God. Can you explain what actually happened that day at the private airport?"

"Well first and foremost I didn't see any faces plus, I'm a business man. I wouldn't recognize anyone in that fashion of trade anyway."

"Agent Giles stated, if I may quote, that you're one of the most infamous criminals unknown to the public. They have been trying to catch you in the act for years. What do you have to say about that?"

"Agent Giles sounds like a fool to admit to the people who are paying his salary that he has been after me.

Well...here I am in Philly, enjoying the hospitality of my own home."

Roc, at the sound of his words shook his head from side to side, hitting redial and getting no response, *"Damn, I almost forgot how crafty you really are old head,"* he said under his breath while watching the word 'Live' written at the top of the screen. He continued to listen to Mr. Holmes attentively.

"Now here I am having a nice time, playing a few games of black jack with an old friend," Mr. Holmes *lowered his head in disbelief as he wiped away a fake tear,* *"God bless his soul, Don Antigeo, sat down beside me and I could see he was in trouble. Because when you truly care for someone you can tell when they're not being themselves. He then indicated that he had been indicted for reasons of a set up and that the police were trying to kill him."*

"Wait, did I hear you right...you said the police?"

"Yes, Molly that's why it took me so long to come back from Mexico because I knew I would be as good as dead if I didn't come here and stayed there to get a level of understanding first."

"Did he state which officer?"

"Yes one, Detective Michael Johnson of the 39th precinct."

Roc eased up from his seat making eyes contact with Lil Mac before stepping out into the hallway. Lil Mac waited five minutes then followed his brother's lead. Roc held the elevator door open for him and once inside, they both remained silent, waiting on the door to close completely when Haffee stepped in saying, "Count me in, Roc. This life of a square I'm living is not for me."

"What are you talking about Haffee? I'm done like you, I'm now retired. I'm sorry my heart just isn't in it no more. My family has won and the streets lost. I just don't have the edge to win no more; I'm second guessing my decisions and someone may get hurt following my orders. So if I can't lead them right, I won't lead them at all. I'll be calling Mr. Holmes telling him I accept his level of understanding."

Haffee stood there perplexed because the look he saw over a hundred times before in Roc's eyes was one of a mystified determination to win at all costs. "Thank you, Roc." Haffee slowly turned in the direction of the voice behind to find a tearful eyed Gizelle.

"You're welcome, now tell everyone to get ready. We're moving location."

"Why, Roc?" asked Lil Mac.

"Because Mr. Holmes knows we're here."

"How you know?"

"Because he never was in Mexico, we are and he was talking about us."

Back in Philly, a quarter mile away from Mr. Holmes's house. Lucifer dressed in camouflage fatigue sat in a tree, letting his binoculars scope the area. He gradually moved from the left to the right s he examined the two C.V.T.V news vans parked in the driveway, the four heavily armed men that secured the perimeter, and the bright light glowing from the living room.

"He's in there," Lucifer's eyes stopped on a silver box that hung on the bridge of a telephone pole. *"Watch it, the box will be rigged with a high voltage power line that will kill you the instant you touch it."* Lucifer remembered the instructions of Roc and let his binoculars continue to flow, *"Follow the left wire coming from the box, that's the real hot wire and it will lead you to the security system."* Lucifer smiled as he spotted the second box hidden in the ground at the base of the fence. He dropped from the high tree rolling on impact to lessen the sound. At the stolen van he retrieved the weapons and tools needed to complete his mission and placed them in his back pack before sliding the two blood stained rings onto his finger.

Lucifer checked his watch with ten seconds remaining in the guard's rotation to restart. He began to say, "I will attack them from the front," then took off running at full speed, needing to beat the time of one minute and twenty seconds or his cover would be blown. He would then lose what may be the only chance to catch Mr. Holmes by surprise. He reached the fence with only 30 seconds to spare as the strong buzzing sound of the flow of electricity vibrating through the metal fence, warned him of danger.

Swiftly, he slid one hand under the bottom wire that was only separated by two inches from the other. The power made the hair on his wrist stand up as his watch showed the remaining seconds, 25…24…23, while his other hand crept between the wire towards the box, 22…21…20. He popped the steel top, "*You must be careful; Mr. Holmes changes his colors, placing them in reverse.*" Lucifer looked at the red then the black ground wire, killing the buzzing sound immediately, 19…18, with a push from the ground he was back on his feet moving across the remaining acre.

"*They're connected to the guest room that will be your best entry point.*" Looking up at the all white stone balcony, estimating the distance to be about twenty feet, Lucifer sent the grappling hook flowing through the air. The steel object made contact in between two bars. He pulled hard testing his weight, content he whispered, "I will attack from the side," while moving up the rope with his legs spread wide and using only his hands, one over the other, pulling his body through the air with each touch until he reached the top.

Bending down, concealed behind a lounge chair with his head poked out just above the edge of the balcony, he paused…01…01…00. His watch vibrated just as the two armed men walked around the corner. "*Right on time*" The second group of men followed in a thirty second delay. Lucifer knew his time for revenge had finally come. He slightly pulled the glass divider back, stepping into the pitch black room. Taking in a deep breath, he smelled nothing, *"That's a strange emotion."* He moved slowly down the hallway as he heard the voice of Mr. Holmes saying, *"I'm telling you this, Molly, for only one reason and that's because Don Antigeo was a true friend of mine."*

"Mr. Holmes, aren't you afraid for your life?"

"Why should I be, Molly? Because if I have any say in the matter, I'll live a long time."

Lucifer grinned, *"Well, once I behead you, there won't be anything to talk about,"* he said quietly, spreading the rings to reveal the razor sharp wire. Making his way down the steps, where he spotted the shadow of Mr. Holmes, Molly and the camera man through the heavy lights placed around the room, Lucifer began to taste his revenge while visualizing his attack. *"I'll kill him then the woman, leaving the camera man for last, not to let the viewers down. Then I will disappear like a thief in the night."*

He hit the last step and dashed for the living room, taking three large steps and he was in the air as the sound of feet moving behind him echoed. The moment Lucifer's feet hit the carpet; he went into the action sending a round house kick to Molly's face, knocking her from the sofa while wrapping the wire around the head of Mr. Holmes. He tightened his grip and pulled, disconnecting it with ease; a little too easy for Lucifer as he looked down at the cardboard head, recognizing that he had just been set up by seeing the small tape recorder on the back of the card board body with Mr. Holmes's voice continuing to play.

Roc's statement then entered his mind, *"But be extremely cautious because this man is like no one you have yet to meet."* Raising his head, Lucifer was met counter clock wise by Stevie Blue and Sammy 'Big Block' Gators who stepped in from the top right side door. Money Bags exited the stairs and posted in the center of the room. The left side door swung open with Travis walking through as his palms held a 9 mm in each hand like every man in the room.

Mr. Holmes was the last to appear, dressed in a cream suit and the same devilish smile upon his face that he had when he killed Lucifer's brothers. "A stratagem," Lucifer stated at the sight of him. "Did you really think you were good enough to get me alone after I killed your two brothers?" questioned Mr. Holmes while leveling off his Ruger at Lucifer's head and before Lucifer could answer, all five weapons exploded until they kicked back empty. 'BOOM-BOOM' Money Bags and Stevie Blue quickly took on the job of cleaning up the body.

Mr. Holmes approached Travis and removed the gun from his shaking hands. "Now you have your revenge on the man who killed your nephew Paul. Now how are you so different than these men?" Mr. Holmes left Travis puzzled, and headed for the master den with Sammy 'Big Block' at his side and ready to continue their game of chess then Mr. Holmes's phone started to ring.

"Hello?"

"Mr. Holmes."

"Roc, you know I had a feeling you were going to call"

"Well, I did and I think it would be best that I take you up on your offer of understanding to stop everything here and now."

"That's great because it doesn't feel right going to war with you anyway. But, you still have the issue with the corporation and you didn't hear it from me. This morning they scheduled another hearing on you for those two killings. The day after tomorrow in Miami"

"I know, they already called me."

"I hope you win, Roc, I really do"

"Me too but whatever they do to me, I can handle it. I just wanted to make sure you and I are fine."

"M word son, I and my men are done!"

'The same here, everyone is hands off...bye."

"Oh, and Roc, before you go, thanks for delivering Lucifer to me, hhaaa-haa," Mr. Holmes laughed.

"No, thank you."

Mr. Holmes's laughter stopped immediately. "For what?"

"Nothing really, I'm just saying thanks because he tried killing my brother also so in a way, it's like you did me a favor. But it would have been nice to know that it was a recording. Even with lines like, *'I'm here in my own home if someone wanted me, I am here.'* I still didn't catch it and you practically told me what to do. Then I turned around and told him what to do. But if I did that it would mean that I know your moves before you make it, like the first time I forced you to sweat but a true player never falls for the same move twice. One can dream though, can't he?"

Mr. Holmes looked at the disconnected phone thinking, *"Roc is something else, it's a shame he has to die.* He entered the den telling Sammy 'Big Block', "Get the pieces ready while I make this quick call."

Relaxing in his leather chair, Mr. Holmes dialed Diego El Sovida who picked up on the second right. "Holmes, my friend, what is it that I can do for you?"

"He called."

"Just as we planned."

"Now all you have to do is handle your business with Sunan Kudari before the haring and his run will have ended."

"That's already done; M-Easy had a change of recollection, right, M-Easy?"

"You're damn right, for 1.5 million," M-Easy's voice said from the background while Diego continued, "Everything is in place. There will be fifty armed men like before along with our top twenty unseen men, so don't worry old friend. After tomorrow, our troubles will be no more. Then the almighty lesson would be taught, never bite the hands that feed you."

Ending the call, Mr. Holmes turned his attention to Sammy 'Big Block' Gators who had a confused look on his face. "Sammy, are you ready for this ass whipping?"

"I don't know about all of that. I do know you're going to give me my money for touching this chess board when I was cleaning your clock."

"I didn't touch it, I left when you did"

"Well, someone did."

Mr. Holmes looked to the board, finding all the black pieces still in tact but the white pieces which were his favorite, had a piece missing and the king was broken in half, lying in the center. He slowly bit down on his bottom lip trying not to show emotion while hitting the intercom and activating the speakers through out the house. "Everyone check all the exits, there's another intruder and I need to know where he's at and what's missing, now!" Mr. Holmes demanded.

"How can you be sure, Money Man? Lucifer could have done this?"

"No, he did what Roc wanted him to do and that was to die." Mr. Holmes looked at the empty space where his knight used to be and said, "No, Sammy, this was personal." Letting out a deep breath, Mr. Holmes could hear once again Billy D telling him as a youth, *"Today you showed me that you have the heart for revenge, that's one lesson that I couldn't teach you. This is why you are the knight, the knight, the knight…"*

"Sir, sir" a voice brought Mr. Holmes back from his thoughts. "Yes, Travis?"

"The house is clean and nothing is missing."

"Then what did you come for, Roc, even after you called a truce?" Mr. Holmes said out loud as his mind raced knowing that with Roc, any mistake still could prove to be deadly.

23

After staying for hours at Temple Hospital until he was certain Detective. Michael would be fine and understood the shooting was an accident, Detective. Brian returned to the 39th station in search of Officer Dell. "Hey Lisa, has Dell been back around here?"

"No I haven't seen him but how are you holding up?"

"You heard?"

"Yes and if you need someone to talk to, I'm here."

"Thanks," Detective Brian moved through the station maintaining his search for Officer Dell, having the feeling that they need to talk about what took place earlier. "No Brian, I don't know where he is, have you paged him?" questioned Officer Bynum, head of the undercover Division. "Several times and he still hasn't responded."

Detective Brian was positive that Officer Dell was not going to be found there and headed for Detective Michael's desk where he quickly explored the drawer contents. *"I'm going to break this case myself. Now come on Michael where did you put it?"*

Coming up empty handed, he looked around the station making sure his actions remained unnoticed as he began to read the notes left on Michael's desk. *'Have to appear in court on the 17th', 'Don't forget Shelly's 41st birthday on the 6th,' 'Talk to the confidential informant for an update on the drug trade in North Philly.'*

"Damn it! Court case after court case…a whole bunch of nothing but I know it's here. Where, is the question." Rechecking his surroundings, Detective Brian turned on the power to Michaels' computer. He began typing and trying to break the six digit access code. He repeated the act and still couldn't figure it out until his detective skills took over. "Michael, you almost had me." Detective Brian grabbed the note on the desk and typed in the month, date and year of Shelly's birthday. *"You've got mail."* A smile appeared through the glow of the computer screen as Detective. Brian spotted what he was looking for. The screen read:

> *Detective Michael,*
> *I'm sending you the information that I received from the DNA on the apple. It's*
> *Strange, the person who bit it was a man called Shanke MuJahid Sabar and I ran*
> *the name twice...he's been dead for over ten years. That's what I don't*
> *understand. So contact me ASAP.*

"And you won't ever understand until I'm finished," Detective Brian switched the Shanke's name with Paul's. Once finished, he stood to his feet taking one last look at the picture of Detective Rayfield that sat in the center of Michael's desk, thinking, *"If he's telling the truth, why didn't you just take the money?"*

Back at his own desk, Detective Brian began to attack the case against Roc with a passion, looking for any weak spot as a call came over his walkie talkie. "All available cars, several shots have been reportedly fired at club Soldi. Approach with caution, owner is known to be armed and extremely dangerous." *"Here we go again,"* Detective Brian snatched his coat from the back of his chair as he headed straight for his car. "If it ain't one damn thing, it's another."

Outside club Soldi, there was a strong scent of burning wood with the continuous cloud of black smoke flowing into the air. Alexis screamed at the top of her lungs, "Y'all lazy mother fuckers are just going to sit there and let his club burn down to the ground!" she was directing her words to the eleven police officers and firemen that sat on the hood of their vehicles paying her threats no mind. "Okay, we'll see who the hell is laughing when you cracker bastards get yours!"

Inside the back seat of the Range, Boggy's eyes flickers before opening to the sound of Alexis screaming to see Inch staring at him in the face. "I see you're finally up."

"Yeah, but I know that's not Alexis screaming."

"That's her."

"Then who's giving her a problem?" Boggy reached for his gun that was no longer there while starting for the door. "Aaaahhh," he yelled as a sharp pain shot through his whole body, stopping him from proceeding. He sat back in his seat, "Shit...what happened?"

"You and this fool here," Inch pointed to Fox who was still knocked out cold on the opposite side of Boggy. "Jumped out the second floor window like you was superman, you should have seen that shit. You had fire coming from your clothes. I wouldn't be surprised if you didn't break something. Then when you stopped, dropped and rolled...that was live. But I held you down. Me!. I got y'all in here just before the cops pulled up on the scene. Alexis decided it would be a good look to be driving away from a burning building."

"Now she's out there making a scene?"

"I guess."

Boggy looked out the tinted window at the many cops just watching the flames like they were attending a casual bond fire as Soldi burned to the ground. "Don't worry, pussies, we'll rebuild better then ever. I promise you," he mused, finally spotting Alexis with her five-foot-seven, 130 pound physique and beautiful dark skin that had a glow to it which usually had men doing a double take when she walked by. Today was no different as Boggy thought, "Damn, I got to hit that again," before speaking out loud to Inch. "Yo, get her in the car and let's get out of here so I can find out who had the balls to do this."

"Okay, I'll get her but Roc said don't move until he calls back."

"Roc called you?"

"No, he called you," Inch handed Boggy back his phone and weapon. "He's been trying to reach you all day to tell you that Mr. Holmes is going to try and kill you or something about half the problem."

"No shit," Boggy remembered the moment he saw Roc's number sending all his calls to voicemail. Becoming angry at him self also, Boggy yelled, "Man, fuck them cops. Where's the weed at and you get the fuck up hard rock." Boggy back handed Fox hard across the face."

"What, what"

"You're wanted for murder, that's what," Boggy responded taking a deep inhale of the blunt.

"So!" Fox yelled while rolling over on his other side, trying to get comfortable as he felt the pain going through his body also. Boggy let the smoke escape and shook his head with a smile at the new wild generation. *"Look at this fool with the police only a parking space away, he goes back to sleep. Dumb but still gangster, ha-ha!"* Boggy thought.

After enjoying half of the blunt, Boggy for the last ten minutes had been telling Alexis how much he couldn't live without her. "I'm serious woman, every since you walked out on me Alexis, leaving me in the room nude, I haven't been the same. Then you didn't answer my phone calls, it just killed me."

"That's because you were in there getting it on with them two trifling strippers. So don't mess with me please! It's been a long day."

"I'm not your ..." Boggy's words were cut short to answer his phone. "Talk to me."

"Who's this?"

"Boggy, Roc what's good?"

"Damn! Look how a few minutes can change a person. I just called and you were knocked out like a baby. They said something about R-Kelly and you believing you could fly," Roc said laughing. "I leave you by yourself for a few days and cats got you jumping out of windows, they blow up my shit."

"This shit ain't funny at all, Roc, and when I see that old head of yours I'm going to…"

"Do nothing," Roc interrupted.

"What! That old bastard tried to kill me."

"I know but I just called a truce, meaning I, along with my people can't touch him or be touched."

"And when did this happen, a second after his old ass tried to kill me?"

"I understand your pain but if you could se me now you would know how good it feels to be retired."

"So you're really going to step away?"

"If they let me."

"If who lets you?"

"The meeting has been called." Closing his eyes, afraid of the answer Boggy asked, "Where's the location?"

"Miami, six o'clock"

"I get it, you meet on neutral ground. Somewhere they know our power is strong but not strong enough to over power the situation. Well, I'm coming."

"I knew you would say that. Look out your window; you'll see Raja close by."

Boggy looked with his practically open eyes, over the large crowd of spectators that formed until he spotted Raja leaning up against Lucifer's stolen van. "I see him."

"Okay, he has two tickets, one for you and Fox. Your plane departs at midnight…one"

"Wait, Roc?"

"Yeah?"

"You know they're going to try and kill you right?"

"Maybe but what can I do?" The line was silent on both ends until Boggy spoke up and said, "Don't go, fuck it, I'll give the streets up and we can take our families and go anywhere you want. I'll make that shit a hood!"

"You'll do that for me?"

"Without question. It's two faces one tear always and I know I can't enter the meeting to cover you."

"I know, I will be alone but I must go."

"Why, Roc?" Boggy screamed, ready to break the phone. He already knew Roc's answer as he mumbled the words as Roc's said them, "Because I gave my word and my word is worth more than gold."

"But is it worth more than your life?"

"Yes because I must show the integrity of a man at all times so that Mac will know how to be one and show his kids. If he has to in the end, show my son. Just not in this game because it ends with me," Roc said firmly.

"You're right; we must teach the youth…have another ticket waiting at the front desk. I just got another young comrade in my sight." Inch smiled, having a plan of his own in mind. Alexis went down the crowded street with Raja right behind her just as Detective Brian pulled onto the scene. Detective Brian looked from the Range Rover to the damage of Roc's club that was now nothing but ashes, stating, *"Someone is sure to die for this if I don't get to the end of this first."* He quickly made a u-turn in pursuit of the Range Rover.

24

A hundred miles off the Gulf of Mexico on a leveled off mountain, there was a 9, 500 square foot piece of land with a thirty room, two swimming pool mansion. One hundred armed men divided into three shifts securing the compound. They changed positions every two minutes to make sure their boss Diego El Sovida was well protected at all times.

As he sat at the edge of his all white leather sofa, watching his 65 inch rear projection TV, Diego El Sovida yelled as if his losing horse could obey his command, "Andale, ándale, nooo, nooo mucho quicker ándale, no!" shaking his head in disbelief as M-Easy stated, "Come on, El Sovida, don't take it too hard. You should have known better than to think a Mexican horse name Rosy was going to win," while taking the fifty thousand in euro off the marble table for their bet.

"Okay, you have won a few victories but your winning days will end," Diego El Sovida replied, surfing through the channels with his wireless remote when he saw a car race. "Ahhhh, speed and very fast…my favorite. I love how they sound, zoom-zoom. Now pick M-Easy and the first one to do three laps wins a hundred grand."

"You know me; all you got to do is say it and it's a bet."

"Then bet."

"I'll take the red ca…"

"KNOCK-KNOCK," a knock at the door paused M-Easy as he noticed Diego El Sovida gliding his hand onto his 9 mm Berretta and releasing it from his waist line. He then gave a head nod directing M-Easy to move toward the door in front of him. For anyone to be a member on Diego

El Sovida's compound, they had to pass over two hundred extraordinarily difficult tests given by the top F.B.I. agent in Mexico. But Diego El Sovida still didn't trust many people.

Approaching the door, M-Easy removed his own weapon with one hand while opening the door slightly with the other and spotted Rafael, Diego El Sovida's personal assistant and next in command. M-Easy returned the nod as Diego El Sovida lowered his gun from the closed section of the door frame. "It's Rafael, what do you want me to do?"

"Let him in," Diego El Sovida replied. Rafael entered the room with two large suit cases. "Sir Sovida and Senor M-Easy, your luggage and the plane will be ready for take off in ten minutes." M-Easy looked at his classic Brequet watch that he also won from Diego El Sovida and said, "Right on time. Let me go get my Mexican green for the ride. Miami, here I come!" M-Easy rubbing his hands together, raced through the master dining room into this living quarters. Diego El Sovida turned to Rafael once he was sure M-Easy was out of the room and asked, "Is everything in place?"

"Yes, Sunan Kudari," replied. "Once he receives the testimony he is on board then our problem will be solved."

"And?"

"And our friend Senor M-Easy will have a little accident before you leave from Miami."

"Very well, even though I hate to do it but any man who will turn on a friend for money, can never be trusted"

M-Easy searched his bedroom until he found his last box of Philly blunts, "There you go." He took a pound of weed also and started back to meet Diego El Sovida, passing the surveillance camera in the living room when a slight motion grabbed his attention. Pausing, he looked intensely at the screen and noticed four men dressed in all black with cables wrapped around their waist making there way up the side of the mountain. The leading man moved with extreme speed up the center as another followed right behind him with a wing man on each side. Recognizing the masked men's attacking position, M-Easy said, "Triangle offense!" He then ran off to notify Diego El Sovida, finding him with his suit case in hand and preparing to leave he yelled, "Wait, we have a problem with Roc."

"I know, but not for long my friend."

"No, you don't understand, he's here."

"What! Where?"

M-Easy pointed at the glass wall where a great view of the compound could be seen. Diego El Sovida identified four men rushing onto his property, catching several of his guards by surprise. "I must commend him for his efforts and consistency to want to die as a solider. Tonight, he will be rewarded," Diego stated while pushing the button to activate the transparent bullet proof shield that lowered down over the glass. He kept his eyes on the activity for five minutes, in shock but impressed at how Roc and his men fought with such heart until he had seen enough. El Sovida slowly removed his phone, demanding, "Rafael, send them now!"

Outside as the smashing sound of the waves slammed into the base of the mountain below, above on land, the muffling sound repeated as it came from the silencer of Roc's gun that rapidly fired on the body of Diego El Sovida's last guard. Spinning it through the air, Roc without waiting to see the body drop, screamed into his mouthpiece, "We only have a twenty minute gap to finish Diego, so let's get moving!" Roc was thirty yards away from the mansion with his feet aggressively moving over the freshly landscaped grass. He raised his head to find that he was met with Diego El Sovida's stare that showed pure confidence.

"We've been made, Mac move with me, Haffee, you and Manny take the left side," Roc ordered, lifting his gun and pulling the trigger twice. The first one was for M-Easy as the hard impact to the shield made him jump. The second left a ricochet mark landing an inch from the center of El Sovida's head.

"Bullet proof. Damn!" Roc with Lil Mac his side, dipped wide right, blending into the shadow of darkness. Haffee and Manny did the same on the left to cover both sides of their perimeter. Haffee quickly took the position as the point man, he whispered, "Clear," and they slowly crept low, rotating their weapons in constant motion ready for any sudden action. Roc was just feet away from the entrance when he raised his open hand in the air which was the sign to pause. "Roc, ten minutes, why are you stopping?"

"I know but something isn't right about this, it's too quiet." Roc went off his instincts and eased a clip from his jacket pocket, tossing it high into the air at the door. At the sound of it hitting, seventy rounds of ammunition ripped through the door's infrastructure. "Retreeeeeeaaatt!" Roc yelled as the four men dashed for their escape route in a criss-cross movement. They passed the window and Diego El Sovida, witnessing his small army in hot pursuit of Roc said, "M-Easy, we will no longer have to wait until we reach Miami till your old friend is finished. His head will be in my hand in minutes, get the champagne; let's celebrate."

"You think so?" questioned M-Easy, taking a seat on the sofa and puffing on a blunt with his eyes closed. He hid his emotion, hating the fact of what he had to do to a friend in this game in order to win. He stood to his feet and spoke, "I really think he's going to get away."

"That's impossible," Diego El Sovida responded, turning to face M-Easy, being met by a black forty five automatic that was pointed at his face. M-Easy corrected, "Not if his plan was to retreat becoming the bait so that I could get away. Now with your whole army chasing after them, there's no one that can stop this."

Without hesitation, M-Easy pulled the trigger placing two bullets in each of El Sovida's knee caps and watched his six foot body drop to the ground. "Aaaaahhhh, okay stop! Okay whatever he's paying you I'll double it. I swear no tricks," Diego El Sovida cried.

M-Easy grinned while he pulled the trigger twice more hitting his target in each shoulder, responding, "That's what you never understood. Money can never replace loyalty. Y'all shot Lil Mac six times and I must return the favor." The last two shots entered El Sovida's head, flipping him over on his back, "Sorry, friend." M-Easy took his suitcase, placed the blunt between his lips and exited through the side door where Rafael waited. "Is everything done?" Rafael asked. "Yes, you are now the boss," M-Easy confirmed. "Thanks Senor M-Easy. You're the only one who could have completed this mission I've requested of you. El Sovida trusted no one."

"Don't remind me."

"Don't be upset, Señor, you did a good thing. Mexico will be different from now on. There will be no more drug wars, there's enough money for everyone. Now, what can I do for you?"

"Just what I asked you for."

"For you, friend, yes," Rafael handed M-Easy a piece of paper. "Are you sure that's all you want? You know I am now the richest person in Mexico."

"I'm sure, now get me out of here. I'm hood sick!"

25

Several hours later, just pass 4:00 am, the inside of Miami International Airport was still packed with people coming and going to enjoy everything from the party scene, luxurious women, or to just to relax in the beautiful weather it had to offer. But all these things were the farthest from the mind of the several men who exited flight 41 without any luggage to claim and their fake identification in hand. Raja, Boggy, Fox, Inch, and Mohammed cleared customs, "Thank you, gentleman, and welcome to Miami."

They blended in perfectly with the crowd as entrusted to not draw any unwanted attention by the undercover FBI, DEA and CIA agents posted through out the eleven walls. Boggy looked down in frustration at the colorful flowered shirt, cotton slacks and close toed sandals that made up his wardrobe instead of his usual wheat Timbs, jeans, t-shirt and custom jewels. "Man, fuck this gay shit!" he said, pulling the t-shirt from his back when Mohammed tapped his shoulder, "Leave it!" "Alright but I don't want to hear a peek out of you niggas about this shit when we get back."

The double glass door remotely opened as the men stepped out into the clean 70 degree night air to see a stretch limousine. On top sat Roc, disguised looking to be in his mid fifties and dressed to impress in his Isaiah navy blue three piece suit. The blue and white tie he wore, matched the Laura hat that sat tilted to the side on top of his head.

He jumped down to have his men surround him in celebration. "Mr. Jones! What's happening?" One by one Roc gave the men that for years put everything they had on the line for him, a hug thanking them as if it may be the last time they enjoy each others company. "Raja, I'm glad you're here."

"If I could be any place in the world, I'd still choose to be here." They embraced in a half hug with Roc sliding a large envelope into his hand. "Thanks for everything, now in the back there's something special waiting for you." Raja entered the limousine as the chauffeur held the door.

"Fox, I owe you an apology. Boggy told me what happened and you have proven in a time of war that you could never be the weak link and a soldier must be rewarded." They embraced, with Roc giving Fox his envelope and Fox's curiosity got the best of him as he opened the box in a hurry, seeing the two large bricks of thousand dollar bills. Fox raised his head with widened eyes, looked at Roc and said, "You my nigga, man. You're always doing something big! First that red hat shit on that rat ass nigga Fatel, now this! You the man for real!" Fox gave Roc a hug before jumping into the limo screaming, "And we got bitches! Man it's on!"

Roc looked at Inch with disbelief asking, "What are you doing here?"

"He's with me," Boggy yelled.

"Inch we'll talk later, now go," Roc shook his head asking in a silent prayer as Inch joined the others, *"God, when will this cycle stop?"* Speaking out loud, he greeted, "Manny my man…we came a long way and it's like the first time you saved my life and you've been doing it ever since. I know I don't say it much but I am truly thankful for everything."

"I know, Roc, but is everything alright? Is something wrong?"

"See, there you go again," Roc repeated the act as Manny with his envelope in hand, paused at the door while turning to look back at Roc hugging Mohammed who had refused to take the money. Mohammed mentioned something about Allah would be providing for him. Manny thought, *"If something is wrong, Roc I'll be there...you can count on that."*

Boggy was the last and only person who really knew what Roc was truly going through. Just before Roc began to speak, Boggy spoke first, "Don't. We can have this conversation after we come from the meeting because I'm getting in there."

"So that means you don't want this paper?" Roc flashed the envelope.

"We can die together but don't get it fucked up, until then I'm going to be about my bread!" Boggy took the money from Roc. "Now shoe me some love," they embraced with Roc using all the strength he had to hold back his tears, knowing if his gut feeling was right...he would truly miss the friend he had when he didn't have anything. The same friend he had now that he possessed everything and if he was ever to go broke with just Boggy's help, he knew he could gain it all back again. A single tear ran down Roc's cheek, landing on the shoulder of Boggy. Not wanting to see Roc tearful, Boggy headed for the limo without turning around, using the back of his hand to wipe his own.

Back at the Waldorf Astoria Hotel, in the presidential suite, a party was in full blast with all the top celebrities as the D.J. screamed, "We the best," spinning the song, *Just like me.* Lil Mac danced with his mother as she showed him some moves, "You don't know nothing about that son, this is before your time," laughed Mrs. Miller as she threw her hip into Lil Mac, doing the bump.

Top Dollar, a few feet away spun Gizelle around and dipped her low to the ground just as the beat broke down. Across the floor, deep in the crowd, M-Easy stood with two bottles of champagne held high in the air with the ashes of the best Mexican weed dropping from the blunt onto the back of a pretty light skinned woman who was bending over, moving her round backside up and down on his manhood. "Damn it feels good to be back!" he thought before yelling, "I'm rich, bitch!"

Roc walked through the confluence room shaking hands while loving the sight of the people he cared about most having the time of their lives. The sudden vibration of his phone made Roc take a look at his wrist reading his Rolex, 5:30 am. He gave the D.J. a nod as the smooth mellow tone of Freddy Jackson made its way through the speakers, *"Hey girl, long time no see. Do you have a little time to spend with me?"* Roc tapped Top Dollar on the shoulder, "Excuse me, may I cut it?"

"Without question, you dig. Gizelle, thank you for a lovely dance."

"The pleasure was all mine," Gizelle showed Top Dollar her beautiful smile.

"Ah, that' enough, baby. You can't give an old player too much or he might fall in love." Roc interrupted while wrapping his hand around her waist and pulling her close.

"Who said I haven't already," Top Dollar stated, taking the hand of a woman passing by who resembled Stacy Dash. "Wait, young sugar, you look like you need an old player up in your life, you dig, and I mean deep in it."

Gizelle could only smile as she interlocked her arms around Roc's neck. "You know he's playing our song," Roc stated. "Yes, I wonder how that happened."

"I guess he knows it was pass time you should have been in my arms. Also, I must say you're stunning this evening, you know that?"

"No, but I'd love for you to tell me what you see." Silence was in the air until Gizelle said, "I guess the cat got your tongue."

"No, it's your beauty. It's so hard to define in such few words. From the lovely sparkle in your eyes that reflect from the fire in your soul that saved me back in the day. Back in a time when I was selling five dollar caps and the police chased me to your house and you refused to let them in."

"Baby, you remember that? That was a long time ago. I'm sure you know by now that there is nothing in this world I wouldn't do for you."

"Sweetheart, truthfully I remember everything you do for me. Even the first time you let me taste those soft lips of yours," Roc gently ran his finger across Gizelle's lips and she leaned in and gave Roc a long passionate kiss like it was their first and last time. Then Roc continued speaking, "It was your pretty smile that made me stop you when you were walking by that day but it was your beauty within that forced me to make you my wife. Therefore, all that I am and all that I have could never be, without you. So to answer your question…what I see is the most beautiful thing that ever happened to me."

"Aaaaww, baby, please stop…you're making me cry."

Roc removed his silk handkerchief and wiped away each drop from her glowing face. "Roc, I love you so much. I need to feel you inside of me." Roc looked at his watch again, 5:47 am, and then let his eyes move in search of Mohammed. Not seeing him, Roc tightly wrapped his arms around her. The feeling of Roc's power always made Gizelle feel safe from the world in his arms as he pulled her through the crowd, "Come on!"

While across the room, Boggy watched Roc's every move, paying the women who threw themselves at him, no mind. Roc went passed the many people trying to get jobs, a favor, money or protection from him until he came to a side room placing his finger to his lips, "Ssshhh." Quietly he pushed the door open and walked through the first section to the back where he saw Mohammed performing his morning prayer.

Roc noticed the binoculars on the back drawer right where they were supposed to be. He patiently waited until Mohammed finished. "Boss you have two minutes," stated Mohammed, leaving the room and placing his prayer rug over his shoulder.

"Two minutes! Roc, what can you do in two minutes?" questioned Gizelle, seated on the bed. "Own the world, now come on," Roc replied. He walked pass her taking the binoculars and stepped onto the terrace. "Will you come on, we only have a minute."

Gizelle followed and quickly covered her mouth in awe while taking in the extraordinary scene of twenty peach roses that set in a gold and crystal vase. There was a large bottle of Don P chilling on ice. The Miami night light twinkled in the distance, making her 6ct. platinum wedding ring that Roc clutched in his hand give off a blinding sparkle as he got down one knee.

"We only have 30 seconds so will you marry me, again?"

"Yes, yes, baby!" not trying to hold back her tears this time she raced into Roc's arms. After placing the ring on her finger, Roc stepped behind her and whispered into her ear as he hugged her and began the count down, "4...3...2..1," he pointed out into the sky and like a personal trick, the sun began to slowly rise. "Here's the sun, next will be the moon."

Speechless, Gizelle enjoyed the sunrise as if she had actually watched it recharge her world. Roc lifted the binoculars to his face and right on time at 6:00 am sharp, a hundred yards down the strip in front of the Epic Hotel, Adrian Cortez exited the back seat of the Range Rover in an all brown suit. Roc recognized the extra heavy security of six armed men escorting him into the building, thinking, *"Whatever is in that suitcase is what's going to do me in. I guess it's time to find out."*

Roc kissed his wife on the center of the neck quickly, hoping his words wouldn't be the biggest lie he ever told her. "Baby, I'll be back. I have to go to the restroom." Once inside the master bedroom, Roc stopped in front of the full length mirror removing his forty five from his hip. Staring at the weapon that had the power to take life, he said, "I now understand in war, victory is only in the eye of the beholder but for a solider who witnesses a drop of blood shed, there is never a winner."

Repeatedly cocking back the chamber of the weapon, ejecting the bullets from it until it was empty, he tossed it without hesitation into the waste basket. He ran his finger over the smooth fabric of the black suit he bought just for this occasion. *"I wonder what your next move is."* Roc turned on the hot water to the shower and vanished behind the steam.

Back out in the party that was still going strong, Boggy waited for Roc to appear knowing something was going on. Twenty minutes passed when Mohammed stepped out with Boggy there to meet him. "Yo, Mohammed, have you see Roc?"

"When?"

"Come on, Mohammed, don't play with me. I saw him whisper something to you earlier, what's going on?"

"Nothing," Mohammed started to walk away when Boggy gripped his arm firmly saying, "I love you, man, but I love Roc more and we've been through shit before. If something's up with him and you're not telling me, we can go through it again, right now!"

"Get your kafur hands off of me and we didn't go through nothing remember he saved you or you would be dead, like all the rest. I'm glad you feel so deeply about boss because whatever is happening has to be big. He cares for you also and the only thing he told me was to not tell Boggy I'm in the back room on the terrace but you didn't hear it from me."

Mohammed walked off without another word, leaving the side door open. Boggy entered fast, moving through the suite and spotted Gizelle. "Gizelle, wake up; where's Roc?"

"Huh?"

"Where's Roc?"

"In the bathroom."

Boggy aggressively knocked on the bathroom door getting no response. He opened the door and let the fresh steam escape, finding the room empty. Seeing Roc's weapon and bullets in the waste basket, Boggy yelled, "Hello no! Not like this homie." He reloaded it in a hurry before tucking it in his waistline and running for the elevator.

"What floor would you like, sir?"

Boggy wiped the sweat from his forehead due to the hot bathroom and replied, guessing, "The same floor you dropped the man before me off."

"Oh, Mr. Jones, he went to the lobby, nice guy. He gave me a hundred dollar tip."

"Then that's enough for the both of us."

Boggy in a panic, strolled out into the morning air searching the faces on the street and sidewalk as he recalled Roc's words, *"They scheduled the meeting for 6:00."* Boggy instantly became upset at himself for not being on point. "Why didn't I think AM?" Knowing when it came to the Corporation, there was no room for mistakes. Boggy looked at his watch, 6:31 am. Hearing Roc's voice once again, *"Boggy, the only thing I want to be later for, is my funeral."*

26

Roc stepped from a taxi as his eyes darkened with no security, no weapon, and no one knowing his whereabouts...so he thought. He stopped at the hotel entrance, breathed deeply before pushing the swinging door open with authority. Just as the sudden sounds of screeching tires of flour black Hummers pulled to a stop inches away from him. Roc never paused his stride, "Sir, welcome to the Epic, do you have any luggage I can help you with?"

"I'm already used to that trick now get away from me." At the front desk, the receptionist slid a gold key across the counter to him, "They've been waiting on you," she said. Roc took the key and noticed the woman's Corporate ring, answering, "I know they are."

He made his way across the matching marble floor where three Corporate guards waited at the front of the elevator. After being searched, Roc rode to the top floor in silence, considering, *"No matter what the outcome is, I've lived the life of a man."* He walked down the extravagant hallway to see several more armed guards lined up on both sides of the wall. Being at peace with him self, Roc smiled while proceeding to the conference room. But he stopped to take time out to study one of the well constructed paintings that hung from the wall. It was a replica of Leonardo DaVinci's, The Last Supper, his favorite because of the way DaVinci made fun of the same people who praised him in their faces without them even seeing it.

Roc was escorted into the large room where five tables covered with every breakfast food imaginable were laid out for the Corporation. Roc saw his section and walked over to his seat with each member standing up one by one in a show of their respect. He gave a short head nod to Adrian

Cortez, Sunan Kudari, and Rafael as he passed, taking a bite of a strawberry. Roc said, "Shall we get this over with?"

"If you're ready," stated Sunan Kudari.

"More than ever."

"Very well then, fellas will you please excuse yourselves and let him know we are ready to begin." The waiters quickly exited the room, leaving nothing but Corporate men present. Moments later the door swung open as Billy D strolled in with twenty specially trained dressed in all black masks covering their faces and leaving nothing to be seen but their eyes. Billy D stood in the center of the room giving a signal with his hand that made his men spread out through the room as Detective. Brian whispered to Foxy, "I haven't worn this suit since we had to save Shake MuJad Jabar."

"Only to have him die at the hands of him," Foxy's eyes locked on Roc before returning her attention back to Billy D who said, "This is a sad day when the men I personally appointed to control what many have said was uncontrollable and we have proven them wrong. Now, one of our own has disrespected the code of our brotherhood and I refuse to let it go with out being punished to the fullest extent."

Billy D's voice became deeper as he continued through tightened teeth, "Roc, we are here today because you're being accused of killing two of your fellow brethren. Do you understand these charges?"

"I do," Roc answered without standing. Billy D, while beginning to circle the room, stated, "When I first heard of the issue, I didn't believe there was enough evidence to call this meeting and then I received a call that changed my mind, along with the fact that Diego El Sovida is no longer with us. You wouldn't know anything about that, would you?"

Roc quickly shot his eyes in the direction of Rafael, who shrugged his shoulders. "I should have known not to trust you." Roc was feeling his plan slipping away right in front of him as he began to speak, "I…"

"Don't!" Billy D said firmly, "Just look." He pushed a button on the small remote that dimmed the lights. A large projector screen lowered to a stop from the ceiling. Billy D hit another button and the vision of El Sovida in his last moment appeared on the screen, standing alone watching Roc run pass the window. Moments afterward, Diego El Sovida slowly turned to face a person whose back was only captured by the camera. "They really got me set up for the kill and I gave them every piece of their plan," Roc thought to his self.

'BOOM-BOOM' the sound erupted as Roc slammed his fist down hard onto the table the second that Diego El Sovida's head exploded. "Rafael, did you have anything to say about this because I believe you were there at the time?" Roc questioned.

"Yes, Roc, didn't…"

"Wait!" Adrian Cortez interjected. "If I'm not mistaken, Rafael is here to replace Diego El Sovida in this Corporation."

"You're correct," Billy D answered.

"But he hasn't been approved as of yet, which I don't have a problem with doing but until then his word is no good here. When a Corporate man's life is on the line, only Corporate men can have say in ending it, Rule IV."

"True. Fellas, please escort Rafael from his seat at the moment until he's officially one of us."

Rafael, with two men locked on each of his arms, turned towards Roc and motioned his lips saying, "I'm sorry, I tried."

"But if he didn't cross me who would have access to El Sovida's cameras?" asked Roc.

"Come on, Roc, think fast."

Roc battle with his thoughts before jumping up to his feet, "Billy D, there's also rule 15 that Adrian Cortez forgot to mention. There must be an anomalous vote of three Corporate men before there can be any action taken."

"Is that what you're requesting?" asked Adrian Cortez.

"Yes."

Billy D was in disbelief in reaction to Roc's answer. If Roc would have just said no, the issue would have been finished because a substitute can only be added by request of the person being accused. "As you wish, please go get him." A masked Foxy headed out the door as Roc asked, "Who?" and his questioned was quickly answered at the sight of Mr. Holmes entering with a look of high confidence. He walked smoothly to his section with the Corporate men standing one by one as he went by, showing him respect. Mr. Holmes returned the gesture by shaking the hands of each man he passed and looking them in the eyes.

He approached Roc with a smile and his hand out, "Son." "Teacher," Roc replied and they interlocked hands with Roc pulling Mr. Holmes into a half hug. On the embrace, Roc said in a whisper, "This was your plan the whole time, from you arranging M-Easy to go away to Mexico, and then telling NayNay the number to the upper room. That wasn't a mistake, you did it on purpose."

"Maybe."

"You knew I was in Mexico but yet you didn't warn him. All this was never about Lil Mac or me, we were the bait. It was about Diego El Sovida the whole time. You wanted him dead."

"How else would he get a chance at power?" Mr. Holmes answered, tightening his grip as Roc asked, "So you used me as a pawn?"

"I told you, struggle builds strength but if you want to look at it that way then check, because the game isn't over but it's near." Mr. Holmes lightly kissed Roc on the forehead and with a smile said, "Your move."

"I knew I should have killed your old ass when I had the chance."

"That's a shame, but I'm not going to miss mine. Just watch with hands off because words are way mightier than the sword."

Roc fell down to his seat in a daze, not really paying the words Billy D was saying any mind as he filled Mr. Holmes in on the events of the past. Once finished, Billy D asked, "Now Holmes, we all know how much you love Roc but you're a man of integrity and there's wrong and there's right. So you must go with the honest judgment."

"You know I don't think that's possible, Billy D."

"And why is that?"

"Because he told me that he killed them"

"Killed who?" Billy D inquired, baffled.

"Apollon and Balial"

"Haaahhh!" Laughter filled the room.

"What's so funny, Billy D?"

"You, old friend! It's great to know even in a time of danger you still have jokes."

"Can we get this over with," Roc shouted, standing up with a smile on his face and beginning to walk around.

"If you're ready."

"More than ever," Roc gave Billy D a nod and the room went dim again as he asked Mr. Holmes, "Teacher, do you know the penalty for killing one of your fellow brethren without cause?"

"Yes, the act is worse than death, it's where you get one wish and it can be anything in the world for someone other than yourself. Before they make you into the half a man you really are by disconnecting every limb on the right side of your body from your feet to your eye, leaving your penis for last. Then you will be locked away for ten years, given animals to kill or be killed for food. I'm so sorry for you, Roc."

"I'll be fine but what amazes me is if you knew this, then why would you do it?"

"Do what! And why are you asking me questions when it's you that is on trial here, not me."

"So you don't know?"

"Don't know what and someone better tell me something or I'm leaving!" Mr. Holmes urged as he looked at the faces of his fellow brethren, in search for an answer when he recognized the masked men responding to his threat by clutching their weapons.

Billy D was the first to speak, "Holmes, as I just explained earlier, Roc has been accused of killing one of our own and I didn't believe there was enough proof to take action until he called me asking that I schedule this meeting quickly because he had new evidence on the killer that would clear his name."

"But what the hell does that have to do with me and why did you call me saying you needed me to fill in for Diego El Sovida?"

"Because I do, he is dead and someone must be penalized for this crime of disloyalty."

"How dare you talk to me like that and all you have is the word of this man whose fighting for his life, he'd do anything to save himself."

"Old head, you know me better than that; I would never push a piece unless there's a checkmate that follows," Roc replied. Billy D raised his hand and on command, four guards clinched Mr. Holmes by the arms. Billy D pushed play with the vision of Lucifer surrounded by Holmes and his gang with their guns aimed. The deep voice of Mr. Holmes echoed through the room, *"Did you thin you were good enough to get me alone after I killed your two brothers?"*

Roc handed Billy D the note left by Lucifer that was taped on the bodies of his brothers that read, "Look at what you have done; now you and Holmes must pay for your sins." Once Billy D finished reading, Roc said, "That's the reason Diego El Sovida is not here, because I promised Lucifer that I would honor his word if he died. Now he's the last part of that," Roc pointed to Mr. Holmes. "Don't worry about him; I will see that he gets what's coming to him. You may watch me at work if you'd like."

"Nah, I'll pass," Roc replied and walked up to Mr. Holmes as Sunan Kudari questioned him. "What is your wish? To be sure your family is taken care of for life?"

"No, if my family isn't prepared for this world then I wasn't the man I was supposed to be, my wish is to free Cyrus from the federal ADX in Florence."

"It's done," assured Sunan Kudari.

Roc looked Mr. Holmes dead in the eyes while using his hand to wipe the sweat from Mr. Holmes's forehead. Looking at the wet substance on his finger tip, Roc said, "I know this is not sweat…you said that's a display of weak emotion based off an overreaction to an illusion of power and pressure that no strong man should allow another person to possess over him. Well, this means it's real."

Digging into his pocket, Roc sat something on the table, stating, "Checkmate," and walked off. Mr. Holmes looked down to see his missing knight. "*See Vernon, you're going to make it, that's why I called you the knight,*" Billy D had told Mr. Holmes as a kid. "You motherfucker!" Mr. Holmes hollered while quickly pulling his arm out his suit jacket and leaving it in the hands of the guards as he snatched the hidden Ruger from his waist and raised it to the back of Roc's head, pulling back the trigger. The gun clicked just as several shots penetrated into his frame. Roc turned around and thought he noticed a smile on the face of Mr. Holmes, seconds before his body collapsed to the ground, dead.

27

After a week and just as Mr. Holmes's will requested, his funeral was small but lovely with only the few people he took care of and that took care of him present. The location was a little local church in North Philly. Roc sat in the back row, not believing he deserved to be in the front row with the rest of his family because for the past week his mind had been all over the place as he recited Mr. Holmes's words in his head a hundred times and they still hadn't made sense to him. Then there was that smile as if it was an abstract message he didn't get.

"Roc, baby" the gentle touch of his mother's hand took Roc out of his daze. "Baby, you look so drained, you're even losing color in your face. I know how much you cared about him but dear, that man didn't mean us any good in the end. So don't trouble your head over spilled milk."

"I know, Mom, but I didn't think he really meant to hurt me at all. Even when he died, the gun in his hand was on safety and he doesn't make mistakes like that, ever!"

"If he wasn't trying to harm you, then what?"

"That what got me."

"Well come on and lets pay our respects to the person that helped you become the man you are today, he deserves that much," Mrs. Miller held Roc's hand tightly as they walked down the aisle to the open casket. Unbeknownst to them, Travis observed Roc's every move closely. Roc was known for being hard all his life literally since the age of thirteen. But at the sight of his mentor who held so much life in him, in his clean cream Armani suit and white tie and matching shoes, Mr. Holmes lay there in a permanent still, like Roc had never seen him before. Roc didn't fight the tears running in his mouth as he talked,

"Damn old head. The bull shit ain't nothing, this should have never come to this." While talking, Roc could feel the stares of Stevie Blue, Sammy 'Big Block' Gators and Money Bags Merrick, who really didn't know what happened but they wanted to place their pain as well as their anger on Roc, and take action. The only thing that stopped them was Mr. Holmes having told them that everything was cool between him and Roc before he'd left for Miami.

Roc resumed, "Somehow I feel there's more to your side of the story that you haven't told me but how and you're gone? Please know old head, even with everything that happened…I love you. I know you taught me better than to be up here crying like a bitch but nothing could have prepared me for this feeling of losing everything I knew." Roc slowly turned from the casket, removing his tears with the back of his hand, missing Travis's sudden movement, who met him just as he completed his turn.

Travis in one quick movement removed something from his back pocket and stuck it to Roc's chest. Roc, not caring anymore just looked Travis in the eye emotionless, prepared for his fate. "Here, he wanted you to have this." When nothing happened, Roc looked down to see a brown envelope resting on the center of his chest. "Read it when you're alone." "Thanks," Roc stated. With the letter in his hand he could feel the power of Mr. Holmes once more.

The sun shined high in the sky as Roc's Maybach led several vehicles through the steel gates with one man standing on the side, "Wait. Stop." The driver touched the brake with Roc lowering the window and asking the unrecognized guard, "Who are you and where are David and Marc?"

"They came down with the pig flu, I think you call it. I'm not for sure, I'm new to America."

"And you are?"

"Kotov, sir, the new protector I would call me."

Roc thought, *"Alright,"* while giving his driver the okay to proceed. The cars continued to go through the private cemetery slowly and stopped along side the clear road. Mr. Holmes's body was lowered into the ground as twenty white doves were released into the air to represent a moment of peace at the end of life. Once the two hour event was finished, one by one each visitor said their goodbye's to Roc who was standing in a trance, staring down at the fresh dirt that now covered the new home of his mentor.

Mrs. Miller saw enough of the mental hurt in her son's face and headed for Roc when Billy D stopped her. "Wait, Carmen, let him be."

"No, Billy D, that's enough. He must leave so he can begin to heal."

"And he will when the man is ready and not a moment sooner. So take your family and his friend and go home. I'll make sure he gets there safely. Plus they're scaring me," Billy D looked in Boggy's direction as Boggy had his eyes dead locked on him with his hand in his pocket. Billy D was sure there was a powerful weapon in there.

"Billy D, are you positive my baby's going to be fine?"

"Carmen, do you remember the day you had Roc and we was all there?"

"Yes, it was you, Top Dollar, Mr. Holmes and Odell. We were so proud."

"Do you remember what Odell said when he first let me hold Roc?"

"That Roc would be the one, but you know Odell like any father, he praised his first born."

"Well to this day he hasn't lied to me," Billy D walked off and stood next to Roc in silence as Mrs. Miller got everyone into their car. "That goes for you too, Boggy. I said he's going to be fine, now come on!"

"Okay, Mrs. Miller, but if he's not…"

"I know, baby, you're going to kill the whole world and I'm going to help you. Now will you help an old lady to her car?"

After an hour of preparing himself for the last conversation he would ever have with Mr. Holmes, Roc slowly raised his head from his daze, sensing the presence of Billy D and asked without looking in his direction but focusing on the sky, "Do you ever feel like you were forced into a game that you had to play to win and the very moment you didn't give it your all, you would lose everything?"

"All the time," Billy D answered truthfully understanding Roc's pain way too much. Roc turned to make eye contact with Billy D, "Then why is it when you become victorious it hurts worse than when you lose yourself?"

"Roc, you know a lot of times we lose sight of our goals and begin to live for others that are near to our heart, so when they lose…"

"Our heart knows no difference," Roc finished the sentence.

"Exactly, but always remember this," Billy D placed his arm around Roc's shoulder as they headed for his black Phantom with Foxy behind the wheel. "Leadership is the art of getting someone else to do something that you want done because he wanted to do it."

Not really understanding the reason, Roc paused asking, "Why did you say that?"

"I just thought I would."

The two reached the vehicle when the sound of a roaring engine of a Bugatti descending through the private cemetery came to a stop along the road. Roc watched Todd intensely and became shocked to see his tearful eyes as he stopped in the same spot that he was just standing and questioned Billy D, "Who's that?"

"You don't remember him?"

"No."

"Are you sure?"

"I'm positive."

"You will; he's the newest member to our Corporation."

"I thought we were voting Rafael in?"

"I know but there can only be four and as the rules state, when a member is killed and hasn't been voted out, his power and position go to his next male offspring."

"So he's Diego El Sovida's son?"

"No. Mr. Holmes's."

"What!" Shocked, Roc's mind quickly flashed to Mr. Holmes smiling as he said, "How else would he get a chance at power."

Todd bent down placing a few flowers on top of his father's grave. "Rest in peace, Pop, but I swear to you if there is more to the story that Billy D told me, I'm going to handle it."

"Well, you won't have to wait long," a stranger's voice said from behind that had Todd standing up immediately, coming face to face with a man in a cemetery uniform. The hatred in Todd's eyes was evident as he asked, "And who the fuck are you?"

"I'm Kotov but my few friends call me Cyrus, the same as your father."

"You knew my father?" Todd inquired anxiously.

"Yes, and he wanted me to give you this. Once you're done reading, we shall begin." Cyrus handed Todd a brown envelope. Todd looked down at it and smiled seeing his father's handwriting.

From the back seat of the Phantom, Roc hidden by the tint, watched Todd receive the same envelope he had sitting on his lap and questioned, "What's his name?"

"Todd."

"Todd…Todd, Todd," as the name rolled off Roc's tongue, his eyes darkened while he remembered the letter he spotted at Billy D's on the locker, computer and table. He asked, "So it was him that was supposed to replace me?"

"Yes."

"So what happened, why didn't I know about him until now?"

"Because once your name began to buzz in the street and I saw that you were a step ahead of what I had planned for you, I pulled his training against Holmes's wishes who then sent Todd away to get some of the best schooling around the world. The whole time, stating that he had hoped I made the right choice. The last I heard, he had become wealthy as the sole owner of his father's company."

Roc slowly removed the envelope and began to read the front as his mentor's voice played ever clearly in his mind, just as Todd did the same. They started to read out loud, "Are you my begotten son?" Simultaneously they answered, "Yes," while ripping open the letter.

The End

An Excerpt from

THE DEFINITION OF A MAN

A novel by Zoe & Yusuf Woods

COMING SOON

Chapter
III

At Graterford penitentiary Dro stepped out of cell 128 on D block with a razor sharp hair cut that made his jet black curls look like silk. His brown D.O.C. uniform was tailored and pressed meticulously as always. His footwear only consisted of one thing, Mr. 23 Michael Jordan and he had over twenty pair. D block housed 830 inmates on its tier with only two Correctional Officers to keep the order, if there was any. This block, like the other five was a world within itself and there wasn't anything you couldn't get for a price.

"Yo get your fagot ass away from my cell!" yelled Dro. "Ain't nobody by your cell," said Apple, speaking in a girls voice as he and another gay guy named She-he stood three cells down. "Man, what did I say? I don't want to see you gay ass niggas anywhere around my cell. Take that shit on the other side of the tier or at least thirty cells down. If I catch you standing anywhere around this end I'm going to put something up in you all right," Dro said as he flashed his 10 inch knife that still had blood on it from his last victim. The two gay men took off down the tier with one of them saying, "Oh no he didn't!"

Dro hated gay people more then he hated cowards, and he couldn't stand them, for he saw how down low brother's were killing their families. They would be there sleeping with men and no protection, then go to visits or back out into the world and be with their wives and kissing their kids. Dro shook his head as he walked down the tier that was about half a city block long, thinking to himself how he got stuck in this nightmare he was now living. He saw it so clearly as if it was only a moment ago...

"Throw the jab, that's right. Jab your way out. Stop dropping your right hand," yelled Matty who was Dro's corner man and trainer. "Time" Dro exited the ring slowly, exhausted from the ten rounds of sparring.

"Put some life in your step kiddo, the biggest fight of your life is in three weeks and after we win that, what is it?" Matty asked.

"The title fight."

"What?"

"The title fight."

"So act like it. I want you to give a hundred and ten percent at all times, not only in the ring. I need that same effort and determination when you're on your way to the gym, running, hitting the bag or if it's when you're just walking out the ring."

Matty leaned in and whispered the rest in Dro's ear, "You're going to be the next champion of the world and that's without question in my eye but the only person that can stop you is you. I'm telling you this because I love you. Dro, we have come a long way together. When you first came in here you didn't know the difference between your right cross and an uppercut. To top it off you were in those damn streets but we worked through it. I kept you out of the street and you kept me out of the old folk's home."

They both laughed. "Seriously kiddo I'm saying this because you have two lovely children and a wife who loves you. You worked hard for this big pay off that you're about to get but those streets can smell money like Bush can smell oil and they both don't give a damn what they have to do to get it. So stay on your square kiddo and stay away from those two right there because they don't mean you any good." Matty looked in the direction of Bo and Gotti as they waited on Dro. "Don't worry about them Matty they're just some old friends that stopped by to say what's up."

"Old friends! Where were they when you were cleaning up pop's gym at night just so that you could train there after you worked an eight hour shift? Where were they when you were fighting at the Blue Horizon or when you were fighting people 30 lbs over your weight class for a thousand dollars to split it three ways? Now you're about to get three hundred thousand per fight and we've got old friends. Just watch yourself kiddo, that's all I'm saying. Now hit the shower."

Dro hit the shower and then stepped out into the warm crisp Friday night air. "Damn nigga, you was always nice with the hands but you look like Mike Tyson in there the way you were fucking that boy around in the ring," said Gotti giving Dro a handshake and half hug and then Bo did the same.

"You know how we get down. I can't let anybody out shine me in my own gym. So what brings batman and robin all the way down here where it's cold?"

"Man we're down here because of Rell." "Rell? What's up with him? Is he all right, did he get the money I just sent him… man what is it?"

The silence was killing Dro inside. They all were best friends for over twenty years but he and Rell were closer to each other like Bo and Gotti. When Dro ran the street they did whatever it took to make a dollar, from robbery, selling drugs, kidnapping, and shootouts. You name it, they did it until they met Mr. Nate and he showed them how to get money and clean up the streets. There were many times Dro had close calls and Rell was always on time to bail him out. Six months after Dro stopped running the streets to focus on his boxing career, Rell caught his first case and that he couldn't beat. It was for attempted murder and his sentence was 10 to 20 years.

Being that Dro was still willing to keep his connections, they found out with the help of Mr. Nate, where the man whose testimony put Rell away was staying. He was in protective custody. Two weeks after finding the right location, the man signed the affidavit stating that he lied and that the police forced him to say Rell shot him. That was over three years ago and they were waiting for Rell's appeal to go through. Dro never got over the fact that he wasn't there for Rell when he needed him the most so if there was anything he could do now to help, he did it.

"Ya'll clowns still aren't saying anything." Five minutes had passed and neither Gotti nor Bo said what was going on with Rell. They just sat on the top of the black Lincoln Navigator with 26 inch rims, blowing haze smoke from the blunt they had in rotation when suddenly the back door of the Lincoln opened up and a pretty dark skinned woman got out wiping her mouth with the back of her hand. Dro knew he was slipping; he had been out there for over twenty minutes and never thought to check his surroundings. That would have never happened when he was in the game. What he saw next was even more unbelievable.

"Nigga if you would just shut up, I would have been out." Seeing the man's face, Dro rushed to the truck. The man fought to keep his pants from falling down as Dro lifted him up in the air. "Damn man; let me button my pants up first. You know a pretty young cat just took care of the kid." Dro released the man as a tear of joy slowly rolled down his face. "Rell when did you get home and why didn't anyone tell me?" Dro looked back at Bo and Gotti. "Don't look at them; I said I didn't want to tell because of this right here." He pointed to Dro's left cheek.

"You're all teary eyed and shit. I know how you get, wanting to throw a party and I needed to slide into town as quietly as possible to find out a few things before people know I've touched down."

"What type of things, you all right...do you need me?" Dro asked.

"I'll holla at you later on that. Your boy's home and we're going out to do it big, you with me? Because it can't be a home coming if you're not coming," Rell replied.

"I wouldn't have it any other way," Dro smiled.

Two hours later they all met up at Soldi II dressed to impress, the only way the A-One team knew how to do it. They were sitting in a lovely back end booth table on the second floor. Soldi II was packed as usual with three live performers on stage. "Now this is what I'm talking about. There's ass everywhere up in here. By the end of the night I might have three kids," Bo said jokingly. "Yeah it's on up in here. I'm glad you said to come here instead of your favorite spot, Touches," said Gotti watching some light skinned woman bend over and touch her toes before she dropped it like it was hot.

"Yeah, what made you want to come here Rell?" Dro asked.

"When I came down to the county jail on writ for my appeal I met this good dude and he said he owned a piece of this place and when I made it out he would make sure they rolled out the red carpet," Rell stated.

"Where is this good dude at now because this is all right but it sure ain't no damn red carpet?" said Bo as they all laughed.

"He's still in the county," answered Rell.

"What's he in for because the man I hear owns this place is bigger then a made man. They say he's the reason the streets is getting so much money now in this recession. The word is that his connection shorted him a few keys so he killed them and took all their coke and money. Now he buys straight from the Columbians," Gotti explained.

"I think they were in on a gun charge."

"There were two of them. Man, get the fuck out of here, two niggas on a gun charge and they didn't make bail? If they did they wouldn't be there but your man owns a piece of this…be real," said Gotti who was unconvinced.

"Man I'm telling you these dudes are men. Ya'll know if anybody could pick out a major player in a room full of nickel and dime hustlers it's me. While I was in the county I didn't want for anything, ya'll kept me straight because real people do real things. But my man had the jail on smash and me being who I am, he put me right in. The man got his ear to the street. It's like he knows everything. Those same cats that did me dirty and I asked you about Gotti."

"Yeah I'm still working on finding those clowns."

"Excuse me, my name is Gizelle, I'm the manager here at Soldi II and I believe a mistake has been made," the pretty woman interrupted.

"A mistake?"

"Yes, your name is Rell correct? You're a friend of Boggy?"

"Yes."

"Well, please follow me."

As they got up from the table, Bo went to grab the two bottles of champagne off of the ice when Gizelle stopped him, "Sir you can leave those there for now. Order whatever it is that you'd like; bottles of Moet, Ace of Spade, or lobster…it's on the house."

Gizelle was looking lovely as ever while she lead them to the top V.I.P. Room. Soldi II had a section taped off with Rell's name on it. As soon as Gizelle removed the tape, six barely dressed women came and stood at the entrance, two black females, two white and two Asian. "They're for you all. Do as you wish. Through those doors down there on the left where the two body guards are standing, is a room with a shower and top of the line clothing if you should need to change. If there is anything else that you need please don't hesitate to ask and oh before I forget, Boggy said to tell you it will always be two faces one tear."

Dro couldn't keep his eyes off Gizelle as she left. He had a thing for beautiful women and she was most definitely a natural beauty. The V.I.P. room was packed with top hustlers, basketball players, rappers and pimps. "What did I tell you? I don't mess with no suckers; I only deal with the real." "Rell all you kept saying was my man this, my man that. If you would have said it was ride or die Boggy, there wouldn't have been anymore rap. Everybody knows the killer of Philly," said Bo who was being led away by a woman he'd been watching. They went to a back room followed by Gotti who was with a woman that had an ass that would put Buffy to shame. More women came but Dro and Rell refused, they needed the time to talk alone.

"Dro watch those niggas dog, I'm telling you." "Watch who?" "Who the hell do you think I'm talking about? Bo and Gotti, those niggas smiles aren't real. You haven't been in the street so you don't have a clue and I didn't want you to come back so I didn't say anything. Not only that but it was late and I didn't have it all together until Boggy's people helped me put the connection in place. One day Gotti called me and said he had this big score on some shake down cat in West Philly. Mind you, you're not there so by now I'm doing my own thing on the side alone, just a step up from hand to hand. I wasn't hurting for anything though so if the numbers weren't right, I was going to pass. He says from anywhere from 400 to over a half a million in cash and drugs and I couldn't get a bigger piece if I put up the buy money which is fifty grand so I was like, bet. We staked out the cat, some Italian dude name Caesar for three weeks watching his every move. By now we had him down so it was time to make the direct connect; the way to do that was…"

"By moving with one of the people that are being shook down," Dro interrupted. "I guess you haven't been retired for that long."

"Something's you can't forget no matter what you try to do." "Well the person that was being shook down is right there just like Boggy said he would be," Rell pointed to Pretty Tony who was sitting in the corner section with about ten people surrounding him, listening to him talk. "Rell I know you weren't putting no work in with that lame ass nigga. While you were gone I had to teach him an old lesson about when you disrespect someone, always make sure you can't be disrespected."

"I knew he was a clown but it was Gotti's call. So we all posted up at the top of the old graveyard in North Philly. It was me, Bo, Gotti, Pretty Tony and two of his people. At the time it was winter. Caesar rolled up in a brand new Audi A8 and got out with two big greasy haired, pizza eating dudes and started talking big shit."

He said, "Hey Tony let me speak to you for a minute over here."

"It's okay Caesar, this is all family. Whatever you got to say you can say in front of them."

"Really, it don't matter you know them extra keys you said you couldn't handle. I'm led to believe different so they'll be an extra 30 in this shipment with a little rise in price and don't make me wait any longer then usual because we wouldn't want to mess up this pretty snow out there. It's all nice and white and we want to leave it like that."

"Caesar then pulled off and five minutes later the shipment arrived and the shit was pure butter. A week later Pretty Tony made the drop of 600,000 G's to the same two slick haired cats. After the drop, me, Bo and Gotti followed their van to the same small row house that we tailed Caesar to on several occasions so the exit routine was already set. Bo hit the front after me and Gotti rushed through the back. I picked the lock and then slid into the kitchen. I could hear Caesar talking to about four other people saying, "I told you that nigger Tony was a work horse, you just got to ride them niggers into the ground and as soon as they can't race anymore you kill them...bang, bang. Two in the back of the fucking head and forget about it."

They started laughing. "I bent down low in the doorway that led to the living room and pointed the inferred on my black Mack 11 automatic to the side of Caesar's head and pulled the trigger. The bullet made contact blowing off the side of his face. One of his body guards said "What the hell?" And before anything else could be said I put two hot slugs into his chest. Gotti entered the living room with a chrome 45 automatic in each hand. He shot the first man to his left with four shots while simultaneously taking out another body guard. The last man stood still shaking as hot piss rolled down his leg."

Gotti said to him, "Are you ready to die, just say the word and I'll take you there." Bo watched from the window with his guns ready in case something went wrong. I let him in after making sure the house was clear. The man told us where the rest of the money was. In the end we were looking at 25 bricks, $800,000 in cash. The mark set in the middle of the three of us when Gotti said, "Look here you pasta eating bastard. You did do what I asked so I'm going to let you live but the next time I see your face, I'm going to put two in it."

"Thank you I promise you'll never see my face again."

"Bang, bang." "Two in the back of the fucking head," said Bo in his best God father voice as he quickly pulled the trigger twice, killing the man. "Now let's get out of here."

"We put the money in the back of Gotti's Tahoe and raced for the exit time which was ten minutes flat. I was behind the wheel making record time with only two blocks before hitting the highway when a Ford Explorer sat parked in the middle of the alley, stopping our escape. We could hear the cops in the distance and the police scanner said that the cops were about three blocks away in the opposite direction but that still wasn't good enough for me. I hit the horn, on the two men talking. The one standing said, "Yo, let them get by," the driver looked back at the truck and replied, "Fuck them, they can get by when I'm done." I could read his lips so I cocked my gun back and jumped out. I approached with my gun tucked behind my leg. The man standing must have felt something wasn't right because when we made eye contact he just walked off. When I made it to the driver's side window I was looking into the face of a masked man with a 12 gage shot gun pointed at my head. The rest happened so fast I couldn't believe it. Another black Explorer raced down the alley blocking us in.

Knowing that it was a set up, I wasn't going out like a sucker. I grabbed my gun tightly then kicked off the truck to give myself room to level my gun off when, "Drop it or I'm going to put your thoughts on the window," was called out.

I closed my eyes, mad at myself as I let the gun hit the ground like a cold sucker while another masked man's gun rested on the back of my head. They pulled Gotti and Bo out of the truck and tied us all up and dropped us off in an abandoned field. So at first I was thinking that they just caught us slipping but there were too many loose ends. Like how did they know we were going to be there unless they'd been watching us as we watched Caesar? The only one that knew were Bo and Gotti, they're blood so I was like fuck it. But two months later I'm at the car wash getting the Benz a bath and I see him.

"See who?" asked Dro slowly as he was feeling good after taking down a bottle of red Moet.

"Sam, he was the one talking to the driver. This cat was there washing a brand new 300 C with 23" shoes on it. I grabbed my gun and called Mark, my little cousin over to get the Benz."

"Mark, the wild young boy that was in the paper for the shooting?" Dro questioned.

"Yeah he's going up state for it but that's my heart. He just wouldn't listen when I was trying to tell him there's another way to get money out here but he just loved the street life.

Anyway, Sam was sitting on the driver's side with his door open blasting his system on some young boy shit. I put the burner to his face, "Move the fuck over." I pulled off in his shit and this clown started crying like a girl. He was talking about, "I didn't have anything to do with it I swear." I asked him who did and he said he didn't know. I pushed down harder on the gas and let one fly, 'BOOM,' he started screaming and cries out, "All right it was Pretty Tony. He said he had a smooth move working on the inside. I just had to supply him with a few young cats that busted their gun and he'll handle the rest."

Sam cried as blood ran out his gut, "So who was the inside man that crossed me, Bo or Gotti," I asked as my body became hot with anger. "I don't know...it's the one who says it is what it is all the time." Man what the hell are you talking about? "One day I was with Pretty Tony and he stopped at a dope house he had doing numbers and the dude was there. That's when he inquired about the plan and all he kept saying was it is what it is." So if you saw him, could you identify him? "No they were in another room. Yo, I got to get to a hospital before I die…please." You don't have to worry about that.

Dro I swore I killed him, I hit him at close range three times in the chest, that nigga has nine lives. I left him in a Wal-Mart parking lot to die after I got the rims from the car. The next morning the cops kicked my door in before I could see that nigga but I got his ass tonight and he's going to tell me which one of my so called partners for life sold me out for a dollar. "Rell, you know I'm with you. You all ready know how we do," said Dro. "We cry together we die together, we chill together we kill together," they both said in unison.

"I know big brother, that's how we used to do but while I was in that cage all I did was read about how my main man could be the next big champion and that's what you're going to be. These streets aren't yours anymore and to be truthful I wish I had the heart to leave when you did," Rell confessed.

"You can still get out Rell and you know I'll help you."

"It's too late family, my soul has tasted blood, it's calling for it and I'm going to give it some starting with that nigga Pretty Tony and anyone else that has something to do with crossing me. If I had to pick which one it was, I would say…"

"You two niggas still here with all that ass they're giving away behind those doors? It's off the chain in this joint; your man Boggy is doing it so big. I had to take my hat off for him," said Bo as he threw an unused rubber on the table making everyone laugh. They all partied for a few hours while Rell watched Pretty Tony's every step. He saw that he was about to exit so he got up quickly and said, "It's getting late fellas and I have to make some moves early in the day, so ya'll go ahead and enjoy your self. I'll catch ya'll in the AM." "Come on with all that, we came together so we're leaving together," said Dro who could feel that something was not right.

Outside of club Soldi II was almost as crowded as the inside with people and cars moving everywhere. Rell, refusing to be denied quickly slid his Mac 10 automatic out of his waistline to put it down beside his leg when he saw that Pretty Tony was now talking with two women. He then checked his surroundings; Bo was off to the left talking to some female that looked like Mary J., while Gotti went to get the Jeep from the parking valet. Dro pulled up to his side so nobody could hear and said, "Man what are you going to do with all these people out here?" "I'm going to show you right now. If you forgot how to put that work in, this is going to be a flashback you won't forget."

"Rell, stop you don't…" Dro stopped mid sentence seeing that it was too late. Rell was already half way across the street waiting on a roll of cars to pass. There were three cars to go before Rell would make someone pay for the nights he had to sleep with his knife taped to his chest to fight off killers in order to keep his manhood. As the last two cars approached, Rell locked eyes with Pretty Tony, "Yeah, nod your head because it's me pretty boy and you're going to tell me what I want to hear or you're going bye-bye," Rell said to himself.

The last car was an old Ford Taurus that came to a stop right in front of Rell's path. "Hey my man, can you tell me how to get to the highway from here?" the driver of the car asked. "Just make a right at the first light, and then bang a hard left and you're right there." "Thanks because I'm going to need it after I kill your nosey ass." "BOOM-BOOM-BOOM, E-Money let off three shots, two of which hit Rell in his chest. The power from E-Money's desert eagle knocked Rell off his feet. E-Money quickly placed the car into the park to finish the job he was paid to do.

Dro heard the shots and looked in time to see Rell fall on his back a few feet away. "Nooooo," Dro yelled and took off running as two men with guns jumped out of the car. "E-Money handle your business and I'll get this brave heart ass nigga," said Dirty Rich as he took aim at Dro's head and fired. Rell saw Money approaching and looked for his gun that was no longer in his hand. He saw it several feet away. Rell fought the pain in his chest to get to the gun and then it was gone. "What the fuck?"

Dro could feel the bullet whiz pass his head as he dove in the air landing not far from where Rell laid and then came up firing. "Boc-Boc-Boc-Boc," Dro's first two shots were way off but on the next ones he started to get his groove back, hitting Dirty Rich in the neck. The next shot told him he was all the way there. The slug crashed dead center into Dirty Rich's forehead. "Sweet dreams." Dro was busting on E-Money before Rich's body hit the ground, "Boc-Boc-Boc," E-Money bit down hard on his lip so hard he tasted blood then he squeezed the trigger "BOOM-BOOM," hitting Dro in the leg forcing him to one knee. Dro tried to put the feeling of the pain out of his mind as he got back up on both feet. He returned fire, "Boc-Boc-Boc," E-Money raced to his car realizing he was now out gunned when a bullet slammed into his shoulder. Bo's Next shot was aimed at E-Money's head but before he could fire, E-Money was racing down the street.

"Rell talk to me man, come on…we cry together we die together. You can't leave me!" Dro screamed. "Dro come on man, we have to get up out of here. The cops will be here any minute," Bo shouted, hearing the sound of sirens getting closer by the second. Gotti's jeep came to a stop right beside Dro, "Get the hell in the truck now. The cops are right behind me." Bo grabbed Dro by the arm. "No I'm not letting him die in these streets alone like this. The same way I wouldn't let you die like this," Dro protested.

"Ya'll got to do something, they're right here." Bo looked up to see the black and white police car turn onto the block. "I'm sorry Dro," Bo ran and jumped in the truck as Gotti hit the gas forcing the truck passed 90mph down the block. Five police officers surrounded Dro and Rell with their guns drawn. "Drop the weapon now." Dro was about to go out in a blaze of bullets when Rell, with the last drop of physical strength grabbed his slowly rising gun arm. Dro looked at Rell to see why he stopped him but Rell's face was now the face of Rasheed and Dashon. "Don't they need you?" said Rell. Dro dropped the gun slowly.

The press was having a field day with Dro's case. The front page of the C.V. Daily Scope read, *"Up and coming Boxer tired of fighting. Local Boxer Jonas Brown was involved in a shootout outside of Club Soldi II Friday that left one person dead and another in I.C.U. on life support. Three others suffered minor injuries. Story continued on page four."* When the smoke cleared, Dro was charged with third degree murder. Many people spoke up for Dro at his sentencing hearing and being that it was his first offence; the judge sentenced him to four to eight years in prison.

"You okay man?" asked old man Scotty, snapping Dro back to reality as a tear descended down his face for Rell. "Nah, I'm good Scotty I was just thinking about finishing the ending of a story told to me by a good friend when the time is right. Why, what's up? "They have been calling you for a visit for the last ten minutes and your team is looking for you too. I don't know why you spend so much of your time helping those two crazy young boys anyway,"

Scotty spat, speaking of Mark and Forty. Dro answered, "Because they were my man's peoples, now they have become mine." Scotty just shook his head as Dro walked off.

It may not be Histeria Lane, but these desperate housewives are fed up with their neglecting husbands. Their sexual needs take precedence over the millions of dollars their husbands bring home every year to keep them happy in their affluent neighborhood. While their husbands claim to be hard at work, these wives are doing a little work of their own with the bedroom bandit. Is the bandit swift enough to evade these angry husbands?

In Stores!!

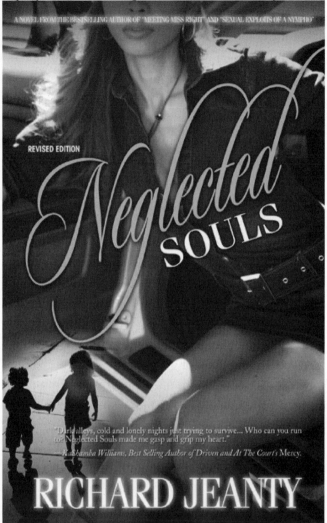

NEGLECTED SOULS

Motherhood and the trials of loving too hard and not enough frame this story...The realism of these characters will bring tears to your spirit as you discover the hero in the villain you never saw coming...

In Stores!!!

Jimmy and Nina continue to feel a void in their lives because they haven't a clue about their genealogical make-up. Jimmy falls victims to a life threatening illness and only the right organ donor can save his life. Will the donor be the bridge to reconnect Jimmy and Nina to their biological family? Will Nina be the strength for her brother in his time of need? Will they ever find out what really happened to their mother?

In Stores!!!

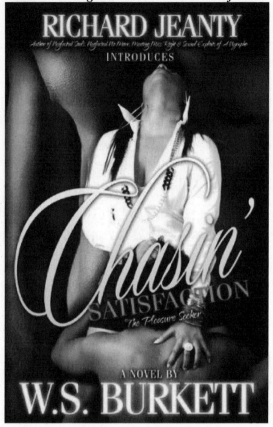

Betrayal, lust, lies, murder, deception, sex and tainted love frame this story... Julian Stevens lacks the ambition and freak ability that Miko looks for in a man, but she married him despite his flaws to spite an ex-boyfriend. When Miko least expects it, the old boyfriend shows up and ready to sweep her off her feet again. She wants to have her cake and eat it too. While Miko's doing her own thing, Julian is determined to become everything Miko ever wanted in a man and more, but will he go to extreme lengths to prove he's worthy of Miko's love? Julian Stevens soon finds out that he's capable of being more than he could ever imagine as he embarks on a journey that will change his life forever.

In Stores!!!

The police in New York and other major cities around the country are increasingly victimizing black men. The violence has escalated to deadly force, most of the time without justification. In this controversial book, noted author Richard Jeanty, tackles the problem of police brutality and the unfair treatment of Black men at the hands of police in New York City and the rest of the country.

In Stores!!!

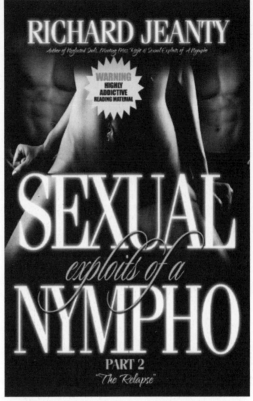

Just when Darren thinks his relationship with Tina is flourishing, there is yet another hurdle on the road hindering their bliss. Tina saw a therapist for months to deal with her sexual addiction, but now Darren is wondering if she was ever treated completely. Darren has not been taking care of home and Tina's frustrated and agrees to a break-up with Darren. Will Darren lose Tina for good? Will Tina ever realize that Darren is the best man for her?

In Stores!!

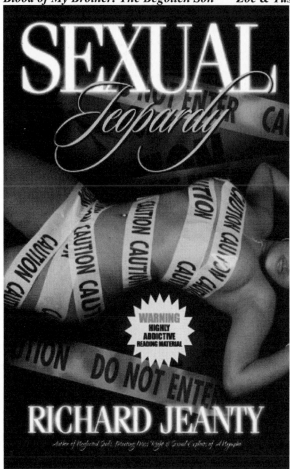

Ronald Murphy was a player all his life until he and his best friend, Myles, met the women of their dreams during a brief vacation in South Beach, Florida. Sexual Jeopardy is story of trust, betrayal, forgiveness, friendship and hope.

In Stores!!!

Tina develops an insatiable sexual appetite very early in life. She
only loves her boyfriend, Darren, but he's too far away in college to satisfy her sexual needs.
Tina decides to get buck wild away in college
Will her sexual trysts jeopardize the lives of the men in her life?

In Stores!!!

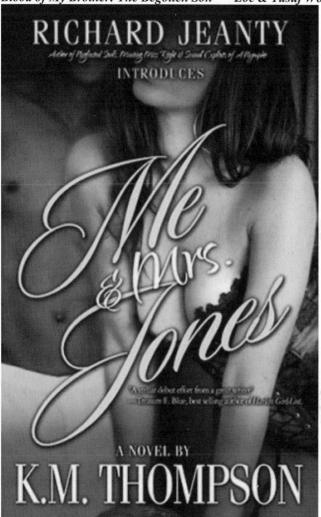

Faith Jones, a woman in her mid-thirties, has given up on ever finding love again until she met her son's best friend, Darius. Faith Jones is walking a thin line of betrayal against her son for the love of Darius. Will Faith allow her emotions to outweigh her common sense?

In Stores!!!

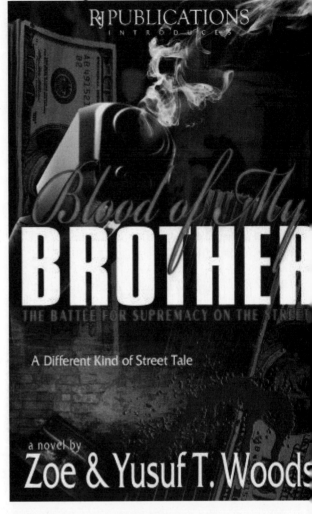

Roc was the man on the streets of Philadelphia, until his younger brother decided it was time to become his own man by wreaking havoc on Roc's crew without any regards for the blood relation they share. Drug, murder, mayhem and the pursuit of happiness can lead to deadly consequences. This story can only be told by a person who has lived it.

In Stores!!!

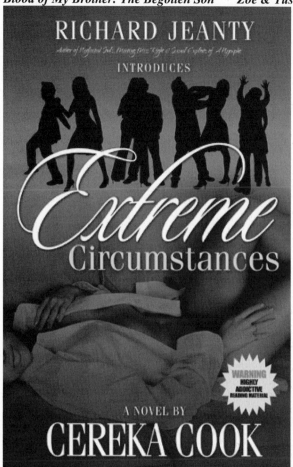

What happens when a devoted woman is betrayed? Come take a ride with Chanel as she takes her boyfriend, Donnell, to circumstances beyond belief after he betrays her trust with his endless infidelities. How long can Chanel's friend, Janai, use her looks to get what she wants from men before it catches up to her? Find out as Janai's gold-digging ways catch up with and she has to face the consequences of her extreme actions.

In Stores!!!

Violence, Intimidation and carnage are the order as Nathan and his brother set out to build the most powerful drug empires in Chicago. However, when God comes knocking, Nathan's conscience starts to surface. Will his haunted criminal past get the best of him?

In Stores!!

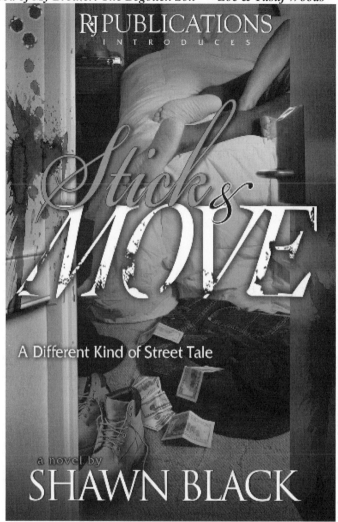

Yasmina witnessed the brutal murder of her parents at a young age at the hand of a drug dealer. This event stained her mind and upbringing as a result. Will Yamina's life come full circle with her past? Find out as Yasmina's crew, The Platinum Chicks, set out to make a name for themselves on the street.

In stores!!

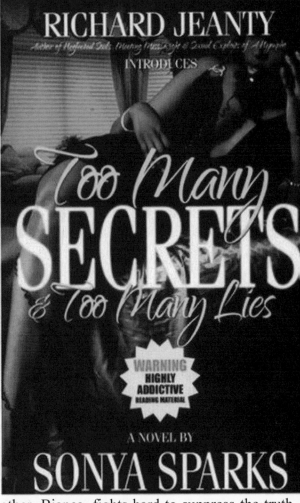

Ashland's mother, Bianca, fights hard to suppress the truth from her daughter because she doesn't want her to marry Jordan, the grandson of an ex-lover she loathes. Ashland soon finds out how cruel and vengeful her mother can be, but what price will Bianca pay for redemption?

In stores!!

Malcolm is a wealthy virgin who decides to conceal his wealth From the world until he meets the right woman. His wealthy best friend, Dexter, hides his wealth from no one. Malcolm struggles to find love in an environment where vanity and materialism are rampant, while Dexter is getting more than enough of his share of women. Malcolm needs develop self-esteem and confidence to meet the right woman and Dexter's confidence is borderline arrogance.

Will bad boys like Dexter continue to take women for a ride?

Or will nice guys like Malcolm continue to finish last?

In Stores!!!

What happens when a woman's devotion to her fiancee is tested weeks before she gets married? What if her fiancee is just hiding behind the veil of ministry to deceive her? Find out as Sean Mitchell takes you on a journey you'll never forget into the lives of Angelica, Titus and Aurelius.

In Stores!!

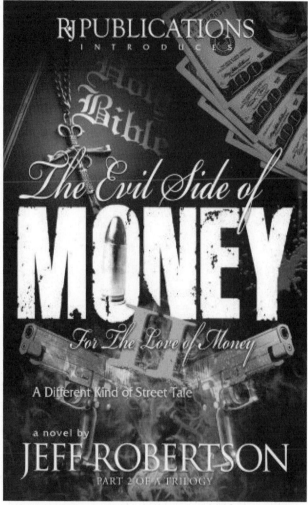

A beautigul woman from Bolivia threatens the existence of the drug empire that Nate and G have built. While Nate is head over heels for her, G can see right through her. As she brings on more conflict between the crew, G sets out to show Nate exactly who she is before she brings about their demise.

In Stores!!!

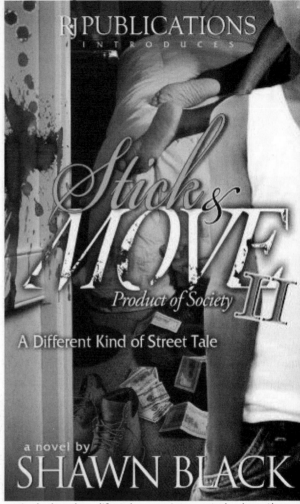

Scorcher and Yasmina's low key lifestyle was interrupted when they were taken down by the Feds, but their daughter, Serosa, was left to be raised by the foster care system. Will Serosa become a product of her environment or will she rise above it all? Her bloodline is undeniable, but will she be able to control it?

In Stores!!

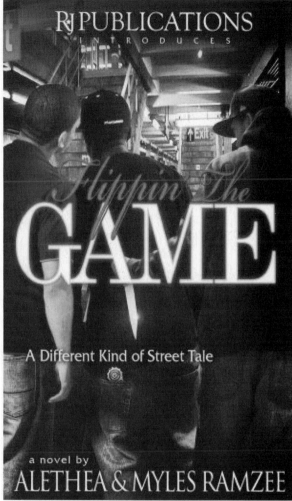

An ex-drug dealer finds himself in a bind after he's caught by the Feds. He has to decide which is more important, his family or his loyalty to the game. As he fights hard to make a decision, those who helped him to the top fear the worse from him. Will he get the chance to tell the govt. whole story, or will someone get to him before he becomes a snitch?

In Stores!!!

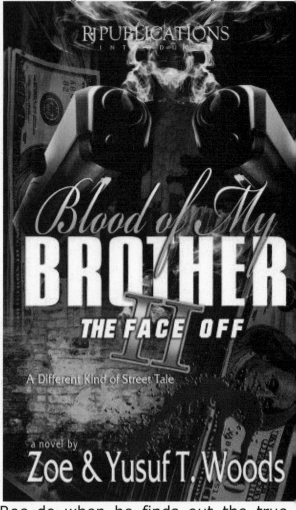

What will Roc do when he finds out the true identity of Solo? Will the blood shed come from his own brother Lil Mac? Will Roc and Solo take their beef to an explosive height on the street? Find out as Zoe and Yusuf bring the second installment to their hot street joint, Blood of My Brother.

In Stores!!!

Dave Richardson is enjoying success as his second book became a New York Times best-seller. He left the life of The Bedroom behind to settle with his family, but an obsessed fan has not had enough of Dave and she will go to great length to get a piece of him. How far will a woman go to get a man that doesn't belong to her?

Coming September 2010

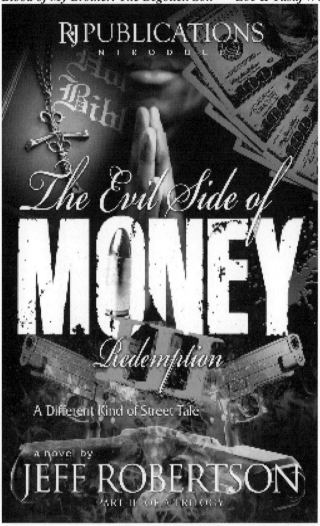

Forced to abandon the drug world for good, Nathan and G attempt to change their lives and move forward, but will their past come back to haunt them? This final installment will leave you speechless.

Coming November 2009

Nafys Muhammad managed to beat the charges in court, but will he beat them on the street? There will be many revelations in this story as betrayal, greed, sex scandal corruption and murder unravels throughout every page. Get ready for a rough ride.

Coming December 2009

Deon is at the mercy of a ruthless gang that kidnapped him. In a foreign land where he knows nothing about the culture, he has to use his survival instincts and his wit to outsmart his captors. Will the Hoodfellas show up in time to rescue Deon, or will Crazy D take over once again and fight an all out war by himself?

Coming March 2010

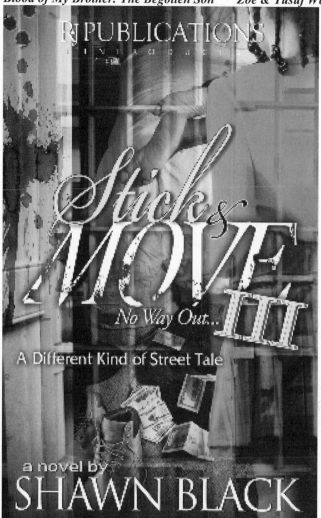

While Yasmina sits on death row awaiting her fate, her daughter, Serosa, is fighting the fight of her life on the outside. Her genetic structure that indirectly bins her to her parents could also be her downfall and force her to see that there's no way out!

Coming January 2010

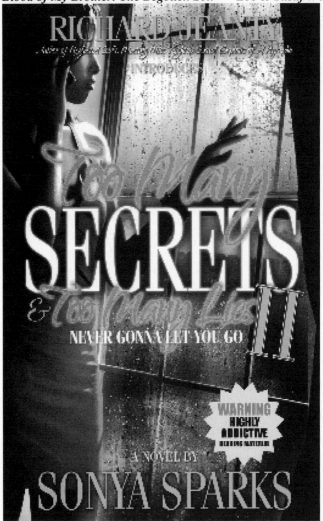

The drama continues as Deshun is hunted by Angela who still feels that ex-girlfriend Kayla is still trying to win his heart, though he brutally raped her. Angela will kill anyone who gets in her way, but is DeShun worth all the aggravation?

Coming September 2009

Buck Johnson was forced to make the best out of worst situation. He has witnessed the most cruel events in his life and it is those events who the man that he has become. Was the Johnson family ignorant souls through no fault of their own?

Coming October 2009

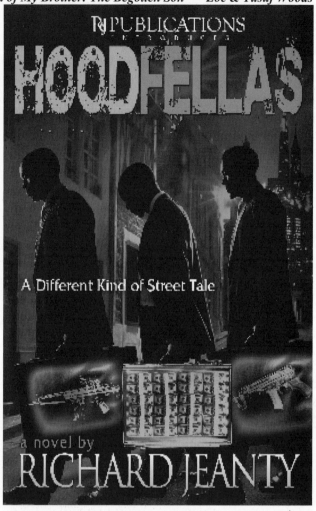

When an Ex-con finds himself destitute and in dire need of the basic necessities after he's released from prison, he turns to what he knows best, crime, but at what cost? Extortion, murder and mayhem drives him back to the top, but will he stay there?

In Stores !!!

What happens when someone falls insanely in love?
Stalking is just the beginning.

In Stores!!!

Use this coupon to order by mail

1. Neglected Souls, Richard Jeanty $14.95
2. Neglected No More, Richard Jeanty $14.95
3. Ignorant Souls, Richard Jeanty $15.00, October 2009
4. Sexual Exploits of Nympho, Richard Jeanty $14.95
5. Meeting Ms. Right's Whip Appeal, Richard Jeanty $14.95
6. Me and Mrs. Jones, K.M Thompson $14.95
7. Chasin' Satisfaction, W.S Burkett $14.95
8. Extreme Circumstances, Cereka Cook $14.95
9. The Most Dangerous Gang In America, R. Jeanty $15.00
10. Sexual Exploits of a Nympho II, Richard Jeanty $15.00
11. Sexual Jeopardy, Richard Jeanty $14.95
12. Too Many Secrets, Too Many Lies, Sonya Sparks $15.00
13. Stick And Move, Shawn Black $15.00 Available
14. Evil Side Of Money, Jeff Robertson $15.00
15. Evil Side Of Money II, Jeff Robertson $15.00
16. Evil Side Of Money III, Jeff Robertson $15.00
17. Flippin' The Game, Alethea and M. Ramzee, $15.00 Available
18. Flippin' The Game II, Alethea and M. Ramzee, $15.00 Dec. 2009
19. Cater To Her, W.S Burkett $15.00
20. Blood of My Brother I, Zoe & Yusuf Woods $15.00
21. Blood of my Brother II, Zoe & Ysuf Woods $15.00
22. Hoodfellas, Richard Jeanty $15.00 available
23. Hoodfellas II, Richard Jeanty, $15.00 03/30/2010
24. The Bedroom Bandit, Richard Jeanty $15.00 Available
25. Mr. Erotica, Richard Jeanty, $15.00, Sept 2010
26. Stick N Move II, Shawn Black $15.00 Available
27. Stick N Move III, Shawn Black $15.00 Jan, 2010
28. Miami Noire, W.S. Burkett $15.00 Available
29. Insanely In Love, Cereka Cook $15.00 Available
30. Blood of My Brother III, Zoe & Yusuf Woods September 2009

Name_____

Address_____

City_____State_____Zip Code_____

Please send the novels that I have circled above.
Shipping and Handling: Free
Total Number of Books_____
Total Amount Due_____
        Buy 3 books and get 1 free. This offer is subject to change without notice.
Send institution check or money order (no cash or CODs) to:
RJ Publications
PO Box 300771
Jamaica, NY 11434
For more information please call 718-471-2926, or visit www.rjpublications.com

Please allow 2-3 weeks for delivery.

Use this coupon to order by mail

31. Neglected Souls, Richard Jeanty $14.95
32. Neglected No More, Richard Jeanty $14.95
33. Ignorant Souls, Richard Jeanty $15.00, October 2009
34. Sexual Exploits of Nympho, Richard Jeanty $14.95
35. Meeting Ms. Right's Whip Appeal, Richard Jeanty $14.95
36. Me and Mrs. Jones, K.M Thompson $14.95
37. Chasin' Satisfaction, W.S Burkett $14.95
38. Extreme Circumstances, Cereka Cook $14.95
39. The Most Dangerous Gang In America, R. Jeanty $15.00
40. Sexual Exploits of a Nympho II, Richard Jeanty $15.00
41. Sexual Jeopardy, Richard Jeanty $14.95
42. Too Many Secrets, Too Many Lies, Sonya Sparks $15.00
43. Stick And Move, Shawn Black $15.00 Available
44. Evil Side Of Money, Jeff Robertson $15.00
45. Evil Side Of Money II, Jeff Robertson $15.00
46. Evil Side Of Money III, Jeff Robertson $15.00
47. Flippin' The Game, Alethea and M. Ramzee, $15.00 Available
48. Flippin' The Game II, Alethea and M. Ramzee, $15.00 Dec. 2009
49. Cater To Her, W.S Burkett $15.00
50. Blood of My Brother I, Zoe & Yusuf Woods $15.00
51. Blood of my Brother II, Zoe & Ysuf Woods $15.00
52. Hoodfellas, Richard Jeanty $15.00 available
53. Hoodfellas II, Richard Jeanty, $15.00 03/30/2010
54. The Bedroom Bandit, Richard Jeanty $15.00 Available
55. Mr. Erotica, Richard Jeanty, $15.00, Sept 2010
56. Stick N Move II, Shawn Black $15.00 Available
57. Stick N Move III, Shawn Black $15.00 Jan, 2010
58. Miami Noire, W.S. Burkett $15.00 Available
59. Insanely In Love, Cereka Cook $15.00 Available
60. Blood of My Brother III, Zoe & Yusuf Woods September 2009

Name_____

Address_____

City_____State_____Zip Code_____

Please send the novels that I have circled above.

Shipping and Handling: Free

Total Number of Books_____

Total Amount Due_____

Buy 3 books and get 1 free. This offer is subject to change without notice.

Send institution check or money order (no cash or CODs) to:

RJ Publications

PO Box 300771

Jamaica, NY 11434

For more information please call 718-471-2926, or visit www.rjpublications.com

Please allow 2-3 weeks for delivery.

Use this coupon to order by mail

61. Neglected Souls, Richard Jeanty $14.95
62. Neglected No More, Richard Jeanty $14.95
63. Ignorant Souls, Richard Jeanty $15.00, October 2009
64. Sexual Exploits of Nympho, Richard Jeanty $14.95
65. Meeting Ms. Right's Whip Appeal, Richard Jeanty $14.95
66. Me and Mrs. Jones, K.M Thompson $14.95
67. Chasin' Satisfaction, W.S Burkett $14.95
68. Extreme Circumstances, Cereka Cook $14.95
69. The Most Dangerous Gang In America, R. Jeanty $15.00
70. Sexual Exploits of a Nympho II, Richard Jeanty $15.00
71. Sexual Jeopardy, Richard Jeanty $14.95
72. Too Many Secrets, Too Many Lies, Sonya Sparks $15.00
73. Stick And Move, Shawn Black $15.00 Available
74. Evil Side Of Money, Jeff Robertson $15.00
75. Evil Side Of Money II, Jeff Robertson $15.00
76. Evil Side Of Money III, Jeff Robertson $15.00
77. Flippin' The Game, Alethea and M. Ramzee, $15.00 Available
78. Flippin' The Game II, Alethea and M. Ramzee, $15.00 Dec. 2009
79. Cater To Her, W.S Burkett $15.00
80. Blood of My Brother I, Zoe & Yusuf Woods $15.00
81. Blood of my Brother II, Zoe & Ysuf Woods $15.00
82. Hoodfellas, Richard Jeanty $15.00 available
83. Hoodfellas II, Richard Jeanty, $15.00 03/30/2010
84. The Bedroom Bandit, Richard Jeanty $15.00 Available
85. Mr. Erotica, Richard Jeanty, $15.00, Sept 2010
86. Stick N Move II, Shawn Black $15.00 Available
87. Stick N Move III, Shawn Black $15.00 Jan, 2010
88. Miami Noire, W.S. Burkett $15.00 Available
89. Insanely In Love, Cereka Cook $15.00 Available
90. Blood of My Brother III, Zoe & Yusuf Woods September 2009

Name_____

Address_____

City_____State_____Zip Code_____

Please send the novels that I have circled above.

Shipping and Handling: Free

Total Number of Books_____

Total Amount Due_____

Buy 3 books and get 1 free. This offer is subject to change without notice.

Send institution check or money order (no cash or CODs) to:

RJ Publications

PO Box 300771

Jamaica, NY 11434

For more information please call 718-471-2926, or visit www.rjpublications.com

Please allow 2-3 weeks for delivery.